Advance P...

'Every decade ... ...es the way we think abou... ..., then Laird Barron, and now Attila ... collection, really unlike anything out there, ...ests a new way forward.'
— Brian Evenson, author of *Song for the Unraveling of the World*

'[Veres'] world is unique, bleak, terrifying, and all his own. Whether it's urban fables of rock music, harvests that claim souls, Aickmanesque situations or an amazing take on cosmic horror, his vision is always stunning. These stories, his debut in English, will blow you away.'
— Mariana Enríquez, author of *Things We Lost in the Fire*

'A stunning parade of terrors surreal and horrors sublime. The uncanny stories in *The Black Maybe* are as originally chilling and imaginatively dangerous as anything you'll read this decade, if not your lifetime, and Attila Veres deserves the worldwide acclaim this inventive work of horror will surely bring him. His approach is genuinely fresh. No maybes about it: this book is pitch black and totally engrossing.'
— Michael Arnzen, award-winning author of *Proverbs for Monsters*

'The ten macabre tales that make up Veres's English-language debut stake their scares on their wildly unpredictable plots. All Veres's stories begin in realistically grounded settings before veering unexpectedly into territory rife with unforeseeable and surreal menaces . . . These tales wear their resistance to conventional horror tropes and formulas as a badge of honor. Readers are sure to be impressed.'
— *Publishers Weekly*

'*The Black Maybe*, by Attila Veres, is a refreshing blast of cold cellar air. The horror is insidious and surreal, slowly chewing away what you think is real until you find yourself surrounded by a nightmare. I love this book!'

— Nathan Ballingrud, award-winning author of *Wounds*

'Attila Veres is fiendishly talented. Certain images in *The Black Maybe* caused me to glance at the darkened corners of my office as I read into the wee hours.'

— Laird Barron, author of *Swift to Chase*

'These stories dwell in the in-between places of life and death, that place where nightmares wait to be harvested. These are your nightmares, or they soon will be, so settle in for an excursion to a horrific mental, emotional, and spiritual landscape like no other. A brilliant work.'

— Elizabeth Engstrom, author of *When Darkness Loves Us*

'Original, brilliant, distinctive. These masterful stories by Attila Veres are a breath of fresh air from out of the darkness.'

— Michael Cisco, award-winning author of *The Divinity Student*

THE BLACK MAYBE

Liminal Tales

by
ATTILA VERES

Translated from the Hungarian by LUCA KARAFIÁTH

Introduction by STEVE RASNIC TEM

VALANCOURT BOOKS

The Black Maybe: Liminal Tales by Attila Veres
First edition 2022

Copyright © 2022 by Attila Veres
Introduction copyright © 2022 by Steve Rasnic Tem
This edition copyright © 2022 by Valancourt Books, LLC
Published by arrangement with Agave Könyvek Kft., Budapest

All rights reserved. In accordance with the U.S. Copyright Act of 1976, the copying, scanning, uploading, and/or electronic sharing of any part of this book without the permission of the publisher constitutes unlawful piracy and theft of the author's intellectual property. If you would like to use material from the book (other than for review purposes), prior written permission must be obtained by contacting the publisher.

Valancourt Books and the Valancourt Books logo are registered trademarks of Valancourt Books, LLC. All rights reserved.

Published by Valancourt Books, Richmond, Virginia
http://www.valancourtbooks.com

ISBN 978-1-954321-69-4 (trade hardcover)
ISBN 978-1-954321-70-0 (trade paperback)
Also available as an electronic book.

Cover by Vince Haig
Set in Dante MT

Contents

Introduction by Steve Rasnic Tem 7

THE BLACK MAYBE

To Bite a Dog	13
Fogtown	33
The Time Remaining	64
Return to the Midnight School	85
In the Snow, Sleeping	116
Multiplied by Zero	135
The Amber Complex	181
Sky Filled with Crows, Then Nothing at All	227
Walks Among You	244
The Black Maybe	282

Introduction

The most enriching aspect of discovering new authors, especially those who toil in the same genre, is experiencing their unique perspectives on beloved themes.

I first read Attila Veres (b. 1985) in *The Valancourt Book of World Horror Stories, volume 1*. His tale, 'The Time Remaining' (included here), begins innocently enough. A grandmother gives her grandchild a plush toy, Vili. But the child never sees the grandmother again, and the mother lies about the reason. The mother lies again, thinking the child too dependent, saying that Vili is dying. Similar lies spread to other mothers and their children, and their plush toys fall 'ill'. What follows is a cascade of extended rituals to keep these toys alive, with powerful visceral descriptions of the toys' pain and the children's involvement. It's a riveting exploration of sympathetic magic and what happens when a fantasy goes on too long. The story was a fan favorite and led to this, Veres' first English collection.

Attila Veres makes his living as an award-winning writer for film and television in his native Hungary. His first novel, *Darker Outside,* was a surprise success. An original blend of the personal and the weird, it falls into that rewarding gray area between genre and mainstream literature.

This was followed by the story collection *Midnight Schools*. Seven of the stories that appear here are taken from that volume. This book emerged at an opportune time, as other younger Hungarian writers began writing about their country and themselves through genre. A *Year's Best Hungarian SFF Short Stories* series began in which Veres has been a regular contributor.

Attila Veres' fiction is rooted in the Hungarian experience. His native readers recognize the seedy urban rock clubs, impoverished farms, and post-Soviet haunted landscapes and experiences as their own, yet Veres twists this reality in bizarre and original ways into unique weird mythologies appealing to an international audience. As someone who has read a great deal of horror fiction, I found myself consistently surprised by these liminal tales.

'In the Snow, Sleeping' is one of my favorites. A young woman travels to a distant spa with her oblivious boyfriend. She knows he carries an engagement ring, which fills her with unease. First they are given a foul, stinking room, and the cracks multiply in their ideal vacation: warnings the hot thermal waters will become harmful, the front door is left open letting wild animals in, the staff disappears. Through the walls she hears banging, crying, and screams. Some of the guests appear injured and bloody. Yet her boyfriend still insists on staying. Veres has a gift for contemporary settings and concerns. These feel like stories of the 'now', interrupted with intimations of the sinister and the strange.

Many of these stories can be classified as either 'urban' or 'rural', illustrating the separation and often antagonism between city and country life in Hungary. The urban stories feature protagonists whose obsessions intensify until a nightmarish climax is reached. Frequently they feature a background of rock or heavy metal.

In the pandemic story 'To Bite a Dog', a man asks his girlfriend about her various cuts and bruises. She has developed a habit of biting dogs, and this proclivity exacerbates as the story continues. In 'The Amber Complex' Gabor, a college dropout living with his mother, decides his natural talent, and mission, is to become an alcoholic. A surprise invitation brings him to a mysterious wine tasting within a vast, labyrinthine cellar. The participants are not tasting wine, but something called 'complex'. Each succeeding color-coded complex produces a hallucinogenic vision, a strategy Veres uses to great effect, transporting the characters into frightening psychological states. Only Gabor is left to taste the final, seventh drink, the Amber Complex.

The rock music-themed 'Fogtown' is told as a series of blog posts, book excerpts, and interview transcripts concerning an unfinished book by a man named Balázs on local rock bands that never released an album. The band Fogtown keeps popping up in these interviews, a legendary group even though almost no one saw them play. Balázs becomes obsessed with Fogtown after discovering people have disappeared, committed suicide, or experienced odd visions following exposure to the band or their music.

'Sky Filled With Crows, Then Nothing at All' is another rock-themed story narrated by a demon created to tell the Antichrist his true nature and purpose. The Antichrist becomes a metal musician after the demon introduces him to the scene, thinking it would facilitate his future role.

Veres makes frequent nods to Lovecraft, but his cosmic horrors are original creations evolving out of his characteristic hallucinatory imagery and religious or cultish visions of horror.

'Walks Among You' concerns a Lovecraftian-like religion originally banned for its use of human sacrifice. The story follows a teenage girl bullied for her faith, a pensioner who helped get the church legalized, and a man married to a church member. Set at the funeral of a woman high up in the church who died of cancer, all three are questioning their faith in the Great Old and Nameless Gods after seeing her cancer-ravaged body.

'Multiplied by Zero' is an extreme portrayal of a descent into Lovecraftian madness. After the narrator's old girlfriend informs him she aborted his child (she argues that a child reduces a woman's value to zero), he takes a guided bus trip into a dangerous and unreal land. The story is told after the fact in the form of a travel guide, with overly deadpan advice given the horrendous events described. It's a suicidal journey for the tourists who sign up.

The rural stories in *The Black Maybe*, inspired by the realities of farming and keeping and slaughtering livestock, continue these themes of cosmic horror by mythologizing those realities, creating weird cosmologies which at times resemble folk horror but which push far beyond.

'Return to the Midnight School' concerns the friendship of the narrator with another boy in his village. The local customs and harvest rituals are explored in loving detail, and it is gradually revealed how unique the biology and the metaphysics are in this region. Locals are born in a pit and some come back from the grave as mindless living dead. The peculiar harvest of their fields is a watermelon-like crop containing animals and humans sleeping in embryonic poses. Their bodies are turned into products from which the villagers profit.

This story was a curious, almost primeval experience, but even more peculiar is the title piece, 'The Black Maybe', one of the weirdest tales I've read in years.

'The young ones collect the snails in the daytime, while the men oil the chains at night.' Emese and her family are visitors living with a host family. They feel lucky to be there during the harvest, living in harmony with nature and discovering the outré knowledge possessed by the local farmers. They learn their roles in the harvest, cooking down the snails for their essence and oiling the silver chains and applying bait to the hooks. The chains and the hooks are dropped into earthen pits and then covered over.

'They bite on it. But not like fish do.'

'I know,' Hugó said. *'Because in fact they don't really exist until they take the bait, right?'*

Emese drinks a metallic booze which makes her speak in an altered voice and levitate. She is constantly pressured to have sex with a local boy, told she'd 'be better off'.

Once they pull out the chains and the catch is delivered, Emese will only have twenty-four to thirty-six hours. Then it will be too late.

Given both the range and the originality of his dark fiction, Attila Veres' career is one to watch.

STEVE RASNIC TEM
January 2022

STEVE RASNIC TEM has published nearly 500 short stories, seven novels, and ten collections during a career spanning forty years. He is a past recipient of the World Fantasy Award and the British Fantasy Award, and his 2014 novel *Blood Kin* won the Bram Stoker Award. Two of his story collections, *Figures Unseen: Selected Stories* and *Thanatrauma*, are published by Valancourt Books.

To Bite a Dog

The room smelled like a used kitchen sponge. It was his flat. They lay in bed, waiting to be aroused again. Mutual attraction was inches away from turning into love.

'Where did you get the scratches?' he asked the girl.

This happened on their third date. It started as a Tinder relationship, but it had gotten off to a bad start. Their first date was at a park. The restaurant where they were supposed to meet was closed due to a sudden, unspecified tragedy. The park was nice, except that their rendezvous was somewhat disrupted by three homeless men fighting over the ownership of half a bottle of red wine. They promised each other a second date, feeling that circumstances had played against them. The second date was uneventful. Maybe even boring. They met in one of those hipster coffee shops that have popped up all over Budapest, promising the illusion of being somewhere abroad. They tried to maintain a conversation, but the coffee machine was shrieking the whole time, and the discussions they overheard seemed more interesting than their own. At the next table, a pair of sisters were talking about their father's recent vasectomy, at another a man was trying to convince his friends to buy a house on the island of Krk, in Croatia, because he could get an excellent deal. Zoltán didn't dare to order a second coffee; he barely had enough money for the first one.

The third date was their last chance, they both knew it. Nikolett arrived with fresh injuries. Scrapes on her knee, on her arm, and minor bruises basically all over her body.

A few hours later they were lying in his room, reeking of sweat and sex. The boy hated the room now for not being more glamorous. Zoltán had wanted to move out of it ever since he moved in, but he never had the money, and now he feared Nikolett would be turned off by the state of the place.

'All right, I'll tell you about the scratches,' said Nikolett. 'But you won't believe it.'

Zoltán shrugged. 'Try me!'

'I bit a dog!' the girl said, giving an imitation of laughter. Her voice shivered from anxiety. The boy got up on his elbows in the bed. Now it was getting interesting. She began her story.

Nikolett had promised a friend of hers she would watch his dog while he was away on vacation at a Croatian ski resort. She wasn't a fan of dogs, but she didn't hate them either. To her they seemed like practical tools. She never got the whole emotional aspect of owning a dog. Dogs were not man's best friend. They were man's subordinates. Still, she liked her friend well enough, and it was no problem looking after his dog for a few days. She and the dog got along well.

The dog was a large mixed breed named Zeus. Nikolett took him to a nearby dog park twice a day. One morning Zeus got into a fight with a smaller but far more ferocious dog. The other dog was called Bandido. The cause of the clash between the animals was unclear. Maybe just as there are people who are meant for each other, there are dogs who are meant to be mortal enemies.

The park turned into a battlefield. Zeus aimed his teeth at his rival's throat, while Bandido attacked Zeus' cheek and nose. It was a chaos of bared teeth, of growling, of blood and violence. A bearded man shouted: 'Bandido, spit it out! Spit it out, Bandido!'

Nikolett threw herself on her knees and, grabbing his collar, tried to drag Zeus away from the fight. She was unprepared for the animal's strength. The dog swept Nikolett off her feet, dragging her along on the gravel. Hence the scratches.

Nikolett panicked, and since she had never had a dog, she

didn't know what to do in a situation like this. Bandido's owner didn't know either. 'Spit it out, Bandido!' he repeated over and over again, and the meaningless sentence became emptier with each repetition. He stood in a pose that made him look like he was about to jump into a pool, but he didn't move.

Finally Nikolett launched herself at Zeus, although in hindsight it was a rather stupid and – considering Bandido's uncontrolled fury – dangerous move. She acted on instinct.

She bit Zeus on the ear. Blood poured out.

The dog let out a surprised howl; Nikolett kept biting until Zeus let go of Bandido. Everyone at the dog park went silent. Even Bandido retreated, tucking back his ears and tail. Nikolett held Zeus and smiled at the other dog's owner, trying to make a good impression before the inevitable argument over who was responsible. Bandido's owner looked at Nikolett, then stepped away from her just like his dog had.

Only later did the girl notice that her teeth were bloody. She had a dog's blood in her smile.

'What did it feel like?' Zoltán asked in bed. 'What did it feel like biting Zeus?'

Nikolett took a deep breath, her mouth open, as if ready to formulate an answer right away. Her mouth hung open, then it closed. She didn't say anything. She didn't need to. She had goosebumps all over her body. They laughed at this, then fucked again, even more ferociously than before.

That date was an icebreaker. Afterwards everything went smoothly. They met almost every day at his place or hers and continued their explorations of each other. Each time they met they found yet unconquered or undiscovered territories, or new pleasures in the lands they had already mapped out. A few weeks later Nikolett lost her apartment because it was turned into an Airbnb. They decided to move in together. With their combined incomes, they could get a bigger and nicer apartment than either could afford on their own.

The new flat smelled like fabric softener and plywood. The

kitchen window and the tiny balcony looked onto a park from the building's seventh floor. One Sunday the sun shone with such magical golden intensity through the kitchen window that Zoltán sat down on the floor looking at the honey-colored light and let the feeling wash over him: he was in the right place. After so many years spent wandering, this was finally home.

Nikolett felt likewise. They bought a bottle of Prosecco at Aldi; they drank it on a Thursday night sitting by the open kitchen window, and when they were sufficiently drunk they confessed their love for each other. They both loved the apartment just as much as they loved each other, but neither of them minded that. After that night, whenever they cleaned the floor or washed the kitchen counter they felt they were caressing the body of some great lover.

It was a liberating feeling to be in a relationship; it made everything easier. At dawn, before work, they would often make love; the warmth they generated in these moments helped them through the coldness of the days. They shared the bills, so by the end of the month they managed to save some money. They hadn't decided yet what to spend it on, but they cherished the idea of savings as if it were some kind of precious seed, from which an unknown, exotic plant would gradually grow. Even when the pandemic started they didn't feel threatened. They switched to working from home and saved even more money by not having to commute. She sometimes needed to go to the office, but she rode a bike.

'Is it this easy?' Zoltán would ask himself from time to time. 'Is it this easy to be happy?'

It seemed like it was, and he hoped that these days would turn into weeks, months, years, and an eternal life.

He was at the greengrocer's picking out onions when he first heard the news of the bitten dog. A middle-aged woman was selecting cucumbers. She recounted the news.

'The Budai family, from the seventh floor,' said the middle-aged woman as she made a grand show out of picking the freshest cucumbers. 'It was their dog. The daughter took it for a walk in the park. She let it off the leash, and after a while the dog came running back to her whimpering. It was bleeding from a wound. A bite, apparently. Terrible, isn't it?'

Surely it had been wounded by another dog. Or some other kind of predator. Maybe a hedgehog acting in self defense, or a cat. These wounds happen all the time in a dog's life.

Zoltán had a hard time falling asleep that night. He watched Nikolett, who was turned away from him, sleeping soundly. He watched for so long that the girl's body parts turned into abstractions in the obscurity of the night. She was nothing but a pale stain here, a small purple blur there. Zoltán watched these abstractions the girl had become in her sleep and searched for any telltale signs of change. He couldn't find any, so finally he fell asleep and dreamed of the park at night.

A few days later a new case of a bitten dog was reported at the grocer's. This second incident gave rise to more concern than the first. It had happened at night again; the dog was bitten on its nose. This bite led to the discovery of yet another incident that had happened the previous night. In that case the animal was bitten on its belly. From these two bites it became obvious that the perpetrator was not a beast – the wounds were shaped in the pattern of human teeth. The owners drifted towards panic and had a million questions nobody could answer. Should they take the dog for a vaccination against infections? Could a man be rabid and pass it on to a dog? Should the police be involved? Do they even handle this sort of case?

Zoltán decided to get his produce at the local Spar, a more impersonal place, in order to stay away from the news and rumors. He didn't have a dog, so he really saw no reason why he should be involved. Still, he was anxious. He knew he shouldn't be; just because Nikolett had bitten a dog once didn't make her the serial dog-biter.

By the shop's counter tiny plush dogs were being sold as

part of some promotional campaign. Zoltán put one of the stuffed toys into his cart, just to prove that he didn't take his own silly thoughts at all seriously. Everyone in line wore a mask, including him. For several months now he had seen human faces only on television, in reruns of old sitcoms and crime shows. He was even starting to doubt whether people still had faces; maybe this last year everyone's faces had vanished, leaving nothing behind but long rows of teeth that everyone covered up now for aesthetic reasons.

Or for safety. Masks are like a muzzle on a dog, protecting us from our own teeth. Zoltán looked at the queue and had a thought that disturbed him. All he saw was hundreds and hundreds of teeth, all standing in line to buy ham and discount laundry detergent, hiding away behind these black and green and blue masks. Before paying, he threw the stuffed toy back where he had found it.

Nikolett was young and cared about her physical fitness, so she often went for a run in the later hours of the night, even if it was against the law now with the curfews kicking in. Legally only people walking their dogs could be on the street after dark. Still, she went running night after night.

She purchased the proper attire for this purpose: black pants, black T-shirt and jumper, and a black mask, so if the police stopped her she wouldn't be fined for not wearing one. As soon as she came back from running, she headed straight to the shower to wash off the grime of physical exercise. Only when she stepped out of the bathroom would she talk to Zoltán, as if she hadn't only washed herself but also changed her face, and if they were to talk before she entered the bathroom Zoltán might see some other Nikolett, the one behind the mask when she was out running in the streets.

Out running in the park.

One night, however, Nikolett didn't enter the bathroom. Zoltán was already lying in bed, waiting for her to return home. The TV was on at a low volume, but Zoltán wasn't paying attention to the program. He heard her enter the flat, kick off her shoes, and head straight for the bathroom. There she paused. She changed direction; Zoltán heard her walking towards the bedroom door. Then she stopped. Zoltán could hear her breathing, but maybe it was just his imagination. There was a long stretch of silence, and Zoltán started to doubt she was out there. Maybe he'd just fallen asleep and dreamt the whole thing. Maybe she was still out there, outrunning the police.

'Turn off the TV!' said the girl in a hoarse, raw voice.

Zoltán reached for the controller, but his hand stopped in mid-air. If he turned off the TV, he would admit to being awake. A thought crossed his mind: maybe he should pretend to be asleep, like the prey that feigns death when the predator approaches. He found this thought dreadful. Nikolett was his girlfriend, they lived in a healthy relationship, in almost complete emotional and financial interdependence. What reason could there be for lying in a relationship like theirs?

Zoltán turned off the television. He went blind in the sudden darkness. He shrank under the blanket, like someone anticipating an attack. The door opened with a quiet creak, and Nikolett entered. The room felt hotter. Zoltán wanted to neutralize the tension with a joke, or ask a meaningless question like 'How was the run?' or 'Home so soon?', but he decided to remain silent instead.

The girl cuddled up to him in bed. She was naked, her skin hot and sweaty. She pressed herself against Zoltán, tightly and possessively. Zoltán suddenly felt sick because over Nikolett's usual smell he could smell something else, something he only perceived with the animal part of his brain and couldn't put into words. The smell of power, the scent the body discharges when it has conquered something, when it wants to declare its superiority over other animals.

That was what he smelled, and the stink of a wet dog too.

Nikolett kissed the boy's face. It wasn't an act of love, but an animal sniffing its mate. Her mouth smelled of blood, and Zoltán thought about the pain of the bite that would be coming soon. He anticipated the sharp pain because he knew Nikolett was going to bite him with her already bloodied teeth.

Zoltán let the girl do whatever she wanted with him. She used him like he was an object, a subordinate. He had no say in what happened in the following hour, he had to take every bit of pain and joy soundlessly.

Later, when Nikolett was asleep, Zoltán lay awake. He had the sense that things were going irreversibly wrong. What was happening now was only the ultimate expression of the nature of their relationship. They both earned money, but the girl earned more. She managed their affairs, took care of the bills and contracts. She was the one to define the direction of their lives. She would also be the one who decided how to spend the savings. Of course she would leave some room for Zoltán's ideas as well, to make it look like he had a say in things, but the important decisions would be up to her. Tonight the girl demonstrated her physical dominance as well. The only question was whether the boy would accept it.

As a man, his answer was supposed to be an absolute no. A man should piss all around his territory. A man should rule, and rule alone in this extra comfortable two-room rental, as well as in the life attached to it. If that wasn't possible, he would have to end this life, break up with the girl and start fresh with a new one, one who was more submissive to a man's needs.

He also knew that the times when men thought this way about themselves were long gone. He wasn't a ruler in this flat; he wasn't a hunter in the jungle. He and she were equals, even though that equality had been upset tonight.

Of course, he could look at it from a different angle. What if Nikolett was sick, in need of some sort of help? No matter how you looked at it, biting dogs was a habit that wasn't widely accepted in society, therefore it could very well be considered a pathological condition. Maybe with some therapy she could be made to give up this new habit, and a new kind of balance could be reached in their relationship, a balance where Zoltán could finally be dominant. But again it meant that when a woman dominated a man it was a sort of sickness to be cured. Zoltán, on an intellectual level, disapproved of the notion, but at the same time, deep down, he agreed with it.

What if one of these nights Nikolett gets caught biting a dog, he asked himself. She would definitely be prosecuted for vandalism or animal abuse or both. In any case, this life would be over, only in a more humiliating manner than if Zoltán walked away right now.

He thought back to the honey-colored Sundays, the Prosecco from Aldi, the extra comfort, and his heart ached with grief. How could he just walk away from all that?

He curled into a fetal position in the bed and fell asleep.

In the morning they didn't talk about it. Nikolett put on her mask and left for work. Zoltán switched on his computer because a call was starting in half an hour.

At night, Nikolett went running again.

Zoltán sat in the window, watching the park, a place that used to promise serenity, offer coolness in the summer heat, leisure and recreation. Now the park seemed like a jungle, a closed ecosystem where two types of beings existed: predator and prey. Somewhere under the disguise of darkness the battle for life is being fought every moment. Zoltán felt thrilled and fearful as the park rose above its own mundanity. He listened carefully to hear the painful whining of a dog from between the trees, to hear the gasp of the dog's owner realizing that their pet had fallen prey. At times he thought he heard something, but it must have just been his imagination.

When she came back from the hunt, in a sense everything returned to normal. There were no secrets anymore, which made both of them feel relieved. The girl's pants were dirty, her lips red from the blood. She sat down next to Zoltán at the kitchen table. She smelled of struggle and blood and he smelled of comfort and soap. He looked at her and understood that he was not going to break up with her; he was too weak to do that. If they broke up the security would be gone. What's safer for a prey than living in unity with a predator?

She told him the entire story.

Zeus was only the beginning. Nikolett hadn't planned on biting more dogs, but the incident haunted her thoughts. As she waited to fall asleep in the warmth of the bed she recalled again and again the moment when she bit into Zeus' ear. There was something utterly compelling about that moment, but she couldn't quite put her finger on it. It wasn't the dog's terror or pain that appealed to her – that was only a necessary element, so to speak. She finally figured out the source of her fascination. It was the moment when the dog shrunk. It was giant before the bite, as if an aura embraced it, an aura that enlarged during the fight, extended far beyond the measurements of its body, though body language was a part of it. It was an invisible sign warning everyone that this dog was dangerous.

This dog was ready to fight.

After the bite, however, this invisible extension shrunk smaller than the dog itself. Zeus was no warrior anymore; he subordinated himself to the will of a creature more powerful than him. His muscles relaxed, his movements became slower, showing no menace, promising submission. Even days later Zeus wouldn't dare to look Nikolett in the eye.

That was it, the moment that fascinated her so much that she couldn't sleep at night. She knew that the moment she bit the dog her own aura grew. That's why Bandido's owner stepped down without a fight. He saw that Nikolett was dangerous. That she was larger than him, even if her physical measurements said otherwise.

She realized that she was just an animal too, and in this jungle only the strong can survive. Mankind had lived in apartments, in the labyrinth of cities for so long, detached from nature, that it took this bite for her to find her way back to her original nature. Having understood this, every day she spent without that high seemed a gray waste.

Of course she couldn't know whether it was a one-off incident with Zeus, or if the experience could be repeated. Whether she could only bite Zeus, or if she could do it to other dogs too.

She bought black clothes and went down to the park to hunt. She hid in a bush, turning her body into a black spot. She waited. She let several dogs walk past the bush. They were no good: either the owners were too close or the dog just wasn't right. Later she understood that there is a definite bond between predator and prey that manifests when the two meet. Her heart skipped a beat when she laid eyes on the German Shepherd; it was a sensation of falling, like when you realize you're in love. This was the dog she needed, this was the dog she wanted, and the dog knew it too because it pricked up its ears and walked over to the bush, sniffing the air. It was a beautiful moment, and she knew exactly what to do. Her instincts kicked in, the instincts of a born predator.

She instantly grabbed the dog and bit it.

The sensation was the same as the first time – the dog collapsed under her teeth, and she herself felt like exploding out of her own body. She became fully herself in that moment, as if her entire life before had been nothing but a dream, an approximation of life. This moment, this was life; it was a moment without fear, without second thoughts. A moment that existed only in itself, separated from both the past and the future. She felt her heart pumping, her muscles tensing, and for the first time she felt completely at home in her own body. Before that, her body served merely as a mask, to make contact with other masks at her workplace, at school, on the street, at the bakery. Every body was just a vessel, a tool. But at this moment her body was a weapon, a clockwork, a miracle. It was not a means to an end, but the purpose itself. Her tongue tasted like adrenaline and she felt she could see in the dark. She waited until the German Shepherd lay down on the ground and quietly started to whimper. It yielded to her completely.

After this act of submission she let go of the dog and retreated to the darkness.

As a hunter she had certain rules to be followed. A dog could only be bitten once. If she had already bitten it on its belly, she couldn't bite it somewhere else. Nor could she pick the same dog twice on separate occasions. Once bitten, the dog was to be left alone on subsequent nights. She never allowed herself to fatally injure a dog; the goal was not killing, but the rediscovery of her true self. The violence against the beasts was only the means to this end.

'But you can't understand it anyway,' said Nikolett. 'Until you try it yourself, you won't get it.'

Over time it created a chasm between the two of them.

Zoltán tried to understand, really, but she was right. What was to understand about it? Eventually he settled on accepting the nighttime hunts as a quirk, or even a necessity, some form of therapeutic activity. It was the time of the pandemic, everyone was under a lot of pressure, pressure that needed release. This was how she found release, so what? After all, dogs are only animals, and they make out pretty well living as our pets. Maybe it was time for them to give back a little bit more to the community. It was only natural. What's the pain of a bite measured against the comforts of a home?

At night, when Nikolett went hunting and Zoltán waited for her sitting out on the balcony, he felt he had made the right decision. They had found a new routine. Their happiness was intact. He learned to accept that everybody needed a hobby, and this was hers.

Only it wasn't a private affair, because it included dogs. Dogs are property, and damaging property inevitably becomes a case. After a short while everyone knew someone who knew someone whose dog had been bitten. Finally it became official, not just a disturbing rumor. Photocopied notes appeared on every entrance and community billboard: 'Watch out! Dog biter on the loose!' It didn't take long before the dog owners tried to ask for help. Naturally, they turned to the police.

The police did nothing – they apparently had more important things to deal with. They made a note of the attacks but also made it clear that upholding curfew laws, monitoring the streets at night, enforcing mandatory quarantines, and dealing with the many cases of sickness all over the country in general and within the force in particular had eaten up most of the time they could spend on such minor cases. To make it clear the police spelled it out for the owners: this was a minor case. So the police directed the dog owners to the local neighborhood militia.

The officials at the militia said the same thing as the police, then directed the dog owners to the Office of Animal Safety and Control, who were completely shut down due to the pandemic, but gladly directed the owners back to the militia, who directed them back to the police. The dog owners finally accepted that no help would be coming. There were laws in this country, but there was nobody left to enforce them. Laws existed, but not for people's protection anyway, and especially not for the protection of their property, the dogs. They felt that laws actually protected the perpetrators from the victims.

They were left to their own devices to defend their dogs. They formed self-protection groups, organized themselves into teams. The dog-walkers from each block tried to walk together. Many of them had armed themselves with makeshift household weapons: kitchen knives, cleavers, sprays. They tried to involve the larger community in the fight against the dog biter, but the larger community was of a different opinion. Dogs are their owners' problem. Those who didn't own a pet, or owned cats, turtles, goldfish, canaries, or other sorts of companion animals felt they needn't threaten their own personal safety for the sake of dogs. Since the dog biter didn't threaten them or their smaller pets, they didn't help, offering only their emotional and moral support to the cause. The dog owners were on edge. If they had to leave home they often took their dogs with them now, fearing that the biter would break into apartments to hunt down the dogs left at home.

Zoltán met one of the bitten dogs at the greengrocer. It was a white pitbull mix. The red bite mark was on its left side. The dog sat by its owner's feet, trembling every time someone walked in the door. Its owner looked at the dog shamefully, like the dog's weakness was his own. He seemed to understand that something was now missing from his beast; that this dog was less than a dog now, and everyone could see it.

That night as Zoltán watched the park from the balcony, he kept thinking about that dog. Nikolett was out there in the night hunting, despite Zoltán's warning of the risks. Who knew what the owners would do to her should they catch her one night. Maybe they would also discover their true selves that had been muted by life in a peaceful society. What would happen to Zoltán then? Would he be free if one night Nikolett didn't return home?

Or on the contrary, would he become lost, like the dog at the produce stand, because he himself would now be less than what he used to be? He took up smoking, hoping that a new habit would help him discover some new, hidden area in himself to claim as his own.

Nikolett didn't get caught that night, but something still changed. She came home, her body hot from the blood, and she drew a line in the sand.

'This can't go on like this!' said Nikolett, taking a cigarette from him. They had agreed not to smoke inside the apartment they both loved, and now the heavy smoke in the kitchen promised a downward turn. Zoltán had known this moment would come.

Several nights passed with her turning away from him in bed, digging a cold ditch between herself and Zoltán. Zoltán knew what this meant. When a person grows uncertain about their relationship but yet doesn't dare to say it out loud, they enter a pupal stage, like a caterpillar, allowing their emotions time to transform until they're ready to make the final decision. Zoltán looked into the girl's eyes, and now, knowing that soon, maybe in a matter of seconds, their relationship could end, she seemed even more beautiful to him than before.

'You can't understand me until you've tried it yourself.'

'What?' Zoltán asked, though fully aware of what she meant. 'What should I try?'

The girl had found a community online, the members of which – like her – had rediscovered a secret, ancient, primordial passion through mistreating pets. Not all of them were dog biters; there were some who, instead of biting, achieved the same effect through asphyxiation or even more exquisite methods which Nikolett didn't want to explain and Zoltán didn't want to hear.

This community had a dating site. Even if she had to go abroad, Nikolett wanted a man who understood her on a deeper level. A man who understood her true needs and didn't just accept them.

'You are important to me. So I'm giving you a chance,' she said to Zoltán. Her arms and thighs had gotten more muscular from her hunts, her gaze calm with the promise of violence. Zoltán loved this girl; he loved her in a way that he couldn't find words for, loved her even if loving her was dangerous, even if this whole thing was madness. Even if she was madness.

He felt safe by her side.

They ordered clothes for Zoltán: a black sweater, matching jogging pants, a cap, and a mask. His socks were black as well. They left for the hunt after eleven. There was some thrill even to this because it was well after curfew and the police or the militia could have easily caught them.

The police, however, didn't care about the area, neither the dogs nor the people. Whoever walked these streets walked them alone, finding their way in the dark, and in a world without police and without militia, without anyone to uphold the laws and protect those who could fall victim, everyone walking these streets was forced to assume the role of either predator or prey.

'I'm a predator! A fucking predator!' Zoltán told himself. He might have even said it aloud in a whisper, but who could tell under the black mask? He told himself he was a predator, but he felt like he was walking in a nightmare.

They reached the park and stepped out of the pale light of the lamps. The girl's posture changed; she moved differently. Her purpose of movement became absolute. Quick steps that found the silent spots on the ground. Her torso bent forward slightly, always ready for a sudden change of direction. She was a hunter now.

In the distance dogs were sniffing the ground, searching for the optimal spot to urinate. Some people conversed in hushed tones, smoking cigarettes. There were many dog owners out that night; like a herd they gathered around the bust of some forgotten state official in the middle of the park. Nikolett gestured for Zoltán to squat down. She threw herself behind a bush a good distance away from the dog owners. They couldn't be seen from where the dog owners were standing, but they could always be spotted by other owners who were patrolling the park. Danger was everywhere.

They waited in the darkness.

Zoltán's heart raced, his muscles ached from so much tension. He felt an urgent need to piss or else his bladder would burst. He envied the dogs who could go about pissing freely, not minding anyone.

Two dogs walked past the bush, but Nikolett ignored them. Zoltán let things run their own course, like in a fever dream. He was sweating under his clothes, and he knew he smelled of fear.

He wanted to run away, but his legs were made of rubber. He wanted to howl, but he was too terrified. It seemed to him that hours, maybe days, passed before the right dog showed up.

Even in the dark he could see that something about Nikolett's posture had changed. She had found her prey and was about to attack. Zoltán thought it would be like seeing someone die. His girlfriend would soon jump out of the bush and, like an animal, start to wrestle with the dog. How could something like that be forgotten, how could he keep going after seeing the struggle?

But what actually happened was in many ways even worse than this.

Nikolett stood straight up behind the bush; she didn't care about being seen. Her figure seemed enormous, and Zoltán understood now what she was talking about before. Nikolett seemed larger than herself, larger than her physical form. This was the strength that was missing from others, this was the force that neither the police nor the militia could control anymore. They preferred to control things smaller than themselves elsewhere, because they were too cowardly to face the world their absence had created.

The girl didn't move, she just stood watching the dog. The dog, a Labrador that looked gray in the dark, stopped mid-movement. It felt a predator's gaze on it.

The dog looked at Nikolett. The distance between dog and human was almost two meters, and Zoltán almost erupted in a joyful shout, because it couldn't happen, it was absolutely impossible that Nikolett could get hold of her victim from that distance. He felt great relief in his heart, because Nikolett had ruined it all, she couldn't triumph from there, she would never outrun a dog.

Nikolett pulled down the black mask to uncover her face. Zoltán knew that face, knew every small detail of it, but he almost didn't recognize her now. It was another mask, or maybe the face she wore during the day was the true mask after all, a mask that had slipped now to reveal the real Nikolett. She looked deep into the Labrador's eyes, then clicked her tongue, and the dog tucked its tail between its legs and started walking towards her.

Zoltán wanted to scream at the dog, yell at it, make it run away, but his body was paralyzed, hypnotized by terror. The dog had just admitted to being prey, a born victim. Victims always lean towards compromise; in order to avoid the greater pain, they offer a smaller one.

The dog stopped in front of Nikolett, then rolled onto its back to show its belly. Its entire body was exposed in a position of ultimate submission. The dog quivered in fear, but it let Nikolett do whatever she wanted.

Nikolett signaled to Zoltán to get closer. He did so on shaking legs. Now he felt more of a kinship with the animal than with his girlfriend. The girl was already opening her mouth for the bite; they had agreed to bite simultaneously, that's why this dog was special. It would be the first with a double bite. Zoltán knelt down by the Labrador and prepared himself for what was to come.

He felt someone's eyes on him. He looked up. The owner of the dog, a man in his early twenties, stood a few meters from them, holding a leash in one hand, a cleaver in the other. He was looking at Nikolett, the trembling dog lying at her feet, and Zoltán, whose face was nothing but a black hole because he never took off his mask.

We're busted, we're busted, a voice screamed in Zoltán's head, but the man didn't move, didn't make a sound. Nikolett looked deep into the owner's eyes, and the man surrendered just like his dog.

After all, if the dog is bitten, he'll be safe afterwards. He only has to go through it once and then it's over.

After seeing that the owner had surrendered too, Nikolett leaned down to the dog's belly and bit it. The dog whined painfully but still didn't run away.

Zoltán did.

He shot out and ran and ran until his lungs couldn't take it anymore, and then he ran some more because he imagined Nikolett running right behind him, mouth open to take a bite out of his face. When he couldn't run any further he stopped by a lamp post, and in the pale LED light he threw up. Then he ran on until he reached the smell of bleach and plywood, the extra comfort, the place of Sunday honey-color and tranquility. His home. Their home.

Her home.

He tore off the black clothes and stood under the shower to wash off the smell of fear and excitement. As he washed himself he kept thinking about the dog and its owner, and he surprised himself when anger startled bubbling up instead of fear and disgust. Why can't these people and their dogs stand up for themselves? Why do they accept being charged the tax of pain at night? Why can't they take control and protect themselves? All they would have to say is no! All they would have to do is lash out at their attacker.

Of course he knew why. He knew because he was just like them. A dog that approaches with knees bent and shaking. A dog's teeth are sharper than its master's and could bite at any time; but power doesn't require sharp teeth, only the will to use violence. And dogs don't have the will; masters do.

He was done showering; when he stepped out of the bathroom, Nikolett was waiting for him in the kitchen.

'You get one last chance,' she said. 'If you don't take it, that's it. It's over.'

Her pants were dirty, her face muddy. In her arms she held a dog, some kind of large mixed breed. She swept everything off the kitchen table and laid the dog down with its belly facing upwards.

'One last chance,' she repeated.

Zoltán stood naked by the kitchen table. The towel had fallen off him somewhere in the corridor. The dog kept shivering on the table, looking at Zoltán, as if asking him to get it over with quickly.

Zoltán looked at the girl, took a whiff of the apartment's scent, which was now mixed up with the smell of dog piss. His own scent was concealed by the shower gel, the smell of comfort and safety. But that smell, he realized for the first time, was only a lie.

There is no safety. There is no one to protect you. There is no one to trust. Everyone is alone in this world, and either you bite or you are bitten.

'I love you,' he said to the girl, then leaned closer to the dog and opened his mouth for a bite.

Fogtown

literarymysteries.blogspot.hu, 2014.08.12, author: Hungarian-Psycho

The time has come to say goodbye. As keri.feri23 mentioned in his previous post, the blog is finished. It will remain searchable, but no more new posts, no more interviews – this mystery is the final one. We have written extensively about the reasons for the suspension in the above-mentioned post, and we've also discussed it on our Facebook page. It basically boils down to how all good things must come to an end. We thank you for having followed us. I believe that this last post is a fitting closure to what we've been doing the past few years. We could even say it's our crowning achievement.

This final literary mystery is about a book that has never been completed. Ironic, given its title: *The Unpublished Books of Hungary*. The manuscript was supposed to have been written by Márton Kopaszhegyi-Kézi and Júlia Nagy. Kopaszhegyi-Kézi was the former editor of a well-known men's magazine, *JCQ*. He is also the author of two small press short story collections: *The Rivers of the Moon* and *Dreamtime*, the latter of which won the short-lived Pompa Prize, awarded by *JCQ* magazine from 2001-2003. Júlia Nagy is known as a journalist and the editor of literary magazines, such as *New Kalifa* (established 1997, ended 2003) and *Litera Magnum* (established 2005, ended 2010). She currently divides her time between ghost-writing music biographies and managing the Adopt Me! animal shelter. Tragically Márton Kopaszhegyi-Kézi passed away in 2012; however Júlia Nagy kindly answered most of our questions, clearing up the picture about their joint project. She also sent us the relevant parts of the unfinished manuscript, which we publish here verbatim, including the editorial notes.

Márton Kopaszhegyi-Kézi's personal notes were made available to us by his widow. We would like to express our gratitude to her here.

The unfinished book, just as the title promises, was supposed to be a catalogue and history of unfinished or unpublished books. Region 2000, a Budapest-based publishing firm, had commissioned the book. Region 2000 achieved its greatest success with volumes on local history from towns all over the country. Later they switched to local art history, then to even more obscure facets, such as the history of local cinemas and theater houses. The publisher was eventually bought out by one of the well-known large distributors, and after a while it was closed down, its assets digested into a larger company.

The idea came about a few years before the buyout and closure. The two authors had already ghost-written several books for Region 2000, although never together. The idea was that people were more likely to read a volume about unfinished books than to read the actual finished and published literature gathering dust on bookshelves.

The authors were chosen because both had the right connections with senior editors, publishing houses, and writers, so they could reach out and compose a list of the most infamous unfinished, unpublished, and lost manuscripts. The Hungarian literary scene is closed and guarded, but once you're within its circles, you just have to ask the right people.

'Most of these unfinished volumes come from the Communist days,' Júlia Nagy recounts in her letter. *'Most of the books we intended to discuss were forbidden items due to their subversive, anti-Communist, or supposedly anarchic content, primarily from the '60s, '70s, and '80s. This would have been the primary market value of our book, since Communism and its sins is always a hot topic. However, in the early stages*

of our research a title came up that at first didn't seem like anything special. It didn't fit into our sins-of-Communism theme either. Still, we couldn't disregard it. It was supposedly an amateur book on rural, small-town bands. It just came up over and over again. People kept mentioning it, but no one had actually read it. Then we learned that there was an actual police investigation about the book at the time. Someone disappeared, we understood, and soon we figured out it was the author himself. He vanished. He's still considered a missing person, maybe he's legally dead now, I don't know. It was enough to mark the manuscript as infamous, so we added it to our list as an interesting counterpiece. Then we hit a wall. In most cases you could talk to an editor or a friend who had read the manuscript and could give you an account of it, even if the manuscript itself was lost or destroyed. That wasn't the case with this one. Although a lot of people had heard about it, the manuscript had never reached the publishers. No editor or editor's assistant had read even an excerpt. Those who supposedly had weren't in the business anymore, and we couldn't track them down. It seemed like they vanished into thin air. I assume they moved abroad, or went underground.'

One day, out of the blue, the problem solved itself.

'*One morning Márton showed up carrying a cardboard box. Inside was a Xeroxed text and a couple of cassette tapes. From the look on his face I knew instantly that it was the book. We had become rather obsessed with it by that time, I must admit.*'

'*How did he get hold of it? That's a good question. Márton never told me. He said he found the box on his doorstep. I think that's bullshit, manuscripts don't just appear when you need them. He wanted to play it close to the chest. He always avoided giving a straight answer. Now we'll never know.*'

After reading through the text, they believed it would definitely make for one of the more exciting chapters in their own book.

'*I'm proud of the work we did. But looking back, I think we shouldn't have signed up for it. It started Márton down a path that led to his end.'*

The relevant chapter is brief, at times lacking style or coherence. It is a work in progress, just like the book the text is about. Presumably it would have been extended and fleshed out in line with the entirety of the book. All dates and city names had been crossed out with a black marker, therefore the two authors make no reference to the city in question in their own manuscript either. Perhaps at the time of final editing they would have provided the name of the location. Júlia Nagy claims that the city is Nyíregyháza, in the eastern part of the country, but she says she cannot be entirely sure. It could be any city or town anywhere in Hungary.

THE UNFINISHED BOOKS OF HUNGARY – excerpts (authors: Márton Kopaszhegyi-Kézi and Júlia Nagy)

Most books don't come about by way of a commission; most books come to be through their author's desire. The final product is like a child born of an illicit relationship, a relationship that is equally joyous and painful. Some authors' desire to write their book is so great it consumes their lives and often the lives of those around them. I believe that was the case with Balázs Peterfy's book, entitled *On the Stage Tonight – Local Rock History*. Most of these labors of love go sour once they hit an editor's desk – they turn out to be amateurish, dire little things that are better left forgotten. This book, however, could well have enjoyed the fortunate combination of both passion and the financial guarantee of publishing. Nonetheless, life had other plans. While in most cases it is either politics, financial issues, or a swift change in readers' tastes that prevents the publishing of a book already accepted by an editor, in this case the work remained unfinished due to the unfortunate disappearance of the writer.

Balázs Peterfy was born in 1980, the only child of a wealthy middle-class family. He went to high school in ―, got good grades, then graduated with a degree in law at ― University. His adult years were overshadowed by tragedy: he lost his parents to a car accident. Two years after the incident he set out to write his book.

During his high school years Balázs' parents guarded him closely to ensure his high grades and academic career. He was never allowed to go to parties, concerts, or the other sorts of outings that are typical in one's teenage years. His classmates lived the nightlife of teenagers, but Balázs stayed at home to study, read, and generally not to be corrupted. Hence there is nothing surprising in the fact that following the loss of his parents he wanted to reenact those wasted teenage years. (*Isn't this a speculation? I know we want to give him motivation, but still. How do we know this? Let's ask S.K. too – the Editor.*)

He was aided in his quest by János Egér. Egér is a mildly successful businessman, owner of a printing company/publishing house as well as a pub called Rathole. He is also an amateur musician. (*N.B.: János Egér's nickname is Rat – the Editor*).

The Rathole is a rather tiny but cozy rock pub (*Márton, it came across as cozy to you? I almost died there, let's be a bit more objective – the Editor*); behind the counter it is often János Egér himself bartending. He is not in the pub business for profit alone.

'*I've always wanted a pub,*' says the successful businessman, who on the outside looks like a member of a motorcycle gang. He met Balázs Peterfy in this pub, though they had known each other from high school. '*We weren't friends in high school. He was a lonely kid. He was always alone, no friends, never came to parties. He wasn't even worth bullying. But as the years go by, you start to appreciate old acquaintances more and more, as friends leave the city or you fall out with them. Or they die.*'

Their acquaintance quickly evolved into a friendship. The men were tied together by a woman: Brigitta Kovács Egér, once the wife of János Egér, who had regrettably succumbed to cancer a few years back.

'We were both grieving, he and I together, that's a strong bond.' (*For fuck's sake, Júlia, this is not an authentic voice. He didn't speak at all like this! – the Editor.* Response: *If we write down what he actually said, this book will never get published.*)

The two men talked a lot about their high school years, and Balázs confessed that as a teenager he had been madly in love with Brigitta Kovács (*no one should write things like 'madly in love'* – the Editor). The fact that Brigitta was not among the living anymore made him depressed, not only because of the personal loss, but also because he felt like his connection to the past had become even fainter with her absence.

'*Brigitta's death upset him a great deal. If Balázs had any friend in high school, it was Brigitta. She told him a lot of stories*

about the shows she had seen, the parties she had been to. I was at those parties too, that's why I married her and he didn't. But now, all these years later, he wanted to live through those times in retrospect. Especially the concerts. But he knew it wasn't possible anymore. The city is not the same.'
(Shouldn't we mention the UFO story here? – the Editor.)

Finally, János Egér, partly out of curiosity, partly to satisfy his friend's desires, offered to publish his book through his publishing house. Balázs wanted to write about the city's underground music scene. He had already amassed a considerable amount of background research by then.

Why and how? We can find the answer in Balázs Peterfy's half-finished introduction to his own book:

I found the first box at a local Sunday flea market. The one right next to the cemetery, by the — housing complex. It was a cold day, the coldest of the year by far. My fingers were red and completely frozen as I searched through the selection. I wasn't looking for anything in particular. Skimming through flea markets became a habit of mine. Finally I found what I had been searching for, even if I didn't know I was searching for it. It was a black shoebox, Nike, size 11. It was full of cassette tapes; all made of white, red, and blue molded plastic. Some had labels handwritten in blue or red ink marking the content; others didn't. I greedily bought up the entire selection. I also bought a cassette player and a Walkman.

Much of the collection was worthless; tape copies of LPs, everything from Iron Maiden to Tiamat to Ossian. But a small portion consisted of demos, mainly from the '90s and early 2000s: amateur or semi-professional recordings of local bands, which no one had ever really listened to aside from a couple of high school students, the proud parents, and maybe the sweaty critics of rock magazines. These were the bands that played at high school parties, nameless pubs, the clubs that were always popping up as something new and exciting and then quickly rebranded into cheap watering holes. All of these places, all of this music, all of these people, had since been eradicated by time. None of them existed anymore, or not in the relevant form. The walls of the buildings remained the same, but not the inhabitants.

Obviously, they were horrible demos. Most of them were recorded in rehearsal spaces or the cheapest studios. The drums sounded like someone beating on a cardboard box, the guitars only squeaked, the bass was so overdriven that it almost blew the speakers. The songs ranged from no good to terrible. Nevertheless, I have never been happier than when I listened to all these tapes. They were pieces of a past that awaited further exploration. This put me on the path at the end of which I had to write this book. The story of the unknown bands of the city, bands that never released a single record.

He had a passion for collecting, and now this passion slowly grew into an obsession. He attempted to catalog the garage bands that were once active in the city, even if they hadn't played a single show. He had taken notes on their members, potential concert venues, bar owners. He hunted for photocopied posters, searched for tapes online and at flea markets. By the time he met János Egér, he had gotten hold of hundreds of demos and had also filled up three notebooks with the names of since-disbanded groups and the contact information for their members. He was trying to draw a map of a time and place that he had co-existed with but never felt a part of. Now, retroactively, he tried to find a place in this past for himself. He wanted to belong. It was only live music that he cared about: metal bands, alternative rock groups, cover bands. He never made any notes on the local techno and house scene, wasn't interested in the history of illegal rave parties. That was a part of the past he erased from his notes by way of omission.

The publishing offer from János Egér only fueled his obsession even more and focused it in such a way that his desires reached a flashpoint. Now he *had* to write the book.

The idea was to reach out to all the band members, the fans, the promoters and groupies (a big word for teenage girls hanging out with their boyfriends) and do interviews with them all.

In several ways Balázs' thinking was disturbing. Judging from his friends' recollections of his behavior, especially in the later phases, he treated the present as a tomb, as if real life existed only in the past and the present was just suspended animation, a trance-like state of drawn-out death. To him the 'relevant form' of the people he interviewed was 'back then'. He looked at them as records of a sort, interesting only because they could talk about the past; in the present they were no more than ghosts wandering in search of their resting place.

The book might have ended up being just like the demos Balázs listened to day and night: amateurish and of interest only to close acquaintances. Still, it would have contained Balázs' desire to recreate the past – even if only for himself.

Nevertheless, the work was never finished. The majority of the interviews had been completed, as was the introduction. Yet the material never reached an editor.

More than ninety-seven interviews were conducted. He recorded all of them with a voice recorder, even when the conversation was on Skype or over the phone. He only wanted to write about bands that had never released any licensed records, just self-released demos or albums without distribution. Balázs wrote short summaries on the subjects and the location of the meeting. He always attached these descriptions to the transcripts of the interviews.

For example:

Name: Róbert Fajan (Tücsi)

Current occupation: car mechanic

Formerly: bass player of the band Ratherd (punk/dirty rock), singer-guitarist of Cyonid (oi punk), singer of Will (hardcore/punk).

Slim, lean man, with a medium-sized Mickey Mouse tattoo on his upper arm (but maybe it's a bat or a Greater Hungary tattoo, I have to ask P.) Black teeth, cigarette in his mouth the whole time.

Location: his garage, Playboy posters and calendars on the wall, the smell of oil.

We cannot know for sure whether Balázs intended to publish the interviews in their raw form or if he would have converted them into a flowing text. He typed out all of the interviews, and he added plenty of comments and notes to them. This seems to underscore his intention of editing.

In any case, this car mechanic in ques-

tion was the very first interview subject,
and Balázs Peterfy consistently stuck to the
system established here.

This interview served as a model for every
interview to come.

...

B: Which was your first band? What was the name?

R: For fuck's sake, you know that! We just talked about it.

B: But I'd like you to say it out loud as well. Now I'm recording.

R: Okay, okay! Ratherd. It was a cool band. Fast and dirty, like my girls at the time.

B: Where did you learn to play?

R: Learn? Nowhere! Me, learning . . . ? (he laughs) It was cool, though. We bought some crappy bass guitar, we connected it to a tape recorder to amplify it, and you know, go! It was overdriven and sounded lousy, but nobody cared.

...

B: How were the parties?

R: I swear to God I don't remember. We always got hammered real good before the shows, you know. I could barely stand. Most of the time, I plucked a single string until I realized that the others were playing a different song . . . so then I started plucking another string. You could say I wasn't no expert player or nothing.

During the interview, they talked through
the history of all three of Róbert's bands.
The man was proud of all of them (altogether they had recorded five demos; Balázs
received a copy of each). They talked about
the popular and cheap studios, the popular
and cheap pubs, the popular and cheap girls.
All of these were thoroughly documented by
the author. This framework was repeated from

interview to interview, and the author gradually gained a deeper insight into the musical scene of his youth. There was no band he was unaware of, even if some had never set foot on a stage or in a studio. One-time musicians turned into lawyers, architects, shop vendors, tax collectors. They outgrew music, outgrew youth. Most of them looked back with a hint of nostalgia; some, with yearning; some, with anger.

That is why the concept of the book is so exciting: it would have been about the growing-up of a generation. However, the truly interesting thing about the manuscript doesn't lie in the wasted potential of the musicians. After thirty-four interviews, it was in the thirty-fifth that a reference was first made to Fogtown, although not yet called by name.

Name: Boriska Schramoweck

Current occupation: magazine editor

Formerly: groupie, girlfriend of the guitarist of Today Bleeds for Roses (emo/hardcore).

Attractive woman, slightly crooked teeth, leather jacket with thigh-high boots. A lot of rings. The flat is minimalist, modern, and rich.

...

B: So you went with them to every concert.

Bo: Yes, I did, but not because it was my duty as a girlfriend or anything like that. I mean, I'm an independent person, I was an independent person even back then, you know. The reason why I went to their concerts was because I believed in what they were doing, that they were conveying an important message to their audience, to the kids, you know. There are so many lost souls that need guidance. I felt like we were starting a revolution.

B: How was the atmosphere?

Bo: Always ecstatic, we really killed it. I think it also elevated the mood that during the concerts everyone wanted to flirt with me, so Tibi (*A red note on the printed paper saying that Tibi is the band's guitarist.*) would play with even more intensity. They always headlined. Except for one occasion, when those idiots played after them. Tibi and the others had a fight with the promoter about it.

B: Which band was it?

Bo: I don't remember. I was a little high by then, I didn't wait for it. It was a bad night, the only bad night I think.

B: Where was this?

Bo: In the gymnasium of the —— high school.

```
Balázs didn't attribute special importance
to this incident. Nonetheless, a certain
change in his focus can be dated back to
around this time period. Although his goal
was to explore the life course of his gener-
ation up until today by mapping a particular
segment of the past, he got more and more
bored by the stories. He wanted more. He
wanted the exact details.
  Not only what happened, but also what stale
beer or an empty street smelled like. How an
ear rang after a show, how the pillow's touch
felt on a hungover morning. What a first kiss
tasted like around midnight. He couldn't get
these details from the interviews, no matter
how hard he pushed. (Márton, where did you
get this from? Is there a journal too? Let's
not write things we can't prove. I want to
delete this - the Editor).
  He became impatient.
  It was in the forty-fourth interview that
the band was named for the first time.
```

Name: Sándor Kiss (Piglet)

Current occupation: event organizer, promoter

Formerly: concert organizer, festival organizer, publisher

Location: cozy cafe at —— Square. (*Why did he cross out the names? Couldn't we fill in at least some of them?* – the Editor).

Leather jacket, sunglasses, tie, shirt. Casual, but elegant guy, always holds a cigarette in his hand, but rarely takes a drag. (Why was his nickname Piglet? He is very slim.)

B: How many concerts did you organize back in the day?

S: There always had to be a party on Fridays and Saturdays, but depending on the season, we could sometimes arrange something weekdays too. But there was always at least one show every week, usually two. For each show I arranged three or four bands. The bigger bands rarely came to town, but there were plenty of local players. The more bands playing on a given night, the more it was worth it for the kids to pay the cover charge. Most of these were, of course, high school bands, so they played for peanuts basically. Most members couldn't even get booze legally, but we paid them in booze tickets anyway.

B: So you knew everyone.

S: Yes, I think so. I wasn't friends with everyone, but I knew everyone, even if by proxy.

...

B: What was your favorite band?

S: I liked Nofertum (instrumental prog rock) as people, they were really cool guys, even if I didn't dig their music. I liked the band Szeged (straight edge hardcore), they were playing some cool music. They were an antidote to that shitfest of a band, something with Roses and Bleeding, and Today, or Yesterday, or whatever. Annoying little self-important pricks. They all became lawyers, no wonder.

B: Which was the strangest, most peculiar band?

S: The Ceiling Puzzle (art rock) were doing some very weird stuff, they wore makeup, played on kitchen utensils. There was dancing too, they went the whole nine yards to be artsy. They weren't in the game for long anyway. Apparently they wanted to be like that other band, Fogtown. Those were the genuine weirdos.

B: Fogtown? What did they play?

S: I don't know. To be honest I never actually heard them play. But a lot of people told me they were good. And weird. There was this little cult around them.

B: Didn't you organize shows for them?

S: No. I think it was the only band I had no contact with. I don't even know who managed them, or if anyone did. That's a good question.

B: Who were the members?

S: I don't know. I guess the regular high school kids. But I really don't know anything else about them.

Balázs searched through his considerable cassette selection, but he found no trace of Fogtown playing. He reviewed the band index one more time, but no luck there either. From that point on, he started bringing up the band's name at every interview.

He got excited: here was a piece of the past that belonged to very few, and if he unveiled it, it could belong to him as well. At the same time, he was worried: what if Sándor Kiss was mistaken about the band's name? What if the band was called something completely different? (*Now you have to stop it once and for all. Or keep going as you wish, but I'll start a new chapter then* – the Editor). A few weeks later he managed to dredge up one member of The Ceiling Puzzle, who by then was working in England as a restaurant manager.

Name: Gábor Kisfalvi Keller
Current occupation: restaurant manager (London)
Formerly: guitarist-trumpeter of The Ceiling Puzzle
Skype call. I don't know what the room looks like, I only see pixels.

...

B: You were an experimental group, right?

G: Yeah, I guess we were. We fooled around on the stage a lot, and we also put together a pretty good single.

B: Did you split up quickly?

G: We played five or six shows. They were good, I think. But then we split up, everyone went in different directions.

B: What was the reason for splitting up?

G: Karcsi. The singer-guitarist. The band was his, and he badly wanted to express something. We were kind of obstructing his self-expression I guess, even though we were his musicians. He was an asshole, and we got bored, so we quit to form another band. We never quite formed it, then we all went to college. That's it in short.

B: I heard that you were greatly influenced by Fogtown.

G: Yeah, I heard that too.

B: Did you like them?

G: I haven't heard a single song from them in my life.

B: So...

G: It was Karcsi who got obsessed with them. We spent all our time trying to be like Fogtown. Trouble was, we had no idea what they played. At first I didn't even believe that the band existed, but then I heard about them from others too. Karcsi worshipped them, but he couldn't tell us what they were like.

B: Why didn't you go to one of their shows?

G: We wanted to, but we could never make it to one, no matter how hard we tried. They were totally nuts. Nobody ever knew when and where they would play. So we never saw them.

B: Who were the members?

G: Listen, I don't know. I don't think anybody I knew knows, maybe only Karcsi did.

B: And where can I find Karcsi?

G: In the graveyard. His heart stopped in his sleep a few years back. By then they say that he had already gone mad from drinking.

```
Balázs looked up all the remaining members
of The Ceiling Puzzle who were still alive.
Two of them didn't want to talk to him and
two of them couldn't provide any substan-
tial new information. He got hold of their
single. It was professionally recorded, but
extremely boring material, with remarkably
feeble lyrics. Fogtown was brought up again
two interviews later.
```

Júlia Nagy has written to us that from this point on she did not take part in the writing of the text because her co-author refused to accept any of her suggestions.

Name: Miklós Janocsek

Current occupation: police instructor

Formerly: singer of the bands Hit'em! (racist metal) and Right of the White (supremacist metalcore)

We meet in his office, at the police station on —— Street

...

B: Have you heard of a band called Fogtown?

M: You bet I have! My girlfriend was crazy about them. My ex. She was the most beautiful girl, but back at the time I dumped her without thinking.

B: Why?

M: First of all, we weren't really a good match, I mean . . . you know. The band members and my buddies weren't exactly happy that . . . you know, that she had Hebrew ancestors. It's really embarrassing to think about it now, I guess I was pretty stupid back then, and my friends were a bad influence on me . . . But that's not the real reason why I dumped her, I mean we could have just denied the whole thing . . . she didn't have a big nose or anything like that, my friends would never have known. And she really wanted it, us being together, she was so much in love with me.

B: I see . . .

M: Anyway. The point is that she would talk about this goddamn band all the time. That we really had to go see one of their shows. That she'd heard something of theirs, or she was at a rehearsal, or her girlfriend was at a rehearsal, whatever, but that we had to go to a concert right away, because it was flaming hot shit, okay? Only there never was any concert at all. No matter how eagerly I searched for them, there was nothing. Nowhere. Only the rumor that there would be a show soon, or there had been one just last Sunday, or something. It was like chasing a shadow. Then I realized: there's no such band at all. They spread word of it as if it existed, when in fact it didn't. Just to fool people, you know. Pulling our legs. And my girlfriend got fooled. She said she had been to a party, but I know that she hadn't been, because that band didn't perform. Never. It didn't even exist, all right? So I got fed up, and I dumped her. Okay, so I actually dumped her because of that, that's what you should write down, all right? I still feel like barfing when I hear that goddamn name. Fog-fucking-town!

After this, Balázs was driven by the sole purpose of finding proof of Fogtown's existence. He looked all over to find the one-time girlfriend; both the girl and her family were gone. He managed to track down a friend of this girl. To Balázs' great surprise, he recognized her: they had attended the same high school, but she was two years his senior.

Name: Eszter Vas
Current occupation: prostitute
Formerly: student, groupie
We are meeting at an apartment, red curtains, tissues, lubricants, a mirror above the bed. Curly, chestnut hair, God, those eyes.

...

B: For sure you don't remember, but we ...

E: I remember. Balázs. Peterfy. You were two years younger than me. You always smiled very kindly at me.

B: Uhm ...

E: I was always waiting for you to finally approach me, but you didn't. You were cute. Never came to any parties, though. Sorry to hear about your parents.

B: ...

E: You're cute still.

B: You ... too.

E: (laughs) This is wonderful! So good that you came to visit, I haven't had such a great time in a while.

...

B: I heard that you had a friend, her name was Y.

E: Yes, I did.

B: Were you two close?

E: We had our ups and downs. We had sex a few times. We were experimenting. She dated Nazis for fun, that really impressed me. She made complete fools out of them. She was a tough girl. She wanted to write a book about her Nazi boyfriends and their sex lives. Most of them are impotent, did you know that? It was all just a prank, but I had so much fun. It's a shame she never wrote that book.

B: What happened to her?

E: She said she had to leave. That was the last time we spoke. She was very upset, she said she had to leave, and that we would meet again someday, later. Then she was gone. I guess she went to Israel with her parents, or somewhere abroad.

B: When did this happen?

E: Three years ago, on August 27th, at 4:38 pm.

B: Do you remember it that well?

E: I remember everything. Literally everything.

. . .

B: They say she was a big fan of the band Fogtown.

E: Yes, she was.

B: Have you by chance been to any of their concerts?

E: No. I only heard them once. They were playing at a school party, without previous announcement, like usual. I'd been dying to go to one of their shows. You know, everyone whispered about them, but nobody had ever seen them. Maybe there will be a show here, someone would say, maybe there, according to somebody else. But you could never know whether they would actually go on stage. But those who went to one of their concerts were not the same afterwards.

B: What do you mean?

E: I don't know. I can't explain it.

B: How come you only heard them? Why didn't you see them?

E: Because I was in a classroom. Me and a boyfriend sneaked in to have sex. He was older than me, he already had a tattoo. He almost got suspended for it. Of course, they couldn't suspend him because he was the principal's nephew. No, not at our school, this happened at —— High. Four bands were announced, the Fruits of Kaboom, the Ocean, the Old Spaceships, and the Intestinal Worms. They were all pretty bad. Do you know them?

B: (presumably he nodded)

E: Then you know. My boyfriend stole the master key from the janitor, or else he bribed him for it. He closed the classroom door. It was winter, and our parents were home. We needed a warm place. By then we had already had sex twice, but it wasn't that good. He didn't exactly have an aptitude for the delicacies of the female body, if you know what I mean. He was like an industrial driller. Actually, it even hurt, but I thought I had to put up with it, that it would get better over time, I just had to get used to it. I wish girls knew that isn't true, that they can say no any time. Anyway. We went up to the classroom when the last band had almost finished. I tried to drink as much as I could, hoping that it would help. It didn't. Then someone said through the mic that there was going to be another band: Fogtown would play at the end. I really wanted to see them, but he dragged me with him. He wasn't sober, and I was a bit scared of him. I thought if I gave it to him quick he would let me see the rest of the show. We went up to the classroom. He threw me onto one of the benches, he ripped off my clothes right away and started with his usual business, hammering away as hard as he could. Then the concert started downstairs. I can't describe to you what it was like. He stopped too. Even though the music was coming through the walls, from one floor beneath us, muffled, we couldn't focus on anything else.

B: What genre was it? Rock, alternative, heavy metal?

E: I don't know. It was constantly changing, but at the same time ... like, it didn't change at all. We only heard an approximation of it, you know. The music echoed through the corridors, it was filtered by layers of concrete. It must have been so much better for those who saw them up close.

B: But in the end, you didn't go down.

E: Of course not. He seemed to adapt to the rhythm of the music. It didn't hurt anymore, quite the opposite. It felt like we were in a dream. We kept on doing it as long as the concert went on. I have no idea how long it took. It felt like days, I swear. Years, aeons even. The next day I couldn't walk. Nothing ever was anything like whatever happened on that bench. It wasn't just sex. That was the least of it. It felt as if we had changed along with the music, I don't know, like we were many things, not only ourselves, but light and time and thought, all drifting though some infinite space ... This sounds stupid, but it was like we were the entire world. It was perfection itself.

B: And since then?

E: Then I thought sex was like that. I tried it again with him. I tried it with others too, but it wasn't the same. Each morning I would wake up crying, because that night in the classroom I experienced a kind of bliss nothing could measure up to. I didn't know how to recreate it. Now you think I'm crazy?

B: No. Not at all.

E: Yes, I can see that. You believe in it, right? You believe that all this really happened.

B: I do.

E: Eventually I realized what was missing. Not the right man or the mood. The music. The music was missing. I focused very hard, and one of the melodies came to me. The only melody, perhaps. I started humming it during sex. And it worked. Nothing came close to the band actually playing, but with the melody I could approximate that original experience. It's only because of this that I'm able to survive. My parents freaked out of course. After all I was a genius, top of the class, I was going to be a biochemist. Then I decided to be a prostitute. I wasn't forced into it like so many others. Do you think it's strange? I like it this way. I can still remember the melody. That's what my clients come for. For me to sing to them. I need them, too. Each time we fly back to the classroom for a little while. Each time they're with me, in that classroom, on that winter night. They're with me and we're young again, touching something that's beyond ... beyond us, beyond what we are, what we see. It pays good money too, but the money's not what I care about.

B: Why haven't you looked up the band?

E: Because if I could experience them raw, I wouldn't want to come back to this world. It wouldn't make sense to go on living. I think that was her problem too. I told her not to go back, but she just kept going to the concerts. Interesting, you know. If you had been to one, you would know when they played next. You would just feel. I don't think she went abroad.

B. Where did she go?

E: I think she's still here. I think she's one with the town. I think she's just beyond.

B: Beyond...

E: Do you want to hear it? The melody?

B: Yes.

E: Come to bed.

B: I don't have money on me.

E: I don't care. You deserve it. You understand... Come.

(at this point it's as if the tape got damaged, there is nothing but static noise)

B: My God. My God.
E: Do you want more?
B: Yes! Show me!

(static noise again)

E: Take off your clothes!

(static noise from this point until the end of the recording)

```
This was when Balázs decided to dedicate
his book to Fogtown. He cared about nothing
but finding the band. He didn't tell anyone
about what happened at Eszter's flat. Nobody
would have believed him, and he couldn't
have explained it either. He reached out to
Eszter multiple times, but the woman didn't
```

want to meet him again. She said it was different for her with Balázs and refused to meet him again. She said she didn't want to go down the path Balázs had started on, but if they were to meet again, she would.

Balázs nearly went mad because of this. He found just what he had been looking for with her, or something very much like it. For those minutes, it was like he wasn't himself. For a moment, he turned into someone he always wanted to be. The worst thing about it was that he couldn't even remember clearly what had happened. He wasn't even sure whether he had slept with Eszter, and if he had, whether it lasted for minutes or hours. He only recalled the melody, but he didn't have a clear recollection of that either.

From the next dozen interviews, he learned that in fact everyone knew someone who knew someone who had once been to a Fogtown show, or had wanted to attend one. He roamed through all the high schools whose gymnasiums could have served as a stage for the band, all the empty basements which once were a club or a pub. One of the interviewees told him that he had heard from someone that in its early days Fogtown used to promote itself on posters, but the posters were blank, only photocopied whiteness. No date, no band name, no location. But those who knew the band understood the message anyway. Balázs found a poster like that in the storage room at —— High School. There was indeed nothing on it, just the blankness of the paper, Xeroxed several times over.

Then he found someone who really knew someone.

Name: Gábor Szabó
Current occupation: locksmith
Formerly: nothing
Dirty flat.

B: So did I understand correctly that you've been to a Fogtown concert?

G: Me? No, I haven't. I didn't go to any concerts, I'm a disco guy. I went to rave parties, techno . . . you know, I went because of the girls.

B: I was told that . . .

G: Yeah, I know why. I'm Big Sabesz. That was Little Sabesz. He liked this shit. The kid was a big artist.

B: Your brother.

G: Yeah. Half-brother from my father's other marriage. We always got along well.

B: So he liked rock?

G: Yep. But there was a minor obstacle. He was deaf as a stone. He had tumors in his ears. The operation resulted in a complete loss of hearing when he was nine. He didn't handle it so well. It caused his death too. He wasn't looking when he was walking and some motherfucker ran him over with a truck.

B: My condolences. But he still went to concerts.

G: He did, poor kid. I guess it was easier to put up with the guitar screeching when you were deaf.

B: And he went to a Fogtown concert.

G: That's what he said. We learned sign language together, but when he got home he was so excited that he just waved his arms chaotically. I had to calm him down so that I could understand him. We went up to my room and discussed it there. I don't know if what he said actually happened. I don't think so.

B: What did he say happened?

G: He was at a school party. I think at —— High School.

That's a very liberal place with a concert hall and everything. My brother went there to a party. You know, local bands playing, the usual. He said it was nice. He used to watch people all the time at these shows. He drew very well. You know, I know nothing about art, but what my brother did always made me ... think and feel. So I guess he was really good at capturing moments, emotions. He mostly drew faces, that was his thing. So I suppose he was observing faces at these parties.

B: Aha.

G: Yeah. So he stood through these awful performances. The place was almost empty by the end of the show, but new people started coming in as if something else was about to happen. So he waited a bit more. And he was right, because suddenly a new band showed up. They weren't on the bill.

B: Fogtown.

G: I think so, yes. They started playing. Poor kid didn't hear a thing, obviously. He said he was watching the stage but he couldn't see the musicians. The place wasn't well lit, so there were only shadows. He said he felt by the tremor on the floor that the concert had started. Then he was watching the people, their faces. He said something changed about them. After that, he spent weeks drawing these faces, then he showed them to me. Unfortunately, I can't show them to you because he had them on him when he died, and ... so I don't have them anymore. But I saw those pictures. Those faces were as if ... I don't know, as if they had been yearning for something, and all of sudden they could have it. They were both sad and happy at the same time. That was the beginning of the party.

B: Mm-hmm.

G: The crowd ... my brother said the crowd went weird. This will sound really stupid, saying it like this, in broad daylight. My brother wasn't a junkie. I asked him if he was on something, just to be sure, but he said no and I believed him. So he told me there was this guy who stepped out of the crowd, he walked up to the stage, and he cut his veins open right there with a broken beer bottle. Blood poured out. My brother freaked out, he called for help. But nobody came. He said it was like . . . like the whole room went one shade darker. But the guy didn't collapse. Blood poured out of him, black blood, because it was so dark. It flew over the floor, covering everything like paint. But the guy didn't collapse. And the crowd started dancing, but that's not even the right expression, because they weren't dancing, they acted like they had all become one, they were swaying, a lot of silhouettes, you know, merging, like trees in a forest. My brother made several drawings of this too. He looked up at the stage and saw that the musicians were not even playing their instruments, they were just standing there. Or they were levitating, or some fucking thing, because apparently their feet didn't touch the stage. My brother looked at the crowd, and they were above the ground too. They were spinning round and round, and writhing, but slowly, as if they were underwater. And they were naked, but their skin looked dark. Not in an unnatural way, more like . . . he said their skin was like night itself. One of these guys turned inside himself while spinning, his whole body twisted and he turned into a big circle, then got smaller, then he was gone. He disappeared into himself. At this point my brother laid down on the floor and pressed his head against the ground so that he could feel the vibration. And he said for a minute he could hear.

B: What?

G: He said it was music. Some kind of music. And crying and laughter. And rain. That's what he heard.

B: And then?

G: Then it was all over. He looked up and the crowd wasn't there anymore. Neither was the band. The lights were up. The cleaning lady was poking him with the mop, telling him to get out because the party was over. She thought he had fallen asleep on the floor.

B: And isn't that possible?

G: Yeah, of course, that's possible.

B: Did your brother change after this?

G: I told you, he would draw all the time, and it was like he tried to hum some kind of melody, only he was deaf. He became quite distracted and anxious. I was worried about him. Not long after that he got hit by that car. There was something weird about it, though.

B: What was that?

G: When he was killed he had headphones on. He was listening to a Walkman. Deaf. There wasn't much left of it, the Walkman I mean, when ... when they gathered up all the pieces of him. But the cassette remained intact. I listened to it, but it was totally blank. A standard cassette, with nothing on it.

B: Do you still have it?

The manuscript ends here. From this point on, we only publish the notes of Márton Kopaszhegyi-Kézi. The reason for writing on paper instead of typing on a computer is unknown, as is the factuality of the text. Maybe everything he writes is speculation. In any case, the cassette existed, according to Júlia Nagy. After the sale of the publisher and the termination of their book contract, Júlia Nagy immediately started to look for new employment, and she didn't reach out to her co-author for a while. "*I will never forgive myself for that,*" she writes. The widow of the deceased writer hardly recognized her husband in his final years. He listened to cassettes obsessively, often going missing for days, until one night he didn't come home at all. These are his final notes.

```
Balázs paid fifty thousand forints for the
cassette. TDK, sixty minutes, transparent
blue plastic. It had been rewound. He lis-
tened to it all the way through. Only the
sound of the empty tape. Emptiness still
comforted him. When side A ended with a sharp
```

snap, Balázs shivered. He flipped the tape over. He took out the interviews that he had already transcribed and printed and read through them. Finally he closed his eyes. He thought of the city that couldn't be his. He thought of Brigitta whom he always loved, not for what she was but for what she represented to him. He thought about the drinks he never drank. The girls he never kissed. The nights that eluded him.

He heard a noise from far off. Something was on the tape after all, it was like the thousandth copy of a copy on minimum volume. It wasn't music, only noise, a shapeless, soft clatter. The more the things he hadn't lived through took shape in Balázs' head, the clearer the sound became too.

The Walkman spun its reels eagerly, as Balázs eagerly spun his dreams in his head. One amplified the other. At last, he could almost make out the melodies, a sort of hypnotic stream, like the sound of a river; a river that's a street, a street that's night and fog. The fog is the taste of cheap booze in your mouth, the neighboring houses are only phantasmagoric sets, just like the sky, just like you. Nothing is real, and yet it's more real than your life. You grab the girl's hand; you fear that the night will end – but you know that dawn will never come. The city is empty and yet filled to the brim with youth; the pubs are all closed and yet they are all open, your money is barely enough for a beer but it also never, ever runs out. Daytime is a distant memory, you're only really alive when . . .

Here the click of the Walkman woke him up. The cassette had ended.

★

The last time anyone saw Balázs was one Friday in the Rathole. He sat by the counter drinking his beer. Rat gave him another one. He asked Balázs how the book was going. Balázs nodded, giving a thumbs-up. He was lying, of course. Nothing was all right. Everything was wrong. He thought about killing himself, removing himself from this desolate, empty age. Maybe tonight. Why wait any longer?

He left the bar around midnight, walking home through the empty streets. A heavy fog was descending, and in his mind's eye Balázs saw his own body lying in the grass, dew settling on it when a passerby finds it in the morning. But how should he do it? A jump? Sleeping pills? A blade?

A person was standing in the fog, waiting for him. Balázs stopped daydreaming about death, because he could recognize this shape out of a thousand.

'Hey. You're late, as always,' said Brigitta, and she smiled. She was just as Balázs remembered her from their teenage years, not yet undone by years and sickness.

He knew he had arrived home.

Brigitta reached out her hands to him.

'Let's hurry, the show is about to start!'

Balázs took her hands; they were cold and wet, as if made from the fog itself. He didn't mind; right at this moment nothing was amiss.

'Fogtown is playing tonight?' he asked.

She laughed.

'You dummy. You know they always play. We just have to find them!'

With that she led him into the fog, and he was never seen again.

This is what happened. This must have happened.

Márton Kopaszhegyi-Kézi was found dead one March morning by a passerby. There were no bruises or wounds on the body, and no sign of toxins in his blood. His body was cold and wet, just as he described Balázs.

At the time they found him, the headphones were still covering his ears. The Walkman had the last tape he must have listened to before his death.

The tape was empty.

The Time Remaining

My therapist urges me to picture a different story, a story in which Vili doesn't die, or at least not like that. But before I can rewrite my past, first I need to face it – recount everything that happened exactly as it happened, up to the point when I lost control.

Vili's death struggle started on a Friday. It was pouring outside, the perfect melodramatic backdrop for the announcement of bad news. The three of us – my mother, Vili, and I – were sitting in the kitchen.

Vili was given to me by my maternal grandmother on the first of May. I remember this because I'd been trying desperately to figure out the meaning of that holiday, but no one could give me a good answer. In a way, the May Day celebration continues to be a mystery to me to this day.

We were headed to the festival, the whole family, my father, my mother, and my grandmother, to enjoy the company of other families, watch the performers on the main stage, and indulge ourselves by buying things we didn't need from the vendors' booths. Early on during the festival a huge storm materialized out of nowhere, devastating the marketplace. My grandmother ran back at the last minute to buy Vili from a seller who was frantically trying to save his stall from destruction. My grandmother grabbed Vili, not even bothering to wait for the change, while the seller was defying the torrential wind.

Grandmother slipped the gift into my hand, yelling – and this was the first time she ever yelled at me, though it was driven only by the need to be heard over the raging wind – to take care of Vili and always remember her. I couldn't understand that request at the time. She was my grandmother, how could I ever forget her? Standing in the windstorm, I suddenly had an eerie vision. I felt like the world was about to fall to pieces, the wind would soon rip through the field and tear apart people and the past and the future, and I would fall into a dark abyss beyond time. I hugged Vili and found his touch rather comforting. He was soft and warm, and he made me feel that together we were solid enough to withstand the violent force of the wind. Vili's charm came from his smile; not a clumsy grin, nor a condescending smirk, not even the bitter, frowning grimace that so often featured on his fellow toys. Vili had a friend's smile, empathetic, approving, encouraging, but also with a touch of adult-like solemnity.

The sense of apocalypse ceased in the car. I clutched Vili in the back seat, and I knew that everything was all right. Grandmother sat next to me. I saw her eyes were blurry with tears, but she smiled at me, assuring me it was only sand. My mother turned around and gave Grandmother that stern look I thought she reserved exclusively for me when I did something wrong, or when she assumed I had done something wrong, which basically amounted to the same thing. I didn't think she could give that look to anyone else, especially not her own mother. They didn't say a word to each other, and I soon fell asleep, clutching Vili.

After that, I saw Grandmother very rarely, until one day my parents explained that she had gone to Australia on a family visit and would not return for a while. They showed me where Australia was on a world map to address my confusion, and they also showed me kangaroos and other peculiar animals in a book, which intrigued me. I hoped we would soon visit Grandmother so that maybe we could watch the kangaroos together. My mother and father agreed that if I behaved well enough all year, this wish of mine might become reality and sooner or later we could visit Grandmother.

I was a kid, that must be the reason why I was so blind to the truth, although they say that children are extremely sensitive to minor changes in their environment. Maybe I'm the exception, or maybe my mother was especially skilled at lying, even to herself. What is important to note is that I was not in possession of that information then: I didn't know that my grandmother had passed away sometime that year. My mother asked her not to visit us, and we didn't visit her either. My mother didn't want me to remember my grandmother as a sick old woman, her illness consuming her body little by little, though I only know this from my father's account. He told me when he was drunk, decades later. I know that my mother was trying to protect me when she decided to lie. I know that she wanted the best for me: what else could a parent possibly wish for her child but the very best? My father, inebriated, made wise by long years of experience, thought otherwise – he believed that my mother was scared to pronounce the words, scared to verbalize that her own mother was dead. In any case, for me my grandmother was a living person for years to come, even though she had long been buried in the ground by the time Vili started dying.

I only understood this later, in adulthood, partially due to my therapist's help. My mother thought I was too attached to Vili. She wanted me to be the best, the most successful, the most confident. In her view, life was an ice-cold forest, and children were wolves in it; they think they form a pack, but at the end of the day they will all aim for the same job, same house, same female. Emotional overreliance on the false sense of security bestowed by a plush toy weakens one's character in the long term, and the weak fall prey to wolves.

We were sitting in the kitchen – two cups of tea steaming on the table, one for her and one for me. Chamomile, to this day I feel sick at the smell of it, but my mother hoped the tea would soften the emotional impact. She didn't make any tea for Vili, from which I deduced that something terrible must be coming.

My mother looked at me, very seriously, as seriously as when I broke something expensive or ran out in the road chasing my ball. In hindsight, and I told this to my therapist as well, I suppose that in those very seconds, before articulating those words, she was thinking of my grandmother, her mother. *I'm going to be straight with you*, she said. *There's something wrong with Vili. Vili is sick, and sadly the odds are against him.*

She went on. *Unfortunately, even plush toys can get sick. Maybe it's genetic, the illness might remain latent for years before it manifests. Vili was manufactured in China, and it's very easy to catch all sorts of nasty diseases in those factories. Vili has been examined by doctors, and the prognosis is clear as day: Vili is going to die.*

I looked at Vili, who was lying on the marble kitchen table resting his friendly eyes on us, and only then did I become aware of Vili's inherent nudity, which made my heart ache. I wanted to cover his little body to protect him from the coldness of the world. I grabbed Vili and squeezed him against my chest. As I glanced at my mother, I could just catch a smile on her face. *You look so nice together*, she said. *I wish I could always remember you like this.*

Vili has two months left, she continued. *Take care of all his needs in the time remaining. The most important thing is to make sure Vili lives out his final days in dignity. Drink up your tea*, my mother said finally, and she wouldn't let me go to my room until I finished my tea to the last drop. That was the last time I drank chamomile tea in my life.

I retreated to my room with Vili. I sat down on the edge of my bed with him, feeling like the world had shrunk around me, like I was locked in a cage from which there was no escape. I could have talked to my father, but I was perfectly aware of the household dynamic. My mother took care of my upbringing, while my father gave her financial stability. I knew that it would be a waste of time talking to him. In a normal situation,

I would have turned to my mother to ask for her help in curing Vili – but she had just assured me that she was unable to help my plush toy.

I laid Vili on the bed, then swept my hand over his body, not looking this time for warmth or safety, but for the symptoms of his disease. I had no idea what these symptoms might look like; Vili's body temperature seemed just fine. I searched and searched, and I could feel that Vili was avoiding my gaze, just as I was avoiding his. In that moment he became actually naked, but not from his lack of clothing – he was naked because my fingers were searching for the end of his life.

I finally found the first rupture in his armpit. The thread had started to loosen, allowing Vili's insides to be seen through a small hole, the white stuffing that was his blood, his flesh. I knew right away that my mother's doctors were telling the truth. Vili's body was sick. I felt like my chest was too small for my lungs, that my brain was swelling and boiling in my skull. The world seemed darker, not in a metaphorical sense, but literally; the edge of my vision went black, I felt I could faint at any moment.

I knew with absolute certainty that death was real.

I grabbed Vili and threw him into the corner with all my strength. Vili bounced off the wall, knocked his head against a shelf, and fell behind my backpack. I couldn't explain to myself the cause of my rage back then, and it took years even for my therapist to convince me that it was a normal reaction to what had happened to me. I tried to rationalize my behavior by thinking that I only wanted to save Vili: I had to hate him because he wasn't alive – and if he wasn't alive, he couldn't possibly die. Perhaps I wanted to save his life by admitting that he wasn't actually alive.

So many years have passed since then that it's time to be honest with myself now. My therapist also encourages me and tells me these things are completely normal until a certain age. I could talk to Vili, and he often talked to me as well – in my head. I believe this phenomenon is often referred to as an imaginary friend, when certain segments of a child's developing personality manifest as a voice or a character. That was Vili to me. He always guided me to do the right thing, to choose the harder path. I often imagined that Vili was a superhero and that he saved others, my parents included, from some perilous situation like a burning car after an accident.

That night I lay in my bed, with Vili still in the corner. I found it hard to fall asleep even though I was exhausted by anger and grief. And then I heard it, I heard Vili's cry. Most likely it was all in my head, but I could clearly hear the voice coming from the corner – he was crying, not out of fear or due to his illness, but because he had let me down: he wasn't a good enough plush toy, so I had had to punish him. Then I realized that I was the one who had failed him; my anger was unreasonable, rather an indication of my own stupidity. I jumped out of bed crying and ran to the corner to hug Vili. I promised him I would never let him down again, I would be by his side for the time remaining.

When I finally fell asleep, Vili wasn't crying anymore.

My mother and other mothers in the neighborhood often socialized, primarily to discuss useful tips regarding the everyday issues of raising children. Thus it isn't surprising in retrospect that soon enough other plush toys at school got sick. I felt relieved because I wasn't alone in this fight – others had to face the same dread as me, and we quickly found each other. I can't recall their names, even though they were my friends. My therapist says it's one of the mind's defense mechanisms. Apart from their names I remember everything about them, so if it's a mechanism, it's not working very efficiently.

The four of us formed a gang, developing a kind of friendship, even if the vast majority of our time together was spent discussing the practical aspects of our toys' dying process. There were two boys and one girl in the group besides me. The fact that our mothers wanted their boys to set aside their plush toys at a certain age was more or less understandable, but I have the impression that parents are less strict with girls in this respect. A girl can play with these toys for a longer period of time – my therapist agrees with me on this – it is socially acceptable for a girl to keep them even into adulthood. Still, the girl's plush toy, Ferkó, got infected with the sickness all the same.

Vili more or less stagnated the first two weeks; only the rupture in his armpit had apparently been growing bigger, and the thread had started to loosen in other areas as well – at his foot, at the edge of his hand where he had black claws made of cotton. By the end of the second weekend his fur started to fade. During this period Vili's voice in my head was calming. He kept my spirits up, as if I were the sick one, not him. I often fell asleep listening to his voice.

Unfortunately during this time I sometimes wet the bed. My therapist says that's normal, it's called regression, an emotional reaction which entails going back to a former stage of development. After a while, I stopped sleeping with Vili because I didn't want to stain his fur. My mother was not very happy with the bedwetting, and I was well aware that it was a sign of weakness. My mother would shake her head impatiently and sigh heavily to express her discontent, and I would stand in the middle of my room in shame, shaking in the coldness of dawn, but Vili's voice gave me comfort even then.

Then things took a turn for the worse.

One day I came home from school and found Vili on the floor, the stitching on his side split open and the white stuffing pouring out of him. My heart sank. I thought Vili had died while I was at school. But I could hear his voice, very quiet, weary with pain, but still clear. Vili was alive. I picked him up carefully in my shaking hands, which only caused him to lose more stuffing; my throat went dry from panic, I could hardly breathe. I laid Vili on my bed and tried to hold his wound together. I couldn't sew, and I despised myself for that. In the end, I applied super glue to the edges of the wound and held the material together while I whispered to Vili that everything was going to be all right, although I knew that nothing was ever going to be all right again.

The next day it turned out that the others had had similar experiences. One of my friends, the boy who always wore black-framed glasses, told us about the deterioration of his plush toy named Nyinyi. My bespectacled friend's thinking was a bit slow and dim – a year or two later he was sent to another school because his learning difficulties had become too severe.

There is a chance – but not a certainty, because I didn't stop to talk to him, I simply walked by as if he was a discarded soda can or a cigarette butt on the cold concrete – that I passed by my friend a couple of years ago, now an adult. My friend apparently lived on the streets, he had a thick blanket wrapped around his waist. There was a tin can by his feet with some coins in it. My friend kept staring straight ahead like someone who had stopped counting the minutes and days long ago and let time flow effortlessly through him. He was still wearing the black-framed glasses, which he kept sparkling clean just like in his childhood. I didn't turn towards him, and I didn't give him money. I wanted to get the miserable man out of my sight as quickly as possible. Maybe it wasn't even my friend, just someone who looked like him.

When my friend was still a kid, he told me how Nyinyi's condition took a turn for the worse. Under Nyinyi's tiny, fluffy tail a hole opened up – it was not even the thread but the fabric itself that loosened, allowing Nyinyi's freshly torn anus to eject thick red fiber onto the floor. My friend tried to push the yarn back, but he only made the hole bigger. My other two friends, the boy and the girl, listened in shock first to my bespectacled friend's account, then to mine. Later that week their own plush toys started to deteriorate as well. One morning the girl found her toy Ferkó with a severed arm – his right arm had detached from his body during the night. The other boy's plush toy, Egyes, went into paralysis. We didn't quite understand what this meant, since we all knew that plush toys don't move by themselves, only when we move them or imagine them to be moving. Well, my friend's toy didn't move anymore. He didn't die, my friend told me; he was one hundred percent alive, only disabled. Soon after, the stuffing started to pour out of Egyes' mouth – the sickness made him vomit up his own guts.

We were all faced with the situation that our plush toys were losing their vital filling, and we knew all too well from movies we had seen that such an excessive loss leads to certain death. We needed a transfusion to keep our toys alive, and for this we had to find other, still-living plush toys.

I fished out some of my old toys from the toybox, those I hadn't played with for a long time – Szilvio, a plush bunny who was given to me by distant relatives for a Christmas years past (I didn't give him this name, it was written on the funny bow he wore); a Disney-franchise plush based on one of their current movie's side characters, which I named Gyuri for reasons unknown, and finally a female fox, Anni, who was my favorite toy for a long time, until I didn't find her fur soft enough anymore, so upon mutual agreement I had retired her into the toybox. Now I spread them out one by one on the floor. I could hear their voices as well, those old voices they used to talk to me in when I still played with them. But Vili's voice drowned theirs out. He begged me not to do it, said that these toys didn't deserve it – but by then Vili had another hole in his body and the stuffing needed urgent replacement. I also knew that no matter how brave Vili wanted to seem for me, he was terrified; I felt it. At this time Vili often talked to me in his sleep. I don't think he was conscious, his words were too confused, too out of character – he would whine in his sleep, often mumbling obscenities; every word reeked of fear.

I smuggled a knife and a pair of scissors from the kitchen

and started with Gyuri, the Disney toy. I never considered him to be too clever, nor very sensitive; on the other hand he was made of an excellent material manufactured somewhere in China. He didn't get sick though, and I was angry at him for that. He didn't deserve to be so lucky. I made an incision with the knife on Gyuri's abdomen – I could hear him screaming in pain, then begging for his life. But at that point there was no turning back. I slipped the scissors into the wound and cut through his skin. Gyuri screamed, and I screamed along with him, or instead of him because he didn't have a mouth or throat to scream out loud. I wanted to give him an actual voice in his final minutes.

My mother asked me during dinner why I was shouting in my room. I told her I was performing surgeries, dissections in order to prolong Vili's life expectancy. My mother was drinking red wine, I recall this because her teeth were black when she smiled. *Good*, she said, *I'm glad that you're taking responsibility.*

That made me happy. My therapist says this is normal, children always want to live up to their parents' expectations, and my mother's expectations were always quite high. She took out a box of ice cream from the freezer and carved out a slice of the delicacy for me. This happened very rarely, only on special occasions. She placed the bowl full of ice cream in front of me and took another sip of the red wine. She kissed the top of my head, another evident sign of motherly love, which nonetheless scared me at that moment. My hair got sticky from drool and wine. *It's important*, she said, *that we take care of our loved ones, that we're by their side even in times of hardship.*

I didn't notice it as a child, but my father says my mother was drinking too much in that period, usually right before bedtime. This made my father unwilling to share the bed with her, bothered by the smell of alcohol. Now he drinks too, of course. Apart from that night I still remember my mother as a sober person though.

My father also told me later, and this gives a special context to my mother's behavior that night, that my mother had abandoned her own mother in the final hours of the latter's life. Or final days. Or final weeks. All in all, my mother kept her distance in the physical, geographical, and emotional sense as well. My grandmother died alone. That night my mother obviously projected her desire to have done it differently onto me. I was, of course, not aware of this at the time. I ate my ice cream and in the following days I butchered my remaining plush toys, screaming and whimpering to vocalize their death throes under the blade of my scissors.

There were times when I would scream for hours, because I didn't finish Anni off right away. We figured that only freshly transfused stuffing was suitable for our plush toys. There couldn't be more than half an hour between the moment of transfusion and the donor's death, otherwise the stuffing would coagulate – it would turn useless and poisonous. But if we only took a handful of stuffing from our donor at a time the donor wouldn't necessarily die; on the contrary, we could keep them alive at our will in order to extract a second and third portion from them, this way prolonging the lives of our favorite toys. I extracted three portions from Anni, and I gave voice to her suffering all the way to the end. I didn't enjoy killing the toys. I hid their remains shamefully in the corners of my room, and early one morning I sneaked out to the street and threw the carcasses into a distant trash can. Then I spent days in terror fearing that someone would knock on my door and confront me with the murder of the three plush toys.

Naturally that never occurred, but my therapist agrees with me that such a fear is an indication of my lack of sociopathic tendencies. I didn't find joy in that sort of torture, and my mind feared retaliation – for I regarded my actions as sinful.

Sometimes I wish I had enjoyed it. Then everything would have been so much easier.

I carefully stuffed the fresh filling into Vili. I knew this was a painful, demanding procedure for him as well, so I sedated him in my imagination. He breathed in anesthetic gas from an old carnival mask made of papier-mâché – obviously this mask was turned into an anesthetic mask only in my mind, but the trick worked. Vili fell asleep; I could hear his rhythmic breathing in my thoughts, but not his voice. Why I didn't do this with the toys I killed I cannot say for certain, but on some primordial level I felt that pain was a necessary element of the process.

I carefully stuffed the fresh, hot filling under his skin with my fingers. I used an office stapler for the stitches. One of my friends, the one without glasses, managed to get a stapler for each of us. His parents were rich and successful. They had some sort of company, and maybe a restaurant too, but I'm not entirely sure about that. Everyone was a little scared of him because his family was so wealthy; even children can sense the power of money. I met him once as an adult. He didn't recognize me, although he was staring right at me – or maybe he did but chose not to talk to me. He quickly looked away and rushed off, perhaps holding the handle of his briefcase a tiny bit tighter. He had an expensive suit, an expensive briefcase, and an expensive pair of shoes. It hurt me a bit that he didn't recognize me, just like I didn't recognize my friend with the glasses.

Anyway, as a child he stole the equipment for us from one of their offices. This speeded up the stitching procedure, which was crucial for me because Vili's sewing loosened more and more every day. No matter how quickly I stuffed in the new filling, when I came home from school or woke up at dawn, he had lost just as much or even more in the meantime.

When we ran out of plush toys at home we had to look elsewhere for resupply. Since we were kids, we didn't have much to spend, except for our rich friend. He was able to purchase new toys and gave us some spare coins now and then, but never enough. With my other two friends I would go through the thrift stores in the hope of finding discounted plush toys. Sometimes we would steal toys from these shops and run through the streets like hyenas with our prey, hoping that no one was following us. These stolen toys smelled like poverty, but they fulfilled the purpose we needed them for. We eviscerated them and stuffed their filling into our own toys. The girl's older sister advised us to mix fresh blood into the cotton stuffing so our plush toys would get stronger. We followed her advice and collected lizards from our school's sunny playground. They were easier to kill than the plush toys because we didn't need to imitate their suffering; they were inherently alive. We slushed their blood onto the cotton wool, but this method didn't bring any visible results.

Not then at least.

The situation soon turned more dire. Vili's skin burst in several places, but not along the stitching like before: the plush itself had worn so much that the wear eventually became a hole, through which the life-giving filling flowed out. These parts were harder to staple because the fabric would often burst or grow precariously thin. Vili's friendly eyes also became blurred. They were covered in some kind of fog, as if his plastic eyes had faded from the inside. One afternoon, as I was trying to close up his latest wounds, Vili's left eye fell out of its place and hit the floor with a thud. I felt like I was going to vomit. Vili was looking at me blindly with his one eye, while where his other eye should have been there was only plush and filling. I wanted to scream, but I bit my arm instead. I didn't dare hug Vili because I was scared his other eye would fall out as well. I tried to glue the fallen eye back, but my efforts were clearly in vain. The eye had nothing to stick to anymore, it would just fall out again along with the stuffing. I knew that Vili's time remaining would soon be up.

At that point Vili was no longer able to sleep from the pain. I would listen to his groaning all night long, his begging, swearing, and cursing. This was not the Vili I knew – my Vili always knew what was right, even if the harder path was the right one. But at night the dying Vili loathed the world that doomed him to suffer – he would either insult everyone and everything with spite, or moan out of terror like a lunatic. He did his best to hold it together during the day, but he spoke less and less. He grew distant, and sometimes I could hear him cursing in the daytime as well.

After a while, his other eye went blurry and eventually fell out. I put red tape in the place of his eyes, so Vili spent his final days with two red X's on his face. The scattered limbs, eyes, and fluffy insides were starting to cause us more trouble. The boys complained that the scattered filling was infecting their other toys with sickness – the wheels detached from their Matchbox cars, their plastic soldiers fell apart, and their Lego pieces didn't fit together anymore. The girl attempted to work out the meticulous protocol of our plush toys' dying process because her parents were doctors. Hence, following the girl's advice, we started to collect the potentially infectious plush body parts in resealable plastic bags, drawing the universal biohazard symbol on the bags with black markers. I placed Vili's eyes, stuffing, and one of his legs that had detached in the meantime into one of these bags.

I was scared to stay alone in my room, especially after I woke up one night to the gaze of Vili's red X eyes. Vili was lying on my pillow, staring right at me, even though at night I would always make a warm, cozy nest for him on the floor, in the first place to protect him from potential bedwetting and secondly because I could barely stand his smell anymore. He smelled of death, and I would choke from it at night. *My eyes*, Vili shouted at me. *Where are my eyes?* I screamed and tossed Vili away, causing him to fall on the floor with a painful groan. For the first time I peed my bed while I was awake. Vili was whimpering quietly on the floor, so I got out of bed, carefully slipped my hands under his head, and placed him back in his nest. Although I was scared, I wasn't angry at him. He was only a sick, demented plush toy. He didn't mean to hurt me, not consciously at least.

Not yet.

The others reported similar stories about their plush toys' disturbed minds. Our rich friend claimed that Egyes had been whispering terrible things in his ear all night about the endless, bleak darkness that swallows everyone like an insane father, and about the Black Emperor who ruled in its guts. The girl stated that Ferkó had attempted to sneak out the window – whether he wanted to escape or kill himself was not entirely clear – but after she thwarted his plan she could feel him pinching her feet and thighs so as to prevent her from falling asleep. After that she would sometimes wake up to find her plush toy lying on her chest with his mouth attached to her skin, as if trying to suck the flesh and the life out of her. Our friend with the glasses recounted that his plush toy walked in circles around the room, cursing and swearing and listing the names of those who had offended him, those who ought to be ended, whose heads should be hung on the wall of the Lego castle, whose blood should be smeared across the television screens.

My therapist maintains that these episodes were no more than violent fantasies, the products of a child's imagination, which we brought to life in order to confront the unbearable stress and confusion we were faced with. Still, after a while I had to tie Vili up at night because he would often crawl into my bed, nauseating me with his foul breath, his burning gaze pointed at me, and clutching a tiny plastic sword in his hand. If I tied him up, nothing of that sort would happen; then I would only hear his painful groaning, his whining that overflowed with his terrible fear of death and his cursing of life. He cursed the one who brought him to life, who forced him to live and die, for he had existed in lifeless unconsciousness until then.

He was cursing me.

Our friend with the glasses was first. One day he found

Nyinyi lifeless on the floor. Nyinyi had passed away in his sleep. Our friend's parents threw Nyinyi's corpse in the trash, and when the body disappeared from the trash can, leaving behind dirty marks on the floor, they resorted to spanking their son, despite his firm insistence that he hadn't touched Nyinyi's corpse. The second night after Nyinyi's disappearance our friend saw him from his window. The deceased toy was dragging a dead cat through the street, disappearing under a garbage bin with his victim. The next day our friend examined the bin and its surroundings but found nothing but used stuffing.

Vili talked less and less; he would instead broadcast a sort of feeling, like a radio station. *I'm ready*, he broadcast to me, *I'm ready to die*. He had suffered enough; his eyes couldn't see anything but red, every single breath was an agony. He asked me both verbally and nonverbally to end it all.

Naturally for a long time I resisted. Though I killed off many other plush toys just so Vili could live, killing Vili was a different matter. On the other hand I also knew that Vili had to die. My mother's prophecy had to be fulfilled, otherwise all this suffering would have been in vain.

Meanwhile, the girl's plush toy died as well – she found him in the middle of her room when she got home from school. The stuffing was still pouring out of his emaciated body, his hands stretched forward as if trying to reach something. The girl read up on the topic, and she found that the only way to prevent our plush toys from being resurrected was to bury them together with an onion – at least that's how I understood it at the time.

She acted according to her theory: she put the corpse in a resealable plastic bag and sprinkled some bits of onion around it. The plush toy didn't return. We all felt relieved when we learned that, except for our friend with the glasses, since Nyinyi was still stalking around his house. Several dogs and cats went missing, and one night someone tried to break into the apartment through one of the ground-floor windows. The policemen who arrived on the scene found only cotton wool.

Vili begged incessantly to die, night after night and morning after morning, hardly allowing me a moment's rest. At the same time a new theory started to circulate among my friends, prompted by Nyinyi's increasingly aggressive activities – that our plush toys crave death because it breaks the bond between them and humans so they don't have to serve us children anymore, and they can roam the world equipped with the power of the grave, equipped with the power of the Black Emperor. We deduced that there must be more plush toys like Nyinyi out there, they might be gathering in the canals and at the bottom of forgotten cardboard boxes, scheming viciously, planning their revenge on us who created them, gave them voice and life, only to eventually take it away from them.

Vili's stench became unbearable, and he couldn't articulate his words anymore. His voice was like a slightly open door through which the coldness of the grave could reach me. I couldn't stand watching him suffer anymore, and I couldn't bear my own exhaustion either.

I used the knife and the scissors. I feel ashamed recalling this – I stood over him for hours with the blades in my hand and I cried. My hands shook; whatever I had done before didn't matter now, only this one act of murder. Vili kept begging me to do it, he tried to catch my eyes with his red, blind ones. At last I did it. I forced myself to cut him open as meticulously as I had with the other toys. After the first cut, for a brief moment, he was his old self again, the old Vili. I chose the harder path, and that made the ensuing hours somewhat easier, the silence in my head, the complete absence of Vili. I howled loudly over Vili's body until my mother found me upon her return from the store. She caressed my head while I hugged her legs, seeking safety and compassion. She soothed me, and then she said that one sentence, which I think made me hate her forever.

Don't cry, it was just a plush toy.

My mother explained to me that you have to make the cadaver resemble its living counterpart as best you can – you can't bury a person with their insides and limbs scattered all over inside the coffin. We reassembled Vili's body, pushing back as much stuffing as possible, stapling his skin together so he would resemble his old self again. He didn't – his body was the most horrible sight; his face was a deformity, his friendly smile now a cut-up grin of insanity. We placed the body in a plastic bag. I demanded that we put some onion into the bag as well – my mother gave in, chopped a bit of red onion and sprinkled it beside Vili. Then we buried the bag in the back yard – I also placed a small cross on the grave. My mother offered me sweets again, then told me to clean my room.

The next morning, I found the cross fallen over and the grave disturbed, as if the earth had been moved from below. My backpack dropped from my hands because I knew that Vili had returned.

Of course, I had alternative theories as well. It could have been an animal that dug up the body, or even a person, a poor child who could only afford dead toys. Perhaps it was Nyinyi who had come for Vili in order to take his distorted body and present it at a gathering of the undead: *Look, this is what mankind does to us.*

The girl explained to me how it happened, not then, but years later, as an adult.

We met in a supermarket. My cart contained nothing but two bottles of vodka and a six-pack of beer. She was the one to notice me and called my name in a tone which suggested she was happy to see me, as if I were a good old friend, a link to a carefree period of the past. When she called my name I trembled as if she had struck me, and I felt ashamed for not recalling hers. I smiled at her as best I could to camouflage my embarrassment. The girl had become a mother; her daughter was standing by the basket with her head down and a plush toy in her hands – Vili. My throat went dry when I saw Vili;

of course I knew it was not my Vili, just another, similar plush toy.

I saw a tiny lesion on the toy's neck. The girl, who was now a mother, smiled at me. *It's like yours was*, she said and leaned closer to me so she could whisper in my ear. *Sadly*, she whispered, and I could smell chamomile on her breath, *sadly, she got infected with some kind of disease. This plush toy is dying, and my daughter has to accept it.*

I dropped the basket, the bottles of vodka smashed against each other, pouring their contents all over the floor, and I felt the urge to throw myself to the ground and lick it all up. *I know why yours came back, I figured it out*, she continued and I wanted to run but my body didn't obey. I listened carefully to what she had to say, and we agreed to have coffee or tea some time, but we didn't exchange numbers, then I vomited in the restroom for hours until the security guards kicked the door in.

I should have used garlic, whereas my mother used onions, which didn't possess any spiritual or symbolic power. Onions are unfit for keeping the dead on the other side, apparently.

I was not aware of this as a child. I was weary and exhausted after finding the disturbed grave. I felt sick, and for a while I had a serious wish to die and have the whole thing over with.

It only struck me that night that Vili might not return in the shape I remembered him. That he might resemble Nyinyi – and I started to be scared. For he swore to come back for me, didn't he? Didn't he plan to take revenge on the one who gave him life and death? I was certain then that he would return for me to drag me with him into the hole I had dug for him in the back yard with my bare hands.

I was not wrong.

The house went dark at midnight – the lights went out on the street as well. Power outage. Darkness surrounded me like thick cotton wool. I was paralyzed. My mother was asleep, my father on a business trip. I started to whimper, but I didn't feel ashamed even back then, for this was the whimper of an animal in the mouth of a predator.

I heard a noise from downstairs, then the voice of something coming up the stairs. The house was filled with the smell of the grave. Some hours earlier I had considered death to be a blessing, but now I felt that death was not the end – something much worse was waiting, and it was coming for me.

I could hear Vili's voice again, louder and louder as he approached.

Only it was not Vili anymore; wherever he was after I had killed him and before he returned, he brought a piece of that place back with him. His voice was the voice of death, like the munching of a thousand worms, no meaning, just emptiness – but to my terror, beyond the sound of maggots and decay it was the voice of my grandmother.

Hail the Black Prince! Vili said. *Hail the Black Emperor!* he shouted, and he showed me what the Black Prince was, what the Black Emperors were, for it was impossible to express their nature with words, only with dreams and images; and I fell on my knees and prayed to them, the Black Lords. I was ready to worship anything just to prevent Vili from taking me to the bottom of the grave as fodder to the Lords, as fodder to my grandmother who, at that time, I didn't even know was dead.

By then I could hear Vili dragging himself towards my door. He smelled of rot and onion, and he tried to speak with a real voice, but whatever he meant to say, death and the earth he was choking on prevented him from doing so. He only growled quietly.

He stopped in front of my room; the stench of death became unbearable. I was struck by waves of genuine hatred coming through the gap under the door. I knew that Vili would take me to where he had come from, and something changed in me.

I'll give you anything, just let me live, I whispered because I couldn't speak, *you can take anything, you can take anyone, anyone but me! Please!*

I wasn't taking the harder path then. Vili wouldn't have approved were he alive. Alas, he was not.

Vili waited a few seconds, then he went down the hallway, and I crawled under my bed and trembled until morning came. I didn't think I would sleep, but exhaustion got the better of me.

In the light of day when I woke up, I thought it had only been a bad dream. Actually, nothing had happened. According to my therapist, everything I experienced or perceived as an experience that night was completely normal, a child's mind struggling with the inconceivable. That morning I decided I would go to school as usual, but I wouldn't talk to my friends anymore. I would leave all this plush toy stuff behind, after all it was indeed time for me to grow up. I crept out from under the bed and went to the kitchen to have breakfast.

She was drinking chamomile tea, I could already smell it from a distance. My mother stood by the counter with a teacup in front of her. I stepped into the kitchen and greeted her, but she didn't reply. The odd smile on her face, some sort of idiotic grin, scared me to death. Her gaze, senseless and emotionless, was fixed on one spot, and I felt a knot forming in my throat. I called to her, but she didn't react. Her hand rested on the mug, but she wouldn't say a word, wouldn't move, and I got furious, since it was all her fault, everything; that I was there, that I was alive, that she killed my toy, killed my childhood, and now she couldn't even say *Good morning*! Something snapped inside me, and I did the unimaginable. I stepped up to her and shook her as if I were shaking a tree to make its crop fall down.

My mother's teeth fell out of her mouth, her glass eyes dropped and clattered onto the counter. Her skin opened up because there was no stitching to hold her together, her hair fell off her head.

Her body unraveled, and there was nothing left in my hands but a handful of cotton wool.

Return to the Midnight School

I live in a village where women usually give birth sitting in a pit. The families who respect this tradition take the mother out to the fields, dig a hole for her, and let her push the baby out into the pit. They lift the baby out of the dirt. They wash it and then bury the pit, its contents along with it.

If the baby is stillborn, they bury it as well. No need to prolong the mourning. It's just meat, and it goes where every other piece of meat does, sooner or later. Under the ground.

If you walk through the village at night you might see the flames of a bonfire out in the fields, a good distance away from the houses – chances are that someone is giving birth. You might spare a thought for the baby that's coming into our world from its own. From the midnight school.

We are born into the dirt of the earth as an act of respect. After all, it is the earth that sustains us. As far as I know I also dropped into one of those pits from my mother's womb, and a pit is where I'll be put again when my heart beats no more. There are some families, especially the ones where the wife comes from some other village or town, who prefer to go to a hospital for the birth. We do not judge or stop them, it's everyone's own prerogative to decide where and how to give birth, if at all. They feel safer at a hospital, although many of them bear their second or third child in a hole dug for them by their husbands.

I don't have children, and at my age that situation is unlikely to change. I don't know what I would have decided, pit or hospital, if I had to face the choice. But as I sit by the window, watching the fields at night – they're darker than black, as if they've merged with the sky above, their depths hiding more secrets than all the seas – I'm thinking it's a blessing to be born in a pit. It's the most natural way. You rise from the ground and then fall back into it when the time comes.

But around here, some people are born from the ground twice. When that happens, we hold a wake for them. You never forget your first wake. I was nine or ten when Uncle Rudolf died. Kids hated him. I hated him too. He had ginger hair and gray, piggish eyes. He was a dedicated torturer of kids. When the other adults looked away he would grab the kid nearest to him and start twisting its nose until the child burst into tears. Like a predator, he would wait for his prey in the cool of summer kitchens or by the shadowy benches along the wall. He would ask for a glass of cold water to get the adults out of sight, then he would look at you and let a pale, terrifyingly cold smile crack on his face. He would draw you in with a beckoning gesture, and you had no choice but to walk up to him. It was a game between predator and prey – a child always does what an adult says (at least they do around here), but that doesn't make them a fool. As for me, I always tried to approach, obeying his order, but remain just out of reach. If I managed to keep my distance until the adult returned with the glass of water, I was safe. Uncle Rudolf was old, but he could lash out quickly and fiercely. He didn't mind if you bled a little. After he gave your nose a good twisting, he laughed as if it had all just been a good joke. As a kid I thought when I grew up I would understand what was so funny about twisting noses. I didn't.

That reminds me of my only memory about Uncle Rudolf which is not related to pain. It was summer – it's as if Uncle Rudolf only lived in the summer, I don't have any winter or spring memories of him. He was sitting in the summer kitchen by the table. He had a soda siphon before him, along with a small glass of soda water, a filthy fly swatter, and a coin. Uncle Rudolf was famous for never drinking or smoking. 'I'll drink in my grave.' That was what Uncle Rudolf always replied when offered a glass of wine or pálinka. I think people offered him a drink every once in a while just to hear him say it.

He was sitting in the kitchen and didn't realize that I was watching him. I was sitting on top of the vegetable cellar. From there you had a perfect view into the summer kitchen through the open window. Uncle Rudolf spun the coin on the table. He watched as it spun gracefully, then the spinning grew sluggish, slower with each turn, like the steps of a chicken bleeding to death. The coin finally collapsed on the wood. Then Rudolf picked it up and spun it again. If the coin was about to veer off the table, Rudolf held his hand under the edge of the table so it would fall into his palm.

I was mesmerized watching the spinning coin, over and over again. I was incredibly excited, on the one hand because I was snooping and snooping is always exciting, and on the other hand because I knew that if he saw me I would be subject to severe nose twisting, or maybe something even worse.

He jerked his head up suddenly, as if he had heard something. He looked at the green door that led to the pantry. As a child I didn't like the pantry because a lot of spiders lived there and the vegetables always smelled rotten. One time my mother sent me in for some jam, and once inside I could clearly sense that something was standing right behind me, watching. When I turned around, of course there was no one there.

The coin just spun and spun while Uncle Rudolf kept staring at the pantry door as if in a trance. This moment seemed to stretch into infinity, like some childhood summers do. Then the door flew open, as if someone had thrown it open with brute force. Uncle Rudolf trembled in fright. There was nobody standing in the doorway. There was no one in the pantry. The coin just kept spinning until it finally spun off the table and dropped onto the floor.

Incidents like this let people know if they're to be born from the earth twice.

I climbed down from the roof of the vegetable cellar, my knees shaking, and from then on I did my best to avoid the pantry.

Not long after this incident Uncle Rudolf died. The sun didn't shine the day he was buried, but no rain fell from the clouds either. We woke at dawn. The entire ceremony was finished before noon. The priest sleepily made a boring speech, and the cheap wooden coffin was swallowed by the hole in the ground. After lunch the adults started the preparations for the wake.

When you're not yet of age they keep you in a house together with the other kids, a house that has been blessed by the priest beforehand. There, crammed into a single room, all the kids have to listen to the screams and wails throughout the night. Some children pee themselves while awake, some in their sleep. Somehow it's worse just to listen without seeing. Everyone dreads the day when they will first have to attend a wake. But there is a curiosity to it as well, especially as you get older. You just have to see it for yourself. Those who say they aren't curious are liars.

This is how it goes.

By nightfall most of the men are drunk. The tables almost collapse under the weight of all the drinks and greasy food. We eat a lot during a wake; it's tradition. All the able-bodied men are present, as well as the female relatives of the deceased and children who are closely related. The rest of the women and children wait it out together sheltered in houses. Someone, usually a civil guard, stays in the cemetery to give a signal. Before my time they used to do it using the church bell, now they also use a whistle, and often a long distance walkie-talkie.

At the wake, everyone is scared, but the most scared are always the first-timers. At my first wake I was given privileges: sweets, watered-down wine, kind and encouraging words. But nothing could wash away the taste of fear. As an adult, I also say kind words to first-timer kids, I give them sweets and wine, telling them that everything's going to be all right. That it's not as bad as it sounds. That it will be over quickly.

I remember sitting by the edge of the fields with Karcsi the following summer, building a maze for the ants. They were massive, yellowish ants, a kind I haven't seen since then. We built the maze out of dirt, and Karcsi looked at me and said he hoped he would come back from the grave after he died. He said it in absolute earnestness. He was always serious about everything. He said he wanted to experience being one of the living dead.

In the village we don't have a definite opinion about the state of living death. We don't talk about it, especially with a person we know will come back. You must never hate the future revenant, but you should still keep a distance from them emotionally. When they come back there's nothing else to do but deal with them. After all, we can't allow the living dead to roam our fields and streets.

Karcsi had weird thoughts and questions about the issue. Like, do the living dead feel? If so, how? What is their vision like? When I saw my first living dead walking in (it was Uncle Rudolf, of course), I couldn't think about anything like that. Most people in the village are unable to do so. For us it's too personal, because it's our dead who walk back to us. No wonder only Karcsi could come up with such things. He wasn't born in the village.

The living dead have a habit of returning to their relatives. Not to the house they had lived in, nor to their lovers or to their animals. They return to their own blood. This is why all relatives gather at the wake. They serve as a sort of beacon for the dead.

If the relatives were scattered all across the village it could confuse the dead. Then we would have to search for it, follow its screaming and wailing for hours on end. That would be terrible.

There are revenants without any living relatives. Andris Béres, for example, didn't have anyone but us, his buddies at work. We knew he would come back, and he knew it too, so after he died we went to Old Béla to ask for guidance. Béla was over ninety at the time, and he had seen all that there was to see. We asked him what to do. He told us.

At nightfall we sat down in Andris' garden with a drink in our hands – his friends and co-workers and some of his old lovers too. We all sang a song Old Béla had taught us that afternoon. It was a rather odd melody. It reminded me of sunsets I had never seen myself because they were before my time, and of sunsets I never will see, because they'll happen long after I'm dead. I found it a very comforting thought, and it made me sing even louder. We kept on singing until Andris Béres found his way back to us from his grave. We felt relief as he crawled in through the open gate, like all the other revenants before him, his mouth open wide in a soundless scream, with the wet earth of the graveyard stuck in his throat.

Karcsi was also there at Uncle Rudolf's wake. He was breaking the rules, of course. He wasn't a man yet, nor a relative. Wakes are private affairs. Nobody should want their loved ones remembered as one of the walking dead. Anyway, he sneaked in and that was the start of our friendship. Everyone called him Karcsi, but he hated that. He wanted to be called by his full name: Károly. He would frown and mutter curses and expletives against the adults under his breath. His vocabulary evolved quickly and constantly in this regard. I called him Karcsi on purpose to annoy him, but he would put up with it from me.

Karcsi was not born in the village, you could tell by looking at him. The hue of his skin was different from ours, his hair was darker. But mostly it was his eyes, which had a strange gleam in them. When he looked at you it was as if he didn't see only the surface, but looked beneath it and even saw through the flesh, muscles and bones, right inside you, saw who you really were.

So it was clear Karcsi was not born in a pit. He was born in one of the big cities. He never told me which one, or if he did I don't remember anymore. The Halász family took him in; they were distant relatives. The Halász family are good people, their daughter now lives across the street from me. She's married with two children of her own. Back then, when Karcsi and I were friends, she could barely walk. It just shows how easily time slips through your fingers.

He was the first one to tell me that the dead didn't come back anywhere else.

'If Mom and Dad came back, there's no way I would kill them.'

This idea had never occurred to me, that the dead wouldn't need to be killed. It was a rainy day, I remember that, because we wanted to play in the fields. Instead we were lying on the floor in my room, sweaty from all the hide-and-seek and chasing each other around the house.

'What would you do with them?' I asked. I always thought of my parents' possible death somewhere down the line, imagining how brave I would be if they came back.

That's why all the men are present at the wake. All of them, not just the relatives. Of course as a kid I couldn't understand this, but the relatives, especially the children of the deceased, are often unable to kill the dead. They just can't bring themselves to do it. If my parents came back I don't think I could have done it either. Fortunately I never had to find out.

'Once I dreamt that they came back,' Karcsi said instead of giving a straight answer. 'I dreamt that I was home, not this home, but the home where I used to live before. In my dream, I was alone in the house, and I heard the doorbell ring, and I knew it was them, that they had died but now they were coming back to me. So I ran up to the door, opened it, and there they were. They were standing in the doorway, but somehow they were still dead.'

He scratched his palm.

'It was a weird dream.'

I thought about it for a little while.

'How did they die?'

'They were shot. In the war.'

I didn't want to seem stupid, so I didn't ask which war that was.

After my first wake, the adults praised me for my good behavior. The next day my parents took me to the cinema, which is several hours away, even by car. I was good because I had watched. Never once looked away.

Many children don't dare to watch. They don't want to see what happens to the dead. Often the relatives also retreat to the house, or turn away and let the others carry out the job. Nobody blames them. It's all right. We sympathize with their pain. A wake is not a pretty sight.

First of all, naturally, the deceased arrives. The dead are buried in light plank coffins so that it will be easy for them to break out. When the watchman sees the dead crawl out of the grave he blows the whistle. As soon as he hears the whistle the sacristan rings the bells in the church too. The whistle and bell sound across the entire village. After this, it takes about fifteen to thirty minutes for the corpse to arrive at the yard where the wake is being held. Animals can't stand the dead, so the corpse's journey is accompanied by howling, growling, barking, and squealing. Most of the relatives have already collapsed by this time, especially if the deceased is a roarer. Not all of them roar; some swallow too much earth when trying to get out of the grave and others just come back mute. A roarer is a terrible thing, painful for the mourners. A child shouldn't hear its own father's corpse roar in the night.

Eventually, the corpse shuffles through the gate, which we leave wide open. The men grab scythes and hooks mounted on the end of long sticks. The dead are not particularly quick, so the men can easily surround them and shepherd them towards the barn. The barn is prepared for the processing of the dead, the butchers are already waiting inside. When the deceased is near enough to the barn, the men step into action.

We swing the scythes and hooks, cutting as deep as possible into the flesh of the returned. The point is to immobilize the body. At times, either intentionally or accidentally, a limb might be cut off, but that is considered disrespectful, because it's a butcher's job. At this point the deceased screams and howls like some kind of animal, writhes and throws himself to the ground, or tries to escape. The butchers do the real job once we've got a steady hold on the revenant and drag it into the barn: they start by hammering a stake into its heart, a stake so long that it pierces through the body and nails it to the ground.

As a child I stepped into the barn when old Rudolf had already been nailed to the floor. His ginger hair had fallen out in patches while in the grave. His face was white. There was a horrible stench in the air. The two butchers commenced the dismemberment of the body, starting with the separation of the legs from the torso. The body that was once Rudolf started to whine, like a trapped animal that had already lost too much blood in the cold night with dawn still far away.

'Twist my nose now, you fucking bastard,' Karcsi said, standing next to me.

That was when we first met.

Since then I have been to several wakes. There was even one time when one of the butchers couldn't make it, so I stepped in as a replacement to help cut up the revenant. The body must be sliced into pieces. The older women who have seen a lot – around half a dozen of them – boil water and meat acid in large cauldrons. As soon as we separate a body part, it gets thrown into one of the cauldrons right away. By the end of the wake, the entire body is boiling in there, and thanks to the meat acid, by dawn it turns into a jelly-like mass. The jelly is then stored in barrels until the time comes to refresh the fields. Then the jelly, which we call *stamen*, is plowed into the fields in early spring. From summer to fall we harvest. That's when the earth gives back what it takes from us during the year. The meat acid is also provided by the earth. Without that we couldn't recycle the bodies into the soil so efficiently. Uncle Rudolf got recycled as well.

The adults were alerted to Karcsi's presence after Uncle Rudolf had been boiling in the cauldrons for some time already. By then everyone was too drunk and tired to care. I gave him some of my watered-down wine, and he gratefully accepted. It appeared that uninvited guests were not showered with gifts, kindness, and alcohol.

Sitting by the cauldrons we exchanged chewing gum stickers with race cars on them. He had a lot more of them than I did because he came from a city. Later on it wasn't so easy for him to get hold of them either. Since we got along quite nicely, the Halász family let me be the designated person to guide Karcsi around the village and show him how the crop was cared for, harvested, and processed. Had the Halász family or anyone else known Karcsi, they would never have let him near the fields at all.

There was one occasion when I had a taste of how it could feel to be Karcsi. We were playing in the fields like we used to do when the weather was good. No doubt because he was born a city kid, Karcsi had a great appreciation for the fields, he enjoyed their infiniteness, the miles upon miles of nothing but sky and earth. Because I could see how much Karcsi loved the fields I looked at them with fresh eyes too, as though I wasn't even born in them, right into their matter. As if the tissues that slid out from between my mother's legs along with me were not buried right there. Sometimes we chased each other, at other times we collected things or made a bonfire. In the summer we were watchers; we had to watch over the crops to make sure the birds didn't eat them up and that nobody else harmed them in any way, intentionally or unintentionally.

It was late afternoon. The crops hadn't grown yet, the dark and rich soil stretched into infinity under the soles of our feet. We were barefoot. That was when Karcsi came up with the game. Later he named it 'Wake the Dead'. It consisted of us lying on the ground, in the middle of the field, our heads resting in the sand. Then Karcsi would say: 'Can you feel it? They're right here beneath us. In the winter they sleep. Now they've awakened, and they know we're here. They're coming upwards. Soon they'll reach us, can you feel it now? They're about to touch us.'

By then Karcsi had become obsessed with the crops and fields. Perhaps I would have been obsessed with them too if I hadn't been born here, if I hadn't lived every day of my life in the endless cycle of winter-spring-summer-autumn, the cycles of feeding-harvesting-processing. There was nothing new about this for me, but he was mesmerized by everything he saw. There were indeed things beneath us when we lay down on the ground. The reason why we plow is to recycle the corpses returned to us. That's what wakes are for – to produce stamen jelly out of them. We believe the revenants are sent by the soil itself because they are the ones the earth wants to possess. The ground hosts the dead until their bodies turn to dust in the coffin. But the relationship is so much more intimate between man and earth when a farmer returns the gelatinized tissues of their own relatives into the soil. That is more than hosting, it's unification. Without stamen jelly the crop yield would be cut in half every year and decline in quality.

In other words, the countless dead of centuries past not only rest in the earth, they are the earth itself.

There is one purpose to it all: the crops.

As a child, I didn't know or didn't understand that the crops were unique to this land. As a child, I didn't understand distance either. I remember when the priest at school talked about Jesus Christ and how he died and was resurrected in a far-off land, Jerusalem, I asked him why we didn't go there to visit. I thought that if the city was a few hours away by car (one full day by horse carriage), then Jerusalem couldn't be much farther, and then we could understand much more clearly what this whole rigamarole with Jesus was all about. Now I know that Jerusalem is far away and that we couldn't have gotten there by car, but as children we perceive distance in a different way. I had almost reached adulthood when it became absolutely clear to me that the crop only grows in our land, or if it grows elsewhere we don't know about it. When I wandered off to villages further away, I noticed that they had a lot more fruit trees than we did, and that they grew wheat, corn, millet, potatoes, and things like that. After a while, I also learned that they had to plant these things, while we receive our crops as a gift from the earth. In other aspects our crops are very similar though: we harvest and process the crops based on the accumulated experience of many generations, just as they do.

In some neighboring villages they started to grow watermelons. Their watermelon fields looked the most similar to our fields. Unfortunately, it seems that watermelons don't tolerate our kind of soil. All the fruits turn out to be sour, and after a while they don't even ripen, they just rot on their stems.

In any case, our crop is watermelon-like in shape, only in most cases much larger than any watermelon you've ever seen, and always black, or such a dark shade of blue or green that it seems black. At first, only tiny black dots appear on the ground, like hundreds of peppercorns. They grow with incredible speed, until the biggest one reaches the size of a full-grown ox. The *legged crop* is the first to ripen, in late spring or early summer; it is then followed by the *toothy* and *sea crops* in July. The peak is in August when the *dreaming crop* is in season, then comes the off season at the end of September, and finally in October we harvest the flesh apples.

The crops do not require any special care, you only have to make sure that the birds don't peck at them too much. The birds only eat certain parts like the tiny tuft on top of the legged crop, or the small seedlings that grow next to the root of the *csirvik*. Otherwise birds die from eating the crops.

When the crop is ripe, we gather it and transport it for processing. The processing is done jointly by men and women. Each part of the crop can be used, so the less that gets wasted during processing the better. The crop is very similar to human skin to the touch, only slightly softer.

There are certain people allergic to touching the crops. Right now there are about a dozen of them in the village. When they touch the crop their eyes lose focus, their vision turns inward. They are no longer aware of their surroundings.

A person must not be touched when they're having an allergic reaction, nor can their hand be removed from the crop, otherwise they will collapse and go into seizures. Depending on the severity they could die from the seizure, but even in the best-case scenario they will be useless for several days. That's one of the first things we teach our children: never touch a person having an allergic reaction. They must learn it very well because most people are revealed to be allergic in adolescence.

So we leave the reaction to run its course. The allergic person, after having touched the crop, stands motionless for a few seconds. Then they start to search for the voice. They emit a strange, atonal growling, not quite singing or speech. At first it's a flat sound, then it modulates, shifting pitch occasionally, as if their throat were an instrument someone was tuning up for a performance. These sounds are rather inhuman in nature, and finding the right voice might take minutes.

Once the proper pitch is found, the allergic person starts to speak. Some think it's simple gibberish, the random interplay of speech organs, not unlike a seizure. Most of us, however, believe it to be a language we can't yet understand and perhaps never will. Some who have seen several such incidents claim they are able to recognize certain sounds, maybe even words that are carried over from one incident to the next. Essentially they claim the allergic repeat the same thing, time after time.

The problem is that this language (if it is one) uses the human speech organs in ways we cannot imitate, no matter how hard we try. Sometimes it reminds me of the dead and their howling. Only the dead never try to express anything. Their bodies are just tools, devoid of meaning. The body of an allergic person, some believe, becomes a vessel for some sort of consciousness beyond human comprehension. Whether that's true is up for debate, but some believe it.

At least, I do.

Naturally Karcsi had always been truly envious of the allergic people. He wanted to see what they could see. Of course that was impossible, because upon awakening the allergic person remembers nothing of the incident. Many have nightmares afterwards, and sometimes when they look in the mirror, for a split second they see a blurry figure standing right behind them. Animals (especially cats) avoid the allergic person for weeks after the incident; some even attack them.

Going back to the legged crop: we put the crop in a bathtub and slice it open carefully with a knife. The tub collects the outpouring white liquid. We separate the shell entirely and put it in a designated bucket, then we take out the seed.

We call it that, but it's not really a seed, as you can't plant it again. We have another, perhaps more appropriate, name for it: *traveler*. In the case of the legged crop, the traveler (or seed) is a spider.

It sits in an organic white sac that is moist and tears easily when touched. The spider hugs its body tightly with its many legs. The body is connected to the root of the crop by an umbilical-like cord. This we cut with scissors, then we lift the spider out and stretch its legs apart. The legs are as long as a grown man's palm from the index finger to the thumb. They are hairless. The spiders are white; those that are not must be burned immediately. The spiders to be destroyed are colorful like a peacock's tail feathers, and their legs are furry. They are extremely dangerous, their bodies unfit for processing. There is a barrel with fire constantly burning during the work process. When we encounter one of these deviant spiders, we have to throw it into the barrel without a moment's hesitation. You have to be quick because these spiders can wake up. They are quick to bite and run away. I have never seen anyone bitten by one and I hope I never will. Anyone bitten by such a spider must be killed on the spot. For that purpose we keep a couple of axes by the fire barrel.

Of course Karcsi was crazy about these spiders. Only once have I ever come across one. I saw its colors as I tore away its organic sac. I threw not just the spider but the whole crop into the fire just to be on the safe side. I think if Karcsi had encountered one of these spiders he would have let himself get bitten.

We process the spiders this way: we separate their legs from their torso, then carve out the major glands from the abdomen. We dry the legs, then we grind them, and with resin and the beeswax extracted from the inner wall of the crop's shell we mix it into a lotion. The lotion has a pain-relieving effect, it also eases irritation, makes skin softer, and cures skin cancer. Usually we produce three hundred kilograms of lotion annually.

We leave the glands removed from the abdomen to rot. We

add sugar to the rot, and later we boil it. If we mix it with alcohol and water it down considerably we get a perfume that makes you seem decades younger. If we leave it in its pure form it's such a strong toxin that it can poison you even through a metal container. It can only be stored in crystal bowls. If someone sleeps next to a bowl containing this toxin, they will have nightmares that poison their life.

Out of the dried abdomen we make spices that go well with meat dishes but otherwise contain no special properties.

Following the legged crops we harvest the toothy crops. Inside the crop there are wolves and foxes rolled up in a fetal position. At first glance there is no difference between these and living wolves and foxes, except the eyes look as if they had turned inwards. You can extract thirty-seven different kinds of products from a wolf and twenty-four out of a fox. The crop in this case is naturally larger than the legged crop, and there is a special kind of additional toothy crop, the *csirvik*. The *csirvik* is a creature that resembles a wolf, but it has six legs and no tail. I have never heard about such a creature in our natural environment. Maybe it's long extinct; maybe it's a species yet to come. Or maybe it's just a weird afterthought of nature, a flawed design that only made its way into our toothy crop.

The toothy crops are followed by the sea crops, which contain mid-size sea animals. These crops (especially the ones containing octopuses) have to be boiled in water before being opened. The liquid surrounding the seeds causes purplish skin rashes, even through gloves, unless the crop is boiled beforehand.

What intrigued Karcsi most was the August crop. The *dreamers*. In this crop human beings, male and female alike, lie in a fetal position, eyes closed, as if in a deep sleep. They are surrounded by a thick, colorless liquid. It takes four or five people to harvest the crop, then three people to process it. These are the base material for the widest variety of products and the most valuable. The skin of these travelers is always covered in tattoos. The pattern of the tattoo is always unique to the individual dreamer.

'Why don't we wait until they wake up?' Karcsi asked when he saw the first dreamer, a black-haired female. Given enough time the dreamers do wake. We cannot let them.

Once upon a time, maybe even long before the days of old Béla, the villagers didn't work in groups. Each house processed the harvest on its own. There was a man who, according to some versions of the story, had always lived alone; other versions said that his family had passed away years before. He did the harvesting and processing by himself. One day the villagers noticed a woman at his house. A tall, gorgeous woman, the story says. They were glad, for the farmer was no longer a man of sorrows. Nobody would have given it a second thought if it weren't for what started to happen around the time she appeared.

According to the story it was the strangest time. Children kept disappearing. Their giggles could be heard coming either from underground or through the walls. Many people claim that animals began to speak like men, uttering in some foul language truths that were too horrible to bear. All the wine turned into blood, and the village was haunted by the presentiment of something awful to come. Corpses disappeared from their coffins and were found sitting at the table at suppertime. There came a day when the sun didn't rise. The villagers were on edge. Many were sure that the end of days had come.

Those villagers who weren't given to overt hysterics suspected that the natural order was upset, that some unspoken law had been broken. Of course, as always, they suspected the one who wasn't one of their own. The farmer's woman.

They were right in their suspicion.

The villagers stormed the farmer's house, and despite his

objections they ripped the clothes off the woman. Her skin was covered in tattoos, recognizable to anyone who had ever processed a dreamer. The farmer had obviously been so tormented by loneliness that instead of processing her he waited for her to wake up. It could have been the start of a beautiful bedtime story. Instead it became a cautionary tale.

The villagers beat the woman to death without any further ado. They dismembered her body but didn't process it. The farmer later took his own life.

Since then, working in groups has become the norm, so that nobody falls prey to temptation. Communal processing is also more economical.

We make one hundred and twenty-four different kinds of products out of the dreamers.

Anyway, as I was lying in the field with Karcsi, playing 'Wake the Dead', the dreamers beneath us were indeed on their way upwards. The point of the game was to stay on the ground longer than your adversary, while he tried to scare you off.

'Can you feel it? That's not your imagination! Something moved underneath. Can you feel that tremor? They're breaking out of the earth right now. *Right now.*'

I always lost at that game.

Karcsi regarded the dreamers and their processing with astonishment, although it's quite a simple process. You peel off the outer skin just like with the other crops, then you cut the cord that connects the dreamers to the root. The dreamers then are lifted and stretched out. Here we don't start by cutting off the limbs like with the other travelers; we slice the torso open and pull out the internal organs, which are then placed in separate buckets. Each organ is used for making a different product. After removing the organs, we peel off the skin and then break off the ribs. We cut the spine open, for the spinal cord is an essential ingredient in a medicine that cures almost all diseases.

The most interesting part, however, is what we call the *grape*. No other seed or traveler has this organ, if it's an organ at all. It's found in the lower part of the cerebellum: an amber ball, no bigger than a grape. Some say this might be proof that the dreamers are different. That the dreamers have souls, the grapes. I don't know, maybe one day these ideas will turn out to be right, and from then on we'll be thought of as murderers. Still, even if that day comes we'll still go on processing the dreamers, the grapes included. We sell the grapes wholesale to a man named Zanó, because however valuable these parts may be, we can't process them. We don't have any recipes.

The rest of the products are transported in trucks to all corners of the world. We sell them off to foreign-speaking merchants. They always come accompanied by a man who translates their wishes into our language. We usually have nothing to talk about but business. We give them the product, and in exchange they give us money or other things we can use. They provided almost all of the TV sets in the village, as well as the cars, the modern ovens, and most of the working tools. We don't ask what markets they bring the products to, and they never tell us. It has been like this for generations, since before my birth, and it seems likely to remain the same in the future. Wars don't reach us, nor the changing tides of politics. It's as if we lived in our own country. The merchants protect us from everything so we can do our work.

Either them or the fields.

Karcsi was always eager to learn more about the crops, and I often tried to impress him with some new piece of information. One day we were hanging out at the school. The school is a simple building, just two large classrooms, a couple of smaller rooms, and a corridor. Actually the adults spend more time there than most of the children because it also serves as a community center. For us children the school is more a place of rest and friendship than a place of study. Our true teachers are the fields.

We enjoyed the cool air and I tried to think of something that might impress him. Finally I told him that deep below the surface, crops are connected to each other with white threads. Every time someone digs a hole, they sever dozens of these connections. That's why we only dig on important occasions, such as births and deaths.

'It's like the human brain,' Karcsi said. 'An infinite number of connections.'

I asked him where he had seen a human brain. He said he had only learned about it. 'These city kids learn strange things,' I thought back at the time. Our only knowledge of the human body came from processing the dreamers.

Once I saw Karcsi eating raw meat. The flesh of a dreamer.

He had cut a piece off during processing and had quickly hidden it in his pocket. When he produced the piece of flesh in the attic where we hid after work I was terrified and angry. He had broken a rule, since nobody is allowed to steal a piece of crop for themselves. Everything must be done communally. I shouted at him but kept my voice down so we wouldn't be heard, which made me sound hoarse. For a moment I thought that was how I was going to sound as an adult. I was not mistaken.

However, I was curious, just like him. Supposedly consuming the raw flesh of dreamers has a tendency to cause allergic reactions, though of a different kind than the one caused by touching the crop. Sometimes when men get drunk, they eat raw dreamer meat on a dare. Some acquire special powers from it. Robi Ajtós, for example, learned to play the violin, but he could only play a single melody. Some sleep for years. Others learn secret things about strangers or themselves. Some die instantly. In most cases, however, nothing happens.

The piece of flesh rested there in Karcsi's trembling hands. Bees buzzed quietly nearby. There was a hive somewhere in the attic, but it felt like it was the flesh itself that was buzzing, like a radio tuned to static.

'If they catch us, we'll get a beating,' I whispered to him.

He grinned at me.

'Then let's do it quickly,' he said, putting the meat in his mouth. He didn't offer me a piece, but I wouldn't have taken it anyway.

Some months before this he had gotten really ill. Some sort of a fever took hold of him. He was carrying water from the well to boil for the sea crops, and he collapsed midway. He was already running a fever that day, but in the bustle of work nobody noticed, and he didn't complain. After he collapsed, his eyes rolled back, his hair was soaked in sweat. We lifted him up off the ground and laid him in one of the bathtubs where we were planning to boil water for the crops. We filled the tub with cold water, then later, when his fever lowered a bit, we took him back to his bed at the Halász family's house. I was told to stay by his side and change the compress on his forehead every once in a while. The adults wanted to get back to work as soon as possible. The processing of the crops cannot be interrupted, or else the whole batch will be ruined.

I kept bringing him fresh compresses all day, wiping his sweaty forehead with a damp towel. In the afternoon Aunt Juli, an old lady who lived on the street, checked in on us, bringing fresh water and some food as well.

'Is Karcsi going to die?' I asked her.

Right by her mouth there was a huge mole with soft hairs sticking out of it like antennae. Her face reminded me of a rotten apple, and every time I looked at her it made me terrified of getting old.

'I don't know, son. Either he will or he will not.'

'Shouldn't we take him to a hospital?'

'We are processing, son. You know we can't.'

Then she left.

In the evening Karcsi started to speak. He was having fever dreams. At first I couldn't understand him. He muttered random words, turning his head from one side to the other on the soaked pillow.

Then he opened his eyes and looked right at me. His pupils were dilated, his eyes unnaturally dark. Some kind of colorless secretion flowed from his nose; I wanted to wipe it away, but I was afraid to disturb him. He sat up in bed, but without leaning on his arms; it looked like someone was pulling him up by a string. I didn't dare to move. I feared that if I moved I would cut the strings holding his body up, and he would fall back dead instantly.

'Mom?' Karcsi asked in the voice of a child. The voice was totally unlike his, and yet I could hear a younger version of him in it. I felt my heart paining for him. I think this was the moment when I first understood his loss, and the façade he had been hiding behind ever since. The façade of a tough kid suffering from a terrible tragedy.

I didn't know what to say.

'Mom?' he asked again.

I started to panic. Karcsi's eyes were filled with despair.

I reached out and held his hand. It was burning hot, like sand under your feet in summer.

'I'm here,' I said.

'Mom! I'm so happy you're here! They said you died!'

He squeezed my hand so hard that I thought he would break it.

'You just had a nightmare. I'm right here. Just sleep now, you need to rest.'

I leaned in and kissed his forehead, like I imagined his mother would have done.

Karcsi smiled. His head fell back on the pillow and he closed his eyes. He fell asleep right away. He regained his strength a couple of days later. Later he didn't remember any of this, but I could never forget.

That's why I couldn't really be angry with him when he stole the meat.

He chewed the piece of flesh and swallowed it with a grimace.
'How does it taste?' I asked.
'I don't know,' he said. 'Like something . . .'
He fell silent. His face went from white to green, like a forest in springtime. He took a few deep breaths like someone about to sneeze, then he threw up. Vomiting is not a typical allergic symptom, but I got scared nevertheless. Karcsi spat, then looked up.
'It was awful. Like raw fat mixed with cotton candy. Disgusting,' he said eventually. He looked at his vomit.
'Stop looking at it, or I'll throw up too,' I said.
'It's not there.'
'What?'
He drew closer to the pool of vomit. He smiled.
'The piece I just ate. It didn't come out.'
I looked. The raw flesh wasn't there.

We waited for the better part of an hour, but nothing happened. It appeared that eating the flesh caused no reaction whatsoever. We got bored in the punishing heat and decided to go out and play.

We ran out of the attic into the burning summer sun, and we drifted away with the breeze, like the seeds of a dandelion.

That was our last really good day.

'It could be like school for them,' Karcsi said, as he stuffed pie in his mouth.

We were sitting by the trunk of a tree, the lukewarm marmalade pies lying wrapped in a scarf. It was an off week during processing. During these weeks the whole village cooks and prepares meals together, waiting for the next batch of crop to ripen. Karcsi and I got our hands on as many sweets as we could and ran away with them.

'School for who?' I asked.

He swallowed the pie.

'For those who want to come across. From the other side.'

This made me think.

'But where is the other side?'

He frowned.

'Well . . . in the afterlife. Where the dead live.'

'But where is that?' I asked.

I couldn't picture the dead anywhere besides the grave. What do they do, get together underground and play cards? If so, how could they be dead? What form do they take? At the time I couldn't imagine a place that wasn't physical. The most extreme form of fantasy, as far as I was concerned at the time, was the idea of America. I knew the place existed somewhere, and I also knew that it was impossible for me to get there because I would have to fly. Flying was also in the realm of fantasy. Since then, of course, I have flown many times to a number of countries.

Karcsi threw the rest of the pie away. He would always just eat the middle, where most of the marmalade was.

'My dad used to say that life was like a school. It trains us for what comes after life.'

My face was a question mark. Karcsi rolled his eyes.

'Life prepares us for death. Death comes after life. But Dad said that death was also a sort of life, only different.'

I shook my head.

'Death can't be like life. Then it wouldn't be death, would it?'

'Dad said we only call it death because we don't know what's on the other side. But there is something, there must be, and here in this life we're getting ready for that life. That's why life is like a school.'

'All right. But how do we get prepared?'

'By living, I guess.'

I took a bite from the next pie, because I didn't understand any of this. I tried to fake the expression of someone pondering over very deep issues, and I kept chewing. The pie was really good. Karcsi went on.

'On the other side they're preparing too, because they're about to come here. Come here to live. Father thinks that when you're born, that's when you come over here from that other school. And in order to be born here, you have to die there.'

This totally confused me.

'What other school?'

'Well . . . the one where the dead are, and those who aren't born yet. Our world is the noon school, theirs is the midnight school, that's how Dad explained it.'

'Midnight school?'

'Yeah. Only they prepare for life by being dead. And they come across from under the earth. To live. That's how they're born here. In the crops.'

I shrugged, I didn't want to argue about it. Crops are just crops, they're neither alive nor dead. They're matter that turns into a different kind of matter, just as fruits are turned into jam.

In my mind I pictured our school at night, with the light of the full moon shining through the windows, the corridor leading into the darkness. I imagined the classrooms as silent crypts with the desks covered in dust. The hands on the wall clock never move, they remain eternally still, always set to zero o'clock in the midnight school.

'That's all bullshit,' I said. I learned that word from him. Bullshit.

'No. I saw it,' he said.

Karcsi leaned very close to me. His lips were white from powdered sugar and shiny with grease.

'The meat worked,' he said, 'just not right away. Only in my dream.'

I got scared. I didn't want him to tell me, but I asked anyway.

'What did you see in your dream?'

'I saw Mom and Dad. They came to me in my dream. Not like before when I used to dream about them, but for real. They didn't look like they used to, and they didn't talk like they did in life. They didn't appear to me as people. They appeared to me as their essence.'

I swallowed hard. He went on.

'They're on the other side, in the midnight school. They told me how to get across to them. This is the place where I can cross. These lands. These fields. This is where the barrier is the thinnest.'

He seemed much older than his years as he told me all this.

'Have you seen the place? The . . . school?' I asked.

'Only the shadows of it. There are no words to describe it.'

I didn't even want him to.

'They said they would try to come over. But it can't be done here. You're here as guards. To stop them from crossing. Killing them.'

'We're not killing anybody. The crops are not alive!' I snapped.

'Calm down. It's good that they can't come over. They wouldn't be themselves. During the transition they would lose what makes them them. That's why I have to cross.'

'You?'

'Yes, me.'

'How?'

'Isn't it obvious? I have to die.'

Very few people commit suicide in the village. Nobody has any real reason to. Sometimes somebody does something that they can't live with afterwards. For instance, Tibi Kovács ran over his own son in his truck. It was an accident, the child was standing in his blind spot. Still, Tibi still couldn't forgive himself. I can understand, I couldn't have forgiven myself either. Tibi hanged himself in the basement of his house. We buried him, just like everyone else. Or sometimes someone has a mental illness. You can sense a sort of melancholy in them, it lingers around them like a scent. They often end their lives out in the fields.

One thing about suicide victims, though, is they always turn out to be revenants. They always come back.

We didn't talk about it for several days. I didn't want to, it all seemed crazy to me. It still does. But you can only avoid an issue for so long before the silence become unbearable. He cornered me one afternoon. We were leaning against the wall of a house, watching as the light of the setting sun painted the land red.

'I wouldn't actually die,' Karcsi broke a long silence. 'I would continue living, but in a different way.'

'I won't help you,' I declared, hoping that I sounded cold enough.

'I can't do it without you. It can't be done alone.'

'I don't care.'

'Then I have to try the other way.'

I looked at him.

'Other way?'

'The usual way. Jump off a roof, or hang myself.'

'Go ahead!'

'Maybe it would work. But Mom and Dad said that the earth would reject me if I did that. That I would return. I don't mind, I'm curious to know what that's like . . .'

'Stop it.'

'. . . but then I wouldn't get across. Those who return from the grave don't get across. That's what Mom and Dad told me.'

'Shut up.'

He didn't shut up. Later we fought too, not as a game, but for real. Our faces bled, our arms were covered with bruises.

At home, my mom and dad also beat me up for fighting and tearing my clothes. They wouldn't let me out of the house for days.

In the end I wound up helping him. I didn't want to see him returned.

I woke up at dawn and slipped out of the house. It was still dark as night, and I was afraid I would trip over something and alert my dad. I shivered in the cold. I regretted not having smuggled a sweater out as well. I met Karcsi at the end of the street. He was holding a spade and a shovel. I had the storm lamps with me in my rucksack. I took the spade from him and we ran towards the fields. I prayed for rain so we would get stuck in the mud and have to abandon the plan. My prayers weren't answered, not then, not ever. We ran, and after a while I felt that we were a good distance away from the houses. The distance a person goes to dig a birthhole.

'It's a good spot,' he whispered in a shaky voice. You could see he was nervous. We lit the storm lamps and placed them on the ground. Karcsi grabbed the spade.

'Don't just stand there. Help me!'

And just like that he dug the spade into the earth.

I started digging too. I thought we'd talk while we worked, but there was no chance. Karcsi worked obsessively, like a machine, piling the dirt up by the side of the hole. I didn't want to lag behind, so I worked even harder than him. It took less than half an hour before we were up to our waists in the pit, sweating and panting.

Digging had never been so easy. I was hoping it wouldn't work, that the dirt would be too thickly intertwined with the roots, that it would be full of gravel and stones, that it would be hard like concrete and that by morning we'd collapse from exhaustion while only standing ankle-deep in a ditch. I was wrong. If anything, it got easier and easier with each shovelful.

The horizon glimmered with bluish light, and we were already up to our shoulders in the pit.

'This will be good enough,' Karcsi said, throwing his spade out of the hole, then climbing out of it himself.

We sat down for a little while by the freshly made pile. I took out a sandwich and handed it to Karcsi. Ham and cheese. I had brought one for myself too. For a while we just ate quietly.

'What if you're wrong?' I asked him finally. 'What if it was only a dream? If it was only a dream and they didn't come back to you?'

He swallowed a mouthful.

'Then I'm wrong.'

I didn't ask anything else after that.

Karcsi studied the pile in the lamplight, reaching into it every now and then to pull something out of the dirt.

'There they are,' he said.

I leaned closer to see what he was talking about. It was the roots, the thin, white threads that connected everything under the ground. Karcsi was smiling now.

'It will work,' he said. 'I know it will.'

He jumped on me and gave me a hug.

He took off his clothes and threw them in. He took one last look around the fields, then jumped into the pit. He looked like an animal that had fallen into a ditch. He lay down on top of his clothes, curled up in a fetal position like the dreamers.

I just stood there watching him. My friend who was about to die.

'Do it already, it's fucking cold down here,' Karcsi urged. 'We have to be done by the time the sun comes up.'

My teeth were chattering like a machine gun in the movies. I couldn't make the first move. There's no way I can do this, I thought. My limbs felt frozen.

'Come on!' he said again.

A strange thought came to me. I thought that if I were moving, I would be less cold. I don't think this thought was my own. I would like to think that it wasn't. It was the field talking.

I grabbed the spade and covered the hole with Karcsi in it. He never even made a sound.

By the time I finished the sun was already crawling up the sky. The air was warming up, the fields had the nice reddish tone of early morning. I appreciated that red, I have ever since that morning. It felt like nothing had changed, like everything was just the same as before he came to us – like Karcsi never even existed. I flattened the earth above the grave, gathered the tools, and left for home.

His disappearance made no waves in our community. The Halász family thought he had run away, and I could tell they were a little relieved. People discussed Karcsi for a while, not his disappearance, but their memories of him.

There were days when I thought I should dig out the pit again. But what would be the point? One way or another, Karcsi got what he wanted. He had gone to the place where the dead go.

Years later a hunger arose in me. I wanted to see what the rest of the world was like. I wanted to study, like kids in other places do. In our community we're even encouraged to go out and learn the ways of the world. When I came of age I moved away. I enrolled at a university and started working in a factory to make ends meet. I visited several of the bigger towns, lived in some of them too. I got married after a summer fling, but the flames of passion turned to ashes soon enough, and by the next summer we were already divorced. After the divorce I moved back home. To the village. Most people do return, often with a spouse. Nowhere else feels quite like home.

Then all those seasons passed, seasons of feeding and

harvesting and processing, one after the other, until I found myself an old man sitting by the window, looking out on the fields day and night.

So many wonders. So many secrets. So much life. My heart always swells up with painful yearning when I think of the fields. They feel like my true home.

I'm waiting for the day when my studying days in the noon school are over and I'm returned to the earth from which I was taken. I hope I won't need a wake and that my grave will remain undisturbed. I hope I will meet my father and mother, my friends and lovers long gone, my neighbors and enemies. I hope, most of all, that I'll meet Karcsi and know for certain that he succeeded, and we'll play together, as if we had never grown up, forever in the midnight school.

In the Snow, Sleeping

Luca couldn't find a rational explanation for why she was afraid of this vacation. She deserved a little rest. Still, she felt anxious. Maybe it was the ring, although she saw no reason to be upset about it; it was the natural way of things.

She had been packing clothes into a borrowed suitcase for herself and Robi, that was when she found the engagement ring among his clothes. It fell out of the back pocket of a pair of jeans. For a moment she considered taking the ring out to the garden and burying it in the ground. It wouldn't have made any sense to plant it in the soil like a seed, yet it seemed such an impossible place that Robi would never find it. She could have also flushed it down the toilet, but then it might clog the pipes. She put it back in the pocket, folded the pants, and slid them to the bottom of the suitcase.

Of course they had gone on vacations together before. They spent a few days at the mouth of the Tisza-Bodrog River two years ago. They had only been together for a couple of weeks at the time. Her most vivid memory was the smell of the sunscreen Robi would oil her back with. Those days they fucked nonstop.

Last year they traveled to Prague. They drank a lot of local beer, far superior to Hungarian products, they had to admit. They saw the museums and bridges and jewelry stores and talked about how beautiful Prague was, feeling a pang of jealousy over it, as Budapest seemed gray in comparison. They brought some weed along with them; at night they rolled massive joints, and only after the second night did they notice that their hostel was right next door to a police station. They laughed.

By the Tisza they forced their way into each others' bodies like impatient explorers into the wilderness. In Prague they made love slowly and calmly, traveling roads now well known. They had all the time in the world.

But now Luca felt like time was slipping through her hands. Maybe a holiday was just what she needed to set her mind straight, to get a grip on things.

They left home quite late. Robi had been out the night before on a company team-building exercise. Luca had stayed home, drinking red wine and watching a documentary about the recycling of rubber tires. She had specifically asked Robi to come home early so they could leave before sunrise to avoid the heat.

He came home late and drunk.

She stayed awake all night, trying to decide whether to make a scene or not. She decided if she was already anxious about being late on the first day of their holiday, that probably wasn't a good sign. You can't be late for a vacation, that's precisely the point of a vacation: it annihilates time. We do not age while we enjoy a holiday. Life just gets enriched; everything stops for a moment so we can indulge ourselves while time is paused, we can focus on ourselves, turn our mind's eye inward, while still to some extent keeping an eye on the landscape, the hotel walls and windows, the bountiful breakfasts, purely for aesthetic and culinary reasons, because these will be the memories to be cherished later on.

That's how Luca saw it by the time they started. She drove. There was barely any traffic, maybe because of the maddening heat, although in the opposite direction there was a traffic jam. Luca pictured the cars as animals running away from a burning forest or a slaughterhouse and now being herded together again by the two-lane highway in order to enter the same burning forest or slaughterhouse through a different gate.

She caught a scent of blood in her nose and tried to divert her thoughts. She turned on the radio. On the local station some male choir was chanting songs without any semblance of a melody.

Robi leaned his head against the window like he was about to go to sleep, but he just stared blankly at the road. He had stubble on his face, and it made him look like a stranger. Robi shaved meticulously each and every morning – except this one. It's because of the holiday, Luca thought, you don't have to shave on a holiday. You just have to focus on yourself. Robi tore his eyes away from the road and looked at Luca.

'What?' she asked. Robi shrugged his shoulders.

Luca knew exactly what was coming. Some brief, shallow chit-chat about last night, who made out with whom at the company, who said what, what minor misunderstandings were settled or created, and who at what point got drunk enough to pull down his pants. They would laugh at the somewhat funnier stories, or shake their heads in disdain at the disgusting ones.

However, this conversation did not take place. They both knew in advance what they would have said, and not uttering those thoughts left a deeper mark in their minds than the sudden collision itself.

The moment it happened they didn't understand a thing. After the impact Luca stepped on the brakes, for the chances of survival are higher in a stopped car than a moving one. A crack stretched across the windshield, limiting vision. She looked into the rearview mirror. There was no other car there, nor could she see a corpse anywhere.

'Let's not tell anyone!' Robi said afterwards. 'At the office, Tomi told me he hit a hare with his mother once at some nature reserve. It just ran right out in front of their car. They reported it and got a fine of half a million for causing damage. When the damn rabbit practically committed suicide! Can you even imagine how much they would ask for a hawk? It was a hawk, wasn't it?'

'It was definitely a bird,' she said, concentrating on her driving. The crack across her line of vision made her tense; her muscles remembered the shock of the sudden noise, the sense of the impact against the windshield, the blur of the winged body bouncing off the car.

There was nothing to report anyway. Luca thought about it long and hard while navigating the empty highway for hours on end. No carcass lay on the asphalt, although it would have been impossible for anything to survive such an impact. Maybe it landed in the grass where they couldn't see it. Perhaps it still lived on for a little while. It might have crawled away, dragging its broken parts like a sack of pain. Then it must have stopped when the pain became too draining. It just lay there, helplessly watching the scavengers circling in the sky. The bird must have known what was coming. It must have hoped for a quick death before those other birds descended to take a nip, then another.

There were no more incidents along the way, and Robi soon fell asleep.

They arrived at the spa in the afternoon. Summer heat rose off the asphalt of the parking lot. The building was glass and metal, all sharp edges and jagged-looking windows. In the lobby there were two leather armchairs and a coffee table covered with brochures and leaflets advertising massage salons, restaurants, wine tours, guided excursions to the local lake, the local hills, the local cemeteries.

Behind the counter a smile awaited them; according to the name tag attached to his polo shirt, the smile belonged to Balázs. The polo shirt was carefully tucked into his dark blue jeans, which Luca found old-fashioned. But who knows, maybe the wellness spa had some kind of rule that everything had to be like 1972.

'Good afternoon! My name is Viktor. How can I help you?' asked the man behind the counter.

Luca peeked at the name tag again because she thought

she'd misread the name. The tag still said Balázs. Could he have two names? Balázs Viktor? Viktor Balázs? Luca decided that his name didn't matter, only his function.

'We have a reservation,' Robi said. 'I've got it printed out.'

Robi reached into his back pocket, and for a second Luca thought he would accidentally conjure up the engagement ring and propose to her spontaneously. The sudden adrenaline rush made Luca feel like she was going to throw up, right there in front of everyone, at least in front of Viktor or Balázs or whatever his name was, then maybe faint. The security cameras would record all this, even Robi standing over her, ring in hand, not knowing what to do with her unconscious body. The cameras wouldn't record the unbearable heat though. Shouldn't there be air conditioning at a place like this?

Robi fished out the crumpled sheet and put it on the counter. He smoothed it out a little with his sweaty fingers. Viktor or Balázs took the paper with a solemn look on his face, typed a set of numbers from it, then broke into a smile again.

'Robi and Luca, five nights, standard double bed.'

They nodded, and Viktor/Balázs nodded with them, and Luca thought everything was all right. At last.

All the walls and carpets were as red as red can be, the carpet thick, the walls too close for comfort. Luca longed for an ice-cold shower.

They received the keycard in a small paper holder. Viktor or Balázs had written the room number on it in black ink.

'303.'

Robi slid the card into the door. Nothing happened. He swore, turned the card upside down, tried again. The door gave a quiet chirp, like a mechanical bird. They entered the room, but even before opening the door Luca knew from the smell that something was wrong.

She wanted to get as far as possible from the stench, so they agreed she would go back to reception. She was terrified of getting lost in the red corridors, since one was just like another

– one wrong turn and you'd end up somewhere other than your destination, while those who wanted to get to the place where you ended up are now left waiting at reception for eternity instead.

Eventually she reached the reception desk, made the complaint, and returned to the room in the company of Balázs or Viktor. The man took a look around the room: the disheveled bed, the filthy mirror, the food scraps lying on the floor, the used needles scattered between the tatters of the bed sheet, the filth on the wall, which Luca believed to be excrement, most probably of human origin.

'I'll put you in another room immediately, of course,' said Balázs/Viktor. 'And I could give you a discount to our weekend sauna event.'

They didn't know what a sauna event was but accepted the offer. They all trudged back to reception, and Viktor or Balázs made a new card for them. He preserved the same paper holder, just crossing out '303' and writing '304'.

They still had time for a swim before dinner. Luca put on the bikini she had purchased for the occasion. She had only tried it on twice: once in the shop, once while sunbathing on the balcony; and now she put it on for the third time, by the wall the other side of which was covered in shit.

The minibar offered tiny bottles of liquor, small cans of Heineken, and chocolate. Robi took out a bottle of vodka, unscrewed the cap and held it towards Luca. She thought about the afternoon, the holiday, the time she could now spend with herself, with herself and with Robi; she took the bottle and downed the vodka. Robi stepped closer and kissed her neck. 'Leave me alone, I just showered,' Luca wanted to say, but remained silent because on holiday nothing matters, only passion, intimacy, the moments to be shared together. The man stroked Luca's belly, his fingers already groping under the bikini bottom, unstoppable like an approaching storm. Luca peeked at the clock: it was only an hour and a half until dinner and they hadn't even swum yet, they hadn't done anything relaxing, and Robi wanted to fuck now! She'd have to shower again afterwards and there'd be no time left to relax at all.

Luca kneeled down and unzipped Robi's pants.

'I want it to be good for you too,' he whispered.

'It's good for me like this,' said Luca, trying not to think of the room next door.

The pools were in the basement. An Olympic-sized pool for the swimmers and several smaller ones filled with hot thermal water renowned for curing a number of chronic diseases. But you couldn't stay in them for too long; each pool had its own warning sign about how long a person could remain in the healthful water before it turned harmful. Luca made a mental note of the dangers of the thermal pools. In one of the pools an old man spread out like an oil spill, his plump arms floating around him, his eyes closed. To Luca he looked dead, but surely he was only resting. Children were jumping into the swimming pool, their piercing screams echoing from wall to wall, even though a sign grimly stated: JUMPING PROHIBITED.

Robi stretched his arms, looked around the swimming facilities with a smile on his face, then jumped into the pool as well.

After a discreet plunge in the water Luca settled on a plastic deckchair, then realized she had left the book she brought for vacation reading up in the room. It was called *Betty and the Aliens*, a bestseller she'd bought at a newsstand even though she was already reading a different book; the book was a success, the kind of book you read on vacation, because a vacation represents success. She had left the other book at home. It was sad, disturbing, not the kind of thing you read on vacation; now it was lying face down like a dead soldier on the nightstand in her bedroom.

A woman sat down on the next deckchair, but Luca didn't

look at her, following the etiquette which dictates that common places are meant to be used commonly but not together, as if Luca were in one room and the woman in another, except that the two rooms happened to share the same space somehow. The woman was wearing a bathrobe. She smelled of chlorine.

'Hi!' she said, thereby inviting Luca into her own room. Luca smiled back and said hi as well. Now they were in the same room. The woman placed her fluffy towel behind her head and opened up a book. '*The Knowledge of Places*', read the title, and Luca burst out laughing.

The woman looked at her.

'Sorry,' Luca tried to explain herself, 'it's only that I'm reading the same book.'

The woman broke into a faint smile.

'I mean, not here, but at home,' Luca continued, although she thought she was imposing now. 'Here I'm reading *Betty and the Aliens*.'

The woman closed her book.

'They were actually written by the same author,' she said, extending her hand. Her name was Alexandra.

After the swim Luca and Robi returned to their room to take a shower and get changed for dinner. Luca hung her bikini out to dry, already disgusted at the thought of having to put the chlorine-soaked garment back on again.

They closed the door behind them carefully and turned to head for the restaurant. They stopped dead in their tracks. A fox was watching them from the end of the corridor, its large ears pointed towards the ceiling. Robi backed away slowly, but Luca didn't move; Robi whispered a swear word, but Luca remained silent, as if the fox had hypnotized her and the animal's muteness had become her own.

The fox must have heard some distant noise, for it turned its head towards one of the windows and ran down the fire escape.

After this they went to have dinner.

'It must have had rabies,' Robi mused at the table. 'Foxes with rabies are friendly,' he added.

She was famished; still, she could barely force herself to eat. The heat in the room was stifling. Elderly Germans fought each other for more meat at the buffet, children laid siege to the cakes, screaming at one another, their mothers sipping wine and chatting about nothing at all.

Alexandra showed up at their table and introduced them to Vajk, a tall, blond man who could have passed for a German. She didn't reveal their relationship. Husband? Friend? Partner? Robi insisted they join their table, and they agreed gladly. They sat close to each other, like they were feeding off each other's body heat. They held hands, which made Luca feel she should touch Robi more often.

Vajk and Alexandra laughed and held onto their anchor of wine glasses. Robi was telling them the story of room 303, and now Luca started laughing as well because it was a funny story indeed. So funny.

Still laughing, Vajk told them that the same thing happened when they arrived; they received the same room three days earlier, and it had already been as trashed as it was now. Everyone roared with laughter but Luca. She found the thought of that unattended room disturbing; it became the rotten core of that place in her thoughts.

After the second bottle of red wine Luca had the idea of reporting the fox sighting to the front desk. Her head was buzzing. She needed to get out of the room; she couldn't sit there enjoying herself when a fox might be running through the corridors all over the building, forever chasing something it would never catch. She wanted certainty that the predator was no longer on the premises.

The reception desk stood empty. Luca leaned on the counter, determined to wait until Balázs or Viktor returned, no matter how long that might take.

The automatic door opened and she looked up. She thought

it must be the receptionist returning to the building.

There was no one in the doorway, only the night. Luca stared down the darkness for half a minute, then she could take it no longer. She ran back to the restaurant.

The automatic door stood open the entire night.

They drank too much, because when people feel good, they drink. Luca was the only one craving her bed, the tranquility of the blanket and pillows, her head dizzy from the wine. The German tourists guzzled down pint after pint, howling with laughter after each sip as if they were drinking jokes.

Vajk drew out a bag of cocaine from his pocket and signaled to Robi to follow him to the restroom. Alexandra joined them, leaving Luca alone at the table. She didn't want to sniff cocaine, she didn't want to drink more wine, and she didn't want to sit either; yet she didn't move. What if they came back and found her vanished like a pile of leaves in a storm? Would they be worried? Would they mount a search? Or would they go back to the bathroom to snort some more coke?

She waited for half an hour, then left the now-empty dining hall.

She didn't even undress, just crawled under the blanket. She latched the door because she found the empty corridor disquieting.

She was dead tired, but she couldn't sleep. From the other side of the wall sounds kept her awake: crying and screams, the sound of a fist pounding on flesh, and laughter. It was the laughter of room 303. She should have banged on the wall – the hotel was a wellness spa, after all, where people came to rest, and rest should be respected – but she didn't. What if the room was actually empty? What if that emptiness spilled over to fill her room with screams and laughter too?

She was just about to fall asleep when Robi started banging on the door. He laughed because his nose was bleeding and he found it funny. He washed the blood off, threw himself onto the bed and fell asleep right away, snoring. She knew she wouldn't sleep anymore. She never could when he snored.

The corpse was discovered at dawn, shortly before breakfast. It was floating in the outdoor pool like a ship adrift at sea, face up. He was a fat man in a red swim brief; Luca felt as if she had seen him somewhere before, then she recalled the man soaking himself in the thermal water. It was the same man. Luca had an irrational thought that made her shudder: what if the man was in fact dead even at that time? Now he had just decided to be dead somewhere else.

A crowd quickly gathered around the pool. The man's skin was pasty white by then, so no one saw any point in dragging the corpse out. Some asked around whether anybody had known the unfortunate man, but everyone just shook their heads. The entire spa hotel was staring at the corpse of a stranger.

The hotel's staff must have already been alerted and gone for help, since the concierge's booth was empty; the reception desk was empty as well. Luca was unsettled at the thought that the hotel might have been unsupervised all night; and it might remain unsupervised from then on indefinitely. She looked behind the counter, which had been clean and empty the night before. Now a half-eaten sandwich lay on the desk, and a magazine called *Teen Pussy*, with its rather disturbing cover exposed to any passerby. Luca thought that kind of magazine must be illegal. She turned away from the desk and left for breakfast.

Most of the tourists followed suit. The restaurant windows looked onto the pool, where the body floated like an iceberg. Luca shivered as she munched on her whole grain croissant. Everyone tried not to pay attention to the corpse; they were all sure someone must have already called for some sort of help.

'Shouldn't we go home?' she asked Robi. He shook his head no. Dark circles cast a shadow under his eyes; he looked tired.

He pointed at the pool with his fork. 'Do you think people don't die everywhere all the time? I bet someone has died in every single room in this building. Dozens must have died in the flat we're living in. The streets that we walk every day used to be filled knee-high with bodies during the war. Still, we don't move out of the city, huh?'

Luca nodded hesitantly.

'We've paid for this,' he said, his tongue dragging a morsel around in his mouth. 'We're staying until the end.'

Alexandra and Vajk showed up, each holding a tray with omelettes and coffee. They seemed fresh and well rested. They sat down at the table without asking permission.

They talked about the corpse outside, then about saunas and the bond market. Luca sometimes glanced out at the pool, at the dead man now on an eternal holiday. Time didn't matter to him anymore; he was just resting, forever resting. We need to rest before we run out of time, she thought, and suggested that they go to the sauna.

In the changing room she looked out the window and saw senior citizens abandoning the spa. Like birds leaving the nest, wings packed into their trolley bags, they plodded towards the charter bus that seemed to have no driver yet. Their time was up, Luca thought. A sudden autumn breeze swept over the pensioners outside; shivering with cold, they gathered their linen summer shirts around their frail frames to preserve some of their body heat.

The swimming pool seemed empty without them. Children were goofing around in boredom by the edge of the water. A mother was reading her magazine on a deckchair; there was no adult around besides her to supervise the kids.

The men were nowhere to be found; Alexandra waited alone for Luca by the sauna, her body wrapped in a towel. However, the sauna was cold and empty, so they decided to go to the steam bath instead.

The world became a foggy maze; how many halls, how

many rooms could there be in one steam bath? In the thick vapor Luca saw nothing but Alexandra's blurry outline. She reached a bench, threw off the towel, and turned towards Luca. Luca dropped her own towel on the bench, but then she had no idea whether to sit or stand. She looked at Alexandra to follow her lead; the woman remained standing, holding a showerhead in her hands. Luca's gaze swept over her naked body. There were scars that she couldn't make out very well in the steam. Luca thought they must have been burns, maybe a car accident or some other tragedy. But no, she realized, those weren't burn marks.

'Bite marks,' Alexandra explained with a smile, turning so that Luca could clearly see the marks stretching over her rib cage and breasts and backside as well. Luca leaned closer to make out the marks through the steam, and now she recognized the pattern of the teeth, dozens of bites mapping out a relationship of pain.

Water burst from the showerhead. Alexandra washed herself and sprayed some water on the wall as well, covering the room in even more suffocating and blinding steam. Her silhouette disappeared in the thick mist, and Luca thought herself lost forever, without any way out of the steam bath maze.

But Alexandra appeared by her side again, so close that her breasts brushed against Luca's arm. She pressed Luca up against the wall. Luca felt the wet, hot tiles behind her and swallowed hard. Alexandra flashed her teeth; they were white, healthy, perfect. She leaned toward Luca's neck, swept over her skin with her tongue, then placed her teeth on her shoulder. She squeezed a little, with the promise of a bite, but she didn't actually sink her teeth into the flesh. Luca wanted to whimper; if she was bitten now the scar would stay there forever, an eternal imprint of the holiday. Instead of memories and photographs, a disfiguration, a defect, so when she looked in the mirror she would always think of the pain instead of the the restful hours.

Alexandra let her go and returned to the bench.

'You two should try it,' she said. 'It strengthens a relationship.'

They relaxed some more in the steam bath, then they set out to find somewhere else to relax.

The lunch was spoiled; they found worms in the meatloaf, you could smell the stench of the chicken tarragon soup from far away, and the Black Forest gateau was covered in mold. The restaurant stood all but deserted, only a handful of tourists loitered around, all shaking their heads at the sight of the rotten food.

Luca went to the reception desk yet again to make a complaint, this time with Robi on her side. But it stood empty as usual, a sign on the counter reading 'Be Right Back'. The sign had been placed upside down.

The weather turned cold, rain coming down heavily in thick, icy drops. A wolf howled in the distance, although Luca was sure no wolves inhabited this part of the country. They wanted to use the outdoor thermal pool, but even that was out of order now.

'We should leave,' she proposed once more, but Robi again shook his head, with Alexandra and Vajk taking his side.

'It's just a minor inconvenience,' Vajk said in a soothing voice. 'Soon everything will be perfectly fine again.'

'Maybe it's all perfectly fine even now! Even if we can't use the outdoor thermal pools, the indoor ones are still functioning,' said Alexandra.

Luca felt like her head was full of wasps; she perceived the world with a slight delay. She needed sleep; she hoped she was actually sleeping now, because then all of this would just be a stupid dream.

'The more we sleep,' said Robi, even though Luca hadn't said a word about sleep, 'the less time we have to relax.'

Luca left the group abruptly and headed to her room,

because despite everything she just wanted her bed. The hell with relaxation! She pressed the elevator button and as she waited she saw a reflection in the elevator door. A woman stood behind her, the mother who had been reading her magazine by the pool earlier. Luca turned to look at the woman. She was in bad shape. Blood dripped from a wound above her eyes, her hair was soaked into a sweaty knot on top of her head, her dress was torn apart, revealing fresh bloody scratches all over her skin. Tears poured from her eyes, eyes that looked like broken crystal, their glimmer dulled by a loss unfathomable to Luca. The woman opened her mouth to say something, one final thing, but no sound came from her throat no matter how hard she tried. She turned away from Luca and ran out the main entrance into the cold rain before Luca could stop her.

The elevator arrived and Luca stepped in. She headed towards their room to put on something warm and then either to sleep or warn the others of an undefined danger. The thick carpet was soaked in stale water; footprints left by bare feet stretched across the hallway, leading from the fire escape all the way to room 303. Under the smell of chlorine she picked up the reek of decay.

She looked down at the outdoor pool from the window at the end of the hall. The corpse was no longer floating on the surface.

She heard a door opening slowly. It wasn't their room. It was room 303.

She ran away as fast as she could.

She found Robi alone in the dining room, fiddling with his phone and complaining about the lack of signal. Luca told him they were getting out of there. Immediately. She made sure to sound as firm as possible and pointed at the empty pool.

'As you wish, darling!' he said.

This word echoed in Luca's head on their way to the exit. She had never been called 'darling' before. She associated this term with an older woman, or a younger one not fully in control of her life. She had never thought of herself as someone's darling, a possession of sorts. She suddenly stopped halfway down the hallway, as if about to make a scene, but she decided this wasn't the right time and kept on walking towards the exit.

One last time they tried to turn to the management for help. Robi thought they could claim a refund for their interrupted holiday; perhaps not immediately, but certainly through some sort of legal process.

They found the concierge's booth empty as usual; the manager's door was locked. There was no staff in the building.

Outside sleet was pouring down and the wind was howling. The electricity was shaky, the lights were failing, going out one second only to return again palely the next. Luca was sure that by nightfall the building would be covered in darkness, and she decided she'd rather sleep in her car than in room 304.

'We should pick up Vajk and Alexandra! I promised them a lift!' Robi said, and Luca wanted to cry.

'Fuck them! Let's just go!' she begged. 'Let's just get out of here, right now!'

Robi shook his head in disagreement. Luca had a thought that she found almost as disturbing as the spa. She thought that Robi's face was dumb. It was the face of an imbecile, an idiot. How could she ever have loved that face, which even now was frozen in a state of indecision about an issue a normal person wouldn't even think about? Had it always been like this? Had he always been like this? Had she always been this blind?

'We'll leave, together with them. We might find another spa or an inn along the way. Wait here!' he said, then ran off down the corridor and up the stairs, and finally Luca burst into hysterical laughter. What fine leisure activities! What great entertainment! She laughed until she cried, laughed until she felt like throwing up.

Half an hour later Alexandra and Vajk arrived. They slowly approached Luca from the other end of the hall, sweaty and naked, teeth sunken into each other's shoulder. Their old wounds had all reopened, their skin was covered in dark blood. They didn't speak, they just groaned like savage dogs as they dragged each other towards Luca. She watched them, this beautiful couple, as they fought each other inch by inch for progress. She felt no fear, only a weird sense of amusement and maybe a pinch of jealousy. Only when she heard the squish of wet soles in the stairwell did she run out of the hotel into the dead of winter.

It was freezing; she had only had time to put on an abandoned bathrobe over her summer dress. She slipped on the icy ground but quickly stood up again and ran towards the parking lot. From the other end of the lot a pack of wolves looked at her; they were feasting on a body which was now nothing but genderless flesh. Beside the wolves were the children who had been jumping into the pool not long ago, now on all fours, naked, their faces bloody, chewing on the same meat the wolves feasted on.

The wolves howled at the sky, and the children howled with them.

There was a Toyota that somebody had left the keys in. Luca jumped in and started the engine. She looked in the rearview mirror. The spa hotel shrunk away as she sped out onto the road; Robi was in the hotel, and thus he was shrinking away too, which she was fine with.

The landscape turned pure white, like a wedding dress. The roads were in horrible shape, but they stood empty for Luca. She saw some cars in ditches, the wrecks now covered with snow. There was nothing on the radio but static noise; under the noise, if she listened carefully, she could hear the voice of a man. She thought she was listening to a sermon; it sounded like a priest's voice, that singsong recital voice they used in churches. But she couldn't be sure, it might have just been her imagination. She found a couple of unlabeled CDs in the glove compartment. She put one into the CD player;

it turned out to be ABBA's greatest hits, which was fine. She hated ABBA but screamed along with the songs anyway.

She ran out of fuel two hours later. She let the Toyota roll until it came to a complete stop, then she laid her head on the wheel so that she could finally get some sleep. In the distance, beyond the snowfall, colossal three-legged giants walked in silence. Maybe they were only trees, but who cared when this car would make such a great bed?

Before she could fall asleep something crashed against the windshield. The glass cracked, like it had cracked before on the highway. Luca let out a scream, her mouth tasted like adrenaline.

She saw Robi in the field. He was standing in the snow, waving at her slowly; his face was obscured in the snowfall, but she would have recognized his posture anywhere. Robi took another stone and threw it towards the car; this time the stone struck the roof. Although Luca anticipated the sound, she still shuddered when the stone hit the metal.

Robi signaled to her again, then turned and walked towards the field.

The temperature had already dropped in the car. She could see her breath. Luca sighed heavily and got out. Her legs sank into the snow. She hissed at the wet cold, but headed after Robi to the field. Wolves and children howled in the distance.

There was a hole. A rectangular hole in the ground, two meters by two meters, in the middle of the snow-covered field. It seemed fresh, the dirt was still black. Somehow she knew it had been dug for her. There was no one else left in the area, perhaps not in the entire world; therefore this hole had to be waiting for her.

She looked down into the hole; Robi lay at the bottom, motionless, face down. He was waiting for her to join him.

All was silent, a supreme silence. The kind of silence that covers you and soothes, silence that gives you rest. She could even hear the sound of the snowflakes.

She climbed into the hole next to Robi and reached into his jeans pocket. She took out the wedding ring and looked at it again. It wasn't ugly, but not particularly pretty either. A simple gold ring. Maybe even too tight for her finger.

It didn't matter; she put the ring on her tongue and swallowed it. Over the edge of the hole she saw the gray sky; she knew they would soon be completely covered by snow.

She hugged Robi and waited for the cold to put her to sleep.

Multiplied by Zero

Goodtravel, travel review
User: Sabesz1984
2016.07.22
Review: Abaddon Travels, Askathoth travel package
Short summary: I'm alive. Hooray.

Summary:

Everything you've heard or assumed about this trip is probably true. The challenges are of an inhuman scale – death or madness is a very real possibility.

The travel agency asked me to describe what happened with the utmost accuracy, explain why I chose this package and what my experiences were, in order to provide guidance for those considering whether or not to embark on this journey. If you don't have the patience to read about my adventures so extensively I will summarize here for you in a few quick words. Three of us survived the trip out of more than a dozen travelers. The survivors' lives have changed irrevocably. Mine in a definitely positive way; I can't speak for the others. Make your decision with this in mind. I believe that it's best to wait until you have nothing left to lose.

Why did I choose this trip?

I work in an office from nine to five at a multinational company. The salary is good. I'm surrounded by inspiring people.

I live for my work. I'm ambitious, my colleagues like me. I spend my nights at my favorite downtown clubs and bars – night after night of boozing with clients and colleagues, punctuated with one night stands and short-lived relationships. Then back to work the next morning, often on weekends too.

I've been doing this for years, on repeat, week after week. Some time ago I realized that I was on the verge of burnout. I couldn't pinpoint the boundary between me and my work, between who I was and what I did for money. At nights, the spritzer and beer weren't enough anymore, I would also down a few shots. If necessary, I would get some cocaine or ecstasy. When I was high I could sense that there was an actual person beyond the office drone that I had become. I needed to make a connection with that person, but the connection achieved through these highs was never permanent, and after a while I started to pay the price. My face got redder, my otherwise lean body became cushioned with layers of fat.

I felt like I was living someone else's life.

I should have been happy. Many people don't have as much as I have. Still, for no good reason at all I sometimes found myself daydreaming about suicide. Of course no one noticed this. I remained just as social as before, I even compensated for the depression at night. I threw away my days like used tissues.

That's when it happened, on one of my nights out. I went to my usual place at Keresztes Square, a club frequented by local office drones and yuppie types. I ran into Erika from accounting. We'd had a series of one night stands, but those nights spent together never evolved into anything permanent. Still, we started chatting again because I hadn't seen her for a while, and I wasn't against one more night of entanglement. I got her a glass of rosé. When I set the glass on the table she looked into my eyes and said that she'd had an abortion a couple of weeks ago.

Last time we'd fucked without a condom. We had a mutual trust in each other, plus we were high, neither of us cared.

Of course when I say there was a mutual trust I mean that I trusted her to have an abortion if she got pregnant. My trust was well founded, apparently.

I asked her if it was mine. Erika shrugged her shoulders. 'Maybe, maybe not,' she said. 'Don't worry about it. It's been taken care of.'

I have no right to judge women, what they do with their bodies or their lives, but at that moment I felt like something had been taken away from me, the possibility of a stable future. Had Erika filed a paternity suit I'm sure I would have thought differently, but still, a gaping hole had opened up in my heart, or maybe it had always been there, but now I could see it, now I could feel it.

I asked her why she would do such a thing to herself. She smiled bitterly.

'Why, would you have raised it?' she asked. 'Would you have become an ideal father? Would you have left your job for a kid?'

I wouldn't, of course. But a woman has to. After all, their bodies were designed for this purpose. They were sacrificed by life from the very moment of their birth. They were assigned an express purpose: to give birth to new beings just like themselves or me. This is of course just my personal opinion.

Erika shook her head in annoyance.

'You men,' she said, 'you just couldn't give a fuck, could you? A child doesn't spoil anything for you, but it nullifies our lives. A child is the multiplier,' she explained, like the economist she was, 'and the value of the multiplier here is zero. Whatever a woman is worth in this equation, the child multiplies her by zero. We become zeroes, while you, you just fuck around more.'

I frowned.

'Why would it be different for men?' I asked.

'Because men aren't worth a damn to begin with,' she answered.

★

I've always believed that a person's worth is determined by how hard they work and how talented they are. Success is the product of talent, perseverance, and luck. After this conversation I decided I would change my life – in small steps at first, so that later, when truly important things came up, I would see them clearly, not blinded by work, alcohol, and drugs.

I had to find a way to separate my work from my free time. So I opted for hiking, in large doses. Around this time I heard from a hiking buddy that he'd scored two tickets to a coveted Abaddon Travels trip, which is otherwise nearly impossible to book.

I'm not a religious person, but my friend assured me that the trip was not strictly religious; lay people and cult members go alike. Anyone could join. I had heard rumors and myths about this journey, and I thought it might be just what I needed to discover the meaning of my life and help me to focus on my own happiness.

There were nights before the trip when I tossed and turned sleeplessly, soaked in sweat, and I almost canceled several times. I didn't look up any reviews or descriptions on purpose so I wouldn't scare myself off. In the end, my hiking buddy didn't join me. He said he'd gotten sick, but he was lying, I know.

He canceled the trip because he was terrified.

The first crossing

The travel agency provides the necessary flight tickets on independent airlines for the first leg of the journey. I went to Ferenc Liszt Airport in the morning, checked in well ahead of time, bought some booze for the flight, and stepped in line with the tourists. If there are any drawbacks, this might be one: in my view an agency of this caliber should ensure that the initial part of the trip lives up to the rest of it in atmosphere and style.

We left the airport twenty minutes late, but I made the connection in Paris, from which we proceeded to Reykjavík on schedule. I had paid an extra fee to avoid economy class, but I didn't find a real first-class section on either of the planes – something to consider for those who value comfort and luxury.

We continued our travel from Iceland on an aircraft owned by Abaddon Travels. It's an ordinary Airbus, painted black. This is the first time you mingle with other participants on the tour, but not everyone is traveling to the same location, and not everyone continues their journey at the same time. I was in the Askatoth package; my ticket destined me for the ancient mountains and caves of Askatoth, but several travelers were en route to the dreamlands of Kal-Kadath or the lost cities of An'samhar Dei. Reykjavík is the only European hub, while other destinations can be reached via different routes from Asia, the Americas, or Antarctica. The Al'r-Dagon diving tour is completely separate from those listed above and requires special diving licenses for safety reasons.

The airplane window shades are kept down throughout the entire flight, so you can't see the landscapes or the clouds. Supposedly it's done on purpose, in order to ensure a successful crossing. The service is somewhat impersonal. The stewardesses never smile. They are pretty, but tired-looking, stern, impatient. They're in desperate need of sleep, judging from the dark rings under their eyes. I assume that this was part of getting us in the mood for the tour, so I don't consider it a drawback. The flight is about four or five hours long, with one meal served, the usual warmed-up airplane food, and one round of salty or sweet snacks. I'd recommend bringing your own sandwich. The consumption of alcohol purchased at the airport is allowed. Smoking is prohibited.

The flight was uneventful, apart from one exception. The language of communication on the plane is English, but all announcements are made in French, German, and some sort of Arabic dialect which I couldn't properly identify and which might not have even had anything to do with any Arabic language.

We must have been a couple of hours into our flight. I had drunk most of the tiny bottles of vodka hiding in my pockets. My head became leaden, my eyelids locked up, the monotonous noise of the airplane engines swamped my consciousness. Luckily I was sitting by the window, so I planned to sleep the rest of the journey, using my sweater as a pillow. That's why I can't be entirely sure whether the following event happened or was only part of a dream.

My heart sank and I clenched the armrest. My body panicked because I was sure that the engines had failed and we were going down. It took me a couple of seconds to identify the sensation. It was not falling; just the opposite. It felt as if we were not flying anymore, as if we had become transfixed in the sky, unmoving, pinned to the clouds. The delicate movement that makes the body aware of having no firm soil under its feet ceased. The plane had become still in mid-air.

It grew dark in the cabin, then even darker. They must have turned off the lights, I thought, even though I could see that the lights were functioning the same way as before. There was light, yet it was dark, like the essence of light had been sucked away. Heaviness settled on my chest, a pressure, as if I'd been pulled upwards with incredible speed.

The stewardesses strolled among the passengers. The captain announced something in that weird Arabic dialect (which was odd because he otherwise spoke English), his voice distorted by the speakers. The stewardesses repeated the captain's words; not to the passengers, but to themselves, muttering under their breath. Droplets of perspiration beaded on their temples, and sweat stains permeated their uniforms as well. The cabin was filled with the smell of fear. The stewardesses tried to hold on to the seats, but one by one they all lay down on the floor, as if taking a much needed power nap. Some of them started crying.

Two elderly tourists were sitting behind me. The man wore a white hat and tinted glasses, with a silk scarf around his neck. His wife, or a woman I assumed to be his wife, wore a necklace of tiny pearls that reminded me of a line of brilliant white teeth. Her face was soft and wrinkly, with too much makeup applied. She had a constant idiotic smile that showed off her flawless teeth. They were speaking in German, although judging by their accent, I was sure they weren't from Germany.

'Blood!' said the man softly. 'He wants blood. He won't let us cross until he's had his fill!'

The woman nodded dejectedly.

'My uncle Rolf made a blood pact, back during the war,' she said, carefully shaping each word like individual clay figures. 'He offered his great-grandson's life in exchange for his own. When little Henrik was born in the spring, I told Eliza right away that she'd better give birth to another one quickly because little Henrik is as good as gone.'

The man smacked his lips. 'That could not happen in our family,' he said. 'A man should take responsibility before the Faceless Lords.'

'But to them, the flesh of innocents is so much sweeter, and innocence is nothing but ignorance,' the woman chuckled.

'Edith, you are living proof that nobody on this Earth is innocent. Least of all the ignorant.'

At this point I was asleep for sure, I must have been. This was only a nightmare.

The hairs on my arm stood on end. The drinks rolled around in my stomach, but not from nausea. The direction of gravity had changed. I felt its force on my back and neck, it pressed me back into the seat. My muscles went numb, I could barely breathe.

He was there with us in the cabin. I couldn't see him, but a vision of him appeared in my mind. He was standing between the aisles, and with his million blind eyes he could see our souls. His countless claws were painted with the dried blood of newborns; flesh-eating worms wriggled in his thoughts. His horns scraped the plane's green upholstery. He walked between the rows, looking for his victim.

'Ar'gtatoth, the servant of the Lord of a Thousand Goats,' the old man whimpered behind me; his withered chest could hardly handle the burdens of altered gravity. Still, he went on. 'It is an honor to share time and space with him.'

'My second husband,' the old woman gasped, 'was a servant to the Great Goat Lord. Oh, the amount of goat shit I had to shovel in my departed youth! The two of them must have met. I wish the Lord had taken my husband's life personally. Then I wouldn't have had to do it myself!'

In my sleep, my head became as heavy as dead meat, drool trickled from my lips. The smell of urine struck my nose; someone beside me was shaking from fear, his teeth chattering as if he were coming down with a fever. I wanted to see, not just imagine, our guest, but I was incapable of movement. I was paralyzed. A scream echoed through the cabin, my eardrums quivered. It was a man, or a woman; I'm not sure, and it makes no difference. Their scream was so filled with terror and despair, so hopeless and painful, that I hoped I would never hear it again outside of my dreams.

Of course, I have heard it several times since.

The screams faded as I dived deeper and deeper into the unconsciousness of dreaming.

I woke up as the plane's wheels touched the runway; I felt an echo of disappointment for having missed the chance to buy from the duty-free catalog.

I looked around and found everyone else waking up just like me, which somewhat alleviated my disappointment. I retrieved my luggage from the overhead bin, my head heavy with fatigue. I sent drowsy smiles at my fellow passengers, which they mirrored with their own tired smiles.

Between the aisles, a stewardess was trying to clean up

a stain from Coke spilled on the carpet. As we went around her with our luggage, we all tried not to notice that it wasn't Coke, but blood.

The second crossing

We arrived at night. Most of the airport's shops had their shutters down, many of the units were empty and for rent. There was a smell in the air I associated with dirty bathrooms. The overhead lights seemed to radiate uncleanliness.

Here is where the groups part ways. Those who are on the way to the Kal-Kadath dream tour connect at this airport. They are escorted to the next flight by the sleep-deprived stewardesses and continue their journey skyward.

The buses going to the Lost Cities usually depart from a parking lot near the building. That night the tour guide arrived to greet his group and lead them to the transport. The guide was a heavy-set, bearded man in military gear. The middle of his forehead was adorned with an odd mark. It might have been a tattoo, a strange symbol inked into his skin. My eyes started to hurt when I looked at it.

In his group there was a child, a blond boy of about ten. Children are allowed on any Abaddon Travels trip, but anyone under the age of eighteen must have an accompanying adult with them at all times. The guide caressed the boy's head, his long nails sinking into the blond locks. The boy turned pale, his eyes filled with confused fear. The parents – an accountant-type man and his wife, a tall, birdlike woman – watched the kid expectantly; evidently the boy was supposed to make the next move, whatever that might be.

The kid's jeans darkened as he pissed himself. A pool of urine gathered beneath his quivering legs. The tour guide burst into laughter just as the urine reached his boots. The parents laughed with him as if it were a good joke. Then their fellow passengers joined in, they all stood around the boy cackling with laughter as the urine kept pouring out of him. He was crying now, frozen in the circle of adults laughing at him.

Anyone planning to take their children on this trip should be prepared for experiences of this kind.

Passing through customs and visa checks is relatively quick. We were warned that border guards can select anyone without any reason or justification and abuse them as they wish. Strip- and cavity searches are the least of your worries. Don't forget that the guards are not only guarding a country; they are guarding a religion and a sacred, holy place. Keep that in mind before joining the trip.

The guards are allowed to cut your tongue out without having to give any reason whatsoever. If they see it as justified and write a report on it too, then they can rape and/or execute any selected person on the spot. The victims of rape are not exclusively women, nor necessarily young. Such atrocities are apparently random; one doesn't need to perpetrate any crime or break any law to be a victim. This is an unavoidable risk tourists face when arriving in the country: the cost of entry includes the possibility of pain, humiliation, and bloodshed. This is a decision everyone must make before embarking on the journey, and if he or she is chosen to be a victim, they have to respect the local laws, even if they don't seem to make sense.

Fortunately, no insult of any kind took place that night. The border guard stamped my passport between two yawns and let me pass. I went through the nothing-to-declare corridor, through a series of automatic doors, and finally arrived at the parking lot where our transportation awaited us, a Volkswagen minibus.

I took a deep breath of the fresh, cold air. I was surprised to notice that the German pensioners joined us as well. I made a gesture towards them, but they chose to not recognize me.

The hotel

The journey was, again, uneventful. When we arrived in the town it was pitch-black night. It's always raining there. Sometimes just a drizzle, often a downpour, so it's wise to pack waterproof jackets and boots. We quickly took refuge against the weather in the hotel lobby. The keys had been laid out on the counter of the concierge's booth, like so many soldiers lying face down in the mud. We each grabbed one without a word and headed for our rooms. The corridors were quite narrow, the bumpy, cracking floor insidiously making you lose your balance.

Every single part of the hotel is made of wood. Yet I have seen no fire extinguishers. Those with a great fear of hotel fires should take this into consideration. On the other hand the hotel building is said to be about two hundred years old. Why shouldn't it last another two hundred years without a fire, especially in this moist air?

A musty smell filled my room. My window looked down on the city from the third floor; still, it felt like being in a cellar. The rooms do not include private bathrooms; the toilet and a line of open shower cabins can be found at the end of the corridor. It's all unisex. Those concerned about this aspect of comfort should take this into account before the trip.

I was drained and could barely stand any longer. I opened the window, accepting the damp cold in exchange for a bit of fresh air, and jumped into bed with my clothes still on. I closed my eyes and listened to the sounds of the town, the miserable melody of fog sirens leading me into my dream.

Someone crawled in through my open window. I woke to the sound of bare feet touching the wooden floor, the boards creaking under the weight of a body. I sat up in bed, squinting. The air was heavy with the smell of fish, mixed with some sort of a damp stink, the smell of wet rot. The intruder swallowed; I could hear the drool sliding down from mouth to stomach.

'Excuse me! Can I help you?' I asked in Hungarian, my sleepiness somehow making me forget that I was abroad.

A girl's voice answered in a language I didn't understand. A peculiar Arabic-sounding dialect, the one I had heard on the plane. It sounded antsy, wired. I could only make out a dark outline, a suggestion of her shape. I switched to English and repeated my question, then in German as well. Knowledge of foreign languages is not an absolute requirement for the journey, but it can be quite helpful in situations like this.

She squatted down on the floor and scampered towards the bed on all fours. I thought about screaming – or shouting, to be more manly. Someone might hear it in one of the adjacent rooms, although the walls, despite being old, were solidly soundproof.

The shape straightened up again near the bed, and with a flick turned on the reading lamp.

'Ar'sh thang' el khammar,' said the girl. It was the sentence the stewardesses repeated after the captain on the plane. Then she sighed, a sigh as tiny as everything else about her. She was two heads shorter than me, her arms and legs skinny. Her skin was stretched taut over her ribs, the delicate bones almost poking through, yet she had a little belly. Her eyes were gray and her long uncombed hair dropped wetly onto her back.

She was naked, shining from dampness, as if she had just stepped out of a bathtub. She was an unhealthy dough-like color, with dark blue veins showing through her skin. She looked like someone who had never seen sunlight.

She climbed into bed next to me. She kept saying words in that exquisite language I didn't understand. The bedsprings creaked beneath us.

'No, no, no,' I protested in every language I knew, but she just kept on talking. She grabbed my hand; her touch was cold and slimy, like an unpleasant November morning. The smell of fish was overwhelming.

'Go away!' I said to her, but she shook her head, spraying my pillows with foul-smelling water. She turned her back to me and covered herself with my blanket. I sighed deeply. I was too tired to argue with a naked local girl. It was a double bed, but still, you have to draw the line somewhere. After all, this was my room, my bed. I paid for it, and there was no place for anyone else in it, especially if they smelled like fish. So I kicked the girl out of my bed, for the first time in my life. I had always thought it was just an expression: to kick someone out of your bed.

Not anymore, not for me. I did it.

My socks got soaked by the slimy wetness covering her skin. The slime felt thick. The girl fell off the bed. For a few seconds she whined on the floor, then tried to sneak back in next to me. I responded with another kick. She settled on the floor by my bed, curled up, whining sadly. Sleepiness made my limbs feel heavy. I couldn't summon the strength to shout out to the neighboring room or look for the night concierge. She was on the floor, and that I could accept for now. I would deal with her after I got some sleep. Or maybe by the time I awoke she would come to her senses and leave.

I woke to a weight on my chest squeezing the air out of me. The intruder was sitting on me, the soles of her feet on my throat, her full weight on my chest. She looked at me with curious black eyes. Only then did I see that her eyes had no white in them, just different shades of black and gray. She screamed as I threw her off. Her head knocked against the floor, but a second later she was on her feet again, angrily flashing her tiny pointed teeth. She hissed at me and I think that was the first time I felt slightly terrified. I saw the time had come to call for help – perhaps this threat, however tiny the intruder was, was too much for me.

A distorted, high-pitched sound came from the street. It made my skin crawl; not with terror, but with a disgust I couldn't explain.

She hissed at me once more, then ran to the window and crawled out into the night.

I looked out on the streets, the hotel walls, the billowing

fog. A tall figure stood in the middle of the deserted street, on his head a deformed diadem, like a crown that had been run over several times by a car. His face was masked by the shadows. He lifted some kind of long whistle up to his mouth and sounded it again. The terrible noise was a call to come home. Crowds of naked visitors left the rooms they had previously penetrated. Apparently I wasn't the only one disturbed by an intruder; there were about a dozen of them. They crawled out of the windows, creeping down the walls of the hotel without the aid of a ladder or rope. They moved like spiders on a wall, quickly, yet without a sound. They approached the tall figure on all fours, kissing his foot one by one in a gesture of submission.

He kicked one of the girls over, then hit another one in the face with the long whistle. The intruders endured the punishment without a word, and when the figure turned and headed towards the darkness at end of the street they followed him on all fours. As soon as they disappeared into the fog and the darkness I went back to bed, and from then on nothing else disturbed my sleep.

The lavatory

In the morning I awoke to the sound of knocking at my door. I felt well rested, although I might have caught a bit of a cold; my nose was a little stuffy. I opened the door, but I found the corridor empty. The hotel is not much brighter in the daytime than at night, however its walls seem even more hostile. I gathered my toiletries and headed for the showers.

The lavatories are located at the end of the corridor on each floor. They are equipped with three open shower cabins and one toilet. Hot water runs out quickly, so early birds get the worm. If you miss your chance, you'll be stuck washing yourself in ice-cold water the rest of the day.

The shower cabins are clean, but the white paint is coming

off the walls, the radiators are rusty, and the pipes cough up sulphurous water from metallic lungs. Those who are sensitive about water quality should be prepared for this.

I took my clothes off, piled them on top of a broken chair in the corner, locked the lavatory, and headed towards the toilet.

The toilet door cannot be locked from the inside; I found that out the hard way, so you can learn from my mistake.

I opened the door and found a woman sitting inside. She was methodically cutting narrow stripes into her thighs with a razor blade, close to her waistline. The woman had covered the toilet seat with paper; she must not have found it sanitary enough. Her jeans and panties were down by her ankles. Blood fell in thick, heavy drops into the toilet water.

'I'm sorry,' I said in Hungarian, then quickly repeated it in English too. Only then did I hear her breathing. She sounded like she was trying to breathe in too much air through nostrils that were too tight. This, I later learned, meant that she was focusing. Right then she was focused on cutting herself.

'Then why don't you close the door?' she asked in English, a strange accent behind the words. I didn't notice any urgency in her voice, merely curiosity.

Why didn't I? I have no idea. The sight was so shocking that it seemed natural; I found escape to be an inappropriate reaction.

Her blood looked black in the half-light. Her thighs were marked with cuts fresh and old alike. She looked up at me but kept the blade over her skin. Her face must have looked old when she was young, and it would look young when she got old. She had tiny, bright eyes, constantly in search of something. Her teeth were small and white. Her slightly crooked nose was a reminder of an old fracture.

'You like to watch,' she deduced, and in that moment I realized that I had already undressed. It was like a recurring nightmare I used to have in which I would find myself arriving to school or work naked. I was getting an erection. She refocused her attention on the razor blade and the wound, like

I wasn't even there anymore. I took a step back, but I didn't take my eyes off the woman, fearing that she might attack me at any moment. She had a blade, after all. She, on the other hand, didn't seem to care about me, I was nothing to her but a momentary inconvenience. She didn't close the door. Finally I turned away from her to get on with my morning.

I took a shower; the water at times felt either too hot or too cold. When I was finished and had switched off the water, I turned around and found her standing right behind me. She had her pants on. No bloodstains showed through the fabric. She tilted her head to the side, a playful half smile on her face.

She stepped closer to me. She had an exquisite smell, like a spice from some exotic city. I wanted to close my eyes and just savor her scent.

'Open your mouth!'

Her words smelled just like she did.

I opened my mouth without hesitation, most likely giving her the impression of someone who was mentally deficient.

'My name is Nora,' she declared, then placed the bloody razor blade on my tongue, like a secret between us. The taste of her blood spread in my mouth.

Nora headed towards the door.

'We will meet again,' she added, then pushed down the door handle in order to leave. The door didn't open, since I had locked it. She tried again, then noticed the key. Her departure, intended to be theatrical, ended up being comical, and I couldn't help it – I burst into laughter. The blade cut my tongue, which only prompted me to laugh even harder. Finally the tiny blade fell to the floor. Blood poured out of my mouth, her blood and mine.

After that, everything tasted like blood.

The breakfast

The breakfast is buffet-style. The selection is somewhat

poor. There is ham and some eggs, both scrambled and boiled. The vegetables are far from fresh. Only white and brown bread is available, no whole grain or gluten-free. There's coffee and hot water in vacuum flasks; the coffee made my stomach hurt, and I wasn't the only one. Many had brought instant coffee powder, which when mixed with hot water turned into a somewhat better quality drink. All coffee lovers should consider this before departure.

Eating hurt. The wound on my tongue opened up every time I chewed. I watched the people around me, and they watched me. I ended up having a conversation with some of them. We took our time in warming up to each other, but I believe this is natural before a tour like this. Still, I treated them all as strangers, and I think I remained a stranger to them. Names and identities are of no importance. The more friends you make, the greater the hurt will be later on.

We met our guide after breakfast. His name was Jufus. He was a man with an anxious appearance, wearing a faded jacket and a pair of horn-rimmed glasses with thick lenses. He had a crown of graying hair around a massive bald spot on the top of his head. It all gave him the air of a failed humanities scholar. He bit the skin on his thumb frequently and eagerly, as if trying to suck out some poison from under his nail. When he smiled, a gap between his front teeth became noticeable.

After breakfast we all gathered in the hall. I drank another coffee despite the objections of my aching stomach and tongue.

Jufus took the floor, adjusted his checkered shirt, then held up both his open hands, as if wanting to appease a deity watching from afar. He remained in that position for a few seconds until there was total silence. Only then did he address us. He spoke English with almost no trace of an accent. He introduced himself, then went through the usual formalities about how happy he was to see us, how much this meant to the town, what our odds were of returning home with a sane mind or unharmed body. His jokes were greeted with laughter in the right places, and by the time he got to the specifics of the upcoming journey, trust had been built. On a tour like this trust is crucial. One's life depends on it. One shouldn't embark on any Abaddon Travels trip without the proper guide.

Eventually Jufus got to the point: we couldn't make it to the hills that day, as the roads were blocked. Some people protested, but Jufus silenced them all. Here is when the question of trust becomes so important: we all believed there was a reason for postponing the tour, and Jufus knew what that was. He didn't have to tell us why. Jufus would protect us, we thought. This is the moment when one still holds out some sort of hope, when one hasn't yet solidly accepted what is to come.

So we went on a sightseeing tour in town.

The town

The town is basically composed of a main street and several unnamed side streets. The outline of the town is pretty clear, it's almost impossible to get lost – each street intersects in clean, 90-degree angles. The town is a line of deserted houses, their windows boarded up with cheap plywood, their walls damaged by the incessant fog and rain. It is not advisable to knock on any of the doors. This is rather a general safety precaution than an actual threat, except at night. There are two streets that are strictly off-limits. They are not marked with any distinguishing signs, therefore you have to be very careful.

It's best to stick to the main street. From there you can see the majestic shadows of the foggy mountains and the dark gray infinity of the sea. The traffic lights on the main street have been out of order since forever, the wind tossing them on their wires like men hanging from a gallows.

There are two restaurants there: a diner where they mostly serve seafood and a hamburger bar. During our visit the latter was unfortunately closed for renovations. The carcasses of several other abandoned restaurants litter the street; two pizzerias, a Greek-Turkish place, and a sushi restaurant peep at the visitors through boarded-up windows. Seafood lovers can rejoice, although the hamburger bar should reopen soon enough. Or so they say.

The Al'hazrad book and antiquarian shop might be of interest for many visitors. If you're lucky and it happens to be open, you can enrich yourself with many exclusive editions – for the Al'hazrad is one of the few stores allowed to produce and sell copies of the *Necronomicon Ex Mortis*, as well as other rare and forbidden tomes. The copying process itself is laborious, as all copies are handwritten and handmade, and the entire process must adhere to strict religious dogmas. Many good men have perished making these copies. Most of the books you find here are of course available as illegal e-books or photocopied PDFs anyway, but for collectors it could be exciting to get hold of one or two originals. You should, however, be prepared for the books to be quite pricey, and the shop won't accept credit cards. Book lovers should consider this in advance. It's equally important to emphasize that fresh copies of *Necronomicon Ex Mortis* cannot be brought into several countries, for the import of products made out of the skin of endangered animals or that of human origin is forbidden. Also, all copies of *Die Mappe aus Carcosa und anderen unheimliches Traumen* are sensitive to light and present a fire hazard if exposed to sunlight. Everyone should be aware of this before shopping. Fortunately, you can also buy postcards and fridge magnets at the shop as more conventional souvenirs.

The church

The pub and the church, like lovers separated by concrete, yearn for each other from opposite sides of the street.

In the morning we visited the Ar'ktak ne Kth'far church. In free translation the name of the church means 'the Sleeping

Dead's Church', or 'Church of the Dead Who Sleeps'.

Both sexes are allowed to visit, though entering the church with your face uncovered is prohibited. At the entrance ski masks and long, loose whole-body veils are available free of charge. The mask I was given had a stale odor; it had the salty smell of tears. It was 100% cotton, although some of the others got acrylic masks that became uncomfortably itchy after a while. You're allowed to bring your own mask and veil, so those with sensitive skin or worries about personal hygiene should be prepared in advance. The bottom line is that the material must be black, and the veil must cover all telling signs of gender.

The church is noisy; some say it's unbearable, although I wouldn't agree with them. The wind blows through holes and pipes made of silver and bone, hence the inside of the church is forever filled with a cacophonous, atonal melody. There are no pews in the church, for one can only kneel before the Nameless Lords; the floor is made of cracked boards, warped from moisture. Walking in the church feels like walking on bones.

According to the brochure that's handed out at the entrance, the church was made of the wreckage of capsized and sunken ships. The locals, on boring foggy days, had set fires along the shore to deceive passing trading ships and make them run aground. The townspeople then plundered the wrecks. If someone was lucky enough to survive the crash, the locals killed them right away. According to local folklore, the cracking of the church is actually the whining and screaming of mariners doomed to a watery grave in the depths of the ocean, where they guard the dream of the Sleeping Great Lord. Of course, everybody knows these kinds of local legends must be exaggerated, but the brochure is undoubtedly an interesting piece of work.

The altar stands in the center, built of dried flesh and boiled bones. For religious reasons, some kind of creature must be agonizing on top of the altar every minute of every day; during our visit it was a mountain goat's turn. Hardly any life remained in the animal as it wriggled on the metal spikes designated for the victim, the spikes showing through its skin. Those who are against animal cruelty should prepare for this, and those sensitive to noise should be ready for the screaming. Rest assured though, it's not only animals that suffer at the altar; they occasionally put people on the spikes too. According to the brochure pain should be evenly distributed among all species.

The high priest was kneeling in front of the altar when we entered. He lost his name during his initiation ceremony, as is customary in the local religion. On his head sat the disfigured diadem that I recognized from the night before. His long fingers crossed over the silver ceremonial stick adorned with pictures of strange animals and deformed humanoid shapes. He knocked on the floor twice the moment he saw us. As he turned to us, many visitors gasped, although any display of emotion is strictly forbidden.

The priest's face is never covered by a mask, although it would be fortunate if it were. It is a mockery of a human face, even if one must admire the priest's fierce determination. One can never discern emotions from these features, because the face is locked in a perpetual grin: the lips have been removed, as well as the nose, parts of the cheeks, the eyelids, and the ears. According to the brochure, during the initiation ceremony the priests must cut their own face, turn it into a mask unfit for any life other than the life of religion. Dedicated people, these.

Many of our group members instantly fell to their knees. I knew right away who they were, despite the masks. One meets these groups on every Abaddon Travels trip. They belong to the Magistrate, a cult worshipping the Nameless Lords; they regularly visit the holy places of their religion. During mealtimes they sit very close together, like they're trying to steal each other's body heat. They murmur like gossipy lovers and in general give the impression of people whose lives didn't work out so well. They're like the members of any other cult, ex-alcoholics and addicts, middle-aged people still living with their parents, kids with severe issues that should be handled by a shrink and not a cult. Still, it's better them than the Jehovah's Witnesses. At least the Magistrate envoys never knocked on my door with the line: 'Can you spare a minute for our lord and savior, the unholy N'arlath'ot'hep?' I've only gotten spam emails from them, but that's something I can deal with.

The high priest looked at the kneeling devotees with what I assumed to be disgust, then he sniffed the air with his mutilated nose, like some kind of strange dog. He turned from the cult members and stepped up to one of our fellow passengers. Outside the wind howled. He leaned closer and sniffed the tourist, then hit her in the stomach with his stick. Like a puppet whose strings have been cut, she collapsed to the floor and curled up.

'Ne'arkh to'parh jan'o frh'ten,' the high priest howled angrily. You could make out his words surprisingly well despite the mutilated lips. But when I heard his voice it occurred to me that he might not be a man at all; this religion makes no difference between genders, and the priests not only cut their faces, but rid themselves of any organ that could give them pleasure or be used for reproduction.

Like a soccer player shooting a penalty, he ran up to give a kick to the person lying on the floor. None of us moved: Jufus had warned us in advance that whatever we saw in the church, whatever the high priest did, under no circumstances should we intervene or even move; however, we must watch at all times. It was slightly uncomfortable though to hear the painful groans, to watch this act of violence perpetrated upon one of our own members, but what could we do? When you visit a foreign culture you must respect it at all times; otherwise you're nothing but a barbarian.

The high priest hit the person in the face twice with his stick. The person showed no sign of resistance, accepting her fate like an animal run over by a car. She cringed on the floor and quivered.

'An'rha k'tfar h'ra k'tum,' continued the high priest, then ripped the mask off the person lying on the floor. It was Nora. She didn't look at anybody, she fixed her eyes on a neutral point so she wouldn't have to look at those non-faces watching her. Thick tears rolled down her bruised face. Her lips were split and blood poured down her chin. The high priest must have detected the same scent I had picked up earlier in the lavatory. The smell of dried spices.

The high priest howled wordlessly, maybe a declaration of his anger, or his contentment. Nora made no movement on the floor, perhaps fearing further punishment, and when the high priest walked away from her we followed him, not minding Nora anymore, not even looking at her so that she wouldn't feel more uncomfortable.

There is one other attraction awaiting visitors in the church, the 'ran th'kum', or in free translation the 'Chamber of Nights'. To enter the chamber you must wear a blindfold. For those who are particularly devout, a silver bowl and a silver spoon with a sharpened edge are also prepared. The brochure says that if one leaves their eyes on the doorstep before entering, they will be rewarded with special gifts in the Chamber of Nights. None of us felt dedicated enough. The cult members discussed the issue in whispers among themselves, finally coming to the conclusion that their original purpose was more important than losing eyes over this.

The group took up the blindfolds and, after paying a small contribution, walked into the Chamber of Nights, led by the high priest. Unfortunately, I cannot recount anything of the chamber because I didn't go along with them. While the priest was handling the cash register next to the entrance, issuing tickets to the Chamber of Nights, I walked over to Nora and helped her up from the floor. I was surprised at how light her body was.

'Take me to the pub!' she ordered.

The pub

Just as people get drunk with their teammates before climbing Mount Everest, the same thing happens during Abaddon Travels trips. One pub located right across from the church specializes in serving the tourists. Its name is Kth'far ne Ak'rhun't, which loosely translated means 'Pub to the Dead Who is Awake' or 'Pub of the Woken Dead'. There are other catering facilities scattered throughout the city; one of them, the legendary Arf'hran, is allegedly to be found in the bay, at the bottom of the sea. That pub is not even frequented by locals, as only at the hour of their death is the pub's location revealed to them. Or so local legend says. In any case, tourists should stay away from any other establishment in town and stick to the Pub of the Woken Dead. Tourists are not welcomed by locals elsewhere.

Nora pulled her finger from her mouth, the tip of it covered with a mixture of blood and drool. She looked at it, then wiped the secretion on her pants.

I put a whiskey in front of her, the product of a local distillery. It is supposedly very popular in Scotland too, as a secret ingredient of certain very rare blended whiskeys. We clinked our glasses, then downed the booze. The wound on my tongue burned and my eyes watered.

'I think my tooth is going to fall out,' she said.

'I'm sorry.'

She shrugged her shoulders.

'Just bring another round.'

By the time I got back from the counter, where a cheerful Spanish bartender served me, Nora was crying. She covered her face with her hands, her thin shoulders shaking from the sobbing. I watched the crying woman without knowing what to do. The bartender was laughing at some joke. I wished he would shut up.

I moved my chair and sat next to Nora. I put my arm around her shoulders; I could feel her trembling. I gave her an awkward hug, trying to give her as much warmth as I could. I felt weird but it seemed to be the right thing to do. Her tears and snot soaked my shirt. I embraced her head as well; her skull seemed to be paper-thin under my fingers.

Nora's crying fit ended just as abruptly as it started. She let go of me and wiped her face with a napkin. I went for one more round.

'I want to die,' Nora announced, then emptied her glass.

We sat in silence for a while, then changed the subject.

In the pub you can buy snacks, nachos and peanuts. There is no hot food. I ordered nachos, but when the Spanish guy brought it out, we found worms in the sauce, crawling in the red liquid. This should be taken into account by those who are fond of snacks with their beer.

I treated the bartender to a few rounds, in exchange for which he offered us a small packet of cocaine from under the counter. We made lines on top of the counter and the bartender cut a straw in half. Nora held up her little finger when snorting her line, and I found this gesture irresistibly charming.

In a while the others arrived from the church, shaking the water out of their hair. Some reacted well to the Chamber of Nights, they saw it as a rollercoaster or a dark ride, where you can only sense but never actually see danger. There were some who didn't feel anything. They walked through a series of cold corridors blindfolded, disregarded the occasional screams and cursing, and in the end the whole thing turned out not to be much of an attraction.

Some, however, were pale and shaking; they claimed to have felt the presence of something and that they had seen things through their closed eyelids, things they either couldn't or didn't want to name.

There is a wide selection of booze, and the taxes on alcoholic beverages are rather low. We drank a lot, a lot more than I thought possible, just like every group before us, and all those who will follow us. It is the last time one can enjoy an evening with abandon, because after this the trip starts in earnest, and then there is no more fun to be had.

We drank to the team. We drank to the Nameless Lords. We drank to the church. We drank to the neverending rain. That's all I recall.

They have first-class red ale on tap in the pub, which I recommend to everyone, but the glasses are often dirty, the edges jagged. Many of us cut our lips on the glasses. When I inquired about it at the counter, the Spanish bartender got into a weird, anxious state. His eyes went empty, his mouth fell. I showed him the broken glass and asked if I could get a clean one, with no jagged edge.

'We don't get nothing,' he answered, his voice hoarse. 'Nothing but you, season after season, until you all die. But I will never leave this place, never – ' he whispered, thick drool pouring from his mouth, ' – they won't let me!' he cried. 'I slit my veins, hanged myself, drowned myself, but they always bring me back, always back! At night they come for me, oh god, what they do to me you can't imagine, nobody can and nobody should!'

His tears were now pouring.

'Ark'nth'fre'ha . . . ne'frah'ten'k,' he sobbed quietly, then he dry heaved, but nothing came out. Finally he sat down on the floor with his head between his legs and kept on crying. While he cried we raided the bar and stole several bottles of spirits.

Fifteen minutes later he was working again, as cheerful as ever. Obviously one should not ask the staff anything about the condition of the glasses or furnishings; similar reactions are to be expected.

Nora wouldn't let go of my hand all night except when I had to go to the bathroom, but I was squeezed out of there by all the couples fornicating in the stalls. I went out to piss in front of the pub, in the downpour. I felt eyes on me from behind the empty windows, from the canals, from the air. Maybe it was the drug taking effect at that very moment, but for a second I felt liberated by the understanding that someone could sneak up behind me at any time and slit my throat. I pulled up my zipper and glanced at my watch, but it had stopped. Later I learned it wasn't just me; everyone's watch stopped at midnight on the dot, regardless of brand or type. Smartphone clocks also froze. Jufus remarked that many watches would never start working again. Therefore bringing your most valuable watch is not recommended.

The group dispersed in the small hours of the morning. We drank our last beer. Jufus was talking to the bartender.

'My grandmother is from here,' Nora said to me. 'She passed away recently. That was when we found out. She escaped. I'm here to find my roots. My true self.'

I didn't know what to say, so I quickly raised the glass to my mouth. I cut my lip. She continued.

'I've often dreamt about the city. It looked exactly like this in my dreams too. After waking up from those dreams I felt a compulsion to cut myself. Or burn my skin. I felt that there was a disconnect between what I was and who I was. Does that make sense?'

I tried to look at her with empathy, so that she would feel that I cared. Back home, this would have been enough for most of my office colleagues, a moment of attention after the end of the shift and they would open up completely, only to close up again when the sun rose.

'The pain created a connection between the two. The dream about the city created the divide, and only in the few moments when I inflicted pain on myself could I close that gap. Have you ever felt anything like that?' she asked.

I thought about my burnout, my nights spent in search of the person I thought I was underneath my life, and I nodded. At that moment, like a faint scent of summer, the thought of suicide came to me again.

'I don't want to be alone tonight,' she said.

We kissed in the hallway. The cuts opened up on my tongue, but she didn't mind. Kissing was painful; by that time everything was.

We spent the night in my room. The window was open, the smell of fish still lingered on the bed sheets. It didn't bother Nora at all. She threw her clothes off but lost her balance when stepping out of her panties and fell to the floor. Instead of standing up again she crawled into bed on all fours, just like the tiny woman the night before. She was all wiry muscles and damaged skin. Scars lined her rib cage like so many frozen waves, long, uneven cuts, the healed flesh pink. On her back the skin was ruptured in several places, marked by different kinds of instruments. Some of the scars looked like cuts and whip marks, others like burn marks. Her body was a map of pain.

I undressed without falling and lay down next to her in bed. I touched her body gingerly. Her flesh was hot like an oven. I dragged my fingers along the scars, taking stock, but it was impossible to count them all.

I found them beautiful. I found her beautiful.

'Did you do all of them?' I asked quietly.

'No,' she said. 'But I wanted them all.'

We kissed for a little while without purpose, since it was clear we wouldn't have sex, then she turned away from me. She licked her palm and fingers and put her hand in between her thighs, rushing herself towards a climax she might never reach. I was incapable of moving, the room was spinning around and around and I was afraid I might get sick from all the booze I'd had that night. The only fixed point in the world was her body next to mine, and I didn't dare to touch her. I stared at the scars covering her back, the muscles working underneath the skin, for a long time before I fell asleep.

The bus

Early the next morning the bus was waiting for us at the entrance to the hotel, like a dormant animal. It might have been bright red once, but the humidity had faded it to the color of tree rot. It had no brand; maybe it was a local make.

Jufus had asked us not to take any luggage with us, only a light backpack with the most essential things. I packed a bottle of water, a box of matches, a flashlight, and a withered apple. Jufus didn't give us any advice as to what was worth bringing on the trip, and I can't do so either. None of the objects I brought was of any use later on.

I settled down next to Nora. On the bus the seats are uncomfortable; the metal frame cuts into your back and bottom. People with back pain, lower back problems, or a hernia had better bring a cushion pillow or lumbar support to make the trip somewhat endurable.

The German pensioners sat right behind me, just like on the plane. I couldn't decide whether this was a good omen or a bad one.

A blond girl decided not to join us for the rest of the tour. She would wait for us in the hotel, she said, and return to the airport with us once we were back. Her face was pale in the morning light, her eyes bloodshot, but her smile was filled with relief. This also serves to demonstrate that those who are not entirely dedicated to a trip like this one should not book any of the tours at Abaddon Travels.

The last I saw of her was her waving goodbye, then returning to the hotel.

We left town. The streets grew even emptier than before. It seemed like a movie set to me, something fake. It reminded me of a slaughterhouse at night, a place that lies dormant, awaiting a new batch of warm flesh to digest in the morning.

The bus driver didn't introduce himself. He was a fat, balding, brown-skinned man. He chewed tobacco and at times spat out the window. A black Magic Trees air freshener hung from the rearview mirror. The radio was tuned to a local station that alternated between broadcasting news in the local dialect and playing the local pop hits, songs written in an atonal key and sung by voices imitating nightmares in the language of gods long dead. I think this kind of pop will be a big hit in the Western world someday, but we're not ready for it quite yet.

The bus was stuffy, the bouncing was relentless. My hangover got the better of me and I drifted into a sort of half-sleep.

I awoke to a disturbance on the bus. All the passengers were gathered by the windows on the left-hand side like a flock of birds, everyone anxious to see. The driver yelled at them in his broken English, but nobody stepped away from the window. Jufus just sat in his seat, a peaceful smile on his face. He paid no attention to the commotion. Someone yelled at the driver to stop; he responded by putting the pedal to the metal. As the sight passed, the tension de-escalated, and the passengers went back to their seats. Nobody talked; they all sat frozen, listening to the top ten local hits on the radio. Behind me the German pensioners were quietly chuckling, and I figured they were laughing at the rest of the tourists – laughing at their shock.

'What happened?' I asked Nora.

She shrugged. She seemed past caring. Her black eyes looked out the window.

'The girl we left behind. The blond one?'

I nodded impatiently.

'She was there in the woods. Like a statue. She was impaled on a stick.'

She made a hand gesture to show the wood was sticking out of the blond girl's body around her collarbone.

Now I understood the silence that had settled upon our fellow tourists.

'I think she was still alive,' Nora said, then kept on staring out the window.

Those who opt for any of the trips with Abaddon Travels must not turn back along the way. First of all because you shouldn't give up halfway through once you've started something. This is a fundamental rule both in business and in private life. Secondly, because if you give up, you definitely won't survive the trip.

The breakdown

The length of the bus journey varies. According to Jufus, you might arrive at your destination in a few hours, or years might pass without reaching it. He claims that the roads are constantly changing, undulating. Here they stretch out, there they contract.

At times we stopped to stretch our limbs. Up to a certain height there is a good view of the sea, the bay, and the town. You can and should take photos, but there's no signal, so it's important to keep your cameras or at least your SD cards until the end of the trip. Bringing actual film stock isn't recommended because the chances of getting the negatives down the mountain undamaged are extremely low. It's also worth mentioning that while the town feels like a dozen streets crossing at right angles when you're down there, from up on the mountain those same streets reveal themselves to be parts of an elaborate maze. Those interested in city architecture should pay extra attention to this detail.

During this part of the trip the traveler is still relatively safe. There was a single occasion when Jufus yelled at us to run back to the bus and we obeyed instantly. As soon as we boarded the bus the driver shot off, his face contorted with terror as he struggled to keep the speeding bus on the road. We looked out the windows but saw nothing. When we counted the travelers, only one of us was missing, but nobody remembered who it was.

This is another reason why utmost trust in the guide is crucial.

'Why are you coming up the mountain?' I asked Nora. 'If you're from the town, shouldn't you be looking for your relatives down there?'

A sad smile appeared on Nora's lips.

'My grandmother was from the mountains. That's where my dreams summon me. That's where the high priest sent me too.'

'The one who beat you up?'

'She blessed me.'

The fog never disappears, but sometimes it disperses so that you can only see its grayness on the horizon. Sometimes it turns into dense rain, then into a milky mass that carries the scent of decay.

'Why are you here?' Nora asked. I guess there's no reasonable answer, or maybe it's too horrifying to admit the truth, so we prefer to lie to ourselves about it. I just shrugged and didn't answer. I knew she understood what I meant.

The bus stopped without any warning, throwing many passengers off balance. We heard a loud bang from inside the vehicle, and the driver stepped on the brakes instantly. The old man behind me slammed into the back of my seat.

'Goddamn this idiot!' he hissed in German.

The driver crawled out of the cabin cursing in his peculiar language. He fished out a wrench and a flashlight from under the seat and jumped off the bus. He hit the side of the bus with the wrench. Several people jumped in fright at the sound. Some saw him crawl under the bus.

We never saw the bus driver again.

Fifteen minutes later some of us got off to see what had happened. We couldn't find him under or around the bus. There was no sign of the wrench and flashlight either. We tried to start the engine but it didn't even cough. It was dead.

From then on, we continued on foot.

The attack

In a certain sense, everyone is already on their own at this point. What happened to my group might never happen to anyone else, while different horrors we never had to face could be awaiting others.

The bus was devoured by the fog and gloom as we followed Jufus down the road and then into the woods as the road narrowed and disappeared. We could feel eyes on us from among the trees, from under the ground, from the cover of the fog. Some of us quietly burst into tears. Jufus, on the other hand, cheered up more with every step, flashing his white teeth ever more often. The more we feared what was to come, the more content he seemed to be.

I grabbed Nora's hand and didn't let go of it.

The trees embraced us tightly, their branches clinging to our clothes over and over again.

You can stumble upon the most curious things in the forest. On this particular trip we were in the woods just when the antlers were in bloom, so we had the chance to see the Garden of Antlers, where they grow from the soil in dense confusion. They say an ancient god sleeps under the earth, and the earth here is merely the excrescence of its skin. From under the skin, when the time comes, antlers break out, they grow and grow, until they shed their skin. Then they fall down and turn into reptiles nobody has ever seen and lived to describe.

If you find yourself in the Garden of Antlers, it is essential that you avoid touching the antlers themselves. When touched the antlers have a peculiar effect. Their victim feels an instant and irresistible desire to lie down on the ground and never get up again. In time, the victim's body and soul will become one with the Nameless Lord's dream, trapped forever in a nightmare.

Jufus had warned us of this risk in advance, so we all avoided such a fate.

We pitched our camp at a relatively safe distance from the Garden of Antlers, but we still worried about its close proximity. Ironic, how we often worry about things that turn out to be unimportant. We lay down on the ground, sharing the couple of blankets and sleeping bags we had brought from the bus, and tried to sleep. Nora cuddled up to me in the sleeping bag, and before I could fall asleep, she pulled down her pants to cut herself. I smelled her blood as I drifted towards sleep.

In my dream I stood on the edge of a gigantic pit filled nearly to its brim with the ruins of once-great cities, the pitiful remnants of human civilization. Ghosts whispered amongst the wreckage, believing their cities still intact and vibrantly alive, while I could see that they were all dead and forgotten. I felt a compulsion to bury it all, to shovel dirt over even the memory of what we once were, to cover the shame of our civilization, so I fell to my knees and shoveled the earth onto the ruins, and I screamed and screamed...

I awoke to a scream. We all woke up, except for those who were already dead by then.

We were being attacked, and it was too dark for me to see clearly. The face of one of our fellow travelers was covered in blood, as if he'd been mauled by a dog. He was screaming, blinded by his own flowing blood. We heard growls from the woods, disgusting burps, giggles. If you choose to take this trip, be prepared for any kind of hostility, be it natural, unnatural, or manmade. The dangers are yet uncounted, but you should look at them as several possible roads leading you to the very same destination.

Something ran by me. I detected a smell, the smell of fish. The attacker moved so quickly that I couldn't get a glimpse of it. Nora pulled up her bloodstained pants, her hands shaking. Someone screamed again: a woman and a middle-aged man from the cult had their ankles tied together with a rope and were being dragged towards the woods. They were both desperately trying to grab on to something, but their situation was hopeless. One of the cult members took hold of the woman's hand, trying to pull her away from her attackers, but then a spear came flying, launched from the forest. The man screamed, his hand reduced to a bloody stump. We watched in horror as the woman disappeared into the woods. It's a strange, unnerving feeling to know you're being hunted, but to my surprise it also brought a sense of calm. I felt I was closer to my goal.

Someone had a gun.

Shots were fired in the chaos; I didn't even know who was shooting, or at what. The attackers retreated, though none of the bullets hit them, or at least we didn't find any bodies. Two of us were injured, however. The man with the mangled hand was hit in the thigh by one of the bullets; the other bullet pierced Jufus body. Our guide collapsed under a tree; he applied pressure to the wound, but blood was seeping out fast. His face grew pale. His lips trembled.

When the chaos had given way to cold contemplation of what had just happened we saw that the gun belonged to a Dutchman with a mustache. When he realized what he had done, that his shooting blindly might well have cost us our lives, he put the barrel of the gun into his mouth. He screamed when the hot barrel burned his tongue. It was an embarrassing moment of weakness, even he knew it, so he tried again. He quickly pushed the gun deep into his mouth, then pulled the trigger before he could feel the pain of his burning flesh. None of us tried to stop him.

Jufus was having difficulty breathing and his eyes had lost their focus. We held on to every second with him, hoping he would tell us which way to go.

'It's no use going anywhere,' Jufus whispered. 'The world moves in circles; there's no way out. Time is a wall, time is prison, and you are a shell . . .'

He kept on going for what seemed like hours. Either he said the deepest things or he made no sense at all. There was just one thing he said that made sense to me. It was his last words to me before he died. His eyes were clear when he said it.

'We'll see each other soon.'

The sacrifice

The wounded slowed us down, but – out of some misguided human compassion – we didn't leave anyone behind. We left a bloody trail for our attackers, and we knew that we could be attacked again at any moment.

We had lost our leader, our direction, and our tools. We were completely alone in a hostile world, and we understood that at best we had days to live.

But this was what we wanted, wasn't it? This was why we came here. This is why you will come here as well. To be lost. To be alone. To vanish.

When we stopped to rest, we could hear the distant, tormented screams of the kidnapped travelers, but we just went on eating quietly. We shared the last of the apples and chocolate that the cult members had on them.

Nora sat in my lap. She was shivering.

'We can't fall asleep now,' I said tiredly.

'The human brain is a huge, complex entity,' she answered in a hoarse whisper. 'There is no single moment when all of its parts are switched on. In a certain sense, you are always asleep. In a certain sense, you are dreaming through your entire waking life.'

We then fell asleep.

By the time we woke up, the members of the cult had committed mass suicide. They had slit their own throats. I felt the same pang of disappointment I had last felt on the airplane when I missed the duty-free. Why did they eat their portion of the food if they planned to kill themselves anyway?

Sometimes I truly don't understand people.

They were all dead except for the man whose hand had been mutilated by the spear earlier. He held the knife in his left hand. He was right-handed, so he couldn't make the strong, clean cut his companions had carried out earlier. He kept wounding himself over and over again, but each wound only caused more pain, not death.

The German pensioners were standing by this final cult member.

'Come and see, my dear!' said the old man with a mirthful smile, a naughty twinkle in his eye as he watched the agony of the last survivor.

The old lady chuckled as she surveyed the bodies. The man knelt down to the cultist and spoke in flawless English. His words radiated glee.

'Your faith is worth nothing,' he said to the wounded man. 'It was invented by a pulp writer to earn the money his fiction never brought him. He didn't have the eyes to see the Nameless Lords himself, but he gave you eyes to see your own suffering. We often drank rum together when I was younger. I was the one who suggested he establish a church. How many miserable bastards he has sent here to die – you can't even count! And you know the best part?'

The old man leaned closer and whispered something into the dying man's ear, then stood up, his joints cracking. He was visibly pleased with himself, and I was terrified of him.

The cult member looked at me, tears welling in his desperate eyes.

'Help me, please!' he begged. 'Do it for me! Use the knife! I can't stand this anymore. I can't stand his words!'

I should have killed him. I should have pressed the blade into his flesh to end his suffering. I didn't do it. I couldn't. It was none of my business, and I had my own imminent death to worry about anyway.

We carried on, leaving the corpses behind. The surviving cultist wailed like a deer with its bones broken in a forest trap. I almost took pity on him, but by that time I was far too exhausted to do anything about it.

Only then did we notice the dozens, if not hundreds, of corpses among the trees, their rotten fingers still clenching the ceremonial knife issued by the Magistrate. Apparently this spot is a fixture in the forest; cultists travel here to die, but their death signifies nothing. It is an empty gesture, which only made their selfish act of eating the last of the food even more annoying.

By then the only ones left were me, Nora, the two pensioners, and a Frenchman in his thirties. The Frenchman stuttered irritatingly, sometimes tugging on his lower lip, as if that would wake him up from this nightmare.

'You know, maybe we're all dreaming,' I said to him. 'Our brain is dreaming every single second, Nora told me. Maybe when we die we awaken in a new life that's not part of a dream.'

He looked at me like I was mad, and I realized I had spoken to him in Hungarian and that he hadn't understood a word.

I never spoke to him again.

The transformation

I began hearing Jufus' voice more and more often from the woods. Once I thought I saw him out of the corner of my eye. I asked Nora whether she had heard or seen our guide too, but she just shrugged her shoulders. Her lips were cracked from dehydration, her skin stretched tight over her bones.

The pensioners walked cheerfully along the impassable roads, their clothes still immaculate. They were committed to their goal; they had a higher purpose, just like Nora.

At last they found the place they had been looking for. Of course it could be that I was only hallucinating from fatigue, thirst, hunger, and madness, but who cares? By this point, the traveler no longer cares about the line between illusion and reality.

'This is the place where the ritual is performed,' Jufus whispered in my ear, coughing up dead air and blood from his lungs.

It was a cave. Around the opening hundreds of wolf skeletons lay scattered.

'They all bring human flesh in their stomachs as an offering,' whispered Jufus, the eternal guide. 'They lie down here and wait to die, that's the only way for them to deliver the offering, in exchange for which they receive nothing. Such is the power of the Lords.'

The ritual of transformation is very rarely seen, as I learned from Jufus, who continued to whisper in my ear. It is rare for maguses of such a caliber to embark on an Abaddon Travels trip, but when they do, it provides an additional wonder to a trip already filled with monstrous delights.

The old people started the ritual right away, paying no attention whatsoever to our presence. In a way, the two of them had always been alone on this journey. We had traveled on the same road, but not together. Especially considering that their goals were opposite to the rest of the group's.

The preparation for the ritual and the summoning of the Servant takes time. It mainly consists of chanting, strange dance moves, fucking, and drawing blood. We watched the whole thing apathetically from the edge of the tree line. By then my attention was mostly focused on my hunger, but I didn't take my eyes off the pensioners, even if I couldn't comprehend what I was seeing.

An important tip: whatever danger you find yourself in, and however tired you feel, you shouldn't miss any chance to admire the horrors of the mountain, since that is why you are there. Even in your last moments you might see and experience things that add to your knowledge and enrich your life. Don't worry about death; it's just an unavoidable nuisance.

In time the pensioners' efforts bore fruit, and a High Servant of the Nameless Lords began to approach from within the cave. The air became thicker around us, worms crawled out of the ground beneath our feet. We heard distant screams coming from the woods as even the cannibal tribes hailed the coming of the Servant from afar.

Eventually, the High Servant stepped out of the cave. My skull nearly exploded with a sudden stab of pain. No matter how hard I tried I was incapable of focusing my vision on the Servant's material body; it always seemed slightly out of focus. This might be a means of self-preservation; the brain refuses to admit what the eyes see, in order to preserve the semblance of the normality of the world.

Nevertheless, let's not forget even now that we had come because we wanted to see. Well, let us see, or at least let us try our best, because the moment we crossed the border into this country we had already paid the ultimate price. We had already lost everything, so there was nothing left to lose.

The Servant had many antlers jutting out from his body, like so many branches of a tree. Its dozen eyes gazed at the pensioners. Its long, muscular tentacles traced signs in the air. In the wake of its footsteps the smell of decay filled the air. As it approached it blocked out the sky.

A boy and a girl hung naked by their ankles from its horns like ripe fruits. They were in their late teens, beautiful and healthy. They wriggled, trying to free themselves from the Servant, but of course it was all useless. The boy howled in fear, while the girl alternately begged and cursed the Servant in a Slavic language I assumed to be Serbian.

The Servant took a rather practical approach to the task at hand. He grabbed the two pensioners and pushed his tentacles down their throats. The woman's dentures flew out of her mouth, the man's remained broken inside his. The Servant was searching for something within the old people's bodies, and when he found it, he ripped it out of them. It was their soul, their essence, a black mess of slimy matter wriggling in the Servant's grip.

The useless carcasses fell to the ground; the worms threw themselves at the meat hungrily.

The human couple hanging from the horns were screaming and crying now incoherently, as all human language is reduced to wordless whining in the last moments of life. The Servant took the young bodies off its horns, forced their legs open and inserted the pensioners' essence into the young flesh through the anus. The bodies shook painfully as a fight took place within for control, but after a little agony the former owners were discharged in the form of black vomit, only to become fodder for the worms as well.

'The cruel beauty of reincarnation,' Jufus sighed behind my back, but when I turned, he was already gone.

The Servant placed the bodies on the ground. The young couple stood up and examined each other. They spoke German, their accent the same as before.

'But my dear, you became a man!' said the girl in awe.

The couple looked at their own bodies, then started laughing as if at a burlesque joke.

'We were put in the wrong bodies,' said the girl. The boy laughed.

'Now you'll know what it feels like to have it stuck in you,' said the boy, then they both launched into a scream-like laughter, but despite the laughs, there was a promise of violence in the air. Then the boy threw himself at the girl.

'No, Henriett, wait!' the girl said, suddenly no longer laughing, but Henriett didn't wait because now he was a boy, a man who waits no more: he punched the girl in the stomach and held down her hands. He inserted himself into her and they fucked among the worms, next to their own shed flesh, crying and screaming and laughing because it was a new sort of ecstasy and a new sort of pain; they were young again, ready for the next lifetime of pains and joys and sorrows.

The Servant laid its many eyes on us, so we decided to move on quickly.

The end of the road

The journey never ends well. Anyone considering going on this trip should take this into consideration. Whether you're happy with the outcome of the trip depends on the extent to which you're happy with your own everyday life. The more you find joy in what you have, the less you'll like what you find at the end of the road, because the journey always ends in tears.

When we reached the gate, it was already open to welcome us.

Nora squeezed my hand. Her skin was hot and damp with fever.

'Never let go of my hand!' she asked.

The Frenchman was whining and trembling behind us. He had been scratching his face; his skin was full of bloody stripes. He had gone mad hours ago.

The gigantic gate was built of flesh; here and there you could make out a face, an eye, a few teeth. I turned around because for a second I thought I might have a choice, but I quickly realized I didn't. My journey, even if I couldn't see it earlier, had led me here, to be with Nora at the gate that was our final destination. I should have been excited, or terrified, but I was neither. I was beyond all that. I was empty. A piece of nothingness, like I had always been.

I entered, together with Nora, the halls of Askatoth, where one of the Nameless Lords lived. As we stepped in, the Lord looked upon us from his throne.

It's important to know that the gaze of the Nameless Lords cannot be tolerated either by the human mind or the human body. This should be taken into account by those whose sole purpose on this trip is to get a glimpse of the Lord. It won't work. Although we established direct eye contact with this Nameless Lord (inasmuch as you can call that nightmare an eye), I couldn't give a physical description of it.

A red fog darkened my mind. I think I must have had a brain hemorrhage, and I died. I fell to the floor, lifeless; the last thing I saw was Nora dancing ecstatically. Maybe she was having a seizure, I thought, then I faded away.

The line between life and death is less strict here than in other places; the presence of the Lords blurs the border. One can cross easily, if the Lords allow.

Or want.

I was lured back to conscious existence by Nora's voice. I opened my eyes as my mind dutifully reoccupied the flesh, the flesh where I no longer felt at home. Nora smiled, not in a dry, sad way like before, but full of joy. She was naked, her stomach disfigured by a fresh wound, a red line, as if she had been cut in half.

'I'm home,' she said. 'I'm finally home and I understand everything! I understand myself!'

I was lying on the ground, and at first I couldn't take in the perspective. Houses and palaces of indiscernible shape hung from the gigantic ceiling; tortured, distorted bodies writhed on the ceiling, and on the walls, tourists and devotees captured and pinned onto meathooks screamed their prayers for the Lords.

'You look happier,' I wanted to tell Nora, but no sound came from my wounded throat.

'Don't try to speak!' Nora caressed my head. 'You have been screaming for days in your death. The Frenchman gouged out his own eyes. He was lucky, they took his offering and let him go.'

She kissed me, the scent of spice filled my nose. From a distance I heard a scream that made my bones quake.

'Listen to me!' Nora went on, grabbing my chin with her fingers. Her grip was strong.

'You have two options. One: you die. If that's your choice

I will make sure that you go relatively painlessly and never return. Do you understand?'

I nodded. I felt a sudden burst of love for her. She was the only person who mattered to me because she was the only one who offered a way out.

'The other option is that you become my husband. They will wed us, and I will be your wife.'

I didn't need time to think it over. I held her hand and kissed her ring finger. Nora blushed.

'Are you sure this is what you want?'

I wanted it more than anything. I came to understand that this was why I had come on this trip. To be nullified, to be made nothing. To be even less than dead. That's the highest reward. That's why we all come.

Nora's smile turned brilliant.

'I will take off the wedding dress now,' she said, then picked up a sharp stone from the ground. I understood why she had been cutting herself. She was just rehearsing for this one particular moment.

She pierced the sharp end of the stone into her flesh between her legs, then carved it along the fresh scab, opening it again, right up to her neck. When the cut was wide enough, she grabbed the edges and tore them apart. I heard the skin tear; she didn't need to be gentle because it was of no use to her anymore. The real Nora crept out of her old shell, accepting her final, true form that she'd been hiding even from herself. That was the first time I really met my beautiful wife and learned her true name: Kth'far Ark'the'k, the niece of a Nameless Lord.

She spilled over the floor, her old shell collapsing on the ground like a worn-out coat. My wife crawled towards me on legs that kept popping up from underneath her new skin; fresh eyes opened up all over her body. She grew bigger with each step, filling up the space around her until she could grow no more. I tried to scream, but I could manage only a painful whisper.

My wife grabbed me by my limbs like a piece of meat; she

was already gigantic by then, her skin wet and hot. She tore off my clothes. From the depths of darkness horrible things dragged themselves out to witness our wedding night. They sang distorted, toneless songs to accompany it. I recognized some of them from the bus; they were singing the local hits.

A new organ emerged from my wife's body and it shattered my flesh and soul. It entered me through all of my orifices at the same time. Resistance was futile, my muscles were no match for this new intrusion. I tried to let go, to relax, understanding that I could do nothing, just try to look at my body from the outside as if I were a stranger to myself. I could hear the cracking of my bones, the tearing of my flesh. That was not me, it was somebody else, I thought. But then I understood – it was me! It was all me, at the hands of something greater than myself, and even though it was painful, humiliating, and destructive, it cleansed me of everything my life had become, even of myself, because now I had become nothing; pure emptiness. It wasn't just the destruction of my body when my wife entered me, she entered my mind as well, my memories, my psyche. She took it all and impregnated it with herself; nothing was left of me but her. There was no hope anymore, and I no longer needed it.

I was home.

When she was done, she tossed me away like the rubbish I have become.

We have been living this way ever since. My house is a wooden cage under the ground. Every once in a while they throw in rotten food. We live in an open relationship; at least she does, as she has found other partners over time. Gender and age are not important; she takes what she likes. She throws them here next to me. If they survive the ordeal and are still capable of speech we often talk. We only talk about her. About our wife.

Although there are now many of us down here, I know that I'm the only one who matters to her. She never asks the others before she takes them. She never offers them a clean death. If that's not a sign of love I don't know what is.

Sometimes she visits me. After that, it takes two to three weeks until I give birth. The babies eat themselves out of my flesh; they crawl out from under my skin. I usually die by the time all of them are born, but here death and life are not so rigidly separated. I'm always brought back. I sometimes wish death would last longer so I could rest a bit, but it's over before I even notice.

My children, dozens of tiny lizards, run around the dark cave in search of hot, living flesh. God bless the tourists we can always capture. Later on, my children enter the pupal stage, and then they gain their secondary form; they become like the girl who visited me in my hotel room. They become the tribe that hunts in the forests.

I don't know what form follows after that.

Sometimes they let me out of the cave to help serve the tourists in the city's restaurants. A centipede lives inside of me in the place of my spine; it watches over me so that I don't escape.

Why would I escape?

I'm writing this report with their consent, what's more, at their insistence. The Nameless Lords kindly welcome fresh visitors who are ready to multiply their lives by zero.

Those who feel determined enough or have abandoned all hope already should feel free to call the toll-free number at Abaddon Travels! Our employees are kind and considerate, they will quickly guide you through the administrative labyrinth.

Those who feel like they are not yet prepared for this journey should by all means choose a more conventional trip.

But even they should not forget: there will be a time when the Nameless Lords feel like taking a break. Just a little holiday; maybe in time when the Sleeping Lords awake.

Soon.

Then we'll come and visit you all.

The Amber Complex

The town is situated in the eastern part of Hungary, a hundred kilometers from the Ukrainian border. As such it is a place of transit, literally and figuratively as well. Most people born here move away; those who stay often face economic instability. Crime, however petty, is often a way of life for those who remain.

In this town miracles rarely happen. Especially around the outskirts, where the poorest live.

This is the story of one such miracle.

The Outskirts Pub was opened in the early '90s by a man named Béla Ózdi and his life partner, Magdolna. They remodeled the three-room house the man had inherited from his uncle. Béla Ózdi believed two things were easy money: women and booze. There was a gypsy camp nearby in a converted Soviet military barracks, as well as the local mill, some half-abandoned industrial areas, and a number of family residences that gave off the stench of their daily miseries.

Yet, no pub in the vicinity.

Béla Ózdi invested the greater part of his savings into opening the pub. He tended to the business himself for three years, until his career was cut short by four bullets, two in the torso, one in the thigh, one in the throat that went through the jaw. Everyone suspected some sort of underworld assassination, but in fact it was his partner Magdolna and her newfound Ukrainian lover. They did it for the money. She was the brains of the operation, he was the muscle. As the police were closing in, the Ukrainian chose not to take any chances. He made a plastic bed for Magdolna and interrupted her disbelieving cries with a single headshot. After the deed he returned to his motherland, and following a couple of adventurous years and a few business missteps he ended up in the concrete foundation of a garage.

In this town happy endings are rare.

The pub was never a blockbuster success, but it wasn't an utter financial disappointment either. All the local alcoholics and gamblers called the pub their home away from home and enjoyed the noise of the incessant sports broadcasts coming from the TV on the wall or the reckless mix of gypsy pop and national rock blasting from the digital Wurlitzer.

Fights were a constant issue. A total of three homicides were committed in the pub or its immediate vicinity, all of them under the influence of alcohol. It was common knowledge that two rapes had occurred there, though neither of them was reported to the police; nor were the countless sexual assaults that are regarded locally as 'just playing around'. Over the past thirty years an ambulance has had to be called 237 times for medical emergencies of all sorts, in twenty-eight of which the patient's road led from the hospital straight to the darkness of the grave. Despite the number of health complications, no one has ever died in the pub of natural causes.

Those who dwelled on the outskirts of town were either manual laborers or living off disability benefits. Many of them didn't last till the age of retirement. The majority died from heart attacks, stroke was the runner-up, and cancer took the third spot. Out of every ten people there was only one who didn't drink on a regular basis and only three who didn't smoke. Each and every one of them begged and cried at night for a brand-new start somewhere else, as somebody else.

This is where Gábor Szeiber grew up. He remembered Béla Ózdi from his childhood. Gábor lived one street away from the pub, in a socialist-style family house. It was shaped like a cube, the ceiling was too low, the rooms cramped, the garden only an afterthought. His father had built a gate out of scrap metal and painted it yellow. This town is known for its outrageous attitude toward colors.

Gábor would often go to the pub to buy cigarettes for his father. One Sunday when the family TV stopped working Béla Ózdi let him watch the afternoon Disney cartoons there. *DuckTales* was interrupted by the news of Prime Minister József Antall's death, an interruption that caused a generational trauma. The boy walked home with tears in his eyes, like so many others that day all over the country. Later the police contacted Gábor because he was one of the last people to see Béla Ózdi alive. He had long considered this to be the defining event in his life, and it wasn't far from the truth.

At the age of forty-four his father bent over to lift up a trailer and collapsed. The runner-up: stroke. The doctors said the tissue in his brain had gotten thin over time. Those forty-four years were all he was given, and they couldn't have done anything to save him. It was a life-altering event for Gábor. After they had discreetly buried his father's body, Gábor vowed to step out of his parents' shadow, move away from his hometown, and make a splendid career in whatever suited his talents.

He did try, and he gave it his all. It just wasn't enough. He got into college, a first in his family. From day one he knew he wasn't cut out for it. He managed to pass the exams, just barely, but he couldn't find any underlying passion or talent, and by halfway through the fourth semester his momentum had run out.

He hung his head and moved back in with his mother, to the old family house with its low ceilings, its cramped spaces, its regrets measured in silences. He thought he'd just push the pause button on his studies. He could recharge, refresh his mind, get some perspective. Of course it was a lie. Deep down he knew that he had actually given up, he had given everything up a long time ago, maybe even the moment he was born.

It was because of that town. The neighborhood, with the vacant lots between the houses, the roads full of potholes, the people in their misbuttoned shirts, the cheap cigarillos, the chemical-flavored booze, the lamps casting weak yellow light on the streets, the nighttime quarrels about money, the screeching rusty gates, the neglected gardens, the laughter ending in coughing fits, the smiles showing missing teeth, the barking of half-wild dogs, and the center of it all, the Outskirts Pub.

That town. That neighborhood. That pub.

Even as a child he knew there was no escape. If you were born there you would have to die there too because the town was a trap.

He was right, of course.

Gábor now worked loading sacks for below the minimum wage. It was simple manual labor that left plenty of time for thinking. Like a prisoner savoring his life mistakes, replaying them in his head to see if things might have turned out differently if he had made different choices. Maybe if he had read more, if he had studied more diligently, if he had chained himself to a passion, then maybe he wouldn't have turned out to be such a failure. To make matters worse, his years at college had made him too polished for harsh physical work. Although it was his own choice to come back, he still felt humiliated. Each bag he loaded with cement was a reminder of those wasted years.

His thirtieth birthday was coming on quickly and one morning he made a snap decision, like steel breaking in the cold, that he would become an alcoholic. Once he formulated the idea, he made a plan and decided to get wasted every single day. Methodically, with determination. It was one thing he should be good at anyway, even if he wasn't good at anything else. Most of the people around him were already alcoholics, or on the road to becoming one, but all of them drifted into that state, they developed the habit day by day without noticing. It came naturally to them. Not to Gábor; he didn't drift into it. It was a mission.

His mother didn't mind. She had turned into the kind of woman who quietly wrings her hands whenever she speaks and hangs crosses on the walls, – not because she believed, but because that's what her own mother used to do – accepting that her value had been reduced to zero with the death of her husband. She would have been a prime candidate for alcoholism too, but her stomach was too weak for it, so her steady depression was uninterrupted by the occasional highs of drinking.

Gábor would have liked to drink in a wine cellar, to give an aura of sophistication to the proceedings. But there were no wine cellars nearby, only the Outskirts Pub, with Christmas lights hanging in the windows, cheap national rock playing over the muted hockey broadcasts, men playing cards in knitted sweaters at the tables. The pub was waiting for Gábor to arrive; it would wait patiently forever, like a good lover.

That November night Gábor cut through the cold with resolve, the remains of his weekly salary in his pocket. He had bought a pack of the cheapest cigarettes. He had given a little cash to his mother for the rent and bills. The rest he had saved for booze.

The low chimneys coughed out smoke; it was cheaper to burn trash for warmth than to pay for gas. The icy, foggy air had a penetrating odor that Gábor had always associated with dawn, autumn, and failure. That's why he had hated autumn, even as a kid.

He crossed the railway lines, passed the spotlights of the mill, then just marched along the wet asphalt, step after step. Gábor had long ceased to think about anything substantial. He told jokes to himself in his head or replayed conversations from long ago, reconstructing them in new ways, imagining what he should have said instead of what he actually had said. He could have listened to music on his phone, but the songs he liked reminded him of how low he had fallen. The music he listened to was considered by the locals to be intellectual and unmanly.

When he saw it he thought it was some kind of animal. First came the sound. A howling. Only animals howl that way, like a dog, for instance, when it's in pain. Then he understood.

Gábor didn't rush to help, but he didn't run away either. He was in shock. He knew this was a defining moment in his life: would he be the one who runs or the one who acts? But he wasn't either of these, he just stood there, in the middle of the road at night, completely frozen.

The murder was taking place a little beyond the roadside ditch. The victim, a man in his thirties, had escaped from his attacker's clutches and was crawling towards the road.

Gábor recognized him. His name was Máté something, a car mechanic and small-time loan shark. He was a short, stocky man wearing a shirt several sizes too small for his belly. It made him look like a pig dressed in a T-shirt. A train rushed along the tracks, casting light on the crime scene. In the fleeting light the blood looked black. He had been stabbed in the neck and stomach. His trousers were darkened by a stripe of urine. He stumbled through the ditch, looked at Gábor, or beyond him, as if already looking beyond this reality, towards the place he would soon enter. Then he collapsed on the roadside, twitched a couple of times, and moved no more.

Gábor looked at the killer, and it occurred to him that he would have to give a description of him when this was all over. He tried to organize his thoughts, quickly record the physical traits so he could reconstruct the scene later and use the most appropriate, most precise expressions to describe the killer. A man in his late twenties, denim jacket, short spiky hair, bloodshot eyes, a twisted nose, as if it had been put on his face wrong. The nose made it click. It was Feri, from the Outskirts Pub. He always drank small spritzers in the corner, two at a time, finishing them off in quick succession. He has a knife, Gábor thought, he has a knife in his hand, dripping with a dead man's blood.

Then he was struck by a chilling thought. There would be no police interrogation. He wouldn't have to describe Feri ever in his life. Gábor kept thinking that he should run. If he outran Feri and beat him to the pub, which was still a good thousand meters away, he would be safe. Or he could stay where he was and try to act like he hadn't seen anything at all.

Feri licked the corner of his mouth.

'I had to do it. He was asking for too much. He broke a promise. A gentleman's handshake,' he said. 'You know how it is. Enough is enough.'

Gábor nodded. His mouth was too dry to speak.

'I know you from the pub,' Feri continued. 'So why don't we just go there, hm? A couple of rounds on me. We'll watch a bit of TV. Forget what you saw.'

Gábor nodded, but Feri stepped closer, tightening his grip on the knife, ready to strike. Gábor knew they would never make it to the pub, that these were his last heartbeats. Soon there would be a breath that would be his last before this whole big stupid system, this body, would become pointless, just a piece of abandoned rubbish by the side of the road. Gábor's voice became awkwardly high-pitched, girly, the kind he would feel ashamed of when he thought about it later. But there was no later.

'But why? I didn't do anything,' he whined as Feri came even closer. Gábor knew that it was futile to start running now. His legs were already shaking, his stomach was cramping, he was gasping for air.

'Relax, I'll do you fast, all right? It won't hurt if you don't resist.'

Gábor retreated towards the side of the road, expecting to trip over a pothole at any moment. He thought of running into the darkness, across the ditch, just as Máté what's-his-name must have tried a little earlier. Then Gábor stopped. He took a deep breath and assessed the situation again.

What's happening here, he thought, is after all only a quicker version of what he had planned anyway. Drinking would take years to kill him, maybe even decades. It hit him, and almost made him laugh, that he would save a lot of money for his mother too.

He looked into Feri's eyes, and the killer smirked. Gábor determined that he wouldn't close his eyes. As long as his eyes could see, he would see with them. The two of them were so caught up in this game, the killer and his victim, that neither saw the car approaching with its lights off. A black Audi that would normally never stop at a place like this unless it had broken down, if that sort of car ever actually broke down. At the sound of the car hitting Feri, Gábor gave a startled jump. Feri spun on his axis, the knife flew out of his hand and embedded itself in the ground. Feri hit the asphalt. The Audi braked with a long screech. The passenger door popped open, and a bald man got out wearing a long, soft woolen jacket. He wore thick horn-rimmed glasses and was clearly drunk. He put a cigarette in his mouth and lit it with a Zippo lighter. He leaned into the cabin, took out a knitted cap, and put it on his head. On the pavement Feri wasn't moving. The bald man looked at Gábor, then leaned back into the cabin.

'He's still here, don't you want to speak with him?'

'What's with the other one?' came from the inside. 'The guy we fucked up with the car.'

'He's just lying there.'

'Dead?'

The bald guy looked at Feri from a distance, and as if waiting for that cue, Feri regained consciousness and started moaning with pain.

'Looks like he's alive. But that's about it. He's not gonna be dancing anytime soon.'

A man poked his head out from the back seat. He looked around, fixed his gaze on Gábor, then grinned and shouted, as if they hadn't just hit somebody.

'Gabika, how's it hanging?'

He got out of the car and opened his arms for a hug. Gábor stared at the man standing there like the crucified Christ, except with a grin on his face. He was a slim man, the same age as Gábor, with a sculpted goatee.

'Feri?' Gábor asked, a rhetorical question.

'Of course I'm Feri! Don't you recognize me? What are you doing here?'

Finally Feri put his arms down. He was getting tired of the pose.

'By the way, was he trying to kill you just now, or what the hell was that?' asked Feri.

'Yes,' answered Gábor. His legs really started to shake, he felt like he was going to collapse any moment now; he became aware of the muscles in his body, the muscles that should be dead by now. The trembling reached his stomach and in a few seconds took over his entire body. His teeth chattered, and Gábor felt he would never be able to speak again.

'I think your buddy is in shock,' said the bald man.

'Yeah. Listen, why don't we take him with us?' asked Feri.

'What?'

'Why don't we take him? There's still room in the car, and Zanó said there would be someone else with us. Someone by accident. Someone who wasn't invited.'

Gábor watched the two men from the bottom of a well as they argued about his life, the life that could be taken at any moment, all you needed was a knife, or not even that, only dedication, a will to kill.

'What if that someone else brings someone else? What will we do with him then, if he's not allowed to come down?'

Feri didn't give up, and Gábor thought he should feel something for Feri right then. That would be appropriate, since his old friend was fighting for him, yet he didn't feel any connection. It was because of the name, he was sure. For this was the second Feri that night; had he only seen the name, the two men could have been the same person. A murderer. How many Feris could be out there in the world? How many murderers?

'Listen, I think it's him. I mean, this was pretty dramatic, wasn't it? What are the odds? Meeting him here, like this? It's him, let's take him.'

Beside the ditch, the Feri who had already killed someone that day was trying to get to his feet. The other Feri and the bald man immediately grabbed Gábor and put him in the back seat. He didn't resist. They gave him a few sips of brandy from a flask. The alcohol soothed Gábor; soon he was almost feeling good. The Audi started to race through the night streets.

The car belonged to the bald man, Mihály. Mihály worked as the VP of an Austrian import-export company. He owned an apartment in Vienna and another one in a fancy part of Budapest. He went on vacation twice a year. One vacation was for fucking in a foreign country. Whether it took seduction or money didn't matter. He had already risen above the exoticism of the different races, and for years now he had been searching for the differences in women by country, or even by region. He considered himself something of an art collector, or a passionate food taster, for whom each occasion is special. He had to have the women in their respective region, in their own terrain, to savor their taste along with the local smells and flavors. It was a passion of his, a fetish, if you will.

His other vacation was for wine tasting. He approached wine and women in a similar manner. Both of them were the product of age, location, and nurture. He liked to taste where the grapes grew, where the juice was pressed, just as he wanted to be together with women in their own land. He wanted to feel the breeze that caressed the bunches, the sunlight that nourished the leaves, he wanted to touch the earth, the minerals that gave flavor to the juice. He would always finish the wine tour in Hungary, always at the same place. The place the car was rushing towards now through the night. Zanó's vineyard.

The car was driven by a woman, Daniella. She had run Feri over, she even stepped on the gas pedal a little to make sure the man was rendered harmless. This was not her first time.

Gábor thanked her, but the woman didn't reply; her blue eyes were fixed on the road. She smoked one cigarette after the other. Her hair was bleached white. A single piece of her outfit was worth more than what Gábor earned in a year. Daniella's parents emigrated at the right time to the right place, and when they were rich enough, with the Kádár regime gone, they returned out of misplaced nostalgia. They had met by Lake Balaton as young lovers, and during a storm they both drowned in the lake as well, leaving their considerable wealth to their only daughter.

After her parents' death she began to search for something she couldn't quite name. She already had everything. She needed something more. More than what she saw around her. More than what she was.

Daniella spoke seven languages fluently. She had degrees in literature, philosophy, economics, chemistry, and psychology. When she couldn't find what she was looking for in her studies, she traveled around the world. She worked for the Red Cross in Africa, in tea fields in Sri Lanka, on a ship in the Amazon, almost retired to a convent in Argentina; instead she became a drug addict, but she kicked the habit soon enough.

Her life was about this incessant search, a hunt for something more, more than possessions, more than the body, more than thoughts. Maybe in Zanó's wine cellar, maybe that's where she could find what she had been looking for. She almost succeeded once. This time she would reach her goal. She always did.

But that was what she dreaded the most. What if she found it? What would be the driving force in her life then?

She lit another cigarette.

Feri and Gábor knew each other from college, they were roommates in the dorm. They would often drink together, watching the city from the dorm window and imagining that youth would never end, that college was forever, that adulthood would be kept at bay by the exams, the parties, the dreaming about the future where everything would magically turn out all right and they would both feel as content and fulfilled as they felt in their dirty dormitory room after three bottles of wine.

For Feri, this future became reality. During college he made connections; the students' union was a perfect platform for this. Just like Gábor, he left school without graduating. He didn't need a diploma, quickly making a career as the department head of a Hungarian-based international live porn site called pornaftermidnight.com. The system was built on the exploitation of women all over the world, but it was legal, and the girls, if they weren't stupid, also got their fair share. Nothing to feel bad about, especially since the company made a fortune, year after year.

He earned as much in a year as his parents had made in their entire lives. Hungarian labor was cheap and expendable, but Feri made himself indispensable at the company. He hadn't turned thirty yet and he'd already achieved everything he ever wanted. For a while he lived a life of pleasure, forming friendships with various drugs, in a stable relationship with alcohol. For a while he slept with a different girl every night, but then he found the one, a girl named Eszter who worked as a prostitute downtown. She charged her clients well above the market rate. Feri paid her a visit out of curiosity.

It wasn't the sex. The girl sang quietly some kind of elusive melody, a melody that took Feri out of time, out of the prison of human sensation, and swept him to a perfect place. Feri had spent a fortune on Eszter. The girl made him addicted, more than any other drug before. He even proposed to her. Money didn't matter, he would have bought her a house, cars, a zoo, whatever she asked for.

They dated for a while, one of the perks of which was that

Eszter sang to him for free. Feri started to think everything was fine, that he had found happiness and that it would stay with him forever. He felt complete. Then one November morning two years ago Eszter hanged herself. The body was discovered by her cleaning lady. A few days earlier someone had sent her a cassette in an unmarked envelope. This cassette was in the tape recorder when she killed herself. Feri played it later, but it was completely blank. He crushed the tape recorder in anger, hysterically tore the tape into small pieces until at last he just wept like a child over the ruins of his life on the cold floor. He fell asleep there.

The next morning he cleaned up, threw out the trash, and accepted that he would never be happy ever again. He would keep running the rat race, he would smoke everything that he couldn't drink, and he would simply live well off until at last he died.

Of course when he told Gábor about his last couple of years he didn't mention Eszter and her melody, only the successes, the wild parties, how he crashed his Bentley last year while drunk, but what the hell, there's always a newer model available. How he bought a house for his parents so big that they regularly got lost in it. How it was worth investing in gold now because the price was going up. He didn't mention the sleepless nights, the panic attacks, the suicide attempt last June. He didn't talk about how the wine tasting they were heading for gave him new hope, a hope that kept the thoughts of suicide at bay.

Gábor kept smoking, one cigarette after the other. His hands were still shaking. Quiet music played in the car, a Nocturne by Chopin, Daniella's choice.

'And what's up with you?' Feri asked. 'What happened to you after college?'

Gábor sank into his thoughts. For years now he hadn't faced a situation like this, where he had to show his best side, appear to be the shining pillar of success, omit every misstep and only focus on the achievements. What achievements? What could he say? What lie could he make up?

'I just want to get drunk,' he said eventually with total sincerity.

Feri burst into laughter, a goat-like sound that was painful to the ears.

'Of course you do, my friend. You could use a drink. We all could. Soon we will.'

Gábor dosed off. He had already lost track of every point of reference, and when he awoke he had no idea where they were. The night was absolute. No city or town nearby. At Mihály's insistence they ejected the Chopin CD and by mutual consensus they put on a Rage Against the Machine album and yelled along with the music in perfect corporate unison. In truth, they were all children. They were teens caught in their thirties, still reeling from the shock of understanding that this was it. This was life, adulthood already, but like teenagers they were still holding out hope that there was more.

All of them, except Gábor. He had given up hope. He was just enjoying the ride.

Gábor didn't care where they were heading or how long it would take, it was just good to be on the way. It was as if he had gotten rid of a heavy chain when he left the town behind, leaving the rigid corpse on the roadside and his mother at the apartment, and now he was returning to those years when the future didn't extend beyond the next party. Like a stone that has a little farther to fly before it hits the ground.

At last they arrived. Gábor didn't even notice they had stopped until the doors opened. He got out, and only then did he realize they were standing at the foot of a mountain. He wasn't aware of any mountain near town, but decided not to think about it too hard.

The clouds parted to make way for the moon, which shed an ivory light over the landscape. The mountain appeared white in the light, like a mountain of chalk. The hills were heavy with trunks of grapevines. The silence all around was deep and soft. Another car was parked there, a Porsche. Leaning on the hood was a forty-something man with a short haircut, an expensive suit, a sweet-smelling cigarillo in his hand. In the back seat was a considerably younger woman with pitch-black hair, the light of her phone shining with a bluish glow as she typed away. The man dropped the cigarillo and pressed it into the cold ground with his leather shoe as he approached the newcomers.

'Gentlemen, good to see you again!' he said and offered a hand to everyone in turn. Nearly all of his fingers were covered with rings. His grip was firm.

'I don't believe we've met yet,' he said to Gábor when it was his turn to shake hands. Gábor felt out of place in his cheap secondhand clothes, which hung heavy on his frame.

'My name is Róbert Kővári, or just Mr. Kővári to my friends.'
'Gábor.'

'Gábor,' repeated Mr. Kővári, as if savoring the name. 'It's a pleasure to meet you, and a surprise. Let me give you my business card.'

He fished out a tiny silver wallet from a pocket of his flawlessly tailored suit, popped it open, and took out a business card. *Winemaker and sommelier*, the card said. Gábor couldn't possibly know, since their lives, their existences, had been unfolding in parallel dimensions unattainable for one another, but the man standing in front of him exported his wines and opinions to all continents at an extravagant price.

'It's your first time in Zanó's cellar, am I right? You are a lucky man. Sometimes I wish I could taste the complexes for the first time. Of course experience doesn't really matter much, since they're different every time.'

Gábor had no idea what the complexes were, but he feared that asking about it would reveal what an uncultured peasant he really was.

'Daniella, you look stunning as usual!' Mr. Kővári turned

to the woman. He didn't offer his hand to shake.

'Your wife looks stunning in the car too. Staying there would suit her well,' Daniella said. It was the first time Gábor had heard her speak.

'Well, yes. You know how it is. The nighttime cold always takes its toll on her.'

'Wouldn't it have been wiser to leave her at home? You don't usually take trash to wine tastings, do you?'

Daniella turned away from the man, who just smiled as if he had been given a compliment.

'I think the rest of us are here too,' noted Mihály. In the nighttime landscape headlights were searching for a way towards the mountain. Mihály lit a cigarette. By the time he finished smoking, the car had arrived. A red Toyota, music roaring at full volume. The driver's face was obscured by the thick smoke that gathered behind the windows. The car finally stopped, its doors popped open, and three figures crawled out from the seats.

'Hey, motherfuckers!' shouted the driver and walked up to everyone to hug them. He had the face of a hyena and smelled of alcohol and pot smoke. 'I don't know you, dude!' he said, turning to Gábor.

'Gábor.'

'Gábor! Yeah. Cool that you're here. Call me Alex. That's what I call myself too.'

At this point he started making a persistent whinnying sound that lasted a little longer than it should have.

'Do you deal in wine, too?' asked Gábor.

'Wine? No. I'm a real estate agent. Do you need a flat? I've got some!'

'Thanks, no.'

'I introduce my dear friends, acquaintances to you.' He pointed towards his fellow travelers.

The guy who crawled out from the passenger seat also stepped up to Gábor.

'Hi, I'm Gábor,' said Gábor, feeling like a preprogrammed robot only capable of repeating the same line.

'And I'm Boss.'

Boss had such a smooth face that he looked like a baby, but in truth he was thirty. His blond hair was cut short and combed to the side. He didn't weigh more than forty kilos. He didn't have a business card, because fuck business cards, if they didn't know who you were then it was their problem. Had he had one, it would have said rock 'n' roll winemaker. He named every wine he made after a rock band, real or imaginary. He'd been on a hot streak lately but felt that he had explored all the limits of winemaking. Maybe his inspiration was abandoning him.

The winemakers were here for the craft. Their guests were here for the fun.

'And that's Cseszi,' said Alex, then burped.

Cseszi was a ginger-haired woman. She didn't introduce herself, just nodded and lit a cigarette. She rolled up her jumper so Gábor could see her tattoos.

'They're nice,' Gábor said, pointing at the tattoos.

'I didn't have them done for you,' the woman answered coldly and kept on smoking. The two of them were in the same boat. It was her first time too.

A door in the hillside opened and a man stepped out of the mountain. Gábor hadn't even noticed that there was an entrance carved into the hillside until then.

'Excuse my delay, I got held up down there. For those visiting my cellar for the first time, I'm Zanó.'

Zanó appeared to be in his forties. His hair was gray all over. He had work boots on and a simple knitted sweater, with linen cargo pants. A plastic bucket swung from his hand, which he tossed aside now to shake hands with everyone. He greeted Gábor as well, and Gábor felt relief seeing that his host wore even cheaper clothes than he did, although he wore them with more grace. The man was surrounded by a strange cellar smell, which Gábor found peculiar, but pleasing.

'You are the one. I told the others that they would bring a stranger. And I was right, wasn't I? You're having a hell of a night, I can see that. Let's go down and you can get to drinking!' he encouraged Gábor as he was shepherded him towards the cellar door.

'Are you a winemaker, sir?' asked Gábor.

'Please call me Zanó, no need to be so formal.'

He spoke fast, following a strange rhythm, sometimes prolonging the final syllables, other times cutting them short. It was a provincial dialect, but Gábor couldn't identify the region. He didn't find it annoying. On the contrary, he noticed that he was trying to imitate the strange intonation in his head.

'Are you a winemaker?' he tried again.

'You might say that, but not quite. There are winemakers, and I admire them, they often make wonderful wine that I enjoy myself. But I don't want to be considered as one of them. I don't wish to take credit for their work. For I don't make wine. I make complexes. A complex is similar to wine, but not quite the same. But you'll soon taste it, and then you can tell me whether you like it or not, all right?'

'Is it alcoholic?'

'Of course it is, young man! What kind of booze would it be without alcohol?'

He laughed at this. The door opened to reveal a spacious hall. An antechamber to the cellar, situated at ground level. At the further end a series of steps led downward, into the belly of the mountain. Gigantic barrels made of wood and metal filled up the wide, cold space. The floor was simple concrete. The walls were carved out of the stone. There were unlit candles on the walls. A green stool stood in the middle of the room, with shot glasses made of finely crafted glass on top of it, all of them filled with pálinka. Once everyone was crammed into the room, Zanó closed the door behind them, then picked up the tray and walked around with it, so that everyone could take a glass. He himself didn't take one.

'Thank you all for honoring us with your presence. Let us drink to celebrate that we are all here and can enjoy the complexes together!' Everyone lifted up their glass and downed the shot. Like drinking hot silk, Gábor thought. After the bleach-smelling rotgut he was used to at the Outskirts Pub this beverage made by adept hands gave him the chills. It was peach pálinka; it went down smoothly and then made a pleasant, lukewarm nest in the stomach. Its aroma lingered for a long time in the area between the palate and the nasal cavity. Gábor savored it with his eyes closed.

'I'd like you to drink it, my dear. We cannot go on until you do.'

'But I don't like pálinka.'

Only then did Gábor notice that Mr. Kővári's wife hadn't emptied her glass. She just held it in her hands, her little finger pointing away. Her black hair was pulled back in a ponytail, and her eyebrows stretched stubbornly above her eyes.

'I'm very sorry, darling. It is one of the prerequisites of tasting. It needs to be drunk for the rest to work properly.'

'I don't drink,' she said.

'Excuse me, my dear, but in that case what are you doing here?'

The woman gave Mr. Kővári a devastating look.

'No problem, I'll drink hers too,' suggested Cseszi.

'No, my dear, it doesn't work like that. Everyone only gets one. But one is obligatory.'

Mr. Kővári turned to his wife.

'I told you to stay home if you couldn't behave,' hissed the man.

'Then go to hell with your wines!' replied the woman.

'Jesus, there they go again!' Mihály rolled his eyes.

Alex looked on with a sardonic grin. It was Zanó who intervened. He sounded pleasant and kind, but Gábor felt a premonition of violence in the air.

'I think it would be best to let the lady go. There is no need to drag her into anything she finds undesirable or displeasing, is there?'

'I'll just go down and watch,' the woman proposed.

'No. You can either stay here or leave.'

'What? Are you throwing me out? And you're going to let him?' She looked at her husband, waiting for help.

'Yes, I am, since you've put me into such an uncomfortable situation. I'm trying to show you something wonderful. And you're acting like this!' said Mr. Kővári.

'As if I cared about your wonders!' yelled the woman.

The man took out a car key from his coat pocket.

'Here's the key. Go now, I'll manage.'

'Your bloody wines mean more to you than I do?'

Mr. Kővári looked the woman up and down.

'It appears so.'

The woman shook her head in disbelief, then ripped the car key from the man's hand and walked out theatrically from the hallway into the night. She tried to slam the door dramatically, but it was too heavy. Zanó poured the woman's drink onto the floor and locked the entrance door with a key.

'We can go down now,' he announced.

The group set off to the depths of the cellar. All of them had to bend over as they started their descent. They could only straighten up when they reached the bottom of the stairs. Gábor had a slight sense of claustrophobia.

A long, narrow corridor carved into the stone led to infinity. Spotlights shone on the walls. Gábor couldn't see an end to the corridor. He had been to wine cellars before, but they were as big as the antechamber they had just come from, usually made of concrete. Just a room to store and drink wine in. This corridor was already more massive in size than any of the wine cellars Gábor had ever seen.

'How big is this place?' Gábor asked, for reasons unknown even to him, in a whisper. Feri answered.

'This isn't a single cellar. It's a system of cellars. Several of them connected by corridors. We drink in a different room each year and we haven't been to the same room twice yet.'

'How many times have you drunk here?'

Feri also started whispering.

'Me, twice. Mr. Kővári has drunk here at least a dozen times. Here comes the creepy part. He says that his father, and even his grandfather, used to taste complexes here. And even back then it was this man who served them.'

Gábor stopped.

'You're pulling my leg.'

Feri grinned, but made no further comments.

The walls were covered with mildew. Occasionally the monotony of these walls was broken by the appearance of a long-forgotten candleholder, or a ledge carved into the rock, housing musty bottles. The corridor came to a fork; Zanó led the group down the right-hand path. There was slightly more space here. The walls were lined with old wooden barrels, some of them with dates carved into them: 1776, 1878, 1606.

The march was quiet, as if the ancient walls, the weight of the mountain, the memories hidden in the stones, had squeezed even the last thought out of the guests. The corridor ended in a gigantic room with barrels covering the walls from floor to ceiling. Gábor stood gaping. It seemed impossible to him that this system of rooms and corridors could have been made by human hands. It would take lifetimes of work, and technology that couldn't have existed at the times suggested by the stored barrels.

'This is the biggest cellar, right?' asked Cseszi.

'No, my dear, I wouldn't think so. There are others much bigger that I know of. Several, in fact, created for special occasions. Of course, every occasion is special, so for each a new space was created long ago. Still, this is nice too, isn't it?'

Several other corridors opened off this room. Zanó led them on. Gábor lost all sense of orientation, he simply walked after the others into a corridor, then into the next one, then back to the one before, or was it a new one? He understood that he was deep inside the belly of a maze. If he got separated from the group he would be lost for good. Yet each corridor and room had its own character and atmosphere. Some of them meandered, like they had been carved out in a state of drunkenness. Other walls were covered in drawings, the work of the shamans of long-dead tribes; in one room an animal skull watched over the visitors, golden chains hanging from its fangs. It didn't look to Gábor like any beast he had ever seen at a zoo or on TV. No one made a comment on the skull and Gábor was worried he was the only one who saw it.

Not long after this, he turned at the wrong corner and ended up in a small room. In the middle there was a hole in the ground, wide enough for three or even four people to jump in. He looked down into the hole, but all he could see was utter darkness. Gábor took a coin and dropped it. He never heard it hit the bottom. Gábor then felt an urge, a dreadful temptation, to jump. He turned and hurried after the others.

At last they arrived in a hall the size of a large room, with a long wooden table in its middle with wooden chairs around it. A wine glass for every chair, made of the same finely crafted material as the shot glasses upstairs. Several other rooms opened off the hall.

'Here we are! Take a seat!' Zanó showed them around. 'Let's start the tasting.'

Everyone chose their seat. Gábor waited so that he could sit down last in whichever chair was left for him. He felt exhilarated just looking at the faces; everyone seemed tense, like zealots about to be given a blessing.

'For those who are not familiar with the routine,' Zanó commenced, 'let me be clear: the complex is not wine. The mountain has been in my family's possession for generations, and we have bred a plant similar to a grape, but not quite the same. Later on I can give you a taste of these complex grapes as well, but they aren't very tasty raw. In my family, we have been perfecting the complex sequence for centuries. And now about the process. The complexes can only be tasted in the exact order I pour them into the glasses. This is rather important, so that the items that come later down the road can also take full effect. Neither more, nor less, is to be consumed than the quantity I pour out, unless someone wishes to quit the tasting to enjoy one of the complexes longer, or feels unwell and wants to stop. None of you should forget: this is not a race, everyone should consume just as much as his or her body and soul desire.'

Gábor looked at his companions, all awaiting the tasting. Mr. Kővári sat anxiously on his chair, playing with a piece of paper. Daniella's hands were shaking. Feri sat with a half-grin, Mihály stared deadpan ahead. Boss pushed his glasses up the bridge of his nose and ceased his constant giggling. Sweat gleamed on his skin. Cseszi turned her glass around and around in her hands indifferently, and Alex fiddled with his phone. He hadn't figured out yet that there was no signal in the cellar.

'Is it all clear to everyone?'

Cseszi raised her hand.

'Yes, my dear?'

'Are you supposed to drink it the same way as wine?'

'Exactly the same way. You can savor it, roll it around in your mouth. It is important that you don't spit it out under any circumstances. You should swallow, otherwise the next complex cannot be tasted. You should enjoy the aroma in your nose. But you'll understand quickly. Any more questions?'

'Will we have the Amber complex?' asked Daniella.

Zanó flashed a reassuring smile that made Gábor uncomfortable.

'Of course, my dear. Every session ends with the Amber. I already have the bottle ready.'

The woman indicated with a nod that she was pleased with the answer. Zanó took out a simple wine bottle from a storage room. The bottle had a blue circle painted on it. He opened it to let the beverage breathe.

'We start with a light, introductory piece. This year's opening item is the Blue. Since last year's overture was a warm item, I chose a cold one for this occasion. I don't want to reveal more, so that I don't influence the pleasure.'

He poured everyone a glass.

Gábor thoroughly examined the beverage in his glass. It was of a pale, yellowish color, although now that he knew it was called Blue, he seemed to discover a slight bluish tinge to it.

The tension in the room was palpable, although Gábor didn't understand why. This was just fancy booze.

He raised the glass to his mouth and killed off the Blue in a single gulp.

It took a second for the true nature of the complex to reveal itself. When it kicked in Gábor thought there was something wrong with him. Maybe his body was having an adverse reaction to the drink. The others were enjoying the taste with their eyes closed. Cseszi was holding on to the edge of the table, her muscles flexed, as if some ferocious wind was about to blow her away. Gábor followed her example and closed his eyes too. The drink, like a slimy snake, penetrated his mind.

A memory came to him, squeezing out everything else from his mind.

The image of a tile. Ceramic, white, smelling like disinfectant, with the smell of mold underneath it.

It wasn't just an image, it wasn't solely visual. There was more to it, a weight, a composition, a sense of being there.

The tile was affixed to the wall of a dark corridor, he could feel the cold on the glaze, he could sense the tiny grooves. The world was composed of nothing but this tile, although in the distance he could sense the corridor and the other tiles that covered it; this tile was one of many, still – it was the absolute focus now.

'It is cold indeed,' said Mr. Kővári. 'But why tiles? It's tiles, am I right?'

'Yes. One tile, with a sense of others,' Daniella laughed. She had a beautiful-sounding laughter, it sounded like falling necklaces. Mr. Kővári continued.

'This not-quite-disinfectant smell is exceptionally subtly positioned, it triggers very precise associations. Mold underneath, huh?'

Zanó nodded with a smile.

'A dark corridor?' asked Mihály.

'Absolutely,' agreed Feri.

Gábor now regretted having swallowed it in one gulp. He came back to his senses, the image that had overwhelmed him before was fading away now, although his memory tried to hold on to it. The others were savoring the Blue in two or three smaller sips. He tried to think back to what had happened exactly. The world was filled with the idea or memory of a tile, a tile he had never seen before until he drank the beverage, but he didn't just see it, he felt it: its smell, its size, its touch, its place in the world.

'The upper left-hand corner of the tile is a little cracked, isn't it?' asked Cseszi, while gasping for air.

Zanó's smile grew wider.

'Indeed,' commented Mr. Kővári. 'Very good observation for a first-timer. Even I had a hard time noticing it.'

Gábor focused. A small piece was indeed missing from the edge of the tile in his mind.

'How are you doing this?' asked Gábor. 'What is this?'

Mr. Kővári burst into laughter.

'I would really like to know that as well. It would revolutionize winemaking!'

'A drug? Controlled association?'

The group paid a few seconds of respectful silence to Gábor for having been able to throw this expression into a casual conversation.

'Maybe,' said Mr. Kővári, shaking his head. 'Not sure.'

Feri poked Gábor.

'Dude, this was only the introduction. It's nothing. Wait till you see the rest.'

Zanó held the next bottle in his hand. This one featured a circle the color of dirty sand.

'This is also an introductory one. I call it Sand. I hope it will compensate for the coldness of Blue.'

He walked around and poured for everyone. The color of the drink differed only by a shade from the previous one.

'I'm warning the first-timers: don't be frightened, but it might feel a little strange.'

Gábor sniffed the drink but didn't smell anything peculiar, only a sweet, alcohol-tinged scent.

'It only works in the mouth,' said Daniella to Gábor in a confidential tone. Her face was flushed from the first glass, her forehead glistened under the lights.

'Cheers,' said Alex, then downed his drink. Everyone followed his example.

Gábor was more careful this time, drinking only half of the drink at first. He let the sip linger in his mouth for a while, then swallowed it. He tried to observe how the trick actually worked, although the experience flooded his senses and memory like a river. At times, for a moment or two he could sense how his own memory was moving and transforming. It felt disturbing, as if his organs were being shuffled around in his body.

Nevertheless he kept focusing because he had to understand. There was a blue sky in the complex; that must be why the complex dredged up a certain long-forgotten memory and ripped it apart. He was six years old, playing on a hillside. Bored, he was watching the sky and imagining aliens attacking Earth. Naturally he had forgotten about this a long time ago, it was just like any other depressing summer afternoon spent doing nothing. However, one of the aromatic components of the complex forced his mind to drag out the memory, extracting the blue sky out of it, while dispensing with everything else. The blue sky had been somewhat transformed, small clouds from other memories appeared added to it, and just like that it became a new sky, but still real in the memory that was not Gábor's own, which had been given to him by the complex by means of flavors, scents, and aromas. Now Gábor understood why these drinks were called complexes. Then he thought no more as the complex took over.

A foreign country. Not Hungary, but somewhere in Europe. Maybe England? Possibly, though no proof. A man stands by the shore of a sea or lake, his brown trenchcoat blown here and there in the wind as if by a mad goblin. He is wearing leather shoes, the left one a little too tight. Horn-rimmed glasses with thick lenses on his nose. A brown leather bag in his hand, a sandwich and some documents inside. He can't remember what's in the documents or if they were even meant for his eyes. The shore is covered with heavy sand, the brownish, wet kind that sucks in your feet and sticks to your shoes. Not far away, a large industrial building. Abandoned. The wind slams a door somewhere inside, again and again. Behind the building, in the distance, a giant industrial chimney points toward the sky. The sky is blue in a dull, dreadful way. No sign of life at all. The man stands by the waterside, contemplating whether or not he should take out the cigarette from his pocket (paper pack, brown filter, on the package the name of the brand with blue letters over a white background), but then he decides not to smoke. The wind would blow the flame out anyway. He inhales the unnatural, chemically overcharged smell of the water.

He doesn't notice, but there is someone in the building, watching him from a window. The watching figure has six fingers on his hand.

Something stirs deep down in the lake. It's coming up towards the surface.

While Gábor could perfectly identify with what the anonymous man was sensing, his own perceptions went beyond the man's sensations or memories. He knew someone was watching the man from the window, without the man's knowing it, but besides that he felt the man's tongue as his own, along with his craving for a cigarette, the sound of his sighs, the feeling of a drop of sweat rolling down his back. He felt the detached fatigue we feel when we encounter something we dread but have faced so many times that the terror has become only dull anger.

There was something under the water. Maybe in a minute, maybe not until the afternoon, or the following day, but it will appear. The man is waiting. He's just waiting forever.

The memory ended here, not like a video recording, but more like a dream, slowly dissipating. The smells and the atmosphere lingered the longest.

'Nicely extended atmospheric quality,' started Mr. Kővári again.

'A little esoteric-apocalyptic,' continued Daniella. 'Isn't it?'

'I can't bear all that mysterious stuff,' Alex announced in a whiny voice.

Gábor drank up the rest of the drink. While the first time the memory was built up mostly sequentially, this time the elements only intensified and could be experienced again. It felt like a snapshot, but it wasn't one; in the complex time passed, but nothing really happened, and then it started again. It was a nightmarish, dreadful moment kept on repeat. Not a snapshot anymore, but not yet a scene either.

'It was the mystery that laid the foundation. It's at the heart of the composition,' said Mihály, as he contemplated his glass with the eye of an expert.

'But which mystery? The thing under the water or the guy with six fingers?' Cseszi asked.

'It depends on the observer. That's what made it exciting. At least in my opinion. No open threat, just a sense of dread.'

Boss grunted.

'Man, I would have really liked to see the monster, or whatever. I wonder, does it eat the guy?'

'I don't think so,' Feri pondered. 'The guy is used to meeting the creature, even though he fears it.'

'Yeah,' Gábor agreed, and he immediately regretted opening his mouth. Everyone else was analyzing and deconstructing, and all he could manage was a 'yeah'.

'Don't worry,' someone said, but he couldn't tell who it was. As if he hadn't even heard it with his ears. Cseszi put her hand in front of her mouth. Was it her voice perhaps? Was it a woman's voice at all?

Zanó spoke, with a new bottle in his hands.

'Now comes the first full-fledged item, the Scarlet complex. It's a little heavier than the ones before, I hope that everyone is prepared. I'm asking the first-timers, are you feeling well?'

Cseszi nodded, smiling. Gábor likewise. He found this new drink exciting and he was also happy to discover that he had the alcoholic buzz he liked so much.

Zanó poured the Scarlet complex.

The first thing Gábor noticed was the presence of the opening drink, the Blue. The tile that filled the entire Blue complex was on the wall, tightly attached to other tiles. This provided the basis for the memory, only the experience of the disinfectant-smell grew stronger. Cold light reflected off the tiles.

The Scarlet complex built itself up at a slower pace than the others.

A man stands in the middle of the room, wearing a long leather apron, like an old-time butcher. On a rolling table lay scalpels, knives, bone cutters, and rib spreaders. Sealed bottles on metal shelves, organs with exquisite shapes swim in opaque liquids. The man in the leather apron is a pathologist. He pushes his metal frame glasses up on his aquiline nose.

There are two autopsy tables in the room. One shines, freshly scrubbed but empty. On the other lies the corpse of a woman. Gray, bloodless skin, curly red hair arranged around her head. The pathologist rolls his autopsy kit closer. He observes the body. There is a scar on the neck. The pathologist examines it. Hanging, presumably suicide, he would say, but he remains mute. If he spoke he would have a deep, raspy voice.

He picks up a scalpel and makes an incision on the skin under the left sternum, drawing the blade straight down to the upper part of the stomach. He repeats the same thing on the other side, then from the stomach down to the groin. He uses his hands to open up the body, as if it were made of paper, and darkness is revealed deep in the body instead of flesh and clotted blood. Something moves, trembles, down there. The pathologist instinctively takes a step back.

Butterflies fly out of the incision, hundreds, maybe thousands of them, in all the colors of the world, the fluttering of their wings slowly being transformed into music, a melody so beautiful one cannot even fathom it.

For the first time in his life the pathologist bursts into tears.

Now it was Gábor who had to hold on to something to remain upright. The pathologist's catharsis kept echoing in his soul. He awoke to the sound of sobbing. Feri was leaning over the table crying, his shoulders trembling, his hands turning into a mask to cover his face.

Gábor knew why he was crying, he remembered Eszter along with Feri. Eszter, the singing girl. He recognized her on the autopsy table, just as Feri did. At first it didn't even hit him that he knew something nobody had ever told him.

No one consoled the crying man. All of them knew his reasons, and Feri knew that they all shared his feelings.

'This was quite a strong complex,' Mr. Kővári observed. 'Although I'm sure it wasn't quite realistic in its depiction of autopsies.'

Daniella nodded. A few tears rolled down her face; she quickly wiped them away with a tissue.

'I guess it was artistic license,' she said.

Cseszi was sipping the drink still. Boss and Alex were smiling at each other approvingly.

'I think we should take a break,' Zanó said. 'There's a room where you can smoke if you wish. Let's say a ten-minute break?'

Gábor felt a thought come to him that wasn't his own. It was not the voice he would hear, for example, when telling himself jokes on the way to the pub. It was not formulated words that took shape but rather a desire, a need. Many of them left for the smoking room. As Gábor stood up too, he felt dizzy.

He didn't go to smoke with the others. He waited in a side corridor until Daniella arrived. He could hear her thoughts in his head just moments before, and he heard them again now. The woman stepped up to him. Gábor embraced her and held her tightly, just as she wished. He could feel her ribs, her tiny breasts, the tremor of her flesh. He couldn't help but think back to the woman lying on the autopsy table, and he was grateful for the warmth of another person's body, just as she was grateful for his warmth.

'Don't think about her!' said Daniella without opening her mouth. 'Hold me tighter!'

They stood holding each other a couple of minutes, then followed the others to grab a smoke.

Zanó left a large ashtray and some lighters in the smoking area, then withdrew. The room buzzed with thoughts and emotions, like a wasps' nest. Nobody talked about the collective opening of their minds, so Gábor thought it best not to bring it up.

'You're free to talk about it,' Mr. Kővári broke the silence. 'Telepathy. It's happening to all of us. It's one of the less useful side effects of the complexes, it will go away after a while. It's not a lasting thing.'

'Isn't it dangerous?'

'What? Opening up to strangers? Sure it is. On the other hand, soon we'll be so wasted that it won't matter at all,' laughed Mr. Kővári, his tongue moving with difficulty as if his mouth were filled with gravel.

'How many complexes are there?' Cseszi asked with a grin.

Mr. Kővári didn't answer, but lit up a new cigarillo instead. It was Boss who answered.

'He always serves seven. But we've never made it to the seventh.'

'Why not?' asked Gábor.

'You give up, dude! You can't take it. For me, six was the max. A few years back. Every year I vow to carry on until the end. But I can't. Impossible.'

'Is it the alcohol?'

'That too. And sometimes you just want to stay with one of them.'

'One of them?'

'Yeah, one of the drinks. If you like it. Like Feri here. He'll stay with the Scarlet now, am I right, Feri?'

Boss poked Feri. Feri nodded, wiping his tear-reddened eyes.

'We're all going for the grand prize,' Boss went on, 'the last one. It's the same every year.'

'What's the grand prize?' Cseszi asked before Gábor could.

'The Amber complex. It has to be pretty wild if it's going to top the sixth one. I drank the sixth once, and I almost burned out on it, you get me? Man, that's a tough one! I don't actually think it can be topped.'

Zanó appeared in the doorway with another bottle of Scarlet in his hands.

'So, what do you say, can we proceed?'

Everyone extinguished their cigarettes and left. Zanó placed the bottle on a bench. Feri nodded gratefully and remained in his place. Gábor was about to turn to leave when Feri grabbed his arm like a drowning man.

'Listen, I'm . . . sorry I didn't keep in touch with you.'

Gábor didn't know what to say. He hadn't thought of Feri for years and Feri knew that.

'No worries, man,' he said eventually.

Feri sobbed. Gábor felt embarrassment for him, even though he knew it was cruel. Feri didn't let go of his arm. Gábor looked around the empty room anxiously. The others must already be sitting around the table. Perhaps the new complex had been introduced by now. He felt an itch to leave for the next round. But Feri wouldn't let go. Finally Gábor pulled his arm violently out of his grip.

'It'll be all right,' he said. They both knew he was lying, but Feri didn't care anymore. He hugged the bottle of Scarlet to his chest.

At the table, Zanó was already in the process of opening the next bottle. Gábor rushed to take his seat, his mind buzzing like a beehive. He was curious about its name but was afraid to break the silence.

'Lily,' Gábor heard in his head. He smiled.

'This one is somewhat lighter, though not less complicated,' said Zanó as he caressed the bottle. Only now did Gábor understand that Zanó's thoughts didn't mix into the telepathic cacophony. Either Zanó kept everything to himself or he was empty inside.

The liquid was light yellow. Gábor smiled when the buzz of the separate thoughts streamed into one single voice as everyone tasted the Lily.

A man in a purple suit. Beard trimmed every morning, his gold-framed glasses hang on a chain around his neck. He stands by an oak table in a gigantic room. He takes a silver watch from his pocket and looks at the time. There are no hands on it. He drops the watch on the table.

There is an enormous, glassless window at the other end of the room. It's pitch dark outside. The man takes off his elegant overcoat and drops it on the floor. He stretches his limbs, the cracking of his joints reverberates through his body. He starts running, eyes fixed on the open window, the air whistling in his ears. His heart races.

He throws himself out of the window. But instead of falling, his nature changes in an instant.

Liquid splashes into liquid.

All senses explode. The guidelines of human perception cease to exist. There is a brief moment of panic, of control slipping, but then there is a sense of letting go. The rules have changed. There is no body any longer. The body is in liquid form now, it is matter of a different kind.

He is a yellow liquid, splashed into pitch black. It's a playful experience. The yellow expands and moves, shifts shape and nature, contracting solid elements within the darkness of its host. He shapes these elements, wears away at them. Time is of no importance; it doesn't yet exist. Only movement matters.

Gábor, as he perceived the complex in the battle and whirling of liquids, understood that the yellow liquid was wind. That he himself had become wind. That moment changed his perception, and now he didn't only see yellow against black, but wind against the world.

He captures a fistful of dust in deserts stretching to infinity, unleashes storms on empty plains. He caresses the tremendous leaves of giant trees the height of skyscrapers, still only toys for him. He tosses ocean waves to shores, where they crash into the rocks with bone-breaking force. He plays with clouds as he pleases. Sometimes he peeks into caves and sings a song among the rocks. There are no animals or human beings in this world, not yet or not anymore. One or two microbes travel with him, ones that he picked up as a favor and then threw away again somewhere, above seas or volcanoes. He ceases to be human, he is liquid and wind, for time eternal.

'This is a very pleasant complex,' said Mr. Kővári, 'with a long-lasting effect.'

He slurred the words, his face all flushed. Cseszi sat with her eyes closed, rocking herself gently, like a child about to fall asleep. Daniella smiled. Mihály scratched his chin. Boss leaned back in the chair.

'Yeah, this is really cool,' he said.

'Can I ask for some more of this later on?' Cseszi asked.

'No, my dear,' Zanó shook his head, 'you cannot go back to a complex, you can only go straight ahead or stay with the last one you had.'

'I'd like to have some more of this.'

'No problem, my dear. There is more. But then unfortunately you cannot taste the other ones.'

'I'll do that next year.'

'All right, my dear. I'll bring you more Lily. Is everyone else ready for the next one?'

Alex quietly fell off his chair. His unconscious body was dragged into a room where a mattress had been prepared for guests who fainted. Gábor thought that maybe now was the time to stop, to give up this binge-drinking race, but he had given up too many things already. What could he lose by continuing? His health? His self-respect? His future? He had already lost these things long ago.

Zanó showed up with a new bottle.

'This is the Indigo complex. It will be slightly heavier than the previous one, but just as exciting, I hope. If you'll allow me . . .'

Then he poured for everyone. Gábor shivered from excitement and knew he had made the right choice.

Red mist.

The senses are still virgin. You are at peace with silence and darkness. No reflection of the self, no distinction between the waking world and dreams. You don't even know that you're alive, because it's the only state you know.

Life is a kind of wriggling, a constant fidgeting deeper into a world that is welcoming, compassionate, soft and warm, a machine that works for you and for you alone. There are others of your kind in this darkness. They are all happy, without understanding what happiness is.

In the womb, before birth, your body moves. You hear a heartbeat, a rhythmic, deep rumble. That is all you have ever known.

Time is of no importance. You could stay here forever, but you are overtaken by a new sense of adventure. You wriggle in the space that now seems to be growing too cramped for you. You later identify this sensation as hunger.

You are isolated in a bubble, but outside another reality awaits, wilder, unpredictable and exciting, providing enough food to kill off this new feeling.

You start to flail, to scratch the wall of the bubble, instinctively drilling yourself ahead. You realize you have a mouth, so you bite and tear your way through this wall. The smell of food pours in through the cracks. Your hunger grows. You are overwhelmed by the excitement of a new world as you struggle, without reflection or reason, just to get out as soon as possible from your former shell.

Finally you're out and food is everywhere, like a sea that doesn't kill but nourishes you. You experience a new level of happiness, the satisfaction of devouring. After a while you devour according to a plan, digging a tunnel in the food, always straight ahead. You sense that yet another world awaits you. You sense others like yourself all around you, doing the same as you.

You reach a new layer. It's not food, but another shell. Again, you have to eat through it.

Finally you succeed. The shell cracks and you squeeze your body through the opening. It is a new world indeed, nothing like the previous one, empty, without food, cold, but somehow still appealing.

You are a spider. A little boy tied to a metal bar screams and watches in horror as spiders eat their way out of his flesh. He might have hours left before his vital organs are eaten up.

You return to eat some more before exploring further.

The complex ended here. Gábor's face was soaked in sweat. Daniella rose from her chair, took two steps running, then threw up. She lay down next to the pool of vomit, shivering. Mihály watched the girl, his face pale white. He didn't say a word. Mr. Kővári wanted to start analyzing the complex but his tongue refused to obey him. Boss covered his face with his palms, breathing heavily.

'I'm giving up. I'm giving up again,' Boss howled.

'Daniella?' Zanó asked the woman on the ground. She looked up at him with tears in her eyes.

'I want some more of this,' she answered.

'All right, my dear, I'll bring some more. Is everyone else ready for the next one?'

Gábor had second thoughts. The world was spinning, his own body felt alien to him. On the other hand, when this was all over, he would have to wake up every single day knowing that the miracle was right there in front of him and he had missed it again.

'I will have some,' he said as slowly and articulately as he could.

Zanó smiled. He looked at Mr. Kővári, who was focusing on not falling off his chair.

'And you?'

Mr. Kővári fixed his bloodshot eyes on Zanó, then nodded sluggishly. Zanó brought another bottle of Indigo for Daniella, who at first eyed the bottle with disgust, then started to drink anyway.

'The sixth in line is the Emerald complex. It's a heavy item, let it flow through you. Don't resist it. I'm really sorry, Mr. Kővári, that your wife couldn't join us, as I selected this one for her.'

He poured the Emerald complex and Gábor, before he could change his mind, took a sip. The drink, however, didn't allow only a single sip. As the first aromatic component spread, it required constant gulping until the glass was emptied.

The complex didn't unfold as a process, in phases. It was like a maze. It was simultaneously sensual and abstract, a maddening mirror game, a labyrinth in which you could easily get lost.

It starts with sunshine, somewhere in a desert, among goats. Heat and dust, long before Christ walked the very same sand. He had a mother, though she didn't give birth to him. She had found him among the stones, the nameless, child-shaped emptiness. Maybe she wanted to fill her own emptiness with him, that's why she took the abandoned baby, although everyone begged her not to. Nobody knows where he came from. Some say the rocks birthed him as punishment.

He was surrounded by nothing but despair, the emptiness of the desert, the carcasses of humans and animals scattered all over. He knew that life was lived somewhere else, that others were alive, but he wasn't. He simply existed, just like the hot sunshine, like the goat shit, like the water you squeeze into your mouth from a dirty rag. He was hungry, forever hungry, and he could never eat enough to feel satisfied. He seemed to be human, but they knew that he wasn't. That he was empty inside and couldn't be killed, though many had tried. He knew it too.

His mother sometimes caressed his head, telling him tales about the moon and the stars. He tried to find out where her voice was coming from, how and why it faded into nothingness, into thin air, how it was born in the warmth of the flesh and turned into cold nothing in the air.

He had a knife by then. One night he cut his mother's throat and devoured her body. That's when he understood his own nature, though he acted on instinct at first.

He left not a single bite, all of it was absorbed by the emptiness inside him. From every bit of tissue he gained memories, feelings, thoughts, until he possessed all of her, and he turned into the mother himself. He had never felt anything that came close to the ecstasy of consuming a life.

At last, he was someone. He lived on as the mother, eliminating his existence as a child. Nobody could tell the difference, his transformation was so complete.

It was then that he first felt love for a warrior. The warrior didn't notice that his lover was not human. They were lying on animal fur, the warrior let his lover ride him, because he saw nothing but a young, beautiful woman, and at the peak of his orgasm, the creature slit the man's throat and devoured his body too.

He was the warrior now, but soon he started to feel bored with this new life. After the joy of devouring there was nothing but emptiness; just because he took someone else's life did not mean he was capable of living it himself. He could only imitate it, and though his imitation was perfect, it didn't satisfy him. He could only experience life through devouring others, one life after the other.

This gave the complex the maze-like quality. Every time the creature ate up a life, he lived through it again: he himself was turned into what he destroyed. As Gábor experienced the life of the creature, he also experienced the lives of everyone it ate. The creature seldom remembered, the knowledge of its past rarely extended beyond the last *two or maybe three lives. But Gábor was still forced to experience and remember all of them.*

He slipped through immeasurable numbers of lifetimes, the first ones from well before the days of the earliest known empires. All of them started the same way: the coldness of the outer world, as the newborn slips out from between the mother's legs. And all of them ended the same way too: the ancient knife slits the throat, the monster looking deep into the victim's eyes before opening its terrible mouth for the first bite.

As the complex unfurled, Gábor, with his last conscious thought, made an attempt to dig his fingers down his throat and throw up, but his hand couldn't find his mouth. He wondered whether he would survive this complex. Then, as Zanó advised, he let go and let the drink take over.

The creature wanted to live through everything, happiness, pain, joy, grief — anything that was real. More real than himself.

Gábor felt a kinship with the creature. He truly did. Maybe that was the way to survive this ordeal.

He had been an emperor, a farmer, a pope, and a foundry worker. He had been a student and an illiterate peasant. He had been a rapist and a rape survivor. In Ancient Rome he ate a crucified person off the cross out of sheer curiosity. He had eaten lunatics who conversed with God in their heads, speechless idiots, beggars, orphans, blind and deaf people, as well as geniuses, athletes, spoiled children, actors, and soldiers. They all provided new points of views, new, unique life experiences he couldn't have harvested from life itself.

The tissue revealed all secrets, all thoughts, even those that the mind had long forgotten. The victims could preserve no part of themselves in death. Gábor lived a thousand lives and died a thousand deaths in the wine cellar.

Even the most seemingly mundane and trivial of lives became magnificently unique as the creature consumed them, and though all lives were special in their own way, there were outstanding gems among them. The creature had selected these, like a fine winemaker, with great care. There was the poet who, whenever writing a poem, caused a rain that wouldn't stop until the poem had been destroyed. His life was inter-

twined in a special way with nature. His senses were different too, he lived in the constant bliss of synesthesia; sight was touch to him, touch was sound, pain was a melody. There was the girl who was raised by a group of owls in the forest. The girl came to resemble an owl herself, both in appearance and behavior. Or the boy who was also six other boys around the world at the same time, sharing one single consciousness. As the creature ate the child, all the rest perished as well; in this way he ate them all. That was quite a feast.

The last lives appeared with clarity in the creature's mind as well, not just Gábor's. A boring philosopher, arrogant, always on his high horse. Then his girlfriend, a law student. Then the girlfriend's childhood friend. Then her twin sister. At last, he approached a woman in a bar: willful eyebrows, pitch-black hair. They went to a hotel room, and the monster took the woman's place.

The woman was Mr. Kővári's wife.

They fucked the night before coming to the cellar. Mr. Kővári didn't notice the difference, he had no idea that his life's worth was being measured, and he was seconds away from being consumed by the terror that had become his wife. During intercourse the creature kept wondering the whole time whether the winemaker was worth devouring. The creature ate his semen to get a taste.

The man was painfully boring, a pretentious asshole, and the creature didn't desire that life at all. Not even the collection of tastes stored on the man's tongue was worth the effort.

The complex ended with the woman sitting in the car, watching Mr. Kővári leaning on the hood of his Porsche, watching the chalk-white mountain.

A car was approaching. Gábor realized that he was seeing himself arriving on the scene, through the eyes of an aeons-old creature.

That's where the complex ended.

The creature adopted every characteristic of its victim: tastes, moods, illnesses. And since Mr. Kővári's wife loathed alcohol the creature declined to be present at the tasting. But had it drunk from the Emerald complex it would have found what it had been seeking for such a long time: its true self.

Mr. Kővári stared ahead, his eyes glassy and empty, like a dead animal's. He slowly slipped off his chair and spread across the floor unconscious.

Gábor felt a desire to lie down beside him and just let go. He burped but didn't vomit. He let the complex wash through him like a wave, purify him, then retreat. He stood up from his chair, which tipped over with a loud clunk. He felt dizzy. He took a hesitant step and grabbed on to the edge of the table. He looked around the room timidly. Mr. Kővári appeared dead. Cseszi was feigning sleep in a corner, but every now and then she would lift the bottle up to her lips and take a sip from the Lily complex. Boss was snoring in a corner. Daniella was drinking the Indigo and masturbating on the floor. The telepathic noise was only a murmur now. Everyone had temporarily lost their conscious self either in sleep or in the trance of a complex.

'It's only the two of us now, my friend,' Zanó smiled. He was the only sober person in the cellar.

Gábor wanted to say something but his tongue wouldn't move. He felt ants running around in his mouth.

'Come with me,' Zanó said. 'Our friends will be just fine here.'

Zanó left and Gábor stumbled behind him through a tunnel. His hands scraped against the wall, seeking support; he remembered his alcoholic grandfather, who could only move around if he was touching a wall the whole time. A few times Gábor lost sight of Zanó, then started to panic, thinking that he would get lost in the cellar system, that he would stroll drunkenly in the darkness forever, until he eventually found the room with the bottomless black hole in the middle, into which he would tumble, falling endlessly as if death were nothing but a soft bed.

At last they arrived in a gigantic room. From wall to wall, from floor to ceiling, it was covered with wine bottles. Gábor couldn't see an end to it. Zanó took a bottle off a shelf, pulled out the cork, and took a sip from the drink. He savored its taste with his eyes closed, then put it down. There was a painted symbol on the bottle. Gábor looked at the marking and it felt like looking into a mirror. The sign meant him. It was not the name his mother gave him; it was his true name, the name that contained his fate and his nature. It was a truer name than any he knew, even though it wasn't meant for human minds.

'This is you.' Zanó pointed at the bottle. 'Your life, from birth to death, in the form of a drink. Now I can say that I know you. Even better than you know yourself. And I believe you should taste the last item. The Amber. In fact, I know you're going to taste it.'

Gábor nodded, as much as his strength allowed. Of course he would.

'Do you know what this place is? This mountain? Do you know what it's made of? I can tell you, so that you'll feel better afterwards.'

Gábor didn't want to hear but couldn't speak anymore.

'This mountain, Gábor, is made up of the dead. Everyone who has ever lived, lives now, or ever will live in this world is here, the bones ground to a fine dust, compressed into stones. You are here as well, in this mountain. My mountain. Your fellows are here too, who came to taste the complexes. They are here alive, because I want them to drink, but they are also here dead. Everyone you know is here, and everyone you don't. Here is where you all end up. And I make complexes out of you all. This is why you exist. The sole purpose of your kind. I want you to remember this when you wake up. It is a peaceful thing to be part of this mountain. It doesn't matter whether you perceive your life as a failure or success. It is all just an aroma, no better or worse than any other. Remember that when this is over.'

Gábor wanted to cry, but he was too drunk. Zanó took the last bottle. It had an amber circle painted on it.

'This is the Amber complex. The last item served tonight.

Very few have ever tasted it.' Seeing as long as his eyes could see, Gábor thought. He didn't hesitate, he downed the complex without thinking.

Everything slipped away.

The experience was beyond comparison. The complex used each and every cell to unfold. It even used the minds of the others who were asleep and dreaming in the cellar; they wouldn't know it, but their minds had become part of the Amber complex, because its formulation required a number of people.

Gábor collapsed on the floor, a pool of urine gathering around him. He lost the better part of his own consciousness, as what the complex showed him went well beyond the limits of human perception.

It was God's point of view.

Gábor himself is the universe. All knowledge, sensation, and memory that had ever existed. The unconscious tranquility of time, the spinning of the nebulae, the self-centered orbiting of existence. The emptiness that stretches between matter, the clash of galaxies, the birth and collapse of suns and planets.

Burning metal and minerals start making love to become planets. On certain planets parasites appear, who demand more than the unconscious existence of matter. Every living creature is such a parasite, and Gábor lives through their lives. He experiences each of their cells as they mingle, divide, swallow up, and produce, not knowing of their own role in the life of a larger organism.

He experiences every grain of sand, every mountain, every drop of liquid, he becomes every storm in the universe, he pierces through nothingness as a comet, only to burn up in the atmosphere of a planet.

He also becomes every plant, each complete in itself, dreaming through life without senses, unfurling from the earth towards the light, or on certain planets from the crystallized clouds of the stratosphere, a million kilometers above the ground. He lives through the lives of all animals too, in an eternal search for food, warmth, and reproduction. He becomes every sound, every wave, every mechanism, every thought, he becomes birth and decay, he becomes every poem, novel, and idea. For him, the decomposition of a cell is equal to the deconstruction of the universe.

The only thing he can't see is Zanó and his mountain made of the dead, with the bunch of grapes that obtain their flavor from lives. It somehow sits outside the realm of the known existence.

And just like before, now he also knows something that the universe doesn't. He can even see that which the universe cannot see. The skin of the grape, the flesh of which is the world we live in, hanging on a stem, waiting for Zanó to come and harvest.

He awoke to find himself shivering on the cold concrete, a hundred meters from the Outskirts Pub. There was a pool of vomit by his face. His nose was filled with the smell of smoke in autumn. He tried to get to his feet, but he felt dizzy. He couldn't think straight, his thoughts scattered before they could take shape and make sense. Finally he rose up and staggered towards the pub, leaning against its wall, then walking on like this, finding stability in the solid matter of the pub. He wanted to enter, for warmth if nothing else. It was too early for it to be open.

From the door his own picture stared at him from a photocopied flyer. 'LOST! We are looking for Gábor Szeiber, who left for the Outskirts Pub on the night of November 3rd.'

This was followed by a description and his mother's phone number. Gábor patted his pockets, searching for his phone. His fingers touched the neck of a wine bottle. He pulled it out; a symbol was painted on the side of the bottle. Gábor's stomach started to cramp at the sight; it was like looking in the mirror. He remembered a gray-haired man taking a sip from this bottle, but he couldn't recollect the entire scene. Maybe it would come to him later, he thought.

He shook his head and set off towards home with unsure steps, hugging himself to keep warm. In the mailbox he found a free newspaper. Judging by the date, nearly two weeks had passed since the night he went out to get a drink, and Gábor didn't want to even start thinking about the implications of this. One thing was for sure: he could kiss his job goodbye.

He saw the yellow gate. For the first time in years he yearned for that dreadful house because it meant sleep and dreaming, possibly forever. He went through the rusty gate, but the door to the house was locked. He found he had lost his keys. He banged on the door. Nobody was home.

He sat down on the doorstep, covering his face with his hand. He was too tired to think. The gate screeched again. Gábor knew it wasn't his mother; he knew the sound of her steps.

'I didn't think you'd have the balls to come back.' Gábor looked up. It was Feri; not his friend, but the killer. One of his arms was in a cast. The other one held a knife. 'You shouldn't have come back. I thought you were smart and disappeared.'

Gábor couldn't speak, he was too hungover for that. He got to his feet with great difficulty.

'I saw you on the street, by the pub,' Feri went on. 'You look like shit. Been out on a binge?'

Gábor nodded and wanted to say something, but Feri approached him in two steps and stabbed him in the stomach.

'I'm sorry, mate, it's got to be done. Always got to be done,' he whispered.

Gábor could feel the hot blood spilling down on his trousers. His flesh was on fire as Feri pulled the blade upwards. Gábor felt debilitated. He had the feeling that he had seen this somewhere before, and a serenity settled over him. It had to be this way. He thought of a mountain, and he felt no fear. His legs gave way and he collapsed into his own blood, which had gathered in a pool.

He wanted to say something, one last thing, anything that came to his mind, but he died before he could do it. He kept his eyes open, to see with them for as long as he could.

Feri watched as life abandoned Gábor. This was his fourth

kill, and he liked it. He enjoyed killing people. He knew he would get caught soon. Everyone always gets caught. He was surprised he was not immediately taken in after the murder of Máté, but the car crash provided a perfect alibi.

He watched the body getting colder, and he thought he should be running. Then he noticed the wine bottle. He felt thirsty, like he always did after a kill. He wanted booze and he wanted to fuck.

He reached for the bottle and uncorked it. He took a whiff of the scent; it smelled like alcohol. Maybe wine, or watered down pálinka, he thought. He poured a sample onto his palm. He wanted to make sure it wasn't antifreeze. Every year a number of alcoholics went blind or died from drinking antifreeze, on purpose or by accident.

But it wasn't that. It was wine. Feri looked around the garden. It was dawn; he had time. He knew he did. And if anyone saw him, so what? He had his knife on him.

Feri took a swig from the bottle. He wasn't prepared for what was about to happen.

Later the murder made the news. The police were careful not to specify what had happened, because there just wasn't any explanation. Gábor's mother found his body and the other body lying right next to it, in the same position as the first one, with the same type of stab wound, although this one was clearly self-inflicted.

The second body was Gábor too, even though the clothes he had on were different. Two Gábors, dead, facing each other with the same expression on their faces.

There was an empty wine bottle lying between the two of them.

Sky Filled With Crows, Then Nothing at All

'The psalm turned into heavy metal
It was not the end, only the beginning!
Devil, brother, keep playing!
I shiver as I listen to your music!'
(Pokolgép, 'Midnight Bell')

I crawl out from underneath his bed. It's midnight and he's asleep, snoring under the blanket, reeking of booze. He drank too much again, beer and shots of pálinka. He should take better care of himself, but it's not up to me to make decisions for him. I sit on the floor and observe the night; I'm hunting for signs in the shadows, in the barking of dogs, in the murmur of the boiler. No message for me tonight. I get up and look out into the street. Everything is still and quiet, almost like before the creation of the universe. Those were good times.

Cassette tapes lie scattered across the floor. He got drunk listening to his old demos again. There is a gutted computer in the corner. I think the video card is broken. Sometimes I have an urge to buy him a new one so he can finish his new album. I wonder how the finished record would sound. I hear it in his head, the ideas of it, but music is not made in the head, it's made in the recording room.

I'm not a heavy metal fan. I listen to it because of him, Csaba, but I prefer Handel and Mozart. Call me old-fashioned. Occasionally I go to Berlin and Vienna and New York to listen to the philharmonics or one of the string quartets that I like. I sometimes go to churches as well, mainly for Bach. A holiday, if you like. Even I need it from time to time.

I give him an hour, then I take out the nightmare. It's hiding in my pocket; I've been working on it under the bed for two days. I shape it into a spider and carefully place it between Csaba's lips. The spider crawls nimbly down Csaba's throat and becomes one with him.

Csaba wakes up roaring an hour later. That's how long the nightmare is; by then I'm back under the bed again, planning the next nightmare.

In the morning he can't see me, but I'm standing right behind him. I watch him as he shaves. He usually doesn't, but now he's going to the welfare office for a subsidy. He won't get it, I made sure of that. I study his face, the wrinkles at the corners of his eyes. I worry. He's a little pale. I wonder if this face is up for second chances. I think yes, maybe. He still has that ferocity in his eyes that used to make women go crazy when he was on stage. He didn't grow a belly, despite eating white bread and sausages all the time, canned beans too if they were cheap in the shop, and he often drinks red wine or beer in the evening. Good genes, I guess.

Still, he is just a shadow of his former self. What a handsome man he was back in the day! Up until his mid-forties he stayed in excellent shape. Then he moved to the countryside and fell apart. I'm not saying I didn't have a hand in it, but at the end of the day everything was his own decision. I only offer him opportunities to divert from the path he originally planned to take, and of course I occasionally put an obstacle in his way. Nothing he couldn't overcome if he truly put his heart into it.

The table is covered with bills. Two months of gas, flat rate for water, a semi-annual fee for trash, and the next installment on the mortgage. Csaba doesn't even look at them. He can't, his stomach cramps at just the thought of them. Every bill represents failure, missed opportunities, a wasted life.

He puts on his Manowar T-shirt. It's a superstition he's been trying to get rid of, but somehow he thinks it will bring him luck. It was given to him by Joey DeMaio before the '94 concert at Petőfi Stadium in Budapest. He only wears it once or twice a year so it doesn't get worn out. He's not even a big Manowar fan. Still, it's a good luck charm.

He heads to the welfare office and I'm left alone. I could go with him, but I know how it will go, and it breaks my heart. Now I'm bored. It's a shame that out of all places he moved to Kál. People only come here to complain about life, then die. In Budapest I could at least always find a church playing a cantata or a fugue. There's nothing here, only a couple of pubs and a post office.

He starts drinking at two. The extra-cheap beer is on sale at the shop. He's bought a dozen cans. I'm sitting next to him. His hands are shaking, a Fecske cigarillo is burning between his fingers. I hate the smell of it, it reminds me of hell. He used to smoke Marlboros, but these are infinitely cheaper.

I feel it's time to try it again. I touch his hand with my claws and he looks at me.

'Again?' he asks. His voice is genuinely annoyed. 'When will you leave me alone once and for all?'

I grin. I don't want to, but it's the custom of my trade. It makes me look more evil, I assume. A few worms fall out from between my teeth. I hate that part, but I can't do anything about it. Worms are part of my nature.

'Join,' I implore him. He already knows what it's all about.

He takes a sip from his beer.

'Go fuck yourself,' he says in a raspy voice. 'I've had enough of you and your bullshit.'

He looks into my eyes and I see emptiness there. This could be a good sign too! It could mean that he is ready to give up on everything in order to gain everything. But maybe he is just bored with my face. Maybe I should change it again, perhaps I would be more successful that way.

'You don't have much time left,' I tell him ominously. 'The Four are standing at the gate.'

Csaba spits on the floor.

'Tell them to go fuck themselves too!' he says, then takes a deep drag from the disgusting cigarillo. When he looks at me again, I'm no longer visible to his eyes. He doesn't think I can see him when he cries, but I do. I'm always by his side when he gets emotional.

I gave him his first heavy metal tape. We could say that it's all been my fault. It was a cassette copy of a record smuggled in from the West, Judas Priest's *Killing Machine* album. Later I got him some more. I always hid them among his father's tapes: the first Accept album, the first two records from Black Sabbath, *Overkill* by Motörhead. I sat there by his side as he listened to them. I heard every song through his ears. Although 'Hell Bent for Leather' and 'Stay Clean' don't measure up to a Bach fugue or a Rachmaninoff concerto, I could still appreciate their harsh energy. I felt Csaba's heart quicken at the rhythm of the drums as he tried to follow the riffs with his fingers. I thought I was being clever. But it only gave him an attitude.

I often think that I should have gotten him books instead of the tapes; words might have made his mission clearer to him. But unfortunately he was born at the wrong time, in the wrong place, enclosed in the cage of the Hungarian language and without the desire to learn another; how could I have arranged for him to get hold of any of the books even of that swindler Crowley? Not to mention the original edition of *Unaussprechlichen Kulten*? No book written by human hands could express precisely what Csaba's role in the world was, but at least they would have created a common language between us. I would have had something to build on. But nothing is available in Hungarian, nothing that could spark his imagination. Reading is despised around these parts anyway.

So music was the only thing left. Music is universal, and yet what a bad influence it has on people.

Later he got some tapes of his own, smuggled in from Vienna: Iron Maiden, Venom, Slayer, Dio, Tankard. He listened to everything with fanatical respect. He was given his first guitar at the age of thirteen, along with a tiny amplifier. He was stubborn even back then, too stubborn for his own good. He could have easily saved himself had he accepted my offer back at that time. But it's kind of my fault too that he didn't.

I made another mistake; I thought if I based my appearance on the visuals of the heavy metal album art he would trust me more. I put horns on my head, I grew a tail and hooves. I wore leather vests like the demons on some of the covers. He was practicing on his guitar when I first revealed myself to him. I even broke a mirror in his room to make my entrance more dramatic. I admit that I should have chosen a different strategy. Perhaps if I had chosen a more attractive look I could have won him over the first time around.

He didn't get scared, or not as much as he should have, seeing a demon appear in his room. I attribute this to the fact that I had prepared him for my arrival with the records. I had read in Western papers that heavy metal was the music of the devil, and I thought that listening to it would lay the groundwork for my manifestation. That's why I put so much effort into the horns. They seemed to make or break a demon.

I got off on the wrong foot about it from the beginning. I only talked about our task, our mission, his and mine. Had I started off in a different way, he might have said yes right away. Because the mission isn't important; it's not the real reason he should say yes, anyway.

I should tell you about the first moment of my life. I had no form yet, but I awoke with a purpose. In that first second I didn't know what I was, but I knew him already. He was the reason I existed. I woke up roaring, born ready, waiting for my work to begin. Waiting for Csaba to be born. The wait alone was several aeons, it started even before Earth was formed from burning-hot rocks.

I lived under the bed while he took shape cell by cell in his mother's womb. I had already seen his dreams back when he was yet unborn. When he slipped out of his mother, I was the first to sniff him and cry from happiness. It was the first time I truly cried, bloody tears pouring from my eyes. In the entire universe he is the only thing that means anything to me, and my sole happiness would be if he took the offer. That's what I should have talked about. How much I loved him.

Is it any wonder he said no? All he saw was a monster, a demon who wouldn't give him a break. All he had to do was take his rightful place on the Midnight Throne, leading the army of the dead against the world. Victory was guaranteed; in the end everything would be his. The power, the glory, life eternal. After that any of his desires would have been instantly satisfied. All he would have to do is burn down time itself as the leader of the dead. It's not a question of right or wrong. He was created for this purpose. The only thing he had to do was say yes.

I explained it to him the first time around. He refused back then, he still refuses now. Yet no one else can sit on the Throne but him. At the age of sixteen, not long after my first manifestation, he gave a concert with his first band, which he named Killing Machine, after the Priest album. His father didn't see the show; they were barely talking to each other by then. But I was there, and I shed bloody tears after each song. I was so proud of him, even though they mostly played covers. At their next show they played a song of their own, called 'War in Hell'. I liked it, although I could also hear that it was a rehash of the main theme from an Accept song. The lyrics in particular appealed to me, and I was sure he would say yes sooner or later. He was still young, struggling with the idea of responsibility. I even supported his musical career in the beginning; I thought a couple of songs like 'War in Hell' would eventually lead him to accept his fate. Back then I thought we had all the time in the world. I was mistaken, of course.

He was nineteen when he recorded his first LP. By then, he had changed the name of the band to Steelbird. The record, called *The First Battle*, was a great success in Hungary. Songs like 'The Child of Plague' and 'Satanic Pact' are still often played in rock clubs. Their next record, *Out of My Way!* was successful too. They were at their peak playing as the supporting act for Judas Priest during the Hungarian stop on the *Painkiller* tour. Before the show I manifested again in the green room. This time I took the form of an attractive woman; my body was covered in tight leather clothes and tattoos, my face was based on models from German magazines. I adjusted the size of the breasts according to Csaba's dreams. I made my offer again.

Once more he said no.

I was disappointed. In him, but mostly in myself. A year later he got married to one of his groupies. Her name was Szilvia. The relationship didn't last a year; it turned out that Csaba was infertile. Szilvia wanted children.

This came as a surprise to them, but not to me. It was my doing, of course, in order to motivate Csaba, nudge him towards the Throne.

The divorce was the beginning of a downturn. I took care of the downward spiral. No major tragedy, just a series of unfortunate accidents, missed opportunities, broken promises.

Now he sits in his room at night and plays the guitar. I recognize the riff, it's the penultimate song on Steelbird's *Night March* album, called 'Undefeated'. His phone rings and sadness grips my heart. I know who's calling and why.

Endre Orsós was the bassist of Steelbird, the only band member besides Csaba who played on every single LP. He was Csaba's friend. Maybe the only one. Now his wife Márta is on the phone; Endre married her after his first heart attack seven years ago. Csaba was their best man.

I sat by his side when he died a couple of hours ago. He

didn't know me, but Csaba's friends are my friends too. A second heart attack, not far from his workshop at the edge of the woods. Nobody noticed he had collapsed, clawing at his chest, gasping for air, only me. I held his hand until he went cold. The dying see; they always see me in my purest form, the form I have never seen myself because there is no mirror to reflect it.

I hope he didn't see me as a monster. I hope I didn't make his last moments even more horrible than they already were.

After the call Csaba drinks through the whole night. He has to borrow money to buy the booze, but he drinks anyway and remembers. He puts on a Steelbird album, the final LP called *To Live or to Die*. He puts the final song on repeat. The only Steelbird song without drums, only acoustic guitars and violin. It's kind of a ballad, titled 'Like Crows in the Sky'. He and Endre wrote it together. Not a very good song, but what Steelbird song is?

I recall the afternoon they wrote it. They were rehearsing in a garage out in an abandoned industrial facility by the edge of the forest. I liked that garage. It almost felt like a kind of a home, since the darkness of the forest was always whispering into my ears, hastening me, 'now-now' rustled the leaves, 'now-now' hissed the snakes. But I knew the time was not ripe. Csaba was not yet ready for the Throne. He sat by the edge of the forest with Endre, each holding a beer. I wished I could sit there with them, I wished I too could sip the lukewarm Kőbányai, like I was one of them. I kneeled on the ground and listened to the two of them talk. We looked up at the sky darkened by crows, our ears filled up with the caws. I gestured towards the sky as a greeting, but nobody saw it. The crows returned to their nests in the woods, resting for the night. That was when Endre dropped the piece of wisdom the song was based on.

'We're just like these crows,' he said. 'For a minute we fill up the sky, then poof, we're gone, not a trace left. Nothing.'

I wanted to hug Endre. This was what I had been trying to explain to Csaba his entire life. This was what I offered a way out from. To become the sky itself, and not just a passing bird against it.

Silence settled upon them. Csaba was quiet. I could feel that deep down in him something was changing. He remained silent a little longer, then said, 'Yeah,' and took another sip.

By the next day they had finalized the song, but the finished version conveyed very little of the atmosphere of the previous night. The audience still liked it. It was often the penultimate song at their shows.

I'm looking at Csaba now. He's sitting by the table crying. I want to hug him, but he would only push me away, even if he saw me crying. Tonight I will be ready with a new nightmare. It will be about the afternoon full of crows, the last conversation between them in Csaba's kitchen, the bills and the welfare office. I hope this will be the push that will finally convince him.

At midnight I put the spider in his mouth and walk out to the garden. I remember his bitterness when he ended up moving here, to this dreadful little village in the eastern part of the country. At the time he wanted to start a post-Steelbird career, but his second band failed. The youngsters were listening to music that he simply couldn't understand anymore. The new, trendy online outlets even saw the legacy of Steelbird as a mere joke, an embarrassment to modern music, made up of elements stolen from here and there. It was revealed that Tibi, the first singer, had been an informer for the Communist regime up until '89. Csaba had had enough, and he couldn't afford an apartment in Budapest anymore.

Csaba spent almost all of his money on this crumbling house, as far from Budapest as possible. But life in the countryside was harder than he thought. He had no talent for anything apart from making music (and not even for that, according to some). He quickly burned through his meager savings.

I sit down on a bench in the garden and listen to the nighttime noises. This time they are sending me a message; every fiber of nature screams it, yet only I can hear. Now I know for sure that I have a heart, because it withers from sadness when I learn the news. I knew this day would come eventually; just as Csaba knew that one day he would grow old. Still, neither of us tried hard enough, we didn't pursue our goals ferociously enough.

Why is he so stubborn? Is it my fault? Did I shape him to be like this with the tapes? I hear his thoughts in my head, I can feel what he feels, as if we were guitar and amplifier connected; and yet I can never fully get to know him. He will forever remain a beautiful mystery to me. I hear screaming from inside the house: Csaba is waking up from the nightmare.

The funeral is held a week later, in Endre's hometown. He is buried next to his parents. It is raining. Everyone wears black, so it's not that different from the crowd at a Steelbird show. Most of the band members are there, even Tibi, the original singer. Nobody cares anymore whether he was an informer or not. The song 'Like Crows in the Sky' plays from the speakers. Everyone is crying by the time the song is over, then they bury Endre. Later on they drink in the pub across the street from the cemetery. They drink and remember, drink and laugh, drink and cry. I wish I could be drinking with them, but I just watch from the dark corners. If I closed my eyes I could imagine them talking to me.

They toss around the idea of getting the band back together again, maybe for a memorial show. Possibly even recording a final album; Csaba mentions that he has an album's worth of songs on his computer. Everyone nods significantly, like they're seriously considering the offer. He only mentions later on to Tibi that he can't even turn on his computer anymore; that everything he has done throughout his life has now turned into ruins, worthless rubbish. Then he throws up.

Later that night he is offered a job. I made it happen. I created the idea through dreams and impressions; my tiny spiders can crawl into any place and any person. The offer is being made by a woman named Betti Csernák; her father was a big Steelbird fan. As a child she often saw them play live. She came to the funeral to pay her respects, and there, understanding Csaba's situation, she makes him an offer. She has a small company, and there is an opening.

It's not a difficult job; he would need to inspect, supervise, and register the merchandise at the headquarters of her export-import company. It would be just perfect for Csaba. He asks for a day to think it over. I know that if he says yes, then he will also take his place on the Throne. With people like him, one small crack in the wall of self-esteem is enough to completely break it down.

He roams the streets drunk the entire night, thinking about the offer. Work, from 8 a.m. to 4 p.m., fixed salary, cafeteria. With the money he could buy a video card, new clothes, could maybe even heat his house properly come winter. The memorial concert and the final album could be arranged, because his life would be in working order again, even if in a limited capacity. I decide that he needs a little push now, so I make myself visible.

He gets a glimpse of me on the surface of a puddle, and he spits right into the water. I don't even need to say a word, he already knows what I want. But this time he refrains from insulting me; he just watches me. Perhaps it's the first time he really sees me. Maybe for the first time he can see what I really am, behind my appearance. Then he steps into the puddle and keeps chasing the dawn. I sit down on a bench and wait.

I feel I'm standing at the gates of success. If he breaks tomorrow, then I might still be in time. Then I might still be able to save the both of us. I touch my chest with my claws. I can still feel the horrible black fingers inside me as they shaped my soul, as they tied it to the life of a mortal. In the darkness before creation I didn't even have eyes, yet I could feel the connection with someone who was just a promise. I was already alive when he was born; yet I took my first true breath alongside him. I cried when he cried.

I can feel the other form hidden deep down inside me; the form I would take if he sat on the Throne. I would be his counselor, his dog, his general, whatever he needed. I could defeat time and space, life and death, memories and dreams. By his side I could be everything. Now I'm nothing. Only a thought, a dream, a possibility. I shiver, my soaked fur quivers. I would like to sleep like humans do; I have never slept in my entire life, only made dreams for others.

I'm lying under his bed at dawn when he wakes up. The director of the Steelbird fan club found Csaba this apartment and let him use it for free for one night so he wouldn't have to pay for accommodation. He washes his face in the tiny lavatory, then sets out to meet with Betti. He has a hard time finding his way around in the city. They meet in a cafe, the deafening shriek of the coffee machines interrupting their conversation from time to time. I don't sit down, I'm walking back and forth around the tables like an excited dog. I strain my ears to detect even the slightest change of tone in their voices.

'I don't accept your offer,' he says between two coughs, as coolly as he can.

Betti nods as if she had expected this, although her eyes are sad.

'I see,' she says. 'We can find you something easier, office work or ...'

Csaba raises his hand to hush the girl. She recognizes the gesture from the concerts. That was how Csaba used to silence the audience when he was about to play an acoustic song.

'It's not about the difficulty,' Csaba explains. 'It's just that I don't want anyone to order me around. No one telling me when I should get to work, what I should do, how I should do it. I don't want anyone telling me anything. Not even for money. I'm a free spirit, you see.'

And at this point, as if he can see me, he glances at me. Of course he can't. I determine when I'm there for his eyes and when I'm not; but he suspects I'm standing there. Maybe even hopes for it. I smile. That attitude! He has always been stubborn; he was raised that way. Always follow your dreams. Life has taught him that, I've taught him that, music has taught him that. It's what he's done his whole life.

Of course he will not ascend to the Throne. Someone told him he had to do it, so of course he won't. In spite of Betti's begging him for half an hour Csaba refuses each and every offer, even those that wouldn't require him to do any actual work. It's a matter of principle. He will be no one's slave, he says, and I recognize the reference to a song on their second album. The song is called 'No Slave for You'. 'I won't be your slave, even if I could be a king of slaves.' This song was written to me, about me. I'm very proud of that.

In the afternoon we sit on the train. He only paid the fare for halfway to save money, now he's hoping the controller won't catch him. He gets lucky.

That night I give it a try for the final time. We've had more than fifty years of this push-and-pull, yet now we only have hours left. I manifest to him and make my offer again.

'Take the Midnight Throne,' I tell him in a sonorous voice. 'Lead the army of the dead!'

Etc., etc., etc.

When he says no, I throw myself at his feet and start begging. This doesn't help. I scold him. I call him a stubborn bastard, a worthless nobody, a terrible musician. He starts throwing insults at me as well, venting the rage left in him. He calls me weak, a piece of shit, a living example of failure. There's truth in his insults, just like there's truth in mine. I exist solely to tempt him, and yet I'm incapable of doing so. What kind of a demon crawls on the floor, kissing the feet of a human? What kind of a demon begs his victim? Still, I don't feel ashamed. I'm doing it all for him. I'm doing it out of love.

Finally I give up. I give up once and for all.

That night I refrain from setting him up with a new nightmare. I know what's about to happen in a few hours, and I'm contemplating the implications of it. I wonder how he'll take the news that is fast approaching.

In the night the birds sing louder, the worms turn anxiously in the soil. A light bulb is switched off in the kitchen.

I think of the last Steelbird concert. It was not meant to be the final one, but a month later everyone had a falling out with everyone else. I didn't enjoy the dissolution of the band, even though I made it happen. I thought it was the only way. Maybe I was wrong, but wrongs don't matter anymore. They were playing in the Wigwam Club for a half-full house. He had already noticed the girl before the concert; she was wearing a Steelbird T-shirt with the sleeves cut off, her messy black hair falling over her shoulders. The lyrics for 'No Slave for You' were tattooed on her upper arm. After the concert they met up. Csaba invited the girl backstage. The girl had long been dreaming about Csaba; I made those dreams myself. No matter how much I was annoyed by the thought, no matter how much I hated to consider the possibility of failure, I needed a plan B. Csaba thought he was infertile.

That was true; he couldn't father children – unless I let him.

That night I did. Neither of them were fans of safe sex. After that night they never met again.

Until now. He sees her approaching the gate and at first he can't quite place her. It's been years. But finally it comes back to him, although he doesn't yet understand, not even when he sees the child.

'She's yours,' says the girl, who is now a woman.

Her name is Ildikó Kőhegyi, and she still has the tattoo on her arm, although she has been checking online to see how she can get rid of it. Csaba is not interested in the woman right now, neither am I. He is watching the little girl. She has her father's eyes, dark green and deeply sad; her mouth is her mother's. A beautiful, beautiful girl. Oh, how I wish I could take care of her. But it can't be so.

Another one like me stands behind her; I greet him with a nod. The thing nods back and reveals his true form to me, and I return the gesture. This is the first time in my life I've met my own kind, and my heart pangs with pain at the thought that he was created in one of the forges of the universe only a few years ago. I had long been roaming the Earth by the time his soul was linked to the girl I created. I felt old. I wonder whether he cried when the girl was born. I wonder whether he will also protect his own as I protected Csaba. I have so many things to ask him, and I sense he feels the same, but we remain silent. We have a lot of questions, but nothing to say to each other; each has to follow his own path.

I failed; it's his turn now to fail or succeed. My time is past. The girl is the new heir to the Throne; Csaba and I have become wasted opportunities. I look at the demon and the girl standing next to each other. They fit together well. They are just as much my children as they are Csaba's. I feel joy and sadness at the same time; I see life and death staring at one another.

Csaba barely speaks a word the entire night. He watches the little girl; he sucks up the stories about his child, one after the other. He doesn't even ask Ildikó why she didn't come back to him with their daughter, why she didn't sue him for child support, why she didn't abort her. How could she have, such a beautiful little girl? Such a little angel? And, of course, I guided Ildikó's hands for a long while.

She tells stories about her. We step on them like stones over a river, we jump from one to the other, until we arrive to the present time. They are leaving the country forever. They're moving to Australia, with Ildikó's new boyfriend; she only wanted the little girl to see her father for the first and last time. It's the demon's work, I know. I nod to the girl's demon.

Skillful. Australia is full of dark secrets, unholy places. It will be easy to navigate the kid towards the Throne. It's lucky she was born at a time when free travel is so easy; she already speaks two languages and is learning a third from her new dad. The child doesn't talk at all the whole night. She sometimes glances at her father and sometimes at me as if she can see me. Who knows, maybe she can. Maybe she can already see everything. Maybe I'm the one who is blind to the world's things, an old monster lagging way behind.

They leave around midnight. As a farewell gift I give a nightmare to the demon, and he gives me a lock of hair from a burnt Barbie doll. Csaba gives a present to the girl as well. I feel my heart sinking when I see that it's Judas Priest's *Killing Machine* album. The first album I gave to Csaba. Csaba transferred the uncontested right to the Throne to his daughter by giving her a present. Now even if he wanted to he couldn't take the Throne.

I will never reach my final form.

They leave, and with that my work is finished.

I could leave here, the whole world is mine. I could go to Vienna or New York. I could take on a human appearance. I could listen to the best performers of Chopin, Schubert, Brahms, and Vivaldi. I could enjoy life for as long as Csaba's life lasts. But all that is emptiness. Csaba is the only true thing for me. The only thing real in this world. When he ceases to exist, I do too; I'll turn into dust and wind the moment his heart stops beating.

Csaba sits on the porch and opens a cheap beer. He watches the night sky. I know he feels that something has changed. That he's lost something by gaining something else.

'Are you here?' he asks.

I don't know whom he's asking, then I realize.

I make myself visible to him. He looks at me from head to toe, then nods at me. He picks up a can of beer from the floor and throws it to me. I catch it.

'Have a drink with me!' he says, and I feel joy I thought I

could only feel standing by the Midnight Throne. I pop up the aluminum tab with my claws and take a sip from the beer. It tastes terrible, but wonderful.

We drink until dawn, telling old stories. We laugh and we cry. At last we are one; he's the only one left for me, and I'm the only one left for him. I promise to get him a new video card. He smiles but shakes his head, he's not sure it's worth it. But I know he'll come around; I know that together we can finish that record.

At dawn Csaba falls asleep. I carefully cover him with a blanket so he won't catch cold. Then I go out to the garden and sniff the cold, fresh morning air. I hear cawing. I look up to the sky. The crows are just flying out from the woods towards the fields. I watch them until they're gone, until nothing is left but the clear gray sky.

Walks Among You

The mourners know the priest is lying, for life is nothing but the absence of truth. Yet they remain silent and listen to his words. Outside the wind is blowing; the temple sounds like a shivering old man.

The woman's corpse lies on the catafalque, her arms crossed over her chest, her eyes covered with black velvet. The mourners stand with their eyes on the floor. The church is full. The air is getting stale.

They all know who she is. She remains Aunt Márti, even in death. Some of them only know her from the TV screen. Many of the mourners remember how she loved having a chat over a cup of chamomile tea.

The mourners are silent. They are silent because the priest is speaking, his glasses on the verge of sliding off his reddish nose. His voice quavers with uncertainty. He looks up as if unsure he's in the right place at all. He continues.

'A funeral is the most beautiful thing in any life,' he says in a sonorous voice, his words echoed by the church walls. 'She, the departed, is here and there at the same time now, standing on a bridge that connects life with death, existence with nonexistence, uncertainty with certainty. The deceased settles amongst our memories, incapable of action, only a passive reminder of the past, a shadow in the fog, which no one pays attention to anymore. She moves from present tense to past.'

He glances at the book lying open in front of him on the consecrated table. He pinches the frame of his glasses between his fingers and pushes it up his nose slightly.

'At funerals miracles happen!' he goes on. 'Whether we see them or not. But miracles are not a matter of perception; they are not for our eyes to see or our minds to understand. Just like the universe, a miracle is independent from us and indifferent to us.'

The priest closes the book and bows his head.

'Let us pray and sing, friends and brethren. And let us not forget that . . .'

'. . . he's always watching! Always watching!'

Her schoolmates yell this at Leila in the locker room. At this point Aunt Márti is practically dead, barely still breathing in a room with her back propped up by pillows, while Leila is preparing for her gym class at school. Soon the old lady will be lying on the catafalque, everyone knows that, though nobody knows when yet.

'He's always watching! Watching your cunt! Watching your asshole! Watching your tits!'

They're getting ready for gym in the sweaty locker room, and it's always the same story. It's mostly the girls who do it, but sometimes even the boys come over from their locker room to toss sandwiches, cans of Coke, rocks, chalk at her and to throw her clothes and bag on the floor. Gym class is the perfect time for bullying. Leila tried to get an exemption from it, but without success. She gets teased and shoved around in the hallways and classrooms too, but the locker room is the real torture chamber. She asks her parents at least once a month to pull her out of this school.

'We must endure these hardships. We must stand up for our faith,' her father always says, his gray eyes piercing through his daughter as if he wanted to pin her to the wall with his gaze. 'We will be expected to make greater sacrifices in the future, much greater than our comfort at school,' he continues, ending the discussion.

We must stand up for our faith, Leila thinks.

Her eyes fill with tears at the mockery of their religious doctrine. It's the basis of her faith, and now they make it sound dirty, sexual. It gets to her every time, even though she tries to deny it. She knows he is watching, always watching. But she imagines he is watching her from above, through the eyes of others, or from dark corners. He watches from inside her heart and soul. But to imagine that he's watching inside her body, watching her orifices, she finds that too disturbing.

She hates the girls for this.

Later that day she finds a dead cat in her bag. Blood from its corpse is smeared all over her books, her snacks, her money, her pocket prayer book. She knows which girl did it, because she smirks when Leila reaches into her schoolbag. A person has to stand up for her faith, so now Leila finally stands up for it. She hits and scratches, she hears nothing except her own raging scream, she feels nothing other than the glorious pain of her nails carving into skin. The other girl screams too, blood flowing down her face. For a moment Leila feels content.

She is summoned to the principal's office afterwards. The principal has a moustache and a bald spot on the top of his head. He keeps a photo on his desk of himself holding an oversized fish in his hands. Leila closes the door, her face still flushed from anger and crying. The principal takes off his gray jacket and places it on the chair. He unbuttons the sleeve of his shirt and stops right in front of Leila. He smells of mint and cigarettes. The girl, her lips quivering, tries to find the right words to explain how it felt to touch the stiff, dead flesh hidden among her books; how she'll never be able to get rid of the stench – how even her holy pocket prayer book stinks of death. How the carcass will forever remind her of Aunt Márti, at home dying. She says none of this.

The principal slaps her in the face as hard as he can. Leila holds on to the desk so she doesn't fall over. She doesn't raise her hands to touch the burning skin on her face, she doesn't want to seem weak, but she's afraid she might be bleeding. She drools from the impact of the blow but doesn't even dare to wipe it off. Silence hangs over the room. She's trembling from the shock.

'How dare you attack my students?' says the principal, filtering the words through gritted teeth. Before Leila can reply, he hits her again. She gasps, and she knows it's a sign of weakness. She knows she is weak. Others surely endure much more than this for their faith and don't make a sound.

There is a third blow coming. With this he achieves the desired effect. She holds up her hand in a gesture of pleading for the punishment to stop. Leila feels like her face is made of rubber, numb from helplessness. She inhales with a whistling sound as if something is stuck in her throat. Her heart beats faster and faster, and she knows that this is a moment that will define her. Her body feels useless, an empty canvas on which strangers can paint wounds.

The principal opens a drawer and pulls out a crucifix, a bronze Christ suffering on black wood.

'I don't like enrolling you people in my school. I told your father that too. I discouraged him from it, actually. By law, I have to accept you because this is a goddamned democracy now, but they can't force me to like you, or your kind. Now kiss this cross. If you do, I will write up a warning for your classmate.'

It's not the punishment administered to her that sticks in her mind, but the image of Christ held before her eyes. The protruding metallic ribs of the crucified figure, the elongated, shiny arms. She feels a desire to kiss it to know what Jesus tastes like, but she knows he tastes of metal, and his touch is cold on the lips, like any dead man's. She refuses because she has to stand up for her own faith.

The principal hits her twice more, then gives her a written warning for assaulting a classmate. For the rest of the week she lets her classmates pull her hair, smash her against the wall, trip her when they're playing volleyball in gym. When they spit on her she doesn't wipe the saliva off her face, for she knows they would just spit on her again. Leila lets go of everything. This is just a body, at the mercy of the world, just a body that is being slowly eaten up by time.

At home she doesn't tell her father about what happened in the principal's office. The bruises are still visible on her face. Her father takes note of them with a cold look, but he doesn't ask questions. She could go to a religious school where the ones like her are in the majority, or to a progressive school where religion doesn't matter. Leila hates her family for putting her through all this, but even her hatred is just a dull pain.

At night she keeps thinking about the body in Aunt Márti's room. The body that is supposedly Aunt Márti. She's been chewed to the bone by the disease. Leila can't even recognize Aunt Márti in that body. How could she still be alive? What keeps her heart pumping? Why is the human body allowed to run on for so long when there is nothing left to run on?

Leila presses her palm against her own chest to feel her heartbeat. She takes off her pajama top and stretches across her bed like the crucified one the principal showed her. Her ribs protrude through her skin, her thin arms tighten as if in pain. She looks at herself and sees no difference between the body of Jesus and hers, except that hers is a girl's body and she can still feel pain, while Jesus is long dead, his suffering transformed into bronze or copper on cheap crosses.

It's Friday night. Leila puts on so much makeup that she doesn't recognize herself in the mirror. The bruises still show. She avoids places where she could meet fellow devotees of the faith. She once tried it with a boy she liked from their community. At that time her body still belonged to her, it held value, so they stopped halfway because she was afraid it would hurt. Since then, her body has become worthless. Now she wants it to hurt.

She drinks fast to loosen up and picks up the first guy who

will take her, even with the bruises on her face. It all happens at his place.

'Hold me down,' she says to the boy, whose name she can barely recall. Her words become slurred, her tongue is heavy from the vodka.

The boy's pants land on the floor, the enormous belt buckle shaped like devil horns drops with a loud clank.

'Hold me down like I'm Jesus,' Leila says.

The boy laughs, but obeys. He pins her arms down above her head. Leila would like him to stretch them sideways, but the boy interprets her struggling as part of the game, so he only holds her tighter. He doesn't ask for permission, his penetration is quick and efficient, unlike the boy she tried it with before.

Maybe this is just how it's supposed to be, Leila thinks. I can't get what I want, not ever. All of her fear and excitement vanishes at the thought that her body is nothing but a piece of meat. It isn't the temple of anything at all. Still, she is surprised by her own pained groans, but these are not her groans, she thinks, just as this is not her life. She is only passing through it. Through this body, through this time.

She doesn't quite remember how she gets home, she only remembers crying by the front door. Realizing that, she slaps herself because crying is a form of weakness.

The next morning she wakes up in her bed. She feels empty. There is dried blood on her tights. Her body aches, but at least it's a reminder that she's alive. She goes down to the kitchen. She finds a piece of paper torn from a notebook with her father's handwriting: 'Aunt Márti died during the night.' Leila finds the drawer where her father hides his cigarettes and takes one out. She smokes it in the garden and when she's finished she puts it out on her thigh.

It doesn't feel bad or good. It doesn't feel like anything at all.

★

The mourners are singing, just like the church itself. The wind grows ever stronger outside, the wood creaks. The song is familiar to all. Most of them have grown up singing it, the words spill off their tongues, although there are some to this day who don't understand their meaning. They are not in Hungarian.

The priest adjusts his glasses again, turns the pages of the book hesitantly. As the song ends he gives a signal for all to be seated. There are no benches or chairs in the church; the devotees can only kneel before the Lords. There is no decoration on the walls, just marks and signs burnt into the wood, which only a hundred years ago ensorcelled anyone who laid eyes upon them. Today they are less effective; they're just for show. The priest opens his arms.

'My brothers and sisters in mourning, let us close our eyes and think of the ebb and flow of the tides, the relentless movement of the planets, the black aether that awaits us out there, beyond earthly life. Let us remember the dreams of the Great Lords, and together let us wait for the eternal awakening. Kth'na'fhre at'hmas . . .'

'. . . ath'ram k'tnass.'

Csabi repeats the sentence in front of the mirror and he feels that something isn't right. It's months before the funeral. He should push his tongue further back to form the right sound when changing between 'h' and 'r'. He feels like punching the mirror, punching his stupid reflection. He can't even manage to do this one thing right. To form one goddamn word the right way.

What was the next line anyway?

He throws away the book in frustration but immediately regrets it. If it were a consecrated, leatherbound copy, he would have had to cut off his fingers as punishment for this offense. Fortunately it was just a student's copy. If it were the genuine article, he would lie to avoid punishment. But then nothing would make any sense. If he ever so much as thought that he could get away with lying, that would mean that He is not watching all the time.

He is always watching, he repeats inside his head. Always.

He sighs and bends down for the book. It has a white cover, with the title also in white for the sake of discretion. You can only read the letters with your fingers. He turns back to the mirror, unable to believe he is actually doing this. He should be working, painting the walls, replastering the whole house, changing the spark plug, doing one of the many things that need doing in the garden. But we sacrifice our time to the gods, if we can't sacrifice something more. He shakes his head and tries again.

Later he sits behind the garage, drinking beer and watching the neighboring lot, long abandoned. That overgrown area has become a symbol of unfulfilled dreams, just like the entire suburb. The weeds are nearly a man's height. There is some ragweed swaying as well, which makes Ágika sneeze constantly. It should be cut down, but Csabi figures it's not his land, so it's not his problem. If he grabbed his scythe and went over to mow, he would wind up taking on all the neighboring lot's problems when he already had enough to deal with at his own place.

But in truth, this is not the real reason he lets the weeds grow. Even now, while he sips his beer, he feels someone watching him. Sometimes at night from the window it sounds like something is rustling among the weeds. Csabi is scared: what would he find if he mowed the weeds? That's why he never dares to look out the window at night. Maybe then he would see it, whatever is watching, would see it clearly in the moonlight. What you see sees you too. It might even kill him. What would Ágika do then?

What would he do without Ágika? He sometimes wonders how much easier his life would be had he not met Ágika. Had he not for some reason clicked on her profile on that dating site. It wasn't love at first sight. On the first date they didn't click. They kept on seeing each other anyway, and it got better and better. On the fifth date Csabi took Ágika home, and since that night they had been inseparable. That first night, as they lay in bed, Ágika told Csabi that she was a believer. Csabi was raised as a Greek Catholic, but his family wasn't particularly religious, and he himself very rarely dealt with issues that couldn't be tackled with one's two hands. One time he said a mental prayer to some elusive God after his father's stroke. His father died the next day, without ever waking from his coma. God didn't listen to his prayer then, but that was all right, since Csabi didn't believe in his existence anyway. If he did exist, he surely wouldn't be fond of occasional believers, just as nobody likes casual smokers who bum cigarettes off them at parties.

Csabi never prayed again. Never, until now.

'Yes,' says Ágika.

It's before all of this. The time when everything seems right.

Outside winter rages. Ágika jumps into Csabi's arms, and he holds her tight. The wedding ring falls out of her hand and clatters across the kitchen floor, landing under the cabinet. They laugh.

'Do you know what this means?' asks Ágika excitedly. 'You'll have to convert. It's the only way.'

Csabi had hoped all along that civil marriage would be sufficient, but now his hopes are shattered. The church was an important part of her life. He tolerated it, but he wanted no actual part in it.

'Will you do it for me?' asks Ágika, already in bed, sweaty from the long, drawn-out sex.

'Sure,' Csabi answers – because what else can he say? – and kisses his fiancée. By the following week he's already attending classes with others who wish to convert. They can marry in the meantime, as he gets a pass for starting his indoctrination. But he knows they're keeping an eye on him. He can't drop out.

Dr. Norbert Vércsehalmi is the head religious teacher in the small church school. Hair grows out of his ears, relentlessly clinking school keys hang on his trousers. He smells of clothes that never quite dry.

'The major tenet of our religion,' lectures Dr. Vércsehalmi to his students, 'is that the universe surrounding us is indifferent to our suffering or joy. We are insignificant, replaceable in the eyes of our gods, who do not care about us. Our duty is to adore them, but we will never be rewarded in exchange. We cannot expect anything from them at all. Expecting any gift is a sin in itself. We can never know whether we are fulfilling our Lords' will. But the Great Lord is watching us in every moment of our lives. Always and forever, even after we die. Maybe even more after our demise.'

That sounds about right to Csabi. You shouldn't expect anything from life, that way you won't be disappointed. The tax authorities are always watching as well, so there's nothing new there either. If only the rituals weren't necessary, that horrible language, the words that tongues and lips used to the simplicity of the Hungarian language couldn't master, the strange symbols that your fingers never could get right. And of course some aspects would remain obscure forever, for example the difference between the Nameless Lords and the Great Lord, plural and singular. Apparently they are one and the same, interchangeable, but not identical. That confuses Csabi even more; but then again, every religion is riddled with such nonsense.

There are seven of them in the group. They had started off with eight people, but one of them stopped attending after a couple of times. She said she couldn't identify with the religious doctrines, the theme and tone of the prayers. She had nightmares from them. No one takes her place, she becomes an eternal memento of absence, of the fact that religion is always a matter of choice. If you don't have faith, you're free to go.

Csabi is thinking about this while he practices the prayer

in front of the mirror. These are just the steps he must take to preserve his marriage, and the Great Lords will either keep an eye on their lives or they won't, who cares?

Later, though, he meets the eighth disciple, the woman who dropped out of the course. He runs into her at the supermarket. He asks her how she's doing, trying to get through the pleasantries quickly so he can go on with his day. But the woman is unable to answer. She has bitten off her tongue one night in her sleep.

Later they visit Aunt Márti. The room smells of medicine, shit, and rot. The nurses are changing her diapers when Ágika and Csabi arrive. Márti stares at him the whole time. Her dry, chalk-white face is pierced by those tiny black eyes, filled with nothing but fatigue and impatience at still being alive. She has no facial features anymore, the skin only outlines the bones beneath. Csabi thinks she looks like one of those Egyptian mummies that museums keep parading around the world. Márti smiles. Her teeth have already fallen out, and Csabi thinks about how he must never ask for anything in life, because asking is a sin.

The priest mumbles to himself and howls in nasal tones. He crouches on the cold plank floor, hitting the planks with his palms, then he hits his head, over and over again. His glasses slide off his nose, but he catches them in mid-air. Leila shudders when she sees this, this premeditated gesture, such control over the falling of the glasses. This is the Mourning of the Twilight, the moment when the priest himself becomes the channel for grief, the mourners' collective sorrow flows through him, out into the black aether where the dead go. The priest screams to the sky, so does the crowd, and Leila cannot help but follow suit, she too screams towards the sky, screams as hard as she can, towards the dead stars, the dead gods, her scream...

... echoes back from the walls. Then Uncle Peter wakes

up. He reaches under his blanket and realizes he's wet the bed again.

'Marika!' he shouts in the dark room. 'Marika!'

He is blind in the darkness, his trembling fingers search for either his glasses or the switch to the bedside lamp, whichever he can find first.

He stops. Even his old lungs stop breathing. Something is hiding under the bed, he can smell it over his own odor, he picks up the smell of clotted blood and worms pouring from the eye socket, he can hear the horns touching the carpet. Under the bed, the Lord is under the bed!

The old man grunts, and a tear rolls down the wrinkles of his face.

'So you came for me, my Great Lord,' he whispers and smiles in the dark.

Now it's time for the awful weight to move under the bed, for the hooves to clatter softly on the floor, for the claws to find their way to the old man's throat or his eyes or his soul.

The door opens and Mari, the night nurse, turns on the light. She is paid by the church to look after Peter. Uncle Peter blinks and screams from the sudden brightness. Mari doesn't greet him, just sets about doing her job. She drops the blanket on the floor and peels the soaked pajamas off him.

'Turn to the other side a little, would you?' she says.

Uncle Peter groans.

'Get out! Under the bed . . . ! It's under the bed!' yells Uncle Peter. 'He's waiting for me under the bed. He's coming for me from below!'

'Who is?'

'The envoy of the Great Lord! The Great Lord . . . !'

Mari peeks under the bed, but all she sees is a bunch of used tissues and dust.

'There's nothing there,' she says.

Uncle Peter bursts into quiet tears. The old man turns on his side so Mari can wash his body.

'I was in prison again,' he says through his tears.

'Have you been dreaming? So have I!' says Mari.

Old Peter shuts his mouth and doesn't say a word. If the Great Lord wants to take him, he has the entire night, and the following one, and the one after that, and on until there are no more nights left in his dried-up body.

'How was it in the prison?' asks Leila the next day. It's Peter's birthday. He has to calculate to figure out how old he is. He remembers the year he was born, but he cannot always recall the current year. On the table before him lies a slice of punch cake, brought from a nearby pastry shop. He hates the taste but he puts another bite in his mouth anyway. Eating is good. There were times when there was no food around. You have to appreciate every bite you can get. Anyway, the strongest weapon against aging is eating. You have to eat even if you don't feel hungry. During the war he saw how easily people give up in the absence of food.

In his mind he's back in prison, in the tiny, cold cell, afraid that the guards will break open the door while he's asleep and beat him for no reason at all.

'It was hard,' Peter says to the girl, but then his words get stuck. He used to talk about those nights so often and with such fervor. He even wrote two books on his prison years. Yet now only silence pours out of him.

'I'm getting bullied too, Uncle Peter. At school,' says Leila. 'The principal wanted me to kiss his cross.'

Peter sighs.

'They always want that. They wanted the same thing back when they locked me up. They wanted it during the war. Now it's what they want again. But I didn't break from the beatings in prison, I didn't break from the torture, I didn't break when they raped me with a broomstick. And you must never break either, little girl.'

Only he speaks no such words. This is what he would say if he could speak now, just as he's already said these things several times before, in the illegal church and in the TV studio, in panel discussions and in his autobiography. Still, he is not capable of speech at the moment.

He thinks about Márti. In his mind he is back in her room, two days earlier. He bursts into tears as he holds her bony hand. Time dries out everything, he muses, and he recalls the night about thirty or forty years ago when they both committed adultery. Márti was so beautiful back then, tall and strong, high cheekbones and legs to make you go crazy, her hair worn in a trendy '80s style, and her eyes, oh, those eyes! The way she could look at you...

His mind drifts back to that moment, that one moment he holds dearest, the moment he wishes could last forever.

'I love you,' says Márti. They're in bed, always in bed together, naked, warm and wet, her dark eyes shine and they are young, so young, even though they see themselves as old already. They are not even forty yet. It's a perfect moment, the most perfect moment of his life, the only time he is truly happy.

Márti believed that compromise was the right way to go. She organized his television appearance. In that studio Peter talked about his years in prison, the grievances he suffered together with other believers, those who didn't make it out alive, or died shortly thereafter. Márti chose him because he was handsome, his eyes bright. He evoked sympathy.

That broadcast in 1986 marked a turning point. They knew it right away from the change in atmosphere in the studio during the taping. From hatred to sympathy. The change was accomplished by Peter, but it was engineered by Márti.

Two years after his television appearance the belief in the Faceless and Nameless and Sleeping Great Lords was no longer punishable by prison in the territory of the Hungarian Republic. The believers were allowed to establish sanctuaries and churches, provided they were outside the city limits and not within a five kilometer radius of any school, prison, church of another religion, or grocery store. Following a lengthy process of tough negotiations even the Sunless Slaves were allowed to remain in the church's possession. Only a few small concessions had to be made for the sake of basic human rights, but – refuting the greatest fears of anti-compromise church members – the Slaves did not legally become full-fledged citizens. With this, most of the believers accepted the new setup.

The only real change was that they had to abandon the rituals requiring human sacrifice.

Márti and Peter went straight to their hotel room from the studio. Starting the next day they began to avoid each other. Márti was pregnant with her third child and didn't want to leave her husband.

She loved him too much, she said, and according to the faith, a spouse cannot be abandoned, only killed.

The priest finally goes silent and rises from the floor. All the believers go on kneeling. The priest raises his arms towards the sky, then points at the corpse lying on the catafalque.

'Now for the last time, with the Great Lord as our witness, let us fill this lifeless body with our memories. Turn your gaze inward, toward the world of remembrance, and reminisce about this woman. At the same time, let none of you forget that the Great Lord walks among you even now. Remember that well . . .'

'. . . because he is always watching,' hisses Ágika as she fixes his tie. Csabi clears his throat but says nothing. He wants to talk about how he woke up in the middle of the night. Half asleep, he felt like something was standing beside his bed, watching him. He can still detect its smell, the smell of cheap perfume. It could have been, of course, that he was only dreaming, but he didn't dare to turn the light on. He feared it was a servant of the Great Lord.

'What should I do then? I don't really get it . . . I didn't know her that well,' explains Csabi timidly, prompting Ágika to sigh. She is getting more and more impatient every day, she even messes up the tie knot, then starts again, while looking at Csabi as if he's to blame. Well, he is. What kind of man can't tie his own tie? The funeral will start in two hours and Csabi still doesn't have a clue.

'I don't know,' says Ágika. 'I don't know what you should do. If I knew, then surely I wouldn't be knotting this fucking tie of yours right now, would I? Then I wouldn't have to . . .'

Ágika's voice breaks and she bursts into tears. Csabi gives her a clumsy hug.

'I loved her so much! Why did she have to die?' cries Ágika.

Csabi puts on the black suit and looks out into the garden. The shirt he's wearing is freshly washed, but it's already soaked with the smell of fear. Csabi doesn't have many options when called upon by the priest to remember. He's supposed to dig out that one single memory he harbors of Aunt Márti. Aunt Márti dying on her bed, nothing but a bag of bones under blankets. That was the only time he met her. Instead his mind recalls Ágika in the church, Ágika, who starts crying over a messed-up tie. Ágika, who sighs in anger just at the sight of Csabi entering the room.

Ágika, who may not love him anymore.

This is Csabi's first funeral. He knows he's doing everything wrong. He tries hard to recall what Dr. Vércsehalmi told him about funerals.

'The ritual significance of funerals is immeasurable,' says Dr. Vércsehalmi in his mind, back at the school. 'For it is at a funeral where the narrow passage between our world and the dream of the Gods opens up for a second. This is the moment when miracles of faith can happen. On the other hand, funerals can also be very dangerous. Or blessed. It depends. Because the Sleeping Great Lord manifests as a mourner at funerals. No one recognizes him, no one remembers him. But the Great Lord walks among the mourners at funerals and gathers their secrets. Nothing can remain hidden from the Great Lord as he walks among you. Nothing.'

In the classroom, Csabi doesn't take these words seriously yet, it doesn't even occur to him that he'll have to attend a funeral sooner or later. He believes that by the time it becomes necessary, he will have understood everything better.

At the funeral, Csabi takes a look around to check whether the Great Lord is standing right beside him. He seeks the gaze, the one that connects with his own, which sees right into his soul where his secrets lie. The eyes of the Great Lord, who is simultaneously dreaming for aeons in the depths of the cosmic seas and harassing mourners at funerals. Would he recognize him if he caught his eye in the crowd? Will his heart be turned to cold glass by terror when he looks straight at the Great Lord, even if the Lord is camouflaged as one of the mourners?

Csabi's hands are shaking. He longs for a cigarette, although he hasn't smoked since high school. He looks around at the circle of mourners and tries to focus his thoughts on Márti instead of Ágika.

Someone is watching him. He feels it. His legs tremble weakly, an ice-cold drop of sweat rolls down his spine. It's a girl. Her eyes are black, her face covered in bruises. Maybe she's the Great Lord. Then Csabi calms down. He remembers that he met her before at a birthday party. The party for the old man, Uncle Peter. But that's not why he calms down.

It's because he can see his own doubt reflected in those eyes.

Leila is watching the man, stupid face, sheep eyes, typical victim. In the church's golden age this man would have been fodder for sacrifices, and yet now he stands here, among them. A sheep among wolves. He doubts. That much is clear to Leila, as clear as her own doubts are. She is filled with shame again. She forces her gaze back to the catafalque, the corpse, and remembers. She remembers the cross. But in her memory she kisses the metallic body instead of enduring the blows. Because if the Great Lord walks among them, then he must see her thoughts, he must see her unfaithfulness. Then retribution would be unavoidable. Punishment.

And if the Great Lord punishes, that's proof he exists. He must exist. She thinks back to the first time doubt arose in her. She thinks back to Richárd.

'What are you supposed to do?' asks Richárd, two years before the funeral. Richárd is her first friend from outside the church community. He wears thick glasses and a T-shirt for a band she's never heard of before. They bond over their love of the Zelda games. Later he moves with his parents to a different city and they lose contact. They fade into memories for each other as if they had died. But for now they're still sitting together under a tent in the backyard, the summer rain dripping slowly outside.

Leila shrugs her shoulders.

'Nobody knows. That's the point. He's among us in the crowd, watching. And we don't know whether we're mourning in the right way. Whether our facial expressions are right, whether our thoughts are right. We can't know what he wants, or if he wants anything. Maybe he'll punish us. Maybe he'll do nothing. But it's also possible he'll produce a miracle.'

Richárd nods along as if he understands.

'What kind of a miracle?'

The girl shivers.

'The kind so terrible you can't even talk about it.'

Richárd lies down across the spread-out sleeping bag.

'If I were you, I wouldn't even go to funerals. It sounds kind of creepy.'

Leila shakes her head. This is the first moment, the first sentence, when she formulates her doubt. Up until now, even if she had any doubt, she kept it so deep she couldn't recognize it. As a child she wanted to become a Magister, to walk around in a hooded gown, with her lips and nose cut off, blind to any doubt or criticism.

There is a long silence before she answers Richárd.

'Nothing happens at funerals,' she says in the tent.

Nothing, she thinks again as he starts to talk about something else, because she knows what she said was true, and she feels like crying.

Later, when she suffers for her faith in school, she often thinks about this moment. How her suffering and shame really means nothing at all.

Uncle Peter sits in the pub. It's three weeks before the funeral. He had planned to drink to Márti's health, but he ends up just drinking, without ceremony. The TV is at maximum volume, a Diósgyőr-Debrecen football match is on. No one's paying any attention. The noise is just for lubricating conversations, like alcohol. Peter has heard these lines so many times from so many different mouths. He shouldn't have come to a church-related pub, but he doesn't know any other.

'We're not as strong as we used to be,' says Károly. 'Since we stopped offering sacrifices to the gods.'

Peter mumbles to himself, but nobody listens, even though it was his presence that triggered the whole conversation in the first place. They know who he is, they know what he did. He himself had doubts in the beginning whether legalization was worth giving up so much for, but all it took to dispel his doubts was the memory of the smell of prison, a smell that stays with you always.

Károly drinks up the pálinka and wipes his mouth with his hand. He's a mechanic, he smells of machine oil.

'Those were the good old days!' he goes on. 'When we were still underground. People only dared to whisper the names of our gods, if they had the courage to name them at all.'

He takes a swallow of his beer, maybe just for effect.

'Blood should be spilled again,' he concludes, looking at

Peter. 'The blood of the innocent. In the South they still do it. They keep to the old faith.'

Peter is right on the verge of getting drunk, his head aching from the drinks and his anger. His old fingers squeeze the beer bottle.

'Have you ever offered a sacrifice?' he asks Károly, his voice louder than the TV. 'A real one?'

Everyone turns towards the old man. They rarely hear him speak. Károly gives a wry smile but says nothing. He doesn't need to. None of his generation ever spilled human blood.

Peter cocks his head. He stands up, letting the chair fall behind him, and takes a step towards Károly. Then gathers a little saliva in his mouth and spits at the man's shoes.

'Of course not. You're just a car mechanic! Not a priest, not a Sunless Slave, not a Magister. Only a damn mechanic.'

Károly shrugs his shoulders and turns away offended. When he's drunk, he truly believes that blood sacrifice would be the right thing to do. This zeal only lasts until he gets home and turns on the TV to see what's on, then the next morning he puts on his overalls and climbs down into the car pit to get to work. He likes to talk big at night, because then for a brief moment he feels proud of being a believer, feels that the dogmas of his faith are as old as human civilization itself. Otherwise, he is indeed only a mechanic, just like anybody else. His faith sets him apart. Now he's drunk. He turns back to the old man and spits back at him.

'And you're a bloody traitor, old man! You turned us into what we are today. They see us as craven cowards. When they should tremble with terror at the bare mention of our name.'

Old Peter puts his glass down on the counter.

'Go on, then,' he says, 'pick someone off the streets. Take him to the woods or wherever, and cut out his heart. Eat it raw, while it's still beating.'

He whispers into Károly's ears.

'It tastes like metal. You need good teeth, for the heart is tough. Kill a child or a newborn. They're softer.'

Károly's hands start trembling. He doesn't want to listen, but now he can't stop the stream of words emerging from old Peter's mouth. The old man now seems stronger, taller, and Károly understands that Peter would still be able to kill him. The knowledge and experience were still there in that old body.

'Do you think it's easy? To pierce through the ribs with a knife, to be deaf to their pleas, to bear the smell of shit when...'

Károly stands up from the table, his chair overturning behind him. He may be hallucinating, but he feels like even the shadows have grown darker than before. Silence hangs over the pub, there's no sound besides the commentator yelling furiously about a missed goal on TV.

'You don't know the taste of human blood,' says Peter. 'So stop talking about what's right and what's wrong! There is no right, no wrong. If you want to do it, do it!'

Károly nods and turns away, and Peter sits back in his seat. He's not supposed to drink, as the doctor warns him all the time. Not that he ever drank much. He feels dizzy, but not because of the drink.

He thinks back to that icy night. It keeps coming back to him, usually before bedtime. He tries to think about Márti, but no. That night is the only thing in his mind. The harsh cold of the altar, the victims crying, the second one, the girl, after watching her brother die, goes limp like the prey in the grip of the wolf's teeth. She doesn't beg, her eyes go empty, her muscles slacken, she is reduced to a body, a doll, to be dealt with as you see fit. She barely makes a sound even when Peter sticks the knife in her at the end of his prayer. She is barely dead by the time Peter drinks her blood.

Seventy years have passed since then and Peter is craving the taste of a child's blood once again. He drinks another sip of pálinka instead and feels bitter because he knows that at the end of the day Károly is right.

'We're going to beat some people up,' says Réka. It's two months before the funeral.

Leila is lying on her belly on the bed, looking at her laptop screen.

'Why?' she asks.

Réka pulls out a pack of cigarettes from her back pocket. She is taller than Leila, her hair curly and blond. She could have been a model, but her hand is disfigured by a long scar, the reminder of a childhood accident. She fell through a pane of glass. Leila stops the video and clicks on another link. The room is filled with the sweet smell of cigarette smoke.

'What do you mean why?' asks Réka. 'Because we can. We have the right to. We're the devotees of the Great Lord. Everyone else is a worm.'

Leila keeps on scrolling through the website of the church radicals, and she doesn't know what's right or wrong. She doesn't care anyway. It's all videos of atrocities committed by church members, their faces blurred. She finds that blurring cowardly, but she's excited to see the violence. No killing though, just roughing people up on the street, usually on the outskirts of towns. It's videos of poor people being abused for being in the wrong place at the wrong time. To Leila, that's not enough. She wants to see people like those bitches from school or their parents bleeding on the ground.

'Is that all? We beat them up?'

Réka tosses the packet of cigarettes onto the bed.

'And we carve the sign of the Great Lord into their foreheads. Let the worms know where they belong.'

Leila closes the laptop, turns onto her back, and looks at the ceiling.

'I know where they belong,' she says. 'I know where all of them belong.'

She looks at Réka.

'In the grave.'

They even choose the knife. The knife they will sink into the heart of the first man they capture, the knife they will use to carve the ancient symbols – the ones the mad Arab scratched onto papyrus with his ink-soaked hands in the depths of long-vanished cities – into the dying man's skin. They choose the prayers they will scream to their sleeping gods, not even hoping for a response. They will be true believers, truer than their fathers.

Eventually, they end up drunk. Six of them sit in the park, teasing each other, but they don't manage to spot a victim. One of them has cheap wine, they pass it from hand to hand until they can barely stand.

'Do you miss your brother?' asks Réka, sitting on the bench, her teeth darkened by the wine. 'I dream about him sometimes,' she continues. 'I think I saw him the other day in the church. I'm not sure, but I think it was him.'

Leila nods. She's too drunk to say a word. She doesn't remember her brother. He was taken so long ago. She can't even recall his name, maybe he never had one to begin with. The night will pass without any bloodshed, she now understands. Leila knows what this means: their faith is weak. It's nothing, it's just like any other church. A lie. The Great Lord is not strong enough to kill for, and there's no real difference between a weak god and a nonexistent one. Around midnight, in the coldness of the park, she presses the ceremonial blade to her wrist to take her own life.

Flesh is just flesh, Leila muses, either living or dead. She can hardly hear anything over the sound of her heart beating. What a curious instrument, the heart, she thinks. She cuts into the skin. The pain is sharp, but not as bad as she expected. Her hands tremble, blood drips down onto her skirt. The cut is not deep enough, but she still has time. A few more tries and she would get it right. She thinks about the miracles she was supposed to see, the miracles that once hid in the depths of cellars to drive the outsiders, the normal people, mad. Now they're the normal people, and it's too much to take.

The world seems unbearably empty. The Great Lord is not asleep deep beneath the seas and the stars. The slaves of Sg'oth'oth are not roaming in the caves of the deserts. The Great Book is nothing but the sick delusions of a crazy Arab, or not even that.

Nothing makes sense anymore. Unless the Great Lord gives a sign. Unless he reveals his existence to dispel all doubt.

Leila finally lowers the knife because she has made up her mind.

At the same moment Csabi brings out two beers and places them on the table. Foam pours out, spilling over the bottle onto Csabi's fingers. The woman takes the bottle, her fingers touch Csabi's own. Her fingers are wet with beer.

She licks it up. She's a distant relative of Dr. Vércsehalmi. She's brought snacks to the party to celebrate a successful exam. Everything happened so fast that Csabi didn't really understand, but he also wasn't trying to anymore. He was lost the moment he laid eyes on the woman.

'What are you thinking about?' asks Aurora. She doesn't drink the beer, just strokes the wet bottle with her fingers.

At first they used the classrooms, but they almost got caught. Since then they've been meeting at Aurora's apartment.

Csabi shakes his head and blushes.

'You're thinking about your wife,' Aurora says, flashing her teeth. Csabi has never seen teeth so white before.

'The woman you're betraying. The one who was promised your heart, but will get nothing.'

Aurora wears the scent of the desert on her skin. Empires have risen and fallen in this smell. She says certain words with a peculiar accent. Her blood, her body, her voice, is half Hungarian, but the other half comes from the source of the faith. From the depths of the deserts.

Csabi nods.

'I've seen everything your teacher talks about,' says the woman. 'The godless places of the desert, the ruined temples. I have been deep down in the sea with an expedition. I've swum in the sunken city. I've reached the icy continent, I've climbed the mountains.'

Aurora knows everything that Ágika doesn't. She knows when to remain silent and when to speak, when to move and when to wait, where a man's boundaries are and how to cross them.

'I've done all the rites local priests only dream of. I've read the manuscripts, in the original language, not those crappy translations you get here. And you know what I've found?'

Csabi shakes his head, mesmerized.

'Nothing. Ruins. The gibberish of madmen.'

She touches Csabi's hands. These fingers are capable of anything.

'Yet I do not abandon my faith,' she continues. 'The lack of evidence changes nothing. If I didn't have faith, then I would have to count on the existence of justice in the world. Morality.'

She leans closer to Csabi, her tongue slightly brushing the man's earlobe. This tongue is capable of anything.

'But if there is morality, then I'm a very bad person. And so are you.'

She sits back and takes a sip of her beer.

'What do I do? Should I divorce her?' asks Csabi, though he already knows the answer.

Aurora smiles.

'Once you have converted, there is only one way to separate from your spouse. And you know it.'

Death.

After this, a series of afternoons and nights passes, all soaked through with the lovers' passion. Csabi doesn't get what the woman sees in him, but he ceased to be in control of his life a long time ago. Perhaps he never had been. The Great Lord dreams through eternity without purpose. The planets and black holes and dead suns drift helplessly through the black mud of the universe. One betrayal more or less has no importance whatsoever in the great indifference of things.

Neither does murder.

The night before the funeral Csabi doesn't get any sleep. He is eagerly waiting for something to show up in the night, something so terrible that he could die at once out of sheer terror. Then he wouldn't need to make decisions anymore. A tear rolls down his face.

If the Great Lord is indeed dreaming, his dreams moving the world, if the faith of the believers is true, then murder doesn't matter. It's a part of life and it's not only forgiven, but welcome. And if there is no Great Lord, then there is only Csabi and his decisions. He decides whether to be a good or a bad person. Whether he'll be a murderer or an innocent man. In that case the indifference of the universe wouldn't redeem his sins. He would have to live with them.

By sunrise Csabi has made up his mind.

Right at this moment Peter wakes from a dream, screaming.

'The prison again?' asks Mari while stripping the soaked pajamas off the old man's body.

Peter nods.

'Prison, prison, yes,' he says in a hushed voice.

It's a lie. He dreams of the children. Of the smell of their fear, their stammered promises as they try to bargain for their lives. The moment the warmth of their outpouring blood corrupts the cold winter air. The sound of their last breath, and the deafening silence that follows.

For a long while his mind has been free of these thoughts,

but now it's as if it happened yesterday. He has been suppressing his desire for such a long time.

The purpose of the sacrifice had been so the family would survive the war, so they wouldn't get packed on trains along with the Jews, or get slaughtered on the main street by passing troops, their houses burned down, their women raped and their children mutilated. It had to be done in order to survive. It had to be done so the eye of the enemy would overlook them.

Peter has never forgotten the required movement. Pushing the blade through the skin between the ribs. The moment of power. The ecstasy of killing, mixed with the ancient words, sanctified by thousands and thousands of years of death.

But which came first? The killing or the prayers? Which is the key and which is the lock? Can one exist without the other? As Marika turns over his old body, Peter wonders why he lied. Why shouldn't he admit that he dreamt of the blood of children, blood spilled by his own hands? What are those two deaths compared to the devastation of war? What makes those two bodies different from the millions lying on the battlefield, starving to death in their homes, flying into the air as ashes?

The difference is that he killed them. Now Peter understands why he wanted to believe Márti. It makes no sense to keep lying to himself. If he hadn't gone public back then he would have wanted to kill again. Not for the Great Lord and the rituals, but to smell the scent of innocent blood. To take a life. At first he would have used the rituals as a justification for his acts, to disguise his true vice. Márti kept him from offering sacrifices by means of her political movement, and Peter was grateful for that.

But Márti is dead now, and Peter knows he will soon follow her to the place where the dead go. What is left to restrain him now? Why couldn't he sacrifice someone to honor Márti's memory, like in the old days? Why couldn't he beg the Great Lord's slaves, his body and soul drenched in sacrificial blood?

The Great Lord would know. The Great Lord would know that Peter was not killing for him. He would know that Peter did everything for his own sake, his own enjoyment.

'Do you have faith?' old Peter asks the night nurse.

'In what?' she asks back.

'In anything.'

She powders the old man's skin with talcum, then unpacks the diaper.

'You've seen dead people, haven't you?'

Old Peter nods.

'So have I. Then why believe in anything?'

Old Peter thinks of the next day's funeral, of death and his desires. He has more strength left in his body than anyone would guess, he knows this, he feels this. If only he could smell the scent of young blood once again, just one more time before the eternal night.

Before he goes back to sleep, he makes up his mind.

At the funeral, it was time for the Jaw of Saturn.

'The Jaw of Saturn,' says Dr. Vércsehalmi in the classroom while Csabi tries to suppress a yawn, 'is that one single minute during a funeral when the sleeping Great Lord might open his eyes for a moment, if he deems the deceased and the mourners worthy. And then a miracle could happen, a horror, which the human mind cannot comprehend.'

Richard wipes his glasses in the tent, the rain slowly pouring in drops. He is waiting for the answer to his question.

'Sometimes the dead come back,' says Leila. 'That happens quite often, they say. There are only stories of what the Jaw of Saturn is like. Nobody I know has ever been to a funeral where a miracle actually happened. If it did happen though, we would go mad. We would die. Maybe the world would come to an end.'

★

Aurora and Csabi are lying in bed. Aurora is leisurely smoking a menthol cigarette. Csabi finds the taste of her menthol-infused kiss particularly appealing.

'One time in Damascus,' says the woman, 'the sun disappeared. A terrible, dark object concealed it. The mourners looked up to the sky, at the absence of the sun, and out of the dark matter, from the depths of the universe, something boiled up. Black spiders fell from the sky like rain onto the mourners' heads, each more venomous than the deadliest snakes on Earth. On another occasion, in France, I believe it was still in the times of human sacrifice, the corpse got off the catafalque and began to speak. He unveiled everyone's darkest secrets, which started a violent fight among the mourners. By the end of the massacre, the talking corpse had disappeared. Some believe the Great Lord had taken him. Others think he still walks among us, poisoning our lives.'

Peter sits in the studio, facing the cameras, and he himself is surprised that his voice doesn't quaver.

'There was a case,' he says, 'when all the mourners went gray at once, and they had the same dream for the rest of their lives. Another time, the Earth refused to accept the corpse; instead, the mourners watched as it twisted itself into a tree of flesh whose fruit was an unending crop of monsters that overran the Earth. And the Sunless Slaves talked for the first time in their lives.'

He knows he is making a mistake. The Slaves should be mentioned as infrequently as possible.

Richárd, Csabi, and the television host all ask the same question, in very different times and spaces.

'Is this true?'

Leila shrugs her shoulders.

'If I thought otherwise, I would be punished by the Great Lord. So it must be true.'

Aurora stubs out the cigarette.

'As true,' she tells Csabi, 'as the resurrection of Jesus Christ and the miracles of Christian saints. As true as Buddha is an overweight, smiling man. As true as God is the Word.'

Peter moves around uncomfortably in his chair for a while, then he opens his mouth.

'For us, naturally it is true. But like most miracles, these cannot be proven with evidence either. We preserve them only in our memories, and in the codex of our Faith. But let me ask you this. Is it any different in other religions?'

The host nods understandingly, and looks at his notes.

'Let's talk about the Sunless Slaves a little.'

Peter ...

... sighs deeply at the funeral. The priest stands up from the floor, his face soaked in sweat, his hands trembling, his face a map of pain. He screams at the crowd in a high-pitched voice.

'Ans'ra'ktha nu!'

The mourners are kneeling in the church, their eyes fixed upon the corpse. This is the time, this is when the Jaw of Saturn opens up and either swallows his children or spits them out. Now is the moment when the miracle can happen, now the Great Lord can open his eyes.

'But there is something else,' says Leila in the tent years ago. 'And this always happens. So they say.'

Richárd pulls out another cigarette from the pack and offers one to Leila as well. Leila doesn't even notice the movement.

'The Great Lord always walks among us in one shape or another, at every funeral. No one knows what his disguise is. No one can see him. But at the end of the funeral he reveals himself to one mourner only. The mourner can never talk about what the Great Lord says or shows him or her.'

Richárd lets out a deep sigh.

'So there is no evidence of that either.'

Leila clenches her fist, her nails cutting into the skin.

★

Silence reigns in the church. The rustling of the wind is the only sound. Leila's every muscle is tense, as if her body were preparing to make an escape. Csabi's heart is pounding so hard that he fears the others will hear it, hear the traitor's heart as it tries to explode from his body. Peter thinks about all the funerals, dozens and dozens of corpses that were not honored by the Great Lord's miracle. But maybe this time, either out of love because Márti has made the faith widely accepted, or out of hate for making the rituals bloodless with that move. The Great Lord certainly cannot remain indifferent now.

His decision is this. If the Great Lord reveals himself, if the Jaw of Saturn closes, if the miracle happens, then Peter will not murder again. If the Great Lord allows the human eye to see his wonders, then old Peter will find comfort in the certainty that his faith is not in vain and deny himself the joy of spilling blood.

Tears flood Leila's eyes, her teeth chatter anxiously. Her mouth is dry. If the Great Lord does not perform a miracle, Leila will conclude that the Great Lord does not exist. In that case nothing makes sense, neither life, nor death; in that case Leila's entire life, her faith, is nothing but a joke. Then she'll take the knife, and this time when she cuts she won't miss.

Csabi squeezes Ágika's hand. If the miracle happens, his actions will be justified by the Great Lord's existence. Then Csabi can kill his wife to live with another woman, since murder is just another ritual. However, if the Great Lord doesn't show himself, then he would just be a murderer. Then he'll sever all ties with Aurora and return to his life with Ágika, so they can march towards retirement age together, man and woman, husband and wife.

Now there is only silence and the whistling of the wind, the anticipation and the pain. This is the moment at every funeral that makes death somewhat bearable.

Hope. Hope for proof.

Hope for a miracle.

★

For a minute they stand in silence, the mourning crowd, people united by faith, all full of secrets, fears, anxieties, and desires. They wait for a minute, every passing second bringing them closer to the lack of certainty and they know it. By the end of the funeral, most of them will neither have gained nor lost anything.

Except for these three people.

The minute goes by, the priest takes a deep breath and shouts out to the crowd.

'The Jaw of Saturn has not closed over us. The Nameless Lords have spat us out, we were unworthy of their attention as we are unworthy of life. Let us then bid farewell to our dead, and let the eternal stomach of the universe devour her body and soul!'

Peter bursts into bitter tears. Csabi's heart aches, for he has lost an uncertain future that he already knows he will yearn for in a few years. Leila sighs, her muscles relax. The stress flows out of her. She accepts her fate because death is nothing but another state for her body to endure.

The priest makes a signal with his hand, and somewhere behind the walls the church superintendent pulls a lever.

Peter is fidgeting uncomfortably in the heat of the lamps, forty years earlier. The lenses, like dead eyes, are all focused on him. He stops fidgeting. In his head, he goes through the words, the arguments that they had agreed upon with Márti and the team.

'The Sunless Slaves are the foundation of our faith. We need them to carry out our rites, both in a sacred and ordinary sense of the word. It is a great honor to be a Sunless Slave. The process itself is not so different from the practice of admitting children to a seminary or educating them to become a Buddhist monk.'

The host scratches his chin.

'Except that there is no education in your religion.'

'Education is a subjective thing.'
'Have you given away a child to be a Slave?'
Peter tilts his head.
'We all have.'

The catafalque opens up as a trap door, and Aunt Márti falls like a stone into the darkness hidden deep within the church. The priest steps away so the mourners can take one last look at the corpse in the depths.

They come one by one to look down into the darkness and cry. They cry because Aunt Márti is disappearing from the world of the living once and for all. They cry because they know that they will all eventually end up like this. And inside, they all tremble at the sound that marks every funeral.

There is always someone who screams.

'Good night, my love,' old Peter mumbles through his tears when he looks into the pit. The body lies on the earth floor, limbs twisted from the impact. Old Peter steps away from the catafalque. Csabi takes his place and looks down. He has prepared himself for the worst, but not this. He doesn't scream because he is too exhausted, but he feels a scream stuck in his throat nevertheless, and he'll have to release it sooner or later.

Leila looks down at the corpse and the Slaves. She wonders if her brother is among them. He must be, if he is alive, although it's impossible to tell the Slaves apart. They have no faces anymore, just scars.

The Sunless Slaves do their work.

Their noises fill up the church, grunting and groaning, the clacking of their teeth as they search the corpse for the softest parts. The skin and flesh are torn with a sound like the snapping of a rubber strap, ligaments cracking as the Slaves pull the limbs to get a piece for themselves.

Leila watches them and thinks that she could have become one of them. If they hadn't chosen her brother instead, then she would have grown up in the darkness as well, with her eyelids sewn together, never hearing a human voice. She would know nothing but the cellars and death and pain. Life would be so much easier that way. With every second there's less and less left of Aunt Márti as the Slaves bite and swallow, chew and gulp, until nothing remains down there but them and the surrounding darkness.

They are starved before funerals so they will finish up the body as soon as possible, a gesture of kindness from the church towards the family of the deceased. When the body disappears completely into the stomach of the Slaves, they close up the catafalque, and the present time of mourning begins to fade again into the permanent past of life.

This is the moment, the only moment, when we are revealed, when we allow ourselves to be seen by one who is watching with eager eyes.

Leila stopped by the catafalque and clutched her chest. She felt like she was falling, even though she knew her feet were planted solidly on the floor. The crowd melted into a faceless mass, a set. These were not people, only puppets, mere stage decoration. Leila was alone in the church, maybe in the entire world, and her heart ached with loneliness.

Her gaze penetrated beyond the walls, for the walls of the church were made of the same material as dreams; the wind blowing outside was nothing more than a sound effect. She saw the sky over the ceiling, and she saw through the sky too, saw the endless darkness of the universe beyond the stratosphere, the dance of dead galaxies following the meaningless, unfathomable rhythm of existence.

And for a moment, however brief that moment was, she could see beyond the aether of the universe, and she saw the Nameless Lords and the Great Lord himself, sleeping with eyes wide open, looked into the awful eyes that coldly contemplate existence without being a part of it. If there wasn't enough suffering for his liking, not enough torment, he would close those horrible eyelids and then the world would cease to exist.

Only as long as those eyes kept watching could Leila and Csabi and Peter and all the people they knew exist. We have to suffer in all sorts of ways, Leila finally understood, so that we can go on suffering at all. Otherwise the Great Lord closes the book, and then there will be no present, no past, no future, there will be nothing but the Great Lord somewhere beyond time and matter, a place that Leila didn't even attempt to understand. She only knew one thing now: that everything belonged to the past in the eyes of the Great Lords, there were no decisions, only the hours and the minutes, which like written words and sentences follow one another to give the Lords the illusion of a story.

Leila screamed and threw herself on the floor, scratched her face, turning it into a bloody mask. The crowd looked at her, some started to pray quietly, perhaps, they thought, perhaps a miracle happened after all. Indeed, it did. Leila crawled towards the priest on all fours, her blood dripping on the floor. She had despised the priest only a minute ago but now she understood that everything was fake in the eyes of the Great Lords, herself included, so now she crawled on the floor and kissed the priest's shoes.

'Take me!' she whispered. 'Let me become the Slave of the Great Lords! I'll cut off my lips and nose, I'll tear my soul apart, just let me serve!'

The priest smiled quietly. Leila's father looked at his daughter through tears of happiness and pride.

'Your wish will be fulfilled if the Nameless Lords want it,' said the priest and placed a knife in the girl's hands.

'Give us one of your fingers to start with,' he continued, and Leila complied without hesitation.

As Leila screamed with pain and joy, the crowd cheered her on, and everyone felt that a kind of miracle had happened; that this funeral was worthy of Aunt Márti's memory, and she would have enjoyed the outcome herself.

★

Csabi looked at his wife in the car on the way back from the funeral. Why would he even want another woman in his life? It all seemed so foolish now that the funeral was over. He decided he would speak with Aurora over the weekend and then never meet her again afterward to avoid falling prey to temptation.

He smiled at Ágika and his wife smiled back at him. Csabi grabbed her hand.

'Everything will be all right,' he said, and he meant it.

Ágika nodded.

'I know.'

That night they ordered pizza because neither of them felt like cooking. Before going to bed, Csabi went outside to smoke a cigarette. He had bought a pack at the gas station on the way home. Ágika made no comment, and Csabi smiled quietly to himself. He knew he would fall in love with his wife again. He looked over at the neighboring lot. He knew he was being watched, that terrible evil eyes monitored his every step. He took a drag off the cigarette and decided not to care. He had to let go of this fear. Maybe he was being watched, or maybe not, but he couldn't spend his entire life in fear just because he had joined the church. If they wanted to watch him, let them, he would go on living his life. He put out the cigarette and went inside to go to bed.

'Do you think that girl really saw something?' he asked Ágika in bed after switching off the lights.

Ágika didn't respond for quite a while.

'She was just imagining it. There are people like that at every funeral. They want to believe too much. They see things that aren't there. I had a friend like that kid. Same thing happened to her.'

Csabi nodded, but no one could see that in the dark. He fell asleep quickly.

It was then that the night moved on the neighboring lot. Ágika got out of bed as quietly as she could and sneaked out to the front door. She opened it. A figure was walking through the weeds towards the house. It occurred to Ágika for a second that she could still close the door, she could prevent what was about to happen.

The figure reached the door.

'Did you bring everything?' asked Ágika.

Károly nodded. He smelled of pálinka and cheap cologne. Ágika had asked him several times to use a different kind, but Károly insisted on his favorite brand.

'Are you sure?' she asked.

Károly nodded again and kissed Ágika. He wanted to kill out of love, and also so that next time he saw Peter in the pub he would be able to measure up to him. He would know the taste of blood too.

Ágika shuddered. It was a strange way to end a marriage. Such a banal thing; but maybe that's healthy. No legal red tape, no attempts at reconciliation, just a clean cut.

'Let's do it then,' she said.

Csabi didn't wake up when they entered the room, which meant he never woke up again.

Old Peter opened his eyes in the dark. This time he didn't shout for Mártika, despite the wet bed. He remained silent, even held his breath. The darkness was absolute. He could sense it lying under the bed. Its horns scratching the floor, blood spilling from between its teeth. Its breath filled the room with the stench of the grave.

'So you came,' the old man growled. 'You came for me . . . ! Finally . . .'

He could feel the horrible creature crawling out from under the bed, he heard it squirming in the dark. The old man curled up, and his face assumed a mask of horror to satisfy his guest. Then he realized that he felt genuine terror.

And he waited.

Any moment now the Slave of the Great Lord could strike

him, it could touch him in the dark, gouge out his eyes, devour his soul. Peter was happy he could receive terrifying certainty before his death. His aged body gasped in the dark room, and besides the sounds of his own body he heard, he must have heard, the voice of the creature. It must be there, any moment now it would touch him, it would slash at him, it would disembowel him.

He would see it if he switched on the light.

But he didn't make a move for the switch. He couldn't take the risk.

'Come! Do it!' he whispered fearfully. 'Do it now . . .'

He lay in the dark for the longest time, waiting. The horror standing by the bed waited along with him.

The Black Maybe

Tradition dictates every step of the harvest. The young ones collect the snails in the daytime, while the men oil the chains at night. Chains are to be dealt with only when cold, because that's when the metal maintains its inner firmness, while the snail yields most of its juice in the daytime heat.

Emese went out to collect snails with Feri. Feri was the son of the host family. His teenage years had stretched him tall and thin, but his face remained pimpled. A snail dragged itself slowly across the burning surface of a stone. Feri pinched the animal between his fingers.

'You have to hold it carefully,' Feri said to the girl, while using his other hand to sweep his sweaty locks out of his eyes. Emese thought she heard a smack when the snail's body detached from the stone.

'You mustn't crush it,' Feri went on. He held the snail up to Emese's face. 'We're looking for huge ones just like this. Look for the red stripe across their side, that sets them apart from other snails. Got it?'

Emese took a good look at the red stripe. The snail was trying to retreat into its shell, but it couldn't; at this phase in their life cycle a thick secretion is generated in their mantle, preventing the animals from withdrawing. This is the fluid essential to the process of harvesting.

'Touch it,' the boy said.

Feri placed the snail on his palm and held it towards Emese. 'No need to be afraid of it,' he said to the girl. Emese took the snail. Its body was hot. The boy grinned, then quickly looked around. All the other kids were farther off, walking among the trees, eyes glued to the ground in search of snails.

'Put it in your mouth,' he told Emese.

'Why?'

'Just put it in your mouth.'

Emese played with the thought of placing the soft, slimy body onto her tongue. She imagined it would taste like overcooked pasta. She put the snail in the basket and shook her head. Feri laughed; he had a hoarse laugh.

'Tourists should always follow our instructions. Didn't my father tell you?' he said.

Emese knew she should have rebelled, rebelled against it all. She should rebel even now for having to suffer the presence of such an imbecile teenager, but she knew she must be a nuisance for Feri as well. A visitor, just someone passing through over summer vacation. She decided there was still time for rebellion later.

'It wasn't my choice to come here, anyway. It's my dad's thing,' she said and started for the woods.

Feri ran after the girl.

'Wait,' he said, and Emese, unwillingly, turned towards him. For a moment she thought she heard desperation in his plea. 'What?' she asked as coldly and indifferently as she could. Feri once more swept his sweaty locks aside; the more he did it, the more Emese found it annoying. The boy sighed deeply, his face reddening.

'We should fuck,' Feri said. 'You wouldn't regret it. I've been with a lot of girls already . . .'

Emese turned and walked away without a word; she reminded herself to bring along the switchblade next time. She had stolen it from her father two years ago and always promised herself she would keep it in her pocket, just in case. The world is a dangerous place for girls, or so she had heard, and a knife could make it a little safer. Despite the promise, she never actually had the guts to walk around with a knife on her.

'You'd be better off!' Feri shouted after her. 'You'll regret it if you say no.'

'Yeah, right,' Emese muttered under her breath, then bent over to pick up a snail.

The men, Gergő and Hugó, worked in the garage at night, oiling the silver chains.

'Tourism helps a lot,' Gergő explained. His voice was flat, always on the verge of sounding bored. 'And of course, what we sell is ours, and the prices are up. But life gets more expensive year after year too. It gets tougher, expenses run higher. Every year it gets harder.'

He worked with the old snail oil expertly, oiling each and every link on the five-meter-long silver chain again and again. He wore a sweater so stained that no amount of washing would ever get it clean. His skin was sensitive to the blade, yet he shaved each and every morning. His neck was always red and covered in pimples; Hugó was looking at this redness now. It wasn't how Hugó had pictured farmers; he had always imagined them as having beards, or at least light stubble. Why should they care about their facial hair, or their lack thereof, when they had no boss to answer to, only nature and the land? Hugó's face was stubbly now, even though he was usually meticulously clean-shaven on workdays. As part of the higher brass of a multinational oil company he couldn't afford the luxury of looking shabby.

Still, as he nodded to the rhythm of Gergő's nodding, a certain formless anger built up in him against things that make life tougher for the farmers. For what is Hungarian life if not the sweet nurturing of the motherland, the preservation of traditions, the production of iconic Hungarian goods? These are the real heroes, he always thought while looking over the account numbers at the firm; these farmers were the flesh and bones of the country, not office drones like himself. Oh, how he longed to be among them every weekday when he looked out his office window. And now, finally, he was here. He was paying for it by the week, but finally he and his family could get a slice of the farmers' life.

'It sure is tough,' Hugó said, to reassure his host of his full agreement.

'Through the links as well,' Gergő said, watching Hugó's movements as the city man used the oil-dripping rag on the chain. 'You have to pull the smaller rag across them, and then through the middle too, so the oil gets dispersed everywhere. Every link has to be well oiled. It has to get inside the metal, be one with the chain's spirit.'

Hugó nodded and wiped his hand anxiously on the North Face sweater which he otherwise used for hiking. When they were packing for this holiday he acknowledged with a sense of guilt that he only owned clothes for business, sports, and the theater; he had never bought any sort of actual workwear. Now he was staining one of his most expensive sweaters, bought specifically for the annual Austrian skiing season. He saw it as a sort of self-punishment, but he knew he would buy a new one soon anyway. He plunged the rag into the bucket full of snail oil and crammed it through the first link of the silver chain. There were a dozen chains in the garage altogether.

'Chains are getting more expensive as well,' Gergő said. 'There are no state subsidies for silver like in the old days.'

Hugó nodded again, then began to speak.

'Yes. Europe doesn't value traditions anymore. They don't care about us,' he said with a hurt pride that wasn't his own.

Gergő finished oiling the first chain. He coiled the metal up carefully on the floor and took out a new chain.

'Well, yeah,' he said. 'Only a few of us still do it the traditional way. Although it was the EU that gave us funding for the guesthouse. That's why we put the EU flag and sign out.'

Hugó cleared his throat; he felt he needed to say something again.

'Well, at least there's some use to those bureaucrats in Brussels,' he said finally.

Gergő nodded and lit a cigarette. He didn't speak again.

They oiled the chains all night long.

Women start working at dawn. They wake before sunrise, consume a light breakfast, and then set out to work in the kitchen in the purple haze of the early hours. They boil the juice of the snail for hours on end, preparing it for later, when it will be used to reach the essence, a most important step in the process of the harvest.

Andrea never got up before nine, but she knew how important this trip was to her husband. She was surprised when she awoke even before her phone's alarm sounded. She dressed and joined her hosts in the kitchen to help with the work. She began chatting to her hosts, since that was the one thing she definitely knew how to do.

'Hugó works at MOL,' she recounted as she plucked fat snails out of their shells. 'He's in the economics department, but he's very intrigued by the world of agriculture. That's why we were so happy to learn that you host visitors during the harvest. We're also saving up for a property in the country for our old age. That's his big dream anyway.'

She sighed deeply, as if she could already smell the bleach-scented happiness of those elderly years, when all their troubles would be behind them. Hugó's constant speeches about the countryside were too abstract to attach emotions to, but this imagined calm she had associated with Hugó's obsession was something she could grasp.

'Watch out, don't let the shell fall into the mash,' Erzsébet said, while rapidly crushing the snails' shells with professional movements, one after the other, like a machine. She wore plastic flip-flops, jersey pants, and a faded Pepsi T-shirt.

'Jesus,' Andrea said with disgust. The snail in her hand was still alive. Its slimy internal organs trickled down her fingers, but it was still moving and writhing, clinging to its crushed life to an unnatural extent. Andrea found the experience disturbing, yet somehow exciting.

'That's perfect,' Erzsébet said. 'Put it in the smaller bowl. These are the ones we're looking for. They're bait.'

Andrea nodded and threw the agonizing animal into the plastic yellow bowl. For one terrible moment she thought the dying body had attached itself to her fingers and would never let go. She shook her hand and the animal dutifully dropped into the bowl to go on dying with its peers.

'What if it dies before the harvest?' Andrea asked, but Erzsébet just shook her head.

'They never die,' she said. Andrea shivered and changed the subject quickly.

'How is life in the countryside?' she asked. 'Living in harmony with nature?'

Erzsébet shrugged. 'We have lived this way our entire life. We live well. Nowadays there's a high demand for our organic products. Gergő never stops complaining, but that's just how he is. If we work hard we harvest well, and that's all that matters. We usually harvest six to eight of them a season, good quality too, and that's enough to live on after the sale. We get nice tax breaks, local and EU too, for keeping up the traditions.'

The soft bodies began heating up under Andrea's hands, as if they were tiny bombs about to explode. Erzsébet went on. 'Last year we added the guesthouse. Now we have to wake earlier to provide for guests, clean up after them, guide them through the harvest. That's additional work, you see. When there are no tourists around, we're still here. We have to nurture the snails and the earth all year. That's the soul of it, the earth. It has to be well fed.'

Silence reigned, and Andrea realized she hadn't said hmm and nodded, hadn't properly signaled her attention. She looked into Erzsébet's eyes to make up for it. 'Don't you have any of *them* at the house?' she finally asked. 'I haven't seen any. Wouldn't they make your life easier?'

Erzsébet shook her head.

'We only produce them,' she said. 'We don't need anything but what we already have.'

Andrea smiled at the thought; how beautiful such a life must be, with no need for anything but the will and eagerness to work and two strong, healthy hands to work with. It was satisfying work, she imagined; at the end of each day a sense of completion awaited.

Andrea heard the door creak. Someone entered the house, and Erzsébet broke into a smile.

'Mama is here,' she said. 'She's forgotten more about harvesting than we'll ever know.'

Boiled snail oil has a strong smell, therefore it is usually heated in the summer kitchen in old pots. While the oil is cooking, the immediate family shares a light lunch before the extended family arrives to carry out the evening tasks.

The immediate family now shared a table with their guests. Andrea and Hugó sat with Gergő and Erzsébet, while Emese sat with the hosts' own children, Feri and his sister, Nóra. Nóra's outfit was from H&M; glittery tops were in fashion at the moment, her clothes lit up the table. She was maybe a year older than Emese, and Emese felt an immediate connection with her.

The lunch was schnitzel with rice and peas. Mama's cooking, the only thing she ever actually cooked. Andrea ate with a smile on her face, but she knew she would put a finger down her throat to make herself throw up later on; the oil-soaked schnitzel was too much for her stomach, and she felt like she was eating snails. Hugó contently filled himself up with the food like it was the best thing he had ever had.

'This is the good stuff, this country food. It's healthier and more nourishing than what we eat in the city,' he said with his mouth full.

The family did not react to his comment, but Nóra grimaced mockingly, and Emese was particularly grateful for the gesture. Emese felt she could grow fond of the girl; after all they were almost the same age, with the same fledgling defiance glimmering in their eyes.

Mama did not eat with them, as she always ate alone. She sat in the kitchen, ears glued to a portable radio, keenly gobbling up the food, almost choking herself on it. She had been eating like this since her childhood. The taste of the food never mattered, the goal was to wipe the plate clean as fast as possible, because only what you had eaten was truly yours. Everything else could be taken away, as history had proven time and time again to people in the country. You had to eat fast, because who knows if there would be food the next day. Her gray hair was covered with a black scarf; she wore knockoff yellow sneakers bought at the market, an old, long skirt and a blue housecoat. She didn't care whether her clothes went together; only practicality mattered. She derived no enjoyment from the beauty of things, or of people. She rolled the meat chunks around in her mouth, silent like the hills. She was listening to a daily program that played music for people over sixty. Apparently that's the age when one starts to listen to operettas, a genre dead for well over a hundred years but kept alive by this one daily show. All the singers performing had been deceased for decades now, but still they kept crooning from scratched old tapes, lulling their audience towards the calm of the grave with songs about nothing at all.

'My darling's heart is filled with sorrow, and so I'm sad too,' chanted the singer now, and Mama listened. She found no joy in music either, but listening to these songs was part of a tradition kept up by the elderly. She had to honor tradition because it was the only thing in the world that mattered.

In the afternoon the family traditionally takes a nap, freeing the mind and the body of that which is unnecessary.

Emese and Nóra hid behind the shed; Nóra took out a pack of cigarettes from a worn backpack. She offered one to Emese too. Emese hesitated. She had never smoked before, and she didn't feel any particular urge to try it just now. What if Mom and Dad sniffed out the smell of cigarettes? But she didn't want to ruin her budding friendship with Nóra, and they had come here to experience rural life anyway. Apparently life in the country involved smoking.

She drew a cigarette out of the pack and let Nóra light it for her. She took a drag and expected her body to be seized with a fit of coughing, like first-time smokers in movies, but it didn't happen. The smoke dipped into her lungs and then left without any issues.

'It's good,' Emese said with a smile. She took another, deeper puff. Her head felt light, like it was filled with air.

'I heard that Feri wants to sleep with you,' Nóra said. 'He says he fucked someone on May Day, but I don't believe him. If that was true, he wouldn't care about fucking you.'

Emese took another drag to hide her embarrassment. Nóra went on.

'I think you should sleep with him. You won't regret it.'

Emese raised an eyebrow. Sex was something obscure, an elusive, wild thing somewhere further on in her life that would surely occur one day, but not this summer. Maybe during another summer like this, when the millionth cigarette she smoked had turned to ash, when all this had become someone else's life, the foundation for another, more experienced Emese who could choose wisely whom to give her virginity to. Let's say two or three years from now. But definitely not now. She still saw herself as somewhat of a child, although she longed to be an adult without quite grasping what that actually meant.

Emese shook her head firmly.

'No,' she said finally.

Nóra shrugged her shoulders.

'Okay. It's your call,' she said, picking up the backpack lying by her feet. She took out a jar filled with some yellowish-brown liquid. There was a spider resting at the bottom of it, its long legs curled around its body in the final posture of death.

'No need to be afraid of it,' Nóra said, tapping the glass to prove that the animal was dead. 'These spiders eat snails, so if you see one, squash it right away. But you can also put them in alcohol if they've already eaten a snail. The booze soaks the snail oil out, and it becomes a potent drink.'

She lifted the jar so the sun shone through the clear liquid. Nóra stubbed her cigarette butt out on the ground, then opened the jar. A metallic smell hit Emese's nose. Nóra placed the mouth of the jar to her lips and took a sip, then tossed the jar into Emese's hands.

'Quick, so we get the rush at the same time,' Nóra said, and Emese knew she had to act now because she would just hesitate and freeze a second later. She took a sip and swallowed without thinking. Warmth spread in her throat and stomach, her mouth felt bitter. Nóra took the jar, carefully closed it again and put it in her backpack.

'I feel it! It's coming,' Nóra said, her voice verging on laughter, and a second later Emese too felt the kick, her mind and body obeying the imperative of the upcoming rush. Her heart raced, she felt electricity crackling up and down her spine. She opened her mouth to speak, to formulate words for the ecstatic joy that was about to erupt from the depths of her soul; but only a deep, resonant voice burst from her throat, a voice she could not recognize as her own. It formed strange words that weren't in any language Emese knew. Nóra tried to speak as well, and her voice became just like Emese's. They both laughed and all of their worries and burdens evaporated.

Nóra ran up against the wall of the shed and kicked herself away: she rose into the air and got stuck at the peak of her jump, in between the earth and the heavens, like a feather carried on the wind. She slowly turned on her axis, cackling in a deep, metallic voice. Emese felt her body tear itself away from the ground, and in a second she was flying around the shed with Nóra, laughing away at the absurdity of it all.

The effect lasted for ten minutes, then both girls hit the ground softly. Emese's head was buzzing and splitting, she felt a tormenting hunger in her stomach, but when she thought about the oily schnitzel, she felt nauseous. Nóra burped.

'You shouldn't drink it often,' she said. 'It's easy to get hooked on it.'

They smoked another cigarette, then went back to the house.

Men traditionally greet each other with pálinka shots while women prepare the bait. The children wait in a separate room while the fresh snail oil cools on the windowsill.

The house was filled with relatives: three families arrived, along with two lifelong bachelors. The harvest was always a family business; they all received a share from the sales. The men toasted with pálinka fermented from peaches.

'Make the beasts strong and fat!' they yelled, downing the drinks with a ritual gesture. The women were threading the still-living snails onto hooks to make the lures. Andrea, although filled with respect for the farmers, couldn't help but be repelled by the sight of the wriggling animals at the ends of the hooks. She wished them dead, even though the purpose of their existence was precisely what she was seeing now. To be half-living bait at the end of pointed metal. A dozen such lures were prepared, for that was how many pits had been dug in the ground outside. The pits were about two meters deep, two meters wide. They used an excavator for the digging; that was the only part of the process done with machines.

While the adults drank and prepared the bait, the children, seven of them altogether, sat in the main hall. Emese was also sent to sit with the children, though she was not counted as one of them. She was there as a guest, and the children of guests usually don't participate in the proceedings and necessities of the harvest; their essence isn't used. Local children were necessary parts of the process though, so now they were preparing themselves mentally for the role they would soon play.

She retreated to an armchair and watched the other children from there. The youngest must have been ten years old, the oldest was a pimpled boy who might even be legally allowed to buy cigarettes. He was staring somberly in front of him like someone willing himself unconscious. The youngest kid was shaking, his teeth chattering, sweaty hands crumpling his trousers. Feri was also sitting among them, trying to act cool, but his breathing was ragged from nervousness. Nóra sat right beside him, smiling victoriously. At this point Emese did not yet understand why.

When the lures were ready, the men went to the shed and collected the chains. They checked the links meticulously once more to make sure all were well oiled. When they were satisfied, they walked up to the pits, dragging the chains behind them.

The women attached the bait to the ends of the chains; Mama checked each of them one by one, then nodded. The chains reminded Emese of fishing lines, and they worked very much on the same principle. Silence reigned above the pits as if a funeral were taking place.

'Let them come!' exclaimed Gergő, throwing a lure into each pit. Two meters of the five-meter-long chains disappeared into the depths, then Gergő laid the remaining length on the ground. The men covered the pits with earth. The smell of manure filled the air.

After this, the women placed mirrors on the ground, right where the chains disappeared into the earth. The extended family and the guests sat around the mirrors and waited. Someone brought along a portable radio tuned to an oldies station. The men smoked and waited. The women carried beer, water, and homemade dumplings to the picnic tables.

Erzsébet brought out a manual drill from the shed; after making sure it was working properly, she placed it on the table beside the dumplings.

Night fell. The men lit lanterns.

Hugó asked Gergő for a cigarette. He didn't smoke, but at that moment he felt that such a manly activity required this manly gesture. Unlike Emese, he coughed when taking a puff.

'Now? Is it now that they take the bait?' he whispered to Gergő.

'In a way, yes. They bite on it. But not like fish do.'

The song 'Beautiful Life' by Ace of Base started on the radio.

'I know,' Hugó said. 'Because in fact they don't really exist until they take the bait, right?'

Gergő ruminated on the words.

'You're right,' he said finally. 'They don't exist, but their elements, their pieces, are already there. That's why we feed the land all year round. The bait only makes them come together. It lures them into life.'

Emese sat down beside the radio; when all the other kids were sent to bed she had managed to get her parents to let her stay. She wanted to see what happened; they had already ruined her summer with this trip, she at least wanted to see everything.

The radio droned on, airing a program called 'Hit Parade': they started with a Wings song, then a rock standard by local band Edda, and then Blondie. It happened during the second chorus of 'Heart of Glass'; Emese felt like she had been punched, she had to hold on to the edge of the table to keep from falling. Her nose started bleeding. From the radio there was nothing but static for a few seconds before Blondie emerged again from the noise.

'It's a catch,' someone said in the dark, and that very moment a mirror broke.

'Here! This one!' Gergő shouted. 'Hold the chain tight!'

The mirror broke in two, its distorted surface reflecting the silhouettes of men as they bent over for the chain. They all grabbed the metal, and Hugó's heart started to race; he was scared he was about to have a heart attack, this close to experiencing the heart of the harvest.

Gergő shouted, 'Heave-ho!'

The men were pulling the chain as one, but it barely yielded.

'Harder!' one of the men screamed.

'Heave-ho!'

Hugó gave it his all, he didn't even care if his hernia came out again; he only heard from far off, through the sound of his own struggling, that another mirror shattered. He felt that whatever was hiding in the depths was slowly giving in to the men's raw strength, and this only made him strain himself even more; he no longer pulled with just his muscles, but with his mind, his thoughts as well. At last the earth moved, and in the light of the lanterns the larva burst forth from the depths. It pushed itself forward on its short, articulated legs. There was no need to pull any longer.

It was a catch.

The men let go of the chain; one of them jumped on the larva, while two men on each side tied up the legs with plastic cords. Hugó was panting but felt like laughing. He saw the larva as a fruit of his physical exertion and felt instant gratification.

A third mirror broke in the distance.

'To the chain!' shouted Gergő, and the men set out to drag the next larva from underground, from nothingness to life.

While her father wrestled again with the depths of the earth, Emese stepped up to the first larva. It was one-and-a-half meters long; Emese would have just fit inside it. The chain disappeared into its body through a hole. She hoped that the larva had found some pleasure in swallowing the bait; although according to some, the larva is the bait itself, only transformed, enlarged, turned into the seed of life.

The women grabbed the larva and turned it upside down. Erzsébet took the drill in her hands and pointed the end of it against the larva's skin.

'What are you doing that for?' Emese asked.

'If I don't make an asshole for it, it will die later on, dear. Every animal needs an asshole, didn't you know that?' She smiled sweetly at the girl, then with a quick movement she drilled a hole into the larva and expanded the opening with a knife. Black blood dripped onto the ground.

'The mouth is no problem, it was created when it took the bait. But we couldn't manage without the other hole. That's where you put the essence in.'

Emese nodded, but she felt sick to her stomach at the sight of the wriggling larva. The next larva was pulled out of the earth, and yet another mirror cracked in the distance.

It went on for hours.

Hugó was tired but radiating with happiness. Although there was a shower in their room he had washed himself in a barrel along with the other men. He felt a kinship with them now. He opened a can of beer. Andrea watched her husband from the bed.

'Are you happy?' she asked, for that was the only thing that mattered now.

Hugó smiled.

'I have never been happier.'

At dawn Nóra sneaked into Emese's room and slipped into bed next to her. Emese smelled the odor of tobacco on her breath.

'What is it?' she asked drowsily.

'Feri is waiting outside,' Nóra said. 'He can do you in the shed. It would mean a lot to him, and it doesn't really matter to you, does it? You're a city girl.'

Emese buried her face in the pillow in annoyance.

'Leave me alone!' she whimpered. 'I'm not sleeping with your idiot brother!'

Nóra shrugged.

'As you wish.'

The essence is traditionally handled by the women in the family; only blood relatives can touch it, usually the mother or the grandmother. The larvae live for twenty-four to thirty-six hours without the essence. The final phase of the harvest must be completed before that.

'Seven mirrors broke last night,' Gergő said. 'That means seven essences for seven larvae.'

Hugó took a bite from the sausage prepared for breakfast. Many of the men were still sleeping on couches and in sleeping bags. The women were up to prepare the day's work.

'What happens when there are more larvae than children?' Andrea asked.

Gergő smiled. 'It doesn't happen often. If it does, it goes to waste unless we get another child quickly somehow.'

The upstairs room was only used at harvest time. Otherwise it was kept locked. Andrea helped to carry the necessary things upstairs. The fresh snail oil had already cooled down.

'We have to hurry,' Erzsébet said. 'It solidifies quickly and then it's no good anymore.'

They fished out seven Tupperware containers from the kitchen cupboards. They filled them with water, threw a magnesium capsule into each, as well as a handful of gravel and two spoonfuls each of salt and sugar. They then spit into all of them. Andrea mixed up the contents of the containers, then took them upstairs. In the upstairs room stood an old bed; generations had stained it with their bodies. On the bed lay handcuffs, attached to chains secured to the floor. The chains and handcuffs were new. Andrea almost dropped the plastic tubs she was carrying at the sight of the bed and the chains.

'It's for the children's sake,' Erzsébet said.

The price that Hugó had paid included room and board, plus participation in the harvest. Working with the essence was the only thing that Hugó was forbidden to take part in. Men were not allowed to be present upstairs, not even the fathers. Entry to the room was strictly limited to Erzsébet, Mama, the given child, and its mother.

Andrea waited outside the door in case they called for her to get something from the kitchen. The children went in one by one. They always screamed; some right away, some quite late in the process. One of them had to be dragged into the room. Andrea felt sick hearing the screams but always felt relief when the children left the room. There was no apparent sign of physical harm on them, aside from the marks of the handcuffs.

When Nóra walked into the room with that subtle smile on her face, Andrea knew right away there was something wrong. She was quickly proven right.

'Up to what age can you do this?' Hugó asked his host downstairs, because he had read contradictory information on the internet.

Gergő gave the question some thought.

'Until twenty-five, give or take. After that you shouldn't touch the essence. But usually by that time you can't anyway. You know how it is with young people, they get spoiled way before that. I got spoiled when I was seventeen. My Erzsébet spoiled me. We got married not long after. You know how it is.'

Hugó nodded like someone who knew.

'You can't start it too soon either,' Gergő went on. 'You can first take it out when they're seven or eight, sooner than that might cause severe harm.'

Upstairs Mama started shrieking.

★

Nóra's face was red where her father had hit her.

'Who was it?' he asked Nóra. 'One of your classmates? That blond one?'

Nóra wiped a tear from her face.

'Does it matter, Dad?' she asked, her voice trembling with suppressed rage and exposed fear.

'Yes, it does, and don't call me Dad, because the daughter I raised isn't a slut! And you had to do it now, right before the harvest? With guests around to watch?'

Nóra murmured something under her nose.

'Louder! So I can hear your excuses!' Gergő shouted at her.

Nóra hit the table, her face contorting into a mask of anger.

'If a boy sleeps with someone, you applaud him, you give him drinks and crack jokes. Why is it reserved just for boys? It's only okay when you fuck?'

Gergő slapped his daughter again.

'Go to your room and don't come out until I tell you!'

'It only works when they're innocent,' Gergő said over a beer. 'If they've done it once, no matter how old they are, they're spoiled. I trusted her too much. Other families check their kids before harvest, you know. The girls, at least. But not me ... not me ...'

He buried his face in his palms. 'We'll lose one now,' he sighed. 'That's one-seventh of our harvest. A terrible loss ...'

Hugó's heart raced; this was his last chance to get close to the farmers in a way few outsiders could.

'What about Emese?' he asked. 'My daughter. Wouldn't she be good?'

A grateful smile spread across Gergő's face.

'Nobody is closer to their children than we are, here, in the country,' Erzsébet said as she rolled up Andrea's sleeves. 'We see their essence. As children, we went through this too, and so will their children as well.'

Andrea gulped. She knew the right decision now would be to run, grab her daughter and run. What would that do to her marriage, though? In a marriage you have to consider the other person's wishes too, not just your own.

'But couldn't it hurt her? I mean . . .' She realized how meek she sounded and she felt ashamed. 'I mean, I've never done this before.'

Erzsébet smiled encouragingly, like an older woman teaching the ways of life to a young girl, even though they were both of the same age.

'You can't get it wrong,' she said, then stirred the snail oil.

Mama arrived, dragging Emese behind her like a dog.

'Let's hurry,' Mama said. 'Night will be here soon, and we don't have anything ready yet.'

Emese's stomach tightened; she felt as if an ice-cold concrete block had been wedged in the center of her body. The room reminded her of a slaughterhouse, though she had never been to one. It reeked of shit and vomit and blood and fear.

She had to detach her tongue from her parched palate so she could speak; she still hoped that all of this was a dream she would soon wake from.

'No,' she said, because that word should still hold some power. She repeated it. 'No.'

But Mama's grip was strong, not the grip of a frail woman but of an ancient kraken risen from the deep. Her voice was an impatient howl.

'Stop being silly, sweetie! Your parents said this would be, so it shall be. Lie down on the bed!'

Emese never understood what terror was until that moment. Her legs were shaking. She looked at her mother: surely she would not put her through the same thing that rural children endure. After all they were from the city, just tourists visiting, beneficiaries and not slaves of the countryside.

'It will be all right,' Andrea said. 'Your father will be very happy with you.'

Emese wanted to scream, but she remained silent. She knew she should have rebelled, rebelled against everything a lot sooner. Anger rose in her because she didn't have the switchblade with her despite her promise to keep it on her at all times. She was again defenseless, like she always had been.

'She'd better take off her clothes,' Mama said.

Emese shook her head.

'I'm not undressing,' she said, then repeated, 'No.'

'It will get nasty,' Mama said with the anger of a woman who has never understood the world apart from her own little slice of it. 'Do you want your mother to keep washing your clothes for the rest of your life? You could do just this one little thing for your parents. They gave you life, you owe it to them not to burden them with any more filth.'

'Let her keep them on,' Andrea requested feebly, her own voice shaky; not a mother's voice, but a child's. 'I'll wash them later.'

But eventually Emese took everything off.

Mama smeared a thick layer of the snail oil onto Andrea's hand and arm, all the way up to her elbow. Andrea felt as if wasps were walking on her arm, hundreds and hundreds of tiny legs.

'You have to be quick,' Mama said. 'Don't fool around, just reach in and take it out. If you wait or hesitate, it will only be worse, both for her and for you.'

Andrea gulped.

'How do I know . . .' Andrea fell silent when she heard the handcuffs click on her daughter's wrists. '. . . when I've found it?'

'If you don't know, then this is not your daughter,' Mama said. 'You are ready. Go ahead.'

Andrea turned towards the bed, her arm oiled to her elbow,

endowed with the strength of gods, yet she felt feeble. She wanted just to grab her daughter and run away, but then she realized that the farmers couldn't run from their traditions, their responsibilities, their job. They had come there with Hugó to get a taste of the country life; well, this was it.

'It'll be quick, my love,' she said to her daughter, but Emese didn't answer, she just squeezed her mouth tightly shut. There was something in her eyes that Andrea interpreted as hate. Not a child's hate, but a woman's.

'Open up, please,' Erzsébet said pleadingly, but Emese just squeezed tighter in defiance. This couldn't be happening, she wouldn't submit her mouth, her throat, not any part of herself to these people. Not even to her mother, who had now become a stranger.

'Goddamn these city people,' Mama hissed, and Andrea felt ashamed because she and her daughter were city people, worthless, and she had no idea what to do. Mama did; she covered Emese's nose with her wrinkled hand.

Emese would have put up a fight to brush the old fingers off her nose, but the handcuffs kept her down, and Erzsébet sat on her legs so she wouldn't kick. Soon she needed air. She hated herself. She opened her mouth.

'Now, for god's sake!' Mama shouted, and Andrea pushed her oily hand into Emese's mouth. She closed her eyes at the last moment as Erzsébet had instructed her, since the sight of it only confuses the heart.

Emese screamed, but her voice was instantly muffled by her mother's hand, her fingers creeping towards Emese's throat. Emese felt as if burning spiders were running around in her mouth and her throat, then she couldn't scream anymore.

Andrea's blouse was soaked with sweat. She knew she mustn't stop, not now, but it was so hard. She tried to take no notice of the body, her own daughter's body, which kept writhing beneath her, struggling with every ounce of its strength. But what right did that body have to fight her?

Hadn't it been torn out of Andrea, the screaming infant pulled by expert hands from her own flesh, just like the larvae were pulled from the ground by farmers? Didn't that make Andrea the owner of Emese's body; doesn't a mother own her daughter's flesh, and with that, her spirit? At that thought, something clicked in her mind.

Now she could feel that her hand had slipped beyond Emese's flesh, beyond her throat, beyond her body. The snail oil had opened the gate separating matter from the essence of life.

'That's it,' she heard Mama's voice from a distance. 'Now search for it.'

She was getting deeper and deeper, unfathomably deep. What would she see if she opened her eyes? For Emese's mouth couldn't possibly open wide enough to accommodate her mother's arm right up to the elbow. Her fingers rummaged in the hot darkness, the thick plasma, and she was just about to figure something was wrong when she felt it. She knew that was it; she had found the essence. She tried to grab it, but the essence slipped through her fingers like a slimy octopus, trying to retreat towards a further corner of the darkness. Andrea made another attempt, not only to pinch the octopus with her fingers but to capture it, to possess it. She had to use her mind, not just her fingers.

She succeeded: the hot slime pulsated in her palm, and she kept on squeezing as hard as she could.

'I got it,' she whispered, her mouth dry.

'Then pull!' Mama said, and Andrea pulled it from the darkness through Emese's throat; she again felt the moment when her hand slipped from one dimension to another. When she pulled her hand out of Emese's mouth a burp broke out from her daughter, but after that she didn't make a sound.

Andrea opened her eyes.

'Beautiful,' she said, although even she could see that the pulsating essence was slimy and shapeless. It was the essence of life, beyond terms of aesthetic conventions. Mama took it from her, and Andrea remembered the first time when her daughter was taken away from her in the maternity ward.

'Well, I told you it would be quick,' Mama said, and walked over to the final Tupperware container. She washed the essence in the prepared liquid, then took up the scissors. Andrea looked at Emese; her daughter remained motionless on the bed, her eyelids half open, the whites of her eyes showing. Her tongue protruded from between her lips, drool and snot dripped from her chin. Her body had let go of everything; the smell of urine and excrement filled the room. She seemed dead, but she was breathing, no matter how faintly. Andrea felt a wintry cold wrapping around her heart, for this was as close to death as she had ever seen her daughter. So she looked at the essence instead; that was her true daughter, right there.

She watched as Mama cut a piece of it with the scissors; the piece fell into the plastic container. Mama washed the wound because blood was oozing from the essence, which now seemed somehow shrunken and withered; but Andrea tried to convince herself that it was just her imagination. Mama turned to Andrea and pushed the wounded essence into her hand.

'Now you can put it back,' she barked, and left the room.

Emese took a shower afterwards. Her thoughts were dead; they stood still and quiet in the icy city her mind had become. She tried to wash everything off; she poured hot water into her mouth to get rid of the snail oil. She tried to vomit, but she couldn't because she was empty inside.

At last she ended up in the same room where the other children were kept. She lay down on the floor, tried to make herself so small as to disappear altogether, and she cried, because that was all she could do, even though she had no tears left.

Feri sat in the corner. He swept the lock away from his forehead; his face was pale, his eyes red.

'I told you we should have fucked,' he said eventually. 'It would have been better for both of us. That at least would have been our decision.'

Andrea embraced Hugó.

'It was so beautiful,' she said. 'Like she was a baby again. I think we purified her entire little soul.'

Hugó sighed heavily and happily.

'You see how these people live? They're surrounded by so much beauty. And we just waste our lives in the office.'

Andrea laid her head in her husband's lap.

'One of these days we'll move out here too.'

Traditionally it is the women who put the essences into the larvae, after having them soaked in the holding liquid for six hours. However, men can also carry out the task.

Andrea saw how meticulous and affectionate Gergő was in his handling of the larvae, how carefully he pulled out the essences from the Tupperware containers, and how skillfully he molded them into a shape, then put them inside the larvae.

'You have to do it through the asshole,' he explained while he was up to his elbow in the larva, 'otherwise it doesn't take root.'

After he secured the essence inside, he pulled his hand out of the flesh and opened up the next container. After the essences are planted, the larvae are left to rest for the night. That's the time the essence needs to take root in the flesh before the final step of the harvest can be observed.

At dawn the larvae are cut up.

Gergő held the larva between his knees and cut into the skin. The larva's shell opened up like a flower greeting the sunshine.

Inside the larva lay a humanoid creature. Its face was

obscured by bodily fluids and dirt, but the chain led to its mouth, disappearing into it. Gergő cut a larger incision around the chain, then pulled the chain out of the body. The entire family watched in silence. It was a moment of success or failure; a moment of life or sustained non-existence.

The creature took a breath through the incision for the first time in its life: its lungs filled with the cold morning air. Then it screamed. It was the most horrifying scream human ears could ever hear, a scream of pain, of grief, of terror. It took another breath so it could scream and scream again, but Gergő was no longer paying any attention to it, as he was busy cutting up the next larva.

'They don't have eyes,' Andrea noticed, but by the time she had said the words, Mama had already bent over the screaming creature and cut two incisions above its nose with a smaller blade.

'Now they do,' she said, wiping the black blood off the blade. The next creature started screaming, and then the next one.

Men poured pálinka for themselves and congratulated each other on the successful harvest; the women set out to cook a celebratory meal. Only Emese cried along with the screaming of the creatures.

'Which one is mine?' she asked through her tears, bordering on hysteria.

'What's wrong, honey?' Andrea asked. She understood the question but wanted to stall for time.

'Which one of them is mine in? Which one has my soul?'

Andrea looked down uneasily, as if looking for the answer on the ground.

'I don't know. They were all in identical containers.'

Hugó caressed his daughter's head like she was still six years old.

'That's only a piece of your essence, not your soul. There's no reason to cause a scene.'

Emese tore herself away from her father's embrace; it was an embrace that meant her harm, she knew that now. She was much wiser than yesterday.

'But why are they screaming?' she asked.

'Every birth is painful,' Andrea said sweetly. 'You cried too when you were born, didn't you?'

Maybe because I didn't want to be born either, Emese thought, but she kept the thought to herself.

The creatures looked at Emese from the other side of the cage through their freshly cut eyes; some of them were still crying, but most were only whining. No hair grew on their bodies, their skin was stone-like, their arms long and muscular. Their eyes were brightly colorful; three of them had blue, three of them red, and there was a single one with black eyes, so black they seemed infinitely deep.

'Those three blue ones over there,' Feri said, 'those are fairly strong and fire-resistant. They're good for manual labor. Factories often buy them. When they're no longer of use, their flesh tastes good too. One of them was given my essence. Mine turn out blue every year, Dad keeps track. The red ones bring luck; if you keep one at your house it protects you from misfortune. A lot of banks use them, did you know that? And the black one ... the black one is the most valuable. There is no limit to what it can do.'

'What do you mean?' Emese asked.

Feri lit a cigarette he had stolen from his sister; he smoked with trembling hands.

'Literally anything. You name it, it does it. It's dangerous too. Too smart. They go on the truck at dawn, we're taking them to the market. You leave in the afternoon, right?'

Emese nodded. Feri smiled sadly.

'Maybe next year then,' said Feri, and walked away.

Emese put her hand into the pocket of her coat to feel the handle of the knife. She had learned her lesson; she would always keep it with her from then on. She scanned the creatures and tried to discover herself in one of them, as if looking for a stranger in the mirror who was at the same time also herself.

One of them was her; it might be a red one, but she hoped it wasn't, she didn't want her new life to be centered on luck. She hoped it was the black one.

Yes, the black maybe.

Because the black is dangerous, and there's no limit to what it can do.

ATTILA VERES (b. 1985) is a Hungarian writer of horror and weird fiction. His first novel *Odakint sötétebb* [*Darker Outside*] (2017) was a surprise success in his native country and was followed by the story collection *Éjféli iskolák* [*Midnight Schools*] (2018). His fiction appears regularly in *Black Aether*, a magazine dedicated to Hungarian cosmic horror, as well as in literary magazines. As a screenwriter he has written several short and feature-length films all over Europe, and he won the Best Television Screenplay award at the 2020 Hungarian Film Awards for the TV feature *Lives Recurring*. He is originally from Nyíregyháza but currently lives in Budapest. His story 'The Time Remaining' was chosen to represent Hungary in *The Valancourt Book of World Horror Stories*, and *The Black Maybe* is his full-length English debut.

CPSIA information can be obtained
at www.ICGtesting.com
Printed in the USA
LVHW020427140922
728282LV00001B/2

9 781954 321700